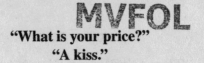

"What is your price?"
"A kiss."

Alexa's face must have betrayed her surprise, for the Wolfhound flashed a rakish smile.

"Haven't you ever been kissed before?"

She sucked in a sharp breath. "O-of course I have."

"Oh, I think not," drawled the Wolfhound.

"Why, you impudent whelp—"

Her words were cut off by the ruthless press of his mouth. He tasted of smoke and spirits—and a raw, randy need that singed her to her very core. Suddenly the Wolfhound swept her into his arms. With several swift strides, he crossed the carpet and pinned her up against the wall, setting off a wicked whisper of crushed silk and flame-kissed flesh.

Alexa meant to cry out, but as he urged her lips apart and delved inside her, outrage gave way to a strange, shivering heat. Against all reason, her body yielded to his touch, molding to every contour of his muscled frame. Broad shoulders, lean waist, corded thighs—Alexa was acutely aware of his overpowering masculinity.

She knew that she should push him away.

And yet, as his hands moved boldly over her bodice, she could not resist threading her fingers through his silky gray-threaded hair. The sensation was sinfully sensuous...

"With mystery, intrigue, laughter, and hot, steamy passion...what more could any reader want?"
—TheRomanceReadersConnection.com

"Another fantastic read from Cara Elliott. Can't wait until the next book."
—SingleTitles.com

To Sin with a Scoundrel

"HOT...Charming characters demonstrate her strong storytelling gift."
—*RT Book Reviews*

"Has everything a reader could desire: adventure, humor, mystery, romance, and a very naughty rake. I was absorbed from the first page and entertained throughout the story. A warning to readers: If you have anything on your schedule for the day, clear it. You won't be able to put *To Sin with a Scoundrel* down once you start reading."
—SingleTitles.com

"Steamy...intriguing."
—*Publishers Weekly*

"Fast-paced...a fun tale...fans will appreciate Lady Ciara as she challenges her in-laws, the Ton, and love with the incorrigible Mad Bad Hadley at her side."
—*Midwest Book Review*

"Delightful...filled with fun and some suspense and lots and lots of sexual attraction."
—RomanceReviewsMag.com

Also by Cara Elliott

Circle of Sin Series

To Sin With A Scoundrel
To Surrender To A Rogue
To Tempt A Rake

Too Wicked To Wed

Cara Elliott

FOREVER

NEW YORK   BOSTON

This book is a work of fiction. Names, characters, places, and incidents are the product of the author's imagination or are used fictitiously. Any resemblance to actual events, locales, or persons, living or dead, is coincidental.

Copyright © 2011 by Andrea DaRif
Excerpt from *Too Tempting to Resist* copyright © 2011 Andrea DaRif
All rights reserved. Except as permitted under the U.S. Copyright Act of 1976, no part of this publication may be reproduced, distributed, or transmitted in any form or by any means, or stored in a database or retrieval system, without the prior written permission of the publisher.

Forever
Hachette Book Group
237 Park Avenue
New York, NY 10017
www.HachetteBookGroup.com

Forever is an imprint of Grand Central Publishing. The Forever name and logo are trademarks of Hachette Book Group, Inc.

The publisher is not responsible for websites (or their content) that are not owned by the publisher.

Printed in the United States of America

First Edition: November 2011

10 9 8 7 6 5 4 3 2 1

For
"The Wenches"
Your friendship and talents are a source of
constant inspiration.

Too Wicked To Wed

Prologue

So *this* is what a brothel looks like. It is not at all what I expected."

"Good Lord in Heaven," muttered Captain Harley Stiles as he blotted the sheen of sweat from his brow. "I would hope that you haven't given the matter a great deal of thought."

"Not a great deal," replied Lady Alexa Hendrie. She turned for a closer look at the colored etching hung above the curio cabinet. "But one can't help being mildly curious, seeing as you gentlemen take great delight in discussing such places among yourselves."

Her brother's friend quickly edged himself between her and the offending print. "How the devil do *you* know *that*?" he demanded.

Despite the gravity of their mission, Alexa felt her mouth twitch in momentary amusement. "I take it you don't have any sisters, Captain Stiles. Otherwise you would not be asking such a naive question."

"No, by the grace of God, I do not." Though a decorated veteran of the Peninsular Wars, he was still looking a little shell-shocked over the fact that she had outmaneuvered his objections to her accompanying him into the stews of Southwark. "Otherwise, I might have known better than to offer my help to Sebastian, no matter how dire the threat to his family."

Alexa bit her lip...

"I, too, am curious." A deep growl, dark and smoky as the dimly lit corridor, broke the awkward silence. "Just what *did* you expect?"

She spun around. Within an instant of entering The Wolf's Lair, she and Stiles had been sequestered in a small side parlor to await an answer to the captain's whispered message. The door had now reopened, and though shadows obscured the figure who was leaning against its molding, the flickering wall sconce illuminated the highlights in his carelessly curling hair.

Steel on steel.

Alexa froze as a prickling, sharp as daggerpoints, danced down her spine. "Oh, something a bit less...subtle," she replied, somehow mustering a show of outward composure. She would not—could not—allow herself to be intimidated. After taking a moment to study the muted colors and rather tasteful furnishings of the room, she returned her gaze to the lewd etching on the wall. "By the by, is this a Frangelli?"

"Yes." Straightening from his slouch, the man slowly sauntered into the room. "Do you find his style to your liking?"

She leaned in closer. "His technique is flawless." After regarding the graphic twining of naked bodies and oversized erections for another few heartbeats, she lifted her chin. "But as for the subject matter, it's a trifle repetitive, don't you think?"

A low bark of laughter sounded, and then tightened to a gruff snarl as the man turned to her companion. "Are your brains in your bum, Stiles? What the devil do you mean by bringing a respectable young lady here? Your message mentioned Becton, not—"

"It's not the captain's fault. I gave him no choice," she interrupted. "I am Alexa Hendrie, Lord Becton's sister. And you are?"

"This isn't a damn dowager's drawing room, Lady Alexa Hendrie. We don't observe the formalities of polite introductions here." The sardonic sneer grew more pronounced. "Most of our patrons would rather remain anonymous. But if you wish a name, I am called the Irish Wolfhound."

"Ah." Alexa refused to be cowed by his deliberate rudeness. "And this is your Lair?"

"You could say that."

"Excellent. Then I imagine you can tell me straight off whether Sebastian is here. It is very important that I find him."

"I can." His lip curled up to bare a flash of teeth. "But whether I will is quite another matter. The place would not remain in business very long were I to freely dispense such information to every outraged wife or sister who happens to barge through the door."

"Is it profitable?" she asked after a fraction of a pause.

"The business?" The question seemed to take him aback, but only for an instant. "I manage to...make ends meet. So to speak."

"Now see here, Wolf—" sputtered Stiles.

"How very clever of you," went on Alexa, ignoring her companion's effort to cut off any more risqué innuendoes.

Smiling sweetly, she shot a long, lingering glance at the Wolfhound's gray-flecked hair. "I do hope the effort isn't too taxing on your stamina."

"I assure you," he replied softly, "I am quite up to the task."

"Bloody hell." Stiles added another oath through his gritted teeth. "Need I remind you that the lady is a gently bred female?"

The quicksilver eyes swung around and fixed him with an unblinking stare. "Need I remind you that *I* am not the arse who brought her here?"

"Would that I could forget this whole cursed nightmare of an evening." The captain grimaced. "Trust me, neither of us would be trespassing on your hospitality if it were not a matter of the utmost urgency to find Becton—"

"Our younger brother is in grave danger," interrupted Alexa. "I *must* find Sebastian."

"We have reason to think he might be coming to see you," continued Stiles. "Is he here?"

The Wolfhound merely shrugged.

Alexa refused to accept the beastly man's silence. Not with her younger brother's life hanging in the balance. "You heard what the Wolfhound said, Captain Stiles. He is running a business and doesn't give away his precious information for free."

Sensing that neither tears nor appeals to his better nature—if he had one—would have any effect, she took pains to match his sarcasm. "So, how much will the information cost me?" she went on. "And be forewarned that I don't have much blunt, so don't bother trying to claw an exorbitant sum out of me."

"I am willing to negotiate the price." Despite the

drawl, a tiny tic of his jaw marred his mask of jaded cynicism. "Kindly step outside, Stiles, so that the lady and I may have some privacy in which to strike a deal."

"I'm not sure, er, that is..."

"What do you think? That I intend to toss up her skirts and feast on her virginity?" The Wolfhound looked back at her with a sardonic smile. "You are, I presume, a virgin?"

"Presume whatever you wish," she replied evenly. "I don't give a damn what some flea-bitten cur chooses to think, as long as I get the information I need."

"Ye gods, Lady Alexa, bite your tongue," warned Stiles in a low whisper. "You are not dealing with some lapdog. It's dangerous to goad the Irish Wolfhound into baring his fangs."

Dangerous. Another touch of ice-cold steel tickled against her flesh. Or was it fire? Something about the lean, lithe Wolfhound had her feeling both hot and cold.

Stiles tried to take her arm, but she slipped out of reach.

"I really must insist—" began the captain.

"Out, Stiles," ordered the Wolfhound as he moved a step closer to her.

Alexa stood firm in the face of his approach. Oh, yes, beneath the finely tailored evening clothes was a dangerous predator, all sleek muscle and coiled power. And ready to pounce. But she was not afraid.

"You may do as he says, Captain. I am quite capable of fending for myself."

Stiles hesitated, and then reluctantly turned for the hallway. "Very well. But I will be right outside, in case you need me," he muttered. "You have five minutes. Then, come hell or high water, we are leaving."

"Do you always ignore sensible advice, Lady Alexa?" asked the Wolfhound, once the latch had clicked shut.

"I often ignore what *men* consider to be sensible advice." The gray-flecked hair was deceiving, she decided. Up close, it was plain that the Wolfhound was a man not much above thirty. "There is a difference between the two, though someone as arrogant as you would undoubtedly fail to recognize it."

"I may be arrogant but I'm not a naive little fool," he retorted with a menacing snarl. "At the risk of further offending your maidenly sensibilities, allow me to point out that when trying to strike a bargain with someone, it is not overly wise to begin by hurling insults at his head."

Alexa felt a flush of heat creep across her cheekbones. "Actually, I am well aware of that. Just as I am well aware that any attempt at negotiations with you is probably a waste of breath. It is quite clear you have a low opinion of females and aren't going to consider my request seriously."

Beneath his obvious irritation, Alexa detected a glimmer of curiosity. "Then why did you agree to see me alone?" he asked.

"To show you not everyone turns tail and runs whenever you flash your fangs." She squared her shoulders. "By the by, why is everyone so afraid of your bark?"

"Because I am accorded to be a vicious, unpredictable beast," he replied. "You see, I tend to bite when I get annoyed. And my teeth are sharper than most."

Lamplight played over the erotic etching, its flickering gleam mirroring the devilish spark in his quicksilver eyes. It seemed to tease her. *Taunt her.*

Alexa wasn't about to back away from the challenge.

"Do you chew up the unfortunate young women who work here, then spit them out when they are no longer of any use to you?"

For an instant, it appeared she had gone a step too far in baiting him. His jaw tightened and as the Wolfhound leaned forward, anger bristled from every pore of his long, lean face.

But just as quickly, he seemed to get a leash on his emotions and replied with a cynical sneer. "You know nothing of real life, so do not presume to think you understand what goes on under my roof," he snapped.

"Perhaps you would care to explain it to me."

The Wolfhound gave a harsh laugh. "Nosy little kitten, aren't you? Seb ought to lock you in your room, before you stray into real trouble."

Alexa fisted her hands and set them on her hips. "Ha! Let him try."

"You have spirit, I'll grant you that." He paused for a moment. "Still interested in making a deal?"

"What is your price?"

"A kiss."

Her face must have betrayed her surprise, for he flashed a rakish smile. "Haven't you ever been kissed before?"

She sucked in a sharp breath. "O-of course I have."

"Oh, I think not," drawled the Wolfhound. "I'd be willing to wager a fortune that no man has ever slid his tongue deep into your mouth and made you moan with pleasure."

"Why, you impudent whelp—"

Her words were cut off by the ruthless press of his mouth. He tasted of smoke and spirits—and a raw, randy need that singed her to her very core. She swayed and suddenly the Wolfhound swept her into his arms. With several swift strides, he crossed the carpet and pinned her up against the wall, setting off a wicked whisper of crushed silk and flame-kissed flesh.

Alexa meant to cry out, but as he urged her lips apart and delved inside her, outrage gave way to a strange, shivering heat. Her protest melted, turning to naught but a whispered sigh. As did her body. Against all reason, it yielded to his touch, molding to every contour of his muscled frame. Broad shoulders, lean waist, corded thighs—Alexa was acutely aware of his overpowering masculinity. The scent of brandy and bay rum filled her lungs, and the rasp of his stubbled jaw was like a lick of fire against her cheek.

She knew that she should push him away. Bite, scratch, scream for help.

And yet. And yet…

And yet, as his hands moved boldly over her bodice and cupped her breasts, she could not resist threading her fingers through his silky gray-threaded hair. Like the rest of him, the sensation was sinfully sensuous.

A moment later—or was it far, far longer?—the Wolfhound finally ceased his shameless embrace and leaned back.

"A man could do far worse on the Marriage Mart than to choose you," he said softly. "For at least he will likely not be bored in bed. Indeed, I might even be tempted to swive you myself, if innocence was at all to my taste."

The crude comment finally roused Alexa from the seductive spell that had held her in thrall. Gasping through kiss-swollen lips, she jerked free of his hold and all of her wordless, nameless, girlish longings took force in a lashing slap.

It connected with a resounding crack.

His head snapped back, the angry red imprint of her palm quickly darkening his cheek.

"*That* was for such an unspeakably rude insult." She raised her hand again. "And *this*, you arrogant hellhound, is for—"

He caught her wrist. "Is for what? The fact that for the first—and likely only—time in your life, you have tasted a bit of real passion?"

She went very still. "Do you really take pleasure in causing pain?"

The Wolfhound allowed her hand to fall away, then turned from the light, his austere profile unreadable in the flicker of the oil lamps. "Most people think so," he said evenly as he moved noiselessly to the sideboard.

"I—I don't understand," she began.

"Don't bother trying," he snapped. "All that should matter to you is the fact that I am a man of my word. You paid your forfeit, so in answer to your other question, your brother is not at present in The Wolf's Lair. And if he were, it would not be for the usual reasons that gentlemen come here." Glass clinked against glass. "Like you, he is seeking information and I've heard word that he thinks I may be able to help him. Should he come by tonight, I will inform him of your quest, and how desperate you are to find him."

Alexa turned for the door, yet hesitated, awkward, unsure.

Taking up one of the bottles, the Wolfhound poured himself some brandy and tossed it back in one gulp. "Now get out of here, before one of my patrons recognizes you. Trust me, the tabbies of this Town are quick to pounce on any transgression. And their claws are far sharper than mine."

"Th-thank you," she said, hoping to show that her pride, if not her dignity, was still intact. "For showing a shred of decency in honoring our bargain."

"Don't wager on it happening again."

Alexa stiffened her spine. "I am not afraid to take a gamble when the stakes are high." She could not resist a parting shot. "And I'll have you know, I am *very* good at cards."

"Here at The Wolf's Lair, we play a far different game than drawing room whist. You have tempted the odds once—I would advise you not to do it again."

"How very kind of you to offer more counsel."

The Wolfhound's laugh was a brandy-roughened growl. "You mistake my sentiments, Lady Alexa. I am not being kind. I am simply trying to stack the deck in my favor. If I am lucky, the cards will fall in a way to ensure that our paths never cross again."

Chapter One

Four months later

amn."

The low oath, though blurred by the shuffling of cards, drew a flash of teeth from the gentleman seated at the far end of the table. "So, the Irish Wolfhound feels the dogs of defeat nipping at his flanks?" he drawled.

The barb drew several sniggers from the small group of cronies gathered around his chair.

"What say you to a last hand?" continued the gentleman. After caressing the pile of blunt he had just raked to his side of the table, he shoved it back to the center. "At, say, double the stakes?"

Their color flickering from silver to slate in the guttering light of the candles, the Wolfhound's hooded gray eyes appeared to focus on the lewd etching on the wall rather than the glittering challenge on the green felt. "Why not?" he replied, the words slurring together, though in truth, Connor Linsley, the Earl of Killingworth, was completely sober, and engaged in a careful calculation of the odds.

As he made a show of fumbling over the last of his banknotes, Connor angled his gaze to the rapidfire cutting of the deck.

Damn.

All night long he had been watching—watching for how the cursed Captain Sharpe, who called himself DeWinter, was managing to cheat. But though the earl was familiar with most every trick of the trade, he had yet to spot any sleight of hand.

Bloody hell—I had better catch it soon, thought Connor grimly. He had lost an obscenely large sum of money so far. Not so much as to completely beggar his purse, but enough to make the coming few months a squeeze, what with the payroll and the routine expenses that must be met in order to keep his doors open.

After a final flick, the cards began to flutter softly through the shadows. The earl—better known in the less glittering environs of London as the Irish Wolfhound—shifted slightly in his chair, angling for a better view of his opponent's hands. Still, no matter how carefully he studied the moves of the other man's fingers and every little shrug of his cuffs and sleeves, he couldn't detect just how he was being fleeced.

But the wool was being pulled over his eyes, as if he were a helpless little lamb.

That was a certainty. As proprietor of The Wolf's Lair, one of the more notorious gaming hells and brothels in Town, the earl was far too conversant with games of chance not to know when the odds were being manipulated. He was also far too canny a player to be suffering such a prolonged string of losses. His ownership of the business enterprise might be a closely guarded secret, but his gambling skills were not, as proven by the profits entered into his ledgers each week.

Tonight, however, he had been keeping careful count and nothing was adding up right.

"Any additional cards?" inquired DeWinter, slapping down two discards.

The earl allowed a small smile. "Just one."

All he needed was a nine or less, in any suit, to play out a winning sequence. Surely it was time for fortune to smile his way. Lady Luck had never deserted him for this long a stretch. And though everyone knew that ladies were notoriously fickle...

The new card flipped in his fingers.

The Queen of Hearts.

Son of a bitch. Why was it that of late, females— especially highborn ones—had been naught but a harbinger of trouble?

As the coach lumbered through yet another tollgate on the London road, Alexa could not help wondering what price she would pay for this spur-of-the-moment decision.

Until several months ago, she had lived a very ordered life. A quiet country existence, defined by the unchanging rhythm of her daily duties on the ancestral estate.

And now?

All of a sudden, two wild, impetuous moves, one tripping on the heels of the other.

The first had been understandable. Her younger brother, a young man whose bohemian spirit had drawn him into the sinister web of the London underworld, might well have ended up with his throat slit if she had not raced hell-for-leather from Yorkshire to alert her older brother of the danger.

Alexa bit her lip, recalling her first real taste of intrigue and danger. As well as her first real kiss. From no less than one of London's most notorious rakes.

For years she had been secretly longing for just such a wild adventure.

So why was she feeling so blue-deviled?

Catching the blurred reflection of her face, dark and brooding in the rain-pelted glass, she expelled a sigh. "I know I ought to be happy," she whispered. "But I am not."

Would that she could explain it.

"I'm lucky—exceedingly lucky—that Papa allowed me the freedom to pursue my unconventional interests," said Alexa to her scowling self. "Just think of all the hours I was free to study mathematics and agriculture instead of needlework and music."

Yes, just think of it. The drumming of the drops couldn't quite drown out the answering voice inside her head. *No wonder that you find much more pleasure in putting your practical knowledge to work on the estate than in attending the local assemblies.*

True. Fashion and flirting seemed so utterly...boring. As did all the gentlemen she knew.

Bland as boiled oats. At times, her life within the confines of Becton Manor took on the same consistency, stirring a longing to experience something out of the ordinary...

Well, she had. In spades.

A loving family, a settled existence, a degree of independence. And, to fill the void between darkness and dawn, a headful of memories of what it was like to be kissed by a notorious rake. What more could a young lady of two and twenty wish for in life?

Indeed, Sebastian had been shocked when she had abruptly announced that she had decided to accept her aunt's longstanding invitation to visit London for the Season. Surprise turning to skepticism, he had expressed his doubts that she would find any enjoyment in spinning through the glittering swirl of Polite Society.

The question, while well meaning, only rubbed raw at a sensitive spot. With an inward wince, Alexa admitted that her behavior—especially of late—was hardly a pattern card of propriety. She was too headstrong, too opinionated. *Too unladylike.* Sparks seemed to fly wherever she went.

However, encouraged by his new bride, Sebastian had surrendered his misgivings with good grace. The letter to Aunt Adelaide had been sent, the trunks had been packed, the coach made ready...

Closing her eyes, Alexa leaned back against the squabs and listened to the sounds of the coach moving ever closer to London. A world of gaiety and glamour. Of polish and propriety. Yet it was the thud of her own heart that overrode the jingling harness and pounding hooves.

Had she made a terrible mistake?

In the angled lamplight, DeWinter's eyes took on a knife-edged gleam as he raked banknotes to his side of the table. "Why, it looks as if the dog has not so much as a bone left to gnaw on."

Laughter sounded from the four tough-looking men who had come in with him.

Connor ignored the attempt to goad him into losing

his temper. He had survived several brutal Peninsular campaigns and his time in the stews by listening to his instincts. And his gut feeling told him that DeWinter's followers were hardened professionals—most likely mercenaries for hire—who looked primed for a fight.

A smile quirked at the corners of his mouth. The blatant provocation might have been amusing—save for the fact that it had just cost him a great deal of blunt.

Most people went well out of their way to avoid a snap of the Irish Wolfhound's jaws, but DeWinter seemed intent on goading him to go for the throat. Connor wondered why.

"Brandy for me and my friends," called DeWinter loudly. "Perhaps I'll give His Lordship a swallow before he crawls off with his tail between his legs."

Connor gave a tiny nod to the two hulking attendants by the door—the Scotsman and the mulatto had been hired for their muscle, though they were rarely called upon to use it.

That the earl actually owned the establishment was a closely guarded secret. His nightly presence had been easy enough to explain by spreading word that he had a special arrangement with the proprietor—a rumor that, unlike most of the ones concerning his affairs, was true enough. Most people accepted that the Wolfhound ran tame in the Lair in return for ensuring that the patrons and play in the gaming rooms were the most interesting in Town. The presence of a notorious rake and gambler was always good for business.

Noting Connor's subtle signal, the mulatto slipped out to the hallway, returning a moment later with a comely barmaid bearing glasses and brandy.

"I'll have a taste of this, too." DeWinter's taunting was now moving beyond mere words. He grabbed roughly at the girl's bodice and exposed a breast.

"Sorry, sir, but ye're te keep yer hands te yerself in here. It's house rules." Experienced in fending off such advances, the barmaid managed to set down the tray without spilling a drop. "If ye wish that sort of pleasure, ye'll have te take yerself upstairs and pay fer it."

"Insolent bitch." Ripping the ruched silk down to her waist, DeWinter struck her hard across the cheek. "I take my pleasure where I please."

Connor decided that things had gone far enough. He was out of his chair in a flash, breaking the other man's hold on the girl with what looked to be no more than a casual flick of his wrist. "You may diddle with me, DeWinter, but no foul play is allowed with the girls. You heard her—the management does not like it."

DeWinter's eyes narrowed. "Are you accusing me of something, you hellhound?"

A low gasp came from one of the other onlookers. The earl's hair trigger temper—and his deadly accuracy with a pistol—were well known. As word of the confrontation spread like wildfire through the other gaming rooms, a crowd quickly gathered at the doorway.

"Bad manners," replied Connor calmly, releasing his grip to brush a mote of dust from his sleeve. "Which to my mind is an even worse transgression than cheating at cards. So I suggest you take your pennies and your prick and spend them elsewhere."

Fury mottled the other man's cheeks to an ugly shade of red, and for an instant, the earl thought that blood was sure to be spilled.

But DeWinter hesitated, his gaze darting from his own companions, tensed and ready to strike on command, to the two house attendants, now reinforced by two burly employees from the adjoining room.

Four former soldiers versus four former pugilists.

The earl's mouth thinned to a sardonic set. *Even odds.* No wonder the greasy maggot was unwilling to play.

"You ought to be grateful for any farthing tossed your way," snarled DeWinter, slowly uncurling his fists. "Seeing as you, like this she-bitch, have been stripped bare."

Connor still had no idea what ulterior motive the other man had in visiting The Wolf's Lair, but as he wasn't likely to learn anything from DeWinter himself, he dismissed him with a shrug. There were other ways of digging up information. "Show this fellow the door, McTavish. In case his memory is not as sharp as his hands."

The Scotsman cracked his knuckles.

"That is, unless Mr. DeWinter feels that gentlemanly honor demands he issue a more formal statement." Connor spoke with a mocking politeness, quite sure the other man had no intention of squaring off in a fair match of pistols at dawn. He was equally certain that the fellow was not entitled to the name and pedigree he had claimed. Indeed, having an excellent ear for accents, the earl rather doubted the fellow was an Englishman.

Jaw clenched, DeWinter—or whoever he was—did not answer, contenting himself with shooting yet another malevolent look before stalking for the door. It was not until he drew abreast of the earl, brushing so closely their shoulders came in contact, that he ventured to whisper, "Every dog has his day. But yours, you misbegotten Irish cur, is fast approaching midnight."

DeWinter's companions followed, each of them turning to fix Connor with a pointed stare before sauntering out the door.

"What the devil was *that* all about?"

The earl slowly looked around at the disheveled figure who was slouched in the shadows. "Haven't a clue."

"Christ Almighty, Connor, are you losing your touch?" Gryffin Owain Dwight, the Marquess of Haddan, was one of the few people who dared to call the Irish Wolfhound by his given name. "I've never known you to play such a bloody awful hand—not even during the worst of the double R's cupshot card games.

Connor grimaced at the reminder. He and Gryff had been friends since their first schoolboy days at Eton, fighting, wenching, and raising holy hell together until finally the dons at Oxford had suggested that their wildness might be put to better use in the military. Their unit had quickly come to be called the Rakehell Regiment for their devil-may-care daring, both on and off the field of battle.

"Mayhap you are getting senile and losing your wits along with the color of your hair," drawled Gryff. "Even when three sheets to the wind—a condition which I have observed on numerous occasions—you have always been able to count to ten."

"I appreciate the vote of confidence." A note of grim amusement tinged Connor's words as he ran a hand through his raven-dark hair, which was threaded with silvery highlights.

The distinctive shade—ranging from soft silver to the steely hue of forged iron, depending on the light—had begun to appear during his year at university. That, along with the fact that his mother had been a noted beauty from County Cork, had prompted one wag at Merton to call him the Irish Wolfhound. Even Connor had to concede the nickname was an apt one. There were plenty of men—both English and French—who would curse him as a fearsome predator.

"However, my losses had nothing to do with my ability to keep track of the cards," continued the earl. "I could have counted until Doomsday and still, I would not have come up with a winning hand."

Unlike the earl, Gryff had imbibed more than a few glasses of brandy. So, it took him a moment to add up the implications. "Are you saying he was *cheating* you?"

"I would wager a monkey on it." With a self-mocking shrug, Connor added, "That is, if I had any damn blunt left in my purse."

"Does that mean you don't have a feather to fly with?" asked Gryff.

"I'm not yet plucked clean." Taking his friend by the arm, Connor guided him past the gaming tables and through a narrow alcove that opened into a small private office. "Like any sensible merchant, I keep a reserve to tide me through any unforeseen setbacks," he said, once the door had been firmly shut.

"By the by, how is business?" asked Gryff.

"Getting better and better," answered Connor with a sardonic smile. Gryff was one of the select few who knew the truth about his activities. "The irony of it borders on the absurd. For me, it's the height of hypocrisy that a titled lord can gamble or swill away an entire family fortune without suffering the slightest snub from his peers. Yet if that the same gentleman is enterprising enough to engage in trade, he is ostracized from Polite Society."

"God forbid that a true gentlemen soil his hands in any useful endeavor," growled Gryff. "Which leaves precious little to excite the imagination."

Pickling one's wits in alcohol did not seem much of an alternative. However, Connor kept the thought to himself. Though his friend's carousing was growing more and more reckless, he was hardly the one to preach reformation. "Be that as it may, my brain has been kept busy these last few months. Thanks to some expert advice, I have implemented a number of little changes that will soon ensure a handsome increase in profits." He poured both of them a glass of brandy. "In the meantime, though, I can ill-afford any more losses."

Gryff scowled as he tossed off the spirits in one swallow. "Bloody hell, if that cursed swine DeWinter was fuzzing the deck, why didn't you shoot him?"

Connor settled into the worn leather of his desk chair. "The thought had occurred to me. However, it would be bad for business if word were to leak out that a winning hand at The Wolf's Lair earned naught but a bullet to the heart."

His friend ran a hand over his unshaven jaw. "I suppose you have a point."

"Furthermore, I was not able to catch him in the act."

The admission drew a grunt of surprise. "Stayed a step ahead of the Wolfhound? He must have been damn good."

"He was."

As Gryff went to refill his glass, the earl began to massage the back of his neck. Feeling weary to the bone, he leaned back and propped his booted feet up upon the corner of his desk.

Mayhap he was getting old, for the strain of the earlier

encounter seemed to have taken its toll from every inch of his lanky form.

Hell, debauchery was far less demanding than doing an honest day's work. Several years ago, having inherited a mountain of debts to go along with the tarnished title left by his reprobate father, Connor had been faced with a decision—marry for money or rely on his own ingenuity to refill his empty coffers. He had seen enough of loveless matches—beginning with his own parents—to shudder at the thought of being legshackled to some demure young chit for the sake of a dowry.

So the choice had been an easy one.

"At least you have a challenge to spark your blood," muttered Gryff. Tugging off his unknotted cravat, he brushed a careless hand over his rumpled coat—which looked as if it had spent several nights careening though the rough-cut alleys of the surrounding slums.

"You might consider publishing your—"

Gryff cut him off with a rude oath. "You aren't the only one who prefers to guard his privacy."

Connor didn't press the matter. "Being the proprietor of a gaming hell and brothel certainly presents its own unique set of challenges," he agreed. "The odd thing is, I rather enjoy the responsibilities of running a business, even though the fact that I now work for a living is a dirty little secret that must be kept hidden from Society."

"Sod the high sticklers," swore Gryff. "Speaking of thumbing one's nose at the *ton*, when is the Bloodhound returning to Town?"

"God only knows," replied Connor with a shrug. "Cam has a knack for sniffing out adventure, and when he's on the scent of something interesting, he could be gone for weeks."

Cameron Daggett had joined the Rakehell Regiment shortly after their arrival in Portugal, and it quickly became evident that he was a kindred spirit who possessed the same biting cynicism and wicked sense of humor as Connor and Gryff. The three men had formed a fast friendship, no matter that Cameron's background remained shrouded in mystery.

Pedigree wasn't worth a spit in the heat of battle, reflected Connor. It mattered naught that they knew nothing about his earlier life. Cameron had proved his mettle many times over, and that was all that counted.

Gryff—who had been dubbed the Deerhound for his relentless pursuit of married ladies—gave a brandy-roughened growl of laughter. "What you mean is, he has a nose for trouble. However, I fear that one of these days, his light-fingered paws are going to land him in serious trouble."

"Don't worry about Cam. Like us, he knows all the filthy little tricks of how to survive in enemy territory."

The Hellhounds made no bones about their wild behavior, and Connor was well aware that the *ton* considered them dangerous, unpredictable beasts. Which suited him perfectly. The swirl of rumors surrounding his name help divert attention from his real sources of income.

Gryff stared moodily at the tips of his scuffed boots. "What about you, Connor?" he asked after a stretch of silence. "Truly—how much of a threat are tonight's losses?"

"DeWinter drew blood, but the wound should not prove mortal." Cuffing a sigh, the earl ended his inner reflections by raising his brandy and watching the candlelight refract off the faceted glass. "After all, I doubt things can get any worse…"

Such sanguine sentiments were quickly knocked to flinders by an urgent pounding on the door.

"Sorry te interrupt, sor." The hulking mulatto was nearly invisible in the dusky shadows, save for the whites of his eyes and a glint of gold dangling from his right earlobe. "But we's got a problem."

"Hell and damnation!" Connor's boots hit the carpet with a thud. "What's the trouble, Rufus? If Singleton is raising a ruckus upstairs again, I'll personally slice off his prick."

"Nor sor, it's nuffing like dat."

"What, then?"

Rufus gave a tug to his earring. "Ye had better come see fer yerself."

Biting back further comment, Connor made to follow. Although Gryff was a trifle less steady on his feet, he took one last swig from his glass and hurried to bring up the rear.

On entering the windowless back office, the first thing Connor saw were shards of glass and splinters of gilded wood from a broken picture frame scattered over the floor.

If Luck were indeed a lady, this evening she was playing devilishly hard to get.

Looking up from the ruined art to the yawing black opening in the wall, he growled a curse. Then he shifted his gaze to McTavish and his head barman, a Dubliner named O'Toole. "I presume you have checked inside the safe?"

McTavish nodded glumly. "Empty as a witch's tit."

"The devil take it," he muttered under his breath.

"Someone certainly has," quipped Gryff.

"Stubble the jokes," snapped Connor, his usual detached sense of humor having disappeared along with all of his banknotes. "At present, I am in no mood for levity."

"I daresay you are not." Gryff leaned over and picked up a black glove that was wedged between the two boxes of old ledgers. "But I would say your thief looks to be a more earthly miscreant."

After a cursory examination, the earl tossed it to McTavish. "Any idea as to who this belongs to? Or how a thief got in here?"

"Nay yet. But when I do..." Balling the leather in his fist, the Highlander gave it a vicious shake.

Connor turned his scowl on the Irishman.

"Begorrah, sir." Smacking a hand to his forehead, O'Toole gave a theatrical wince. "Me and O'Leary did leave our posts to lend a hand with the blades in the gaming room, but we weren't gone fer more than two shakes of a lamb's tail."

"What I ought to shake is your damn skull. Haven't I told you never to leave your room unattended?"

"Er, well, yes, but I thought..."

"Would that your brain were half as powerful as your biceps." Kicking at the broken glass, the earl waved both men away. "Though it's highly doubtful there are any other clues lying around, you might as well make yourselves useful and do a search."

Looking relieved to escape any further snarls, they slunk off.

His gaze narrowed as Connor surveyed the damage. It

looked as if he had been the mark of not one, but two assaults on his finances.

A random coincidence? The odds of that were . . . astronomical. They had to be related.

But how? And why?

The questions were unsettling, as there appeared to be no logical answer. He had made a host of enemies over the years, any number of whom would go for his jugular if given half a chance. But of late, he had done nothing to stir up old enmities.

No cuckolded husbands, thought Connor wryly. *No outraged peers who had found their luscious opera dancers waltzing off to warm another bed.* Hell, he had been far too busy learning the principles of accounting and cost management to have any energy left for amorous activities.

And as for any other exploits . . .

Gryff cleared his throat. "Er, look here, Connor, if you are feeling the squeeze, I should be happy to lend you whatever you need. You know damn well that I have more money than I know what to do with."

Connor felt his jaw tighten.

Sensing the hesitation, his friend flashed a rueful grimace. "Look, I've been drinking heavily and playing with all the skill of a donkey's arse these last few months, and have yet to put a dent in the family coffers. A few more guineas won't make a whit of difference."

Years of poverty had honed Connor's pride to a fine edge. But loath as he was to lean on his friends, he suddenly found himself in a very precarious position. Just a month ago, he had committed a chunk of his savings to a long-term investment, while another obligation had required a goodly amount of his reserve cash. He expected its return shortly, but the theft, coupled with the gambling losses, threatened to bankrupt his business unless he could borrow some funds to tide him over.

"It would only be for a matter of days—a week at most," he muttered.

Gryff waved off the condition. "You may repay me whenever you wish."

"No." The earl gave a dogged shake of his head. "It will be done as a proper business transaction, or not at all." Moving to the desk, he scribbled out several lines and signed it with a flourish. "A promissory note for half of The Wolf's Lair should be sufficient collateral for the funds I require."

"Hell's teeth, Connor. Your word is more than good enough. I don't need some scrap of paper," protested Gryff. "I'll probably only lose the damn thing when I'm in my cups."

"Even corned, pickled, and salted, you should be able to hang on to this." Connor forced the pledge into his friend's hand.

Pulling a face, his friend stuffed it into his waistcoat. "I am not sure it is the best idea in the world to have the prospects for your future riding in my pocket."

"Given the scrapes you have been getting yourself into lately, I can't say as I am enamored of the idea either," replied Connor. "But at the moment, I am at a loss to come up with a better one."

Chapter Two

Was this a foolish mistake?

Alexa could not help but ask herself again as she surveyed the crowded ballroom. Unerring in judgment when it came to matters of estate management, she felt far less sure of her decisions regarding her own life.

Had she really imagined that a tall, aging beanpole with unruly tresses—and an even more unruly tongue— might fit in among all the carefully cultivated blooms of London?

Brushing back an errant curl, Alexa dropped her gaze to the tips of her slippers. As the musicians struck up the first lively notes of a country gavotte, a rueful twist pulled at her mouth. She had certainly had ample time to contemplate her folly. Other than stepping out for a set with Lord Bertram and one with Mr. Hallaway—sons of Aunt Adelaide's bosom bows—she had sat on the perimeter of the dance floor for the entire evening, half hidden between a small group of turbaned matrons and a towering arrangement of potted palms.

The irony of her position was not lost her. It seemed that of late that she had been feeling awkward and isolated wherever she was. As the shadows of the fronds began a gentle swaying in time to the music, she wondered whether she would ever feel in step with those around her...

"Mr. Givens is offering to fetch us some refreshments, my dear." A discreet tap of her aunt's fan deflected such melancholy musings. "Would you care for a glass?"

Alexa forced a smile. "Yes. Thank you." She had no real desire for a sip of tepid punch, but for her aunt's sake, she wished to appear polite.

"And wouldn't you rather join Lady Fiona and her friends, instead of sitting here listening to the boring chatter of ancient crones?" Lady Merton's tone was light as she waved her fan at a group of young ladies whispering together near the card room, but there was a note of concern in her voice.

On the whole, Alexa preferred the company of her aunt and the other matrons, for at least they did not giggle incessantly while discussing the latest bits of gossip. However, she gave a small nod, reminding herself that with the time and blunt her family was spending to indulge her whim she ought to be making an effort to fit in.

"Perhaps just for a bit, if you are sure you will not feel neglected."

"No, no, not at all! Evelyn and I are having a very comfortable coze, so go and enjoy yourself." The brightening of her aunt's countenance made Alexa feel even more guilty. "I am sure Mr. Givens would be happy to provide an escort once he returns with our drinks."

Dear and determined Aunt Adelaide! She did not miss any opportunity to bring her niece to the attention of an eligible young gentleman. Alexa didn't have the heart to point out that an outspoken bluestocking of her years, no matter that she was the daughter of an earl, was not likely to attract a host of admirers.

Now, perhaps if she possessed cherubic little cheeks and a rosebud mouth—preferably one that only opened to voice adoring compliments to any male in the vicinity...

A sharp pinch knotted the strings of her reticule more tightly around her fingers. She must guard against turning too cynical, Alexa reminded herself. It wasn't as if she was hurt by the lack of suitors. So far, of all the gentlemen she had met, there was not a one for whom she felt the slightest glimmer of attraction. Indeed, for all their elegant manners and well-tailored wardrobes, they might as well have been cut from pasteboard. It was hard to distinguish one from another.

Looking up through her lashes, she saw nothing that was going to alter that opinion.

"Lady Alexa..." Her lemonade was proffered with a rather exaggerated flourish. "Allow me to escort you across the room."

Lady Fiona Eversham and her friends, four rather gawky misses fresh from the schoolroom, greeted Alexa's arrival politely enough, but their real interest appeared to be in engaging Mr. Givens in a bit of mild flirtation. The young man lingered, clearly enjoying the attention, until the beginning of a new melody reminded him of a previous commitment.

"He has very broad shoulders," sighed Miss Katherine Wilberton as Givens finished making his bows and edged his way across the dance floor. "And remarkable blue eyes."

"Yes, but Mama says his family is quite *un*remarkable."

By the firm note of her reply, it was obvious that Lady Fiona was looked up to as the authority by the others. "A minor barony is all, and on top of that, he is naught but a second son. Turn your eyes elsewhere, Kitty. We can all look higher."

Though a number of caustic comments came to mind, Alexa remained silent, mildly curious to hear what other words passed for worldly wisdom among the younger girls of the *ton*. But after a short spell, she was heartily regretting the decision to leave her chair. Following Lady Fiona's initial observation, the four of them were quick to begin a whispered exchange of other bits of gossip and rumors, each one more outrageous than the next.

Having heard enough foolishness, Alexa was about to excuse herself when Lady Fiona gave a theatrical flourish of her fan. "And speaking of ineligible gentlemen, you have only to look over *there*!"

She followed the young lady's gaze to the colonnaded entrance of the ballroom.

"The Earl of Killingworth possesses the most wicked temper in Town," continued Lady Fiona in a knowing tone. "He is said to have broken a man's arm just because he did not like the way the fellow was looking at him."

"And I overheard Papa say that he shot his paramour's husband." Lady Lucinda Lassiter was quick to contribute her own bit of scandal. "But as the man was Italian, Prinny did not force the earl to flee the country."

"He is a notorious gamester, and has stripped a number of innocent young men of their fortunes!" added Miss Wilberton rather breathlessly. "It is also said he smuggles brandy."

Not to be outdone, Lady Marianne Dickerson gave a

tiny wave of her fan. "That is not even the half of it." Lowering her voice to a conspiratorial whisper, she went on. "Aside from being a ruthless rake, my brother has heard that the earl was cashiered from the army for conduct unbecoming an officer."

A nervous titter ran through the group.

"La, Mama will fall into a fit of megrims when she sees he is among the invited guests. Lord Killingworth is precisely the sort of scoundrel she forbids me to even look at," announced Lady Fiona. Her eyes, however, remained glued on the tall figure standing in the shadows. "In less polite company, he is known by the nickname of the Irish Wolfhound, and no wonder. The earl is a *very* dangerous beast."

As if the man was going to leap out and sink his fangs into the silly chit's neck, thought Alexa. She drew in a sharp breath, aghast at the viciousness of the rumors that were circulating through Society.

Reckless daredevil, inveterate gamester, notorious womanizer—Killingworth was certainly no saint, but neither was he the devil incarnate. Though her brother Sebastian had been suspiciously loath to discuss his former comrade in her presence, she managed to learn enough about the earl's activities to know for a fact that none of the hearsay that had just been repeated—save for the part about smuggling—was true.

"What utter fustian," she muttered, unable to keep quiet any longer. "As you can see, Lord Killingworth has neither horns nor cloven hooves. In fact when I conversed with him, his manners were perfectly pleasant." That last statement was stretching the truth, admitted Alexa to herself.

All four of the other young ladies turned to stare at her.

"Y-you have spoken with the Irish Wolfhound?" gasped Lady Fiona.

Alexa nodded, finding their expressions almost comical as maidenly shock warred with adolescent awe.

"I—I am certain I should faint dead away were he to address a word to me," stammered Lady Marianne.

Alexa confined herself to a response that was only mildly ironic. "I am certain you have nothing to worry about. Despite all the rumors being bandied about, I don't believe he has ever been accused of despoiling innocent maidens in the middle of a crowded ballroom."

Unsure whether to feel disappointed or relieved, the young lady essayed a confused smile.

"Yes, that's quite right." After an awkward pause, Lady Fiona sought to reassure her friend with a pat on the arm. Nodding vigorously, the other two also gathered around more closely to offer their support. "The gentleman wouldn't dare force his advances on you, Beth. Not with..."

Alexa turned slightly. Having no interest in hearing more schoolgirl prattle, she found her attention wandering back across the room.

Even from a distance, the earl radiated an odd sort of animal magnetism. Chiseled cheekbones accentuated a lean face of angular hardness, and while his mouth—his only feature that did not appear cut from stone—had a sinuous fullness, it was usually twisted in a faintly mocking sneer. Still, there was some primal attraction about the predatory glint in his gray eyes and the hint of raw, masculine power beneath the finely tailored evening clothes that held her gaze in thrall. In contrast, all the other gentlemen of her acquaintance seemed so...tame.

Dangerous and unpredictable. Seeing as her life was the exact opposite, no wonder Alexa felt an unwilling fascination for the rogue.

And so did a number of the other ladies present, she noted, seeing she was not alone in sneaking a peek at the earl.

Alexa quickly looked away, determined not to be caught gawking.

It was, she admonished herself, absurd to be paying any heed to the likes of Lord Killingworth. Common sense said she should forget that she had ever met the dratted man!

But despite the mental scold, Alexa could not help recalling his kiss. With a small swallow, she found that she could still taste the searing press of his mouth, hot with fiery brandy and raw, animal desire. Her skin began to prickle at the recollection of his long, lithe fingers slipping beneath the silk of her bodice with wicked ease.

Hell's bells. A strange heat began licking up at her core.

Suddenly tingling with awareness, Alexa looked up to see that the earl was close by, and moving her way. Drawing a deep breath, she smoothed at her skirts and sought to control the flush of color rising to her face.

Determined to appear cool and composed, she rehearsed a suitably nonchalant greeting...

Only to find that she need not have bothered.

Without so much as a glimmer of recognition, the earl brushed past her to bow over the hand of a statuesque brunette, whose ample endowments were highlighted by a massive diamond pendant dangling at her cleavage.

Bowing her head to hide any telltale burn of color left on her cheeks, Alexa melted back into the crowd and hurried to resume a seat by her aunt.

Connor guided his partner through another intricate spin. "You haven't lost a step, I see," he murmured. "It must have taken a bit of fancy footwork to convince Chatsworth to come up to scratch."

The lady laughed softly, her eyes dancing with the same rich sparkle as her jewelry. "Oh, Drew was more than willing," she said dryly. "However, it took some time to convince the dowager dragon that I was a suitable match for her son. Now *that* required some adroit maneuvering." Moving with a fluid grace that belied her humble origins in the slums of Southwark, she finished off the complicated figure with an added flourish. "But as you know, I'm rather adept at improvising."

A grin tugged at the earl's lips.

"I have yet to thank you properly, Connor," she said, her voice growing more serious as their steps carried them away from the other couples. "For suggesting that Andrew stay at my inn while visiting his cousin."

He gave a shrug. "He was feeling blue-deviled and needed a cheery place to stay. Not to speak of someone who would be willing to lend sympathetic ear."

"I have a sneaking suspicion that my *ear* was not the part of my anatomy that you first mentioned to him." Once his bark of laughter had died away, she continued, "In all seriousness, I owe you a debt of gratitude for so much. Without the initial investment that allowed to me take up a more respectable profession—"

A squeeze of the earl's hand, coupled with an abrupt

spin, forced a pause in her words. "No need to mention it," he said curtly.

"The hell there isn't." Unintimidated by the Wolfhound's growl, the Honorable Mrs. Andrew Blake Chatsworth of Heatherton Close—formerly Suzy Simmonds of The Wolf's Lair—added a saucy smile. "But seeing as it is bringing a blush to your cheeks, I shall leave off any further expressions of gratitude. However, if there is ever anything I can do for you, Connor, you have only to name it."

Connor gave a mock shudder. "I was hoping you would say as much, but don't let Drew get wind of it. Of all my former comrades, he is by far the best shot, and I would rather my lungs and my liver remain intact."

The smile remained, but her brow took on an odd little quirk. "You know, I cannot help remarking that the least little show of tender feelings draws naught but sardonic snarls. Why are you so defensive? Afraid your reputation may be ruined were it to become known you have a heart, as well as gristle and bone, beneath that tough hide of yours?"

Though it was said half in jest, he felt himself go very rigid.

After dancing in a stiff-gaited silence for several moments, Suzy let out a harried sigh. "Forgive me if I have overstepped the bounds of our friendship. I did not mean to tread on a sensitive area—"

"You haven't," he said gruffly. "I have my reasons, however they are not ones I intend to discuss with anyone." Seeing the spasm of hurt that crossed her face, he was quick to retreat to a less touchy subject. "Getting back to your offer, I meant it when I said there was something you might help me with."

Her expression looked a little less pinched. "There is?"

"Has Drew, er, stayed friendly with Brighton and his circle?" The question was a trifle more awkward to ask than he had imagined, for it suddenly occurred to him that a wife, however worldly, might not care for the idea of her husband running tame with a ring of smugglers.

His worry was short-lived, as Suzy laughed. "I might as well still be running an inn, for how often Hogshead Harry and Spotted Dick spend the night at the Close. Why do you ask?"

"I would like to find out what they know of a cardsharp who goes by the name of DeWinter. Medium height, heavyset build, light brown hair." He went on to give a few more physical details. "And an accent that rolls in and out like the tide. Until recently he may have been working on the other side of the channel—mayhap in Antwerp or Amsterdam."

"As it happens, Drew and I are returning home on the morrow. I should be able to send you an answer within a few days." Bemusement left behind, she was now all business. "Any other particulars that would prove helpful?"

The earl pursed his lips. "A good point. Any information on who he has worked for in the past. And more importantly, who might have contracted his services within the last few weeks."

Suzy maintained a thoughtful silence as the violins raced to an echoing crescendo. "Do you mean to say that someone has tried to stir up trouble at The Wolf's Lair?" she asked.

"He did more than try," admitted Connor. "He picked my pocket clean. Not only that, in creating a diversion at the tables, he also afforded an accomplice the opportunity to sneak into the back office and rob the safe."

Her eyes widened. "Who would instigate such an attack?"

"At this point, your guess is as good as mine." His gaze began a slow sweep of the room. "Apparently someone is of the opinion that an old dog's teeth have grown dull from disuse." The earl was about to turn away when his head snapped around for a second look at the arrangement of potted palms. A sharp intake of breath was followed by a muttered oath. Despite the dim light and the overlapping fringe of fronds, the pale profile and twist of wheaten curls was all too recognizable.

"Hell and damnation," he repeated under his breath.

Suzy, now alert for any hint of danger, leaned in closer. "More trouble?"

"In spades," came the gloomy response. "Whoever named Luck a lady was a bloody idiot."

Desperate for a few moments of solitude, Alexa glanced around, then hurried past the withdrawing room for ladies and turned down a darkened side corridor. With its heady swirl of silks and scents, of lights and laughter, the ballroom had suddenly become too oppressive to bear. Every glittering, gleaming detail seemed a mocking reminder of how dull she was.

How different she was.

Alexa pressed her palms to her cheeks, feeling the hot humiliation burn through her thin kidskin gloves. Spotting a set of arched French doors up ahead, she quickened her steps and slipped out to the gardens. The small terrace was deserted, its decorative urns and slate tiles shrouded in shadows cast by the torchieres on the balcony and the full moon overhead.

Drawing in a great gulp of the cool night air, she choked back a sob. Oh, stop indulging in self-pity, she scolded herself. What had she expected? To dazzle the gentlemen of London with her beauty and brilliant intellect?

Hah. With a wry grimace, she blinked the beads of moisture from her lashes. She was a rough-cut bit of country quartz compared to the perfectly polished jewels of the *ton*. To imagine that—

The click of the door latch was followed by a grunt of surprise.

Alexa whirled around. "I'm sorry. I know I shouldn't be out here alone—" she began, and then stopped short on seeing who it was.

"*You*," growled the Irish Wolfhound. "You seem to have a habit of straying to places where you shouldn't go." A breeze ruffled his hair, and the swaying twists of ivy cast a pattern of light and dark across his chiseled face. He looked fierce. *Forbidding.*

Alexa lifted her chin, refusing to be intimidated. "I needed a breath of fresh air, and a garden terrace is a perfectly respectable place for me to be." She exaggerated taking a look around. "Or were you hoping to sneak a quick tup with one of your lightskirts?"

His lips thinned. "You have a saucy mouth, Lady Alexa Hendrie. Take care that it does not get you into trouble."

"It already has—on more than one occasion," she said defiantly. "If you recall, *you* kissed me."

"I have kissed a great many women," drawled the earl.

"And I wasn't very memorable?"

A quicksilver flicker of moonlight flashed beneath his dark lashes. Then his eyes were once again as hard as blackened steel. "What do *you* think?"

She felt a flush steal over her face, and was furious with herself for asking such a stupid question. *Idiot.* Of course he wouldn't remember kissing an awkward country miss. As for her own recollection of the moment...

"Thank God for that," answered Alexa with a mock shudder. "Seeing as I, too, have expunged the unpleasant interlude from my mind." She paused for a moment. "Not that it required much effort, I might add."

"Indeed?" A dark brow shot up. "I was under the impression that you were paying rather close attention to the experience."

"You flatter yourself, sir. Be assured that, as kisses go, your performance was quite forgettable."

"Forgettable," he repeated softly.

"Completely," she assured him.

"Well, then perhaps you need a reminder."

Alexa gave an involuntary gasp. "You wouldn't *dare*."

"I warned you about your mouth—that's exactly the wrong thing to say to a lecherous libertine."

Don't. She stared at the sinuous curl of his smirk. *Don't think about the hot, brandy-spiced taste of his lustful lips. Don't think about the hard, steel-chiseled press of his sculpted muscles.*

"Don't..." she stammered.

Too late.

With a wicked gleam in his gaze, the Irish Wolfhound seized her shoulders and drew her close. Then his wanton mouth was on hers, teasing a terrible, tingling lick of heat inside her. Fire sizzled from her scalp to her toes—and to hidden places she wasn't even aware existed.

This time, his kiss was slower, softer. He suckled her lower lip, his teeth gently nipping the swell of her flesh. Alexa shivered as the earl traced his fingertips along the arch of her neck and framed her face between his palms. Surrendering a tiny moan of pleasure, she opened herself to his delving demand. The slide of his tongue inside her was wildly sensuous. Her pulse began to skitter, her knees began to quake.

Strangely enough, the soft, suckled sighs were not all hers. The Wolfhound's breath tickled her cheeks, and within its gossamer flutter seemed to float a sweet, sweet whisper.

She tried to make sense of the sound but the earl's hands were moving—from slope of her shoulders down the curl of her spine, their touch sending shivering sparks spiraling through her belly.

Oh, oh, oh. This was too wicked—too wonderful—for words.

Overpowered by all the new sensations, Alexa needed a fraction of a second to realize that the earl had released her and moved back a step.

Sucking in a breath, she sought to steady her shaky legs. Every bone in her body seemed to have melted into mush.

"I trust you won't need another reminder to stay within the confines of Polite Society," said the earl, now sounding thoroughly bored. "As you see, danger lurks in every crevasse and corner of London, ready to devour any innocent who makes the mistake of straying into the shadows."

Turning on his heel, he descended the stone steps and disappeared into the mist-shrouded garden. A moment later, Alexa heard the *clink* of an iron gate open and close as he let himself out to the street. A swirl of silvery vapor danced silently through the ivy vines, serenaded by only the plaintive song of a nightingale and the faint whisper of a violin.

Chapter Three

If looks could kill, that poor knight would have expired ages ago."

Making an effort to smooth the scowl from her face, Alexa glanced up from the chessboard. "Sorry. I suppose I have not been very pleasant company."

"No," agreed her cousin Henry. "In fact, you have been quite rotten company." He nudged his pawn into the space vacated by her bishop, promptly putting her king into checkmate. "And on top of it, you have been playing like a pea-brained widget, when you normally rout me in less than a quarter hour. What's wrong? I would have thought you would be enjoying the chance to experience a Season in London."

Why must everyone keep reminding me of that?

Her fingers lingered on one of the ivory figures, then brushed it from the board. She must push aside her odd mopings. Along with the unaccountable daydreams about a certain roguish gentleman. It was only in the pages of a Minerva Press novel that a heroic white knight came galloping in to sweep a lady off her feet.

And the Earl of Killingworth, with his distinctly off-color looks, could hardly be called lily white.

"It's not that I miss moving mountains of manure or digging miles of drainage ditches. But…" Her nebulous discontent was maddeningly hard to explain. "But with Sebastian away in the army and Papa uninterested in mundane matters like money, it fell to me to keep the estate from crumbling into ruin. And strangely enough, the duties proved interesting."

Henry made a face.

"I found the challenges fulfilling," went on Alexa. "However, now those responsibilities rightfully belong to Sebastian and Nicola."

"Seb and his bride would be wise to hire you as their head steward," joked Henry. "How you managed to turn a sow's ear into a silk purse is beyond me."

"That's because I read books on crop rotation and seed hybrids—"

"Ballocks to books!" exclaimed her cousin. "I say that's exactly the trouble. You've been in harness too long. It's time to kick off the traces and have a little fun here in London."

"You forget that gentlemen are accorded a great deal more freedom than ladies," she muttered. "I might as well have taken the King's shilling, for all the rules and regulations that regiment my life. At least I would be getting paid for the aggravation."

Henry laughed. A year her junior, he had shared many a youthful escapade, tagging along on the heels of her brothers, so he was used to her tart candor. "That bad, is it?"

"The drawing rooms are stifling in every sense of the word."

"Sounds as if you could use a breath of fresh air. What say you to a ride in the park?"

"Where propriety dictates we proceed at a sedate walk?" She shook her head. "Lud, what I wouldn't give for a rousing gallop across the moors."

"I know how you feel." Still in the throes of sowing his wild oats, he had narrowly escaped being sent down from Oxford for a schoolboy prank. "Pater has felt obliged to tighten the leash—and the purse strings—of late and it's deucedly annoying to feel..."

"As if you can't breathe?" she suggested. "Ha!" A note of bitterness crept into her voice. "At least you do not have to submit to a corset and endless evenings of dull dances and prosy bores."

A mischievous gleam came to his eye. "Want to cut loose for an evening?"

Alexa knew the sensible response was a firm "no." She had not needed Sebastian's words of warning to know that in London, the slightest breach of etiquette could result in a ruined reputation.

But then, a small voice spoke up in the back of her head.

To hell with the rules. Why could she not enjoy one night free from the fetters of everyone's expectations?

"What do you have in mind?"

Henry grinned. "There is to be a soiree of music and gaming given by a certain lady whose existence is not acknowledged by the *ton*. Having been a guest at her previous gatherings, I can vouch for it being a great deal more lively than your usual entertainments."

"It does sound like great fun." Though sorely tempted, Alexa allowed common sense to reassert itself. "But if you are planning to attend, the odds are that other gentlemen of our acquaintance will be there as well. There isn't a snowball's chance in hell that my presence would go unnoticed. Or unmentioned." She heaved a sigh. "Your conduct would be deemed youthful exuberance, while mine would be deemed an utter disgrace."

Henry's grin grew even wider. "Not if you, too, were to appear as a man."

Alexa blinked. "You're joking!"

"You have pulled it off before. Remember the time you dressed as a groom and came with us to the mill between Belcher and the challenger from Liverpool?"

Henry was right. It would not be the first time she had donned breeches and boots to accompany him to a gathering forbidden to females of her social standing. Yet going unremarked amid a frenzied throng of well-lubricated spectators screaming for blood was one thing. Masquerading as a gentleman at a Town soiree was quite another.

"There will not be nearly the distractions," she pointed out. "The disguise would have to be awfully good."

"I have a friend who is quite skilled in amateur theatrics," said Henry. "I'm sure he can fashion a convincing rig."

"I couldn't...I shouldn't..."

"Come, the risk is not so very great," urged Henry. "The rooms will be dimly lit, and the other guests will be foxed."

Alexa bit at her lower lip.

Her cousin then played his trump card. "You have always said that you wanted to test your skills against serious gamesters. Well, the card room will offer some very interesting opportunities for play."

Did she dare stake her reputation on one night of hijinks?

In managing the estate, she had always been prudent, carefully assessing the risks before making a decision. And she had always erred on the side of caution. Now, with her own future in the balance, Alexa decided to throw caution to the wind.

"Very well—I'll do it."

"Ha! I knew you would come around!" Henry gave a whoop of delight. "I promise you, this will be a great lark. Who knows—with your nerve and your knack for numbers, you may even end up winning a hefty amount of pin money."

"Ha!" she echoed, though in her voice the boyish enthusiasm was tempered by an edge of pragmatism. "Sometimes it takes more than nerve and skill to win."

"Right." Plucking the ebony queen from the checkered board, he tossed it up and watched it turn a slow, spinning somersault before catching it in midair. "Sometimes it takes a dash of luck. But you, my dear cuz, have always been a lucky lady."

The numbers were proving perversely difficult to add up. Connor looked up from the ledgers, admitting that the difficulty lay not with the neatly penned expenses but with his own wandering concentration. He wished he might claim it was all on account of his sudden financial setbacks. However, as the figure in his mind's eye began to take a completely different set of curves than the ones on the page, he was forced to set the book aside.

Hell, he had not been aware that Lady Alexa Hendrie had returned to London. That in itself should not be very surprising, seeing as he paid little heed to the everyday gossip of the *ton*. Yet he had experienced the oddest sensation the other night on seeing her sitting in the shadows. For an instant, the jolt of awareness was almost as if he had been struck by a bolt of lightning.

More likely, he ought to be struck by a punch to the jaw!

The earl shook his head. Normally he would need no such overt reminder that a gentleman of his reputation was expected to stay well away from innocent young ladies. Sebastian Hendrie had not minced words in saying as much several months ago. Not that Connor blamed him. What conscientious brother would allow a notorious womanizer near his sister? But unlike many of the rakes who roamed in his part of Town, Connor had absolutely no interest in the pursuit of such prey. Despite the widespread opinion of Society, he was not lost to all notion of honor.

And besides, dewy-eyed inexperience in the ways of world bored him to perdition.

So why had he kissed her again? Only a fool made the same mistake twice. He had enough down-to-earth problems without allowing quirks of fancy to take flight.

Connor traced the contour of his lower lip with his tongue. It was not the lingering traces of Scotch whisky and Virginia tobacco he tasted, but the tingling memory of her pliant mouth.

Still, he could not quite shake the thought of Alexa Hendrie from his head. Even seated in obscurity, she radiated a unique vitality, her strong, sun-dappled features giving her an aura of individuality among all the bland beauty. Even more intriguing was the spark of her sapphire eyes, hinting at an inner fire.

The rakehell Irish Wolfhound undone by a stolen kiss?

Damn. Connor had lost count of how many women he had kissed. Of all of them, Alexa Hendrie should not be very memorable.

And yet she was.

Maddeningly so. Beguilingly so. He could recall in exquisite detail the shocked shiver of her lips, their initial resistance slowly softening, and the cry of outrage turning to a whispery sigh.

Against his will, he found himself thinking back to their first encounter, and how, for a fleeting interlude, she had opened herself to his intimacies. As if she somehow trusted him, though he had her pinned up against a wall, his body thrust ruthlessly up against hers. The tentative touch of her fingers twined in his hair, the shy flick of her tongue, the hesitant arch of her back—such innocence should have warned him to pull away.

He had meant to teach her a lesson about the perils that lurked in London if a young lady was too bold in bending the rules. Instead, in a moment of madness, he had forgotten all about rules. He had unbuttoned her bodice and rucked up her skirts, feeling a strange need to touch her breasts, to slide his hands over her smooth thighs. Lust did not begin to describe what had come over him. It was something infinitely more compelling. Urgent and yet tender, in a way that defied mere words...

Bloody hell. I'm not only a miserable poet but also a damnable fool.

Massaging his temples, Connor decided to fetch himself another bottle of brandy, no matter that he could ill-afford the drain on his dwindling supply of spirits.

To hell with the cost. He had a feeling it was going to take more than a swallow to douse the strange flare of desire that had come to life inside him.

Peering up from beneath a high crown beaver hat, Alexa stared at the front door.

"Relax. Reggie's idea of casting you as university student, newly arrived from Sweden, was sheer genius," assured Henry. "All foreigners are looked on as eccentric, so any oddities will be excused."

"Your friend has a diabolically vivid imagination," she muttered, pulling the brim a bit lower. "Thank God we talked him out of the idea of turning me into an Indian nabob."

"You would have looked smashing in a ruby red silk turban."

Alexa rolled her eyes. "Right. A perfect choice for someone who does not wish to attract attention."

"We both agreed you had a point. This suits you much better." Her cousin reached for the brass knocker. "Don't worry. All you have to do is remember the few little mannerisms we went over."

Before she could voice any further reservation, the door swung open, and her cousin hustled her inside.

"Show a bit of bottom," he hissed, making quick work of handing their overcoats to the butler. "M'friend here prefers to keep his hat," he announced with an airy wave. In a lower voice he added, "You know the Swedes—queer fish."

The butler nodded gravely.

"Come along, Lars." A tug to Alexa's sleeve pulled her along into the hallway.

"Lars!" she muttered under her breath. "Did you have to choose a name that sounds so close to 'liar'?"

"Put a cork in it," he warned, as the babble of voices and clinking of crystal indicated they were fast approaching the main drawing room.

"Speaking of corks, I think I could do with a glass of champagne..."

Whether it was the wine or just the loosening of her nerves of their own accord, Alexa soon found herself feeling more at ease. Henry had been right—the other guests were too caught up in their own amusements to pay any heed to the new arrivals. The laughter was growing louder, and the conversation more animated.

Out of the corner of her eye, she noticed a gentleman's hand sliding down the bare shoulder of his companion—

"Ahem." With a sharp cough, Henry pulled her away and headed for an arched entryway. "Shall we go have a look at the gaming room?"

"What's the hurry?" Alexa paused as one of the musicians climbed atop a bowfront sideboard and launched into a lively country jig. As two men linked arms and begin spinning in a dizzying circle, she slanted a look around the room. "There don't seem to be many ladies present."

"To tell the truth, I don't think that there are *any* ladies present." Henry helped himself to more champagne, then refilled her glass. "If you get my drift."

Seeing a buxom blonde mount a gentleman's shoulders, her skirts frothing up around her thighs, Alexa gave a low snort. "You needn't dance around the subject. If you mean that most of the females here are lightskirts, I would say that is fairly obvious."

Henry nearly choked on a swallow of his wine. "As if you have ever set eyes on that sort of woman."

"As a matter of fact…" Her mouth curled up at the corners. Henry knew nothing about her brief visit to a house of ill repute and she decided to leave it that way. Sebastian had once mentioned that her cousin tended to turn awfully garrulous when drunk.

"Oh, never mind," she continued. "However, as you well know, my sensibilities are hardly those of a sheltered young miss." Her gaze, still fixed on the dancing, caught the saucy wink that a raven-haired doxie was directing Henry's way. "By the by, if you wish to pursue a more intimate acquaintance—one that might take you upstairs—don't let my presence hold you back. I can find my own entertainments."

Turning a bit green at the gills, Henry promptly drained his glass. "Perhaps this was not such a good idea after all."

"Don't turn priggish now," she murmured. "What goes on between men and women is no dark mystery when one has overseen the breeding of sheep and—"

"Have some rum punch," he mumbled, reaching for a new round of libations.

"No, thank you. I prefer to keep a clear head for cards."

"Cards." Looking relieved at the change of subject, Henry started forward. "By all means, let's see what sort of action is taking places at the tables."

Alexa, however, refused to be rushed. The air, scented with the seductive spice of cigars and perfumes, was intoxicating and she stood for a moment, simply inhaling the tantalizing whiff of forbidden freedoms. Gentlemen had all the luck, she decided. They had so few boundaries.

While ladies were expected to be satisfied living their entire lives within the confines of a tight little box.

And most were. Alexa played with the folds of her cravat. Was she odd, to be longing for something she couldn't quite put a finger on? Looking around again, she knew she should be shocked by the licentious looseness of the crowd. By all rights, the laughter was too loud, the comments too lusty.

And yet, she thought wistfully, they all seemed to be having such fun.

A nudge from Henry finally moved her to follow him into the gaming room.

Despite the low light and haze of cigar smoke, it quickly became evident that the stakes were running a good deal higher than a penny a point.

After glancing around at the taut faces, her cousin was moved to a low whistle. "The play tonight is too deep for a novice," he cautioned. "We'll just watch for a bit, then take our leave."

"No," replied Alexa firmly.

"But—"

"I've enough blunt to take a seat for a hand or two."

He grimaced as his gaze fell on the players seated in the center of the room. "I would not advise it. Northinger and Haddan are notoriously reckless when it comes to betting."

One of the gentlemen at the table suddenly rose and with a curse at the cards staggered off. Alexa quickly slipped into his place, leaving her cousin no choice but to play along with their charade.

"Young Lars here has just arrived from Sweden," announced Henry to the other players as he leaned in over her shoulder. "He wishes to test his mettle against you gentlemen."

"*Ja*," she muttered.

"He doesn't speak much English," explained Henry.

"Neither does Quincy." The dealer's comment drew a good deal of laughter. "Half the time I can't understand a bloody thing he says."

"Kroner, crowns—as long as the lad has ready blunt, he is welcome to play," replied the dealer.

The others nodded in agreement, and after a brief round of introductions, a new game began.

"It's damnably close in here," remarked Northinger. "Why the hat and gloves?"

"For luck," answered Henry quickly.

"*Ja*. Luck," echoed Alexa.

The reply was accepted with naught but a slight shrug. Without further ado, the group settled in for some serious play.

Grateful for the silence that descended over the table, Alexa soon fell into the rhythm of the cards. Undistracted by the flow of spirits or the occasional female who stopped to watch the action, she paid strict attention to every nuance of the unfolding hands. Such diligence soon paid off. The banknotes began to pile up in front of her.

"I'm done." After yet another loss, Northinger slapped down his cards with a grunt of disgust. "Come, Haddan, let's see if the females in the other room will prove more accommodating than the bloody Queen of Spades."

"No, no, m'luck's bound to come 'round." The marquess waved for more brandy. "I'll stay a bit longer."

Northinger laughed. "That's what you always think, Gryff. Especially when the few wits you possess are fuzzed with drink." He turned and clapped an arm around Henry. "I know I can count on you to be up for a little fun."

"Well, er..." stalled her cousin, trying to slip out of the embrace. "That is, I shouldn't leave Lars alone—"

"Ballocks!" With Henry still firmly in his grasp, Northinger moved toward the doorway. "The lad doesn't need a nursemaid. Doing fine on his own."

Alexa, emboldened by her string of successes, waved Henry on. "*Ja.* Go."

Seeing no way out, her cousin allowed himself to be ushered away, but not before shooting her one last look of reproach.

She restrained the urge to stick out her tongue. How glorious it felt to be wickedly, wantonly irresponsible. Like the other free spirits in the drawing room, she wanted to dance a little jig.

The pair tottered through the doorway. But as they rubbed shoulders with a lone figure making his entrance into the room, Alexa felt her stomach do a sudden, skidding slide into her ribs.

Chapter Four

$\mathcal{A}$pproaching the smoke-shrouded table, the Earl of Killingworth nodded a greeting to the players. "Who's the puppy," he growled, his gaze lingering for a moment on Alexa.

Ducking her head even lower, she made a show of studying her cards.

"Lars—he's a friend 'f Sir 'Enry," answered Gryff, sloshing more brandy into his glass.

"Lars appears to be a lucky lad," remarked the Wolfhound, flicking a quick look at the pile of banknotes piled in front of her.

"Nipping at our balls, that's for damn sure," muttered Quincy. "Next he'll be gnawing on my prick."

Leaning a hip against the back of her chair, Connor crossed his arms. "How very embarrassing," he drawled. "I, for one, would never dream of letting such an inexperienced mouth anywhere near my privy parts."

The remark elicited a round of guffaws.

Alexa was suddenly hot all over. Her cheeks flamed, her fingertips burned. But the worst of the flames seemed to be licking at a small spot just below her left shoulder.

Beneath the layers of her clothing her skin felt scorched.

The Wolfhound shifted slightly and the fall of his trousers grazed against her.

Dear God. Dear God. As if she needed any reminder that he was a distinctly male animal.

"Your turn to discard, Lars," chided Quincy.

She threw down a random card.

"Ha! Knew it!" With a slurred smile, Gryff scooped up his winnings. "Lady Luck's finally going to kiss my hand."

"Kiss my arse," grumbled Quincy.

"Perhaps, you ought to quit while you are ahead," said Connor softly, eyeing the pair of empty bottles by his friend's side.

Making a face, Gryff replied with a rude oath.

"Suit yourself," murmured the earl.

Alexa felt the Wolfhound's big, muscled body shift again, and silently prayed that he was taking his leave. A trickle of sweat teased its way down her spine, leaving a trail of liquid sparks.

"What's the matter, puppy?" he snapped. "Am I making you nervous?"

She shook her head, not daring to speak.

"Then stop squirming."

Her limbs tensed and she held herself very still. This was dangerous.

Oh-so dangerous.

But it wasn't just fear that was coursing through her blood like hot buttered rum. It was something far more potent—a heady mixture of excitement, elation, and some emotion she couldn't quite define.

After several long moments of silence, the Wolfhound moved away, but only to stand by the marquess.

"Do you wish to pull up a chair and join the game?" asked Gryff.

Holding her breath, Alexa ventured a peek from beneath the brim of her hat.

"The stakes aren't high enough to tempt me." The Wolfhound appeared to have lost any interest in the players or the card game. As he turned to survey the room, his gunmetal gaze skimmed over her as if she weren't there.

Alexa knew she should be relieved, and yet...

"Have you seen Babcock?" he asked his friend.

"Not that I can recall," answered Gryff.

"If you are searching for company, Lord Killingworth, you need not look too far." A voluptuous blonde slipped around two gentlemen at the dice table and placed a hand on his sleeve. Alexa tried to concentrate on her cards, but she couldn't help noticing that the décolletage of the woman's gown was cut nearly to her navel. And her ample bosom was covered by barely a thread. "I would be delighted to keep you company."

"I've business elsewhere," he replied.

"Business?" The blonde's hand rubbed suggestively along his arm. "But here, you won't have to pay for your pleasures."

Her touch dropped to toy with the fastenings of his trousers. And then her fingers slid lower and cupped a small squeeze.

As the Wolfhound gave a rumbled laugh, Alexa felt her own flesh begin to tingle. His brandy-roughened voice seemed to stir a fresh wave of molten heat that swirled in her belly, then dipped deep between her legs.

With a little purr, the blonde began to tease her palm back and forth.

The earl's reaction was obvious, despite the low light. However, his laugh grew a little louder. "I assure you, my dear, that wherever I go, I am never required to pay for my pleasure."

"Hell, the lad's blushing," chuckled Quincy. "Have you ever tupped a woman, Lars?" he asked with a leer. "You've got more than enough to pay for a prime article like Sally."

"Bloody hell, could we stubble the talk of sex?" grumbled Gryff. "Be a good lass and dangle those lovely tits elsewhere, Sal. You'll frighten the lad away before I've had a chance to recoup my losses."

The woman made a moue of disappointment and flounced away.

"Very well, I'll leave you all to your games." The Wolfhound glanced at Alexa and gave a bored shrug. "Enjoy your evening, puppy. You may blink now and I won't bite off your head."

Gritting her teeth, Alexa watched him walk away. *Damn the man.* The fire inside her cooled somewhat, and yet her blood was still thrumming. *How dare he treat her like a child when she was besting some of London's most notorious gamesters?*

Forcing her attention back to her hand, she steadied her nerves and channeled her pent-up emotion into sharper play and bolder bets.

"Damn, I'd wear *two* pairs of those cursed black gloves if it would bring me such a winning touch," growled Quincy, as he shoved back his chair. "I'm done for the night. Ye better fold them as well, Haddan. Your dish is as empty as mine."

"No, no, I can feel it in my bones—this next deal is

going to change everything." Gryff looked to Alexa. "Any objection t' playin' on, Lars? Say, f'r one hand t' recoup all m' losses?"

She thought for a moment, then nodded in agreement, though the spot in front of him was indeed bare.

Following her gaze, Gryff started fumbling through his pockets. "Bloody hell, must have some more blunt tucked away s'mewhere." A slip of crumpled paper emerged from the depths of his waistcoat. After giving the contents a bleary squint, he dropped it on the table. "This should do it. Worth a demmed sight more'n the bet—and likely cost me m' prick if I lose it. But I don't intend t' lose."

Alexa didn't imagine anyone ever did. But even had she trusted her voice, she would have kept mum. Far be it for her to offer advice to a seasoned gamester, even if a novice could see that tonight was not the night to keep challenging Fate.

"Will y' accept a vowel, lad? 'Pon my word of honor as a gentlem'n, it's good."

"*Ja.*" In truth, she wasn't thinking about the money. The heady thrill of taking a risk, heightened by her earlier encounter, was making her heart race and her breath come in ragged gulps. It was both frightening and exhilarating. No wonder gentlemen frequented gaming hells if it made them feel this... alive.

Gryff took up the deck and dealt the cards.

Alexa paused for a moment, eye to eye with the Queen of Hearts as she waited for the butterflies to cease fluttering around in her stomach.

The marquess groaned in disgust.

A peek at her hidden cards showed the Ace, King, and Jack.

Alexa could scarcely believe that luck had favored her with such an unbeatable hand. She turned the dazzling show of red face up in the flickering light.

"May the Norse Gods be neutered," swore Quincy. "He's done it again."

"Er, so he has." Gryff swore under his breath. "Was sure my luck w's turning."

She gathered in the slip of paper and shoved it, along with the jumble of banknotes, into the pocket of her coat. Touching the brim of her hat in a jaunty salute, she rose and walked off, hoping her mimicking of a masculine stride would hide her real desire to twirl on her toes.

Feeling light as a feather, and free as a bird, Alexa passed through the doorway. In her elevated mood, she saw it as a magic portal. Indeed, it was all like something out of a fairy tale, where the rules and roles had given way to dreams and desires. Her lips, half hidden by the false mustache, curled up in secret delight, but after another step or two, the smile turned rather bittersweet.

All fairy tales had an end. At the stroke of midnight, the laughter would fade, the revelries would die away and the glass slipper—or in this case, the high top Hessian boots—would turn back into ordinary kidskin pumps.

Alexa glanced at the clock, then plucked a glass of champagne from the sideboard and headed out to the gardens. The air was cool, and she stood for a moment in pale moonlight, sipping her wine and savoring the scent of lilac. She meant to enjoy the last few minutes of precious freedom in solitude, but for some unaccountable reason, she found herself wishing she might conjure up a storybook prince for company. One whose hair shimmered with silvery highlights...

"Silly goose," she muttered under her breath. The champagne must be having an odd effect on her brain, for rarely did she indulge in such silly schoolgirl fantasies.

A prince, indeed!

Ha! She may as well kiss the stone gryphon set in the niche of the wall, for all the good it would do her.

"There you are!" Henry appeared a trifle out of breath as he caught hold of her sleeve. "What—what the deuce are you doing standing atop that urn?"

Her boots hit the gravel with a crunch. "Nothing," she muttered, grateful that a twist of ivy covered her embarrassment.

"Step over here. We must talk."

His peremptory tone caused her hackles to rise. Why must he ruin these last few precious moments of freedom? "What is so important that it cannot wait until later?" she demanded.

"The vowel."

Alexa stared at him blankly.

"Haddan's pledge. You have to give it back."

"Give it back?" He meant to rob her of that as well? "But I won it fair and square!"

Henry shuffled his feet. "Er, well, he wasn't quite thinking straight at the moment. He wasn't supposed to risk that particular piece of paper." Clearing his throat, her cousin added, "And, er, had he known he was playing against a female, he would never have made the wager."

It was now righteous indignation that brought fire to her cheeks. "I thought that once a gentlemen made a bet, he was honorbound to abide by it."

"Yes, but..."

Once again there appeared to be two sets of rules. And

as always, the one that applied to gentlemen apparently allowed for far more latitude than did the one that applied to ladies. Her mood already on edge, Alexa reacted with blunt outrage. "Well it's a trifle late for regrets."

Her cousin's face took on a greenish cast. "Be reasonable, Alexa!"

"Why should I?" she shot back.

"B-because it's..." Taken aback by the unexpected resistance, Henry was reduced to an incoherent stuttering. Raking a hand through his hair, he finally gathered enough composure to blurt out the truth. "Bloody hell, Alexa. The pledge happens to be a half-ownership in a gaming hell and brothel!" He gave a nervous laugh. "Surely you can see now why it must be handed over immediately."

She withdrew the paper from her pocket and for the first time took a close look.

The Wolf's Lair. The name was written in a bold script, along with a scrawled signature. *Linsley.*

Wishing to make sure it was not a bend of light or a hiccup of reason that was playing tricks with her imagination, Alexa read it over several times before carefully refolding the foolscap and tucking it away in a more secure place.

For whatever reason, it appeared the Earl of Killingworth had been forced to take a gamble. Her lips set in a grim smile.

Ha! The Wolfhound had held the upper hand the first three times they had met. Now, she was—to say the least—on equal footing with the rogue.

"Alexa? You are going to give it back, aren't you?"

"Absolutely not."

Henry was rendered momentarily speechless. Seeing that pleas were getting him nowhere, he resorted to wheedling. "Pater will have my guts for garters when he finds out—that is, if Sebastian doesn't murder me first and feed my entrails to the wolves."

"There are no wolves in Yorkshire," retorted Alexa. A spasm of resentment caused her fists to clench. Turning on her heel, she started to walk away. "As for the consequences, you will just have to chance them, won't you?"

"Alexa! Wait!"

His lunge caused her to stumble up against a trellis of roses. Caught in the thorns, her hat came off, pulling her tightly wound tresses loose in a scattering of hairpins.

With an angry toss of her head, she yanked herself free. "By all rights it's mine, Henry. Come hell or—"

In the heat of the argument, neither of them heard the approaching steps.

"May Sat'n be boiled 'n brandy!"

Alexa whipped around to find the Marquess of Haddan staring at the tumble of her wheaten curls.

Gryff blinked. "Good God."

"Good God," repeated Henry, in hollow echo of the marquess's surprise. "We are really in the brambles now."

Seeing there was no way to disguise the truth, Alexa reached up and peeled the itchy bit of hair from her upper lip.

"Who—" began Gryff.

"Allow me to introduce my cousin, Lady Alexa Hendrie," said Henry through gritted teeth.

"D-delighted t' make your acquaint'nce," drawled the marquess.

"I highly doubt it," replied Alexa.

"Look, Haddan, I know this looks highly irregular—"

The marquess slid his gaze down to Alexa's snug breeches and allowed a small smile.

"But I beg that as a favor to us—and to your old comrade Sebastian Hendrie—that you will promise to keep this little charade a secret. It was all meant in harmless fun, but if word were to leak out, the lady would be ruined."

"Seb's s'ster?" Gryff's expression sobered. "You have my word 'f honor that I'll say nothing about this."

Alexa waited until the sigh escaping from Henry's lips had run its course. "Speaking of honor, Lord Haddan, it appears we have another rather delicate matter to discuss."

Gryff started to hold out his hand.

"Not so fast." Alexa folded her arms across her chest. "Would you seek to renege on your bet if I were really a gentleman?"

The marquess looked nonplussed. Her cousin stared down at his boots.

"Well?" she pressed.

"No," admitted Gryff. "I wouldn't."

"Then that is the end of it," she announced.

"I fear it's j'st the beginning," replied Gryff slowly. "Unless, o'course, you will let me redeem the vowel at, say, double the value?"

She shook her head.

"Y're a dab hand at cards, Lady Alexa. Appear t' have a clever mind an' steady nerve as well." The marquess smoothed at his rumpled cravat. "Hope ye have a spine o' steel hidden beneath the gent's garb. Y'll need it when the

Wolfhound hears o' this."

"Don't worry about me, sir." She paused as she tucked her hair back under her hat. "As you have seen, I'm not afraid to go *mano a mano* against any gentleman, however fierce his reputation."

Chapter Five

Jaw clenched, eyes narrowed, Connor paced the perimeter of the dance floor, all too aware of his unfortunate resemblance to a predator stalking its quarry. The other guests were quick to slink out of his way, wary yet watchful, their curious gazes following his every move. Already he could hear the faint whispers behind his back. Speculation, no doubt, on what had brought the Hellhounds out to prowl through the inner circle of Polite Society.

The music, a lilting Viennese waltz, set his teeth further on edge. *Damn Gryff and his jug-bitten judgment.* As he stalked past the musicians, Connor was sorely tempted to put his foot through the delicate inlaid veneer of the pianoforte.

Pivoting on his heel, the earl brushed by the colonnaded gallery, his brusque step setting a wave of ostrich plumes to fluttering as several turbaned matrons fled like hens before a fox. He watched them regroup and begin an agitated clucking—which he answered with a black scowl.

On the morrow, of course, the drawing rooms would be humming with the latest example of the Wolfhound's vicious temper. But at least the tale would be true, unlike most of the outrageous ondits.

His mouth stretched taut as the bass string of a viola, he fell in stride with Gryff, who had just finished a turn through the entrance hall. "Any sign of her?"

"No." The marquess essayed a note of grim humor. "But perhaps I should check the card room."

"Perhaps you should check your damn tongue, if you do not wish to have it yanked from your throat and chopped into mincemeat."

The faint smile disappeared. "Sorry. Just trying to add a bit of levity to the proceedings."

"Well, don't," snapped Connor. "The situation isn't remotely funny."

"I know, I know." Looking away, his friend fell to scanning the swirl of bright silks. "I ought to be drawn and quartered, and my head skewered on a pike."

"One can't stick a spike into thin air," he retorted.

Gryff repressed a wince. "Bloody hell, I warned you not to trust me with the cursed scrap, Connor." His fingers tightened around the stem of his glass—which, the earl noted, contained ratafia punch rather than champagne. "I'm aware that my drinking has been getting out of control. But I didn't give a damn about the consequences. Until now."

His friend's face was twisted in such an uncharacteristic look of hangdog remorse that Connor found his anger ebbing away. "You did warn me. So don't cut yourself up about it," he muttered gruffly. "Besides, I fully intend to recoup my losses."

The marquess took a swallow of his drink and grimaced. "You think she will accept the offer you have in mind?"

"How many ladies have you met who can resist the allure of money?" The Wolfhound's mouth curled up at the corners. "What do you think all the primping and posturing is about on the Marriage Mart, if not to sell themselves to the highest bidder?"

"You have a point." A slight furrow creased his friend's brow. "But Seb's sister struck me as somehow... different. I daresay there are those who care for aught than money or material things."

Were there? Connor turned for a moment to watch the dancing couples, aswirl in a vortex of rich silks, costly jewels and polished manners. He supposed he should not be so cynical. However, after all he had experienced in his life, assuming the worst of people had become an ingrained habit.

He was rarely disappointed.

The wife of a duke passed, so close that her fluttering skirts brushed his evening shoes. A tiny turn of her head revealed a fluttering of lashes as well, and a wink. A wink reflected a million times over by the ornate diamond necklace kissing the cleavage of her bosom. The earl had bedded enough such ladies of the *beau monde* to know that beneath many a soft curve and sultry smile beat a mercenary heart.

There were the odd exceptions, he supposed. In his walk of life, he rarely encountered them.

And Alexa Hendrie?

No question she was different. His lips gave a grudging twitch. Not many innocent young ladies would have possessed the courage or imagination to barge into a brothel, undaunted by the danger to her person and her reputation. Just as not many innocent young ladies would have dared dress as a man and risk playing at high-stakes games of chance.

What was she hoping to gain?

He didn't know her nearly well enough to hazard a guess. Their first two encounters had revealed a stubborn streak of loyalty and fierce show of independence—not to speak of a hidden depth of passions. But as for her most recent escapade...

It was, he reminded himself roughly, a matter of complete indifference to him what the chit was after, as long as he got back his damned scrap of paper.

"Every lady has her price," he said softly. "It's merely a question of whether a gentleman is willing to pay it."

Gryff, looking thoughtful, did not reply.

A moment later they were joined by another gentleman. Impeccably attired in elegant evening clothes, he appeared the very picture of patrician elegance—save for the shocking pink neckcloth that frothed down in a perfect Waterfall knot.

"I got your note." Cameron Daggett arched a well-groomed brow at Gryff. "Very amusing. And here I thought that *I* was the one with the lurid imagination."

Of the three Hellhounds, Cameron Daggett was perhaps the most whimsical. And enigmatic. Known for his biting wit and flamboyant style, he gave the appearance of viewing life as nothing more than a scathing joke. Connor and Gryff were among the few people who could stand up to his worldly cynicism. But even they did not know all the secrets that lay beneath the show of detachment.

"Perhaps you ought to eschew your lyrical landscape essays and take up writing novels for Minerva Press," went on Cameron. He pinched a speck of dust from his fuchsia neckcloth. "Now, what's the real story?"

Gryff scowled at the veiled reference to his artistic endeavors. "Swallow your usual sarcasm, Cam. The Wolf's teeth are already on edge." His expression screwed tighter. "By the by, where did you find that garish rag? Wrapped around the thigh of a French whore?"

Unlike his two friends, who appeared in unrelenting black and white, Cameron enjoyed tweaking the rules of gentlemanly dress as well as deportment. "I'll have you know this bit of rare silk cost an arm and a leg," he drawled. "But then, originality is not to everyone's taste."

"Neither is your sense of humor."

Cameron exaggerated a sigh. "The two of you simply have no eye for fashion."

"You look like a bloody Barbary pirate," growled Gryff.

The other man fingered the large diamond stud in his left earlobe. "You don't like my latest acquisition? Perhaps I ought to return it to its rightful owner."

"Dare I ask where you've been for the last sennight?"

Cameron's answer was a cocky smirk. "Just amusing myself." He was deliberately vague about a great many things, and would often drop out of sight for days or weeks, returning just as suddenly with no explanation of where he had been. Or why. "Apparently my games were more profitable than yours."

Normally, Connor would have found the sharp exchange of banter diverting, but his patience was coming perilously close to snapping.

Eyeing the clench of the earl's fist, Gryff was quick to retort. "You won't be finding things any too amusing in another moment unless you bite that devilishly sharp tongue of yours."

"Is it true, then? A lady now owns half of The Wolf's

Lair?" The glint of unholy amusement in Cameron's green eyes darkened somewhat as Connor answered with a grim nod. "Good God, I leave you two alone for a few weeks and all hell breaks loose." He wagged a finger at Gryff. "Naughty dog. One of these days, your taste for brandy is going to suck us all under."

"Don't lecture me on the perils of drink," barked the marquess.

Dismissing the retort with a slight shrug, Cameron focused his attention on the dance floor. "Which one is the Lady of the Lair?"

"Lady Alexa Hendrie has yet to make an appearance," growled Connor. With any luck, she had come to her senses and scampered back to Yorkshire. However, as luck was proving damned elusive of late, he wasn't counting on it.

"Sebastian Hendrie's sister?" Cameron's gaze sharpened as the dancers spun by. "That certainly adds an intriguing twist to the affair," he mused. "In Lisbon, Seb showed me some of her letters—she struck me as a very sensible, intelligent young lady."

"Ha! You might revise your opinion once you have met her."

"How—"

Ignoring the question, Connor turned on his heel. "That's enough jawing. Can the two of you stop snapping at each other's flanks long enough to check around the refreshment tables while I make another turn of the room?"

Alexa was aware of the earl's presence before she looked around. A prickling sensation started at the back of her neck, teasing the tiny hairs to stand on end. A shivering tingle trilled down her spine, as if that piercing gray gaze was a finger of cold steel laid against her bare skin.

It was frighteningly sensual...not that such a thing made any sense at all.

But then, her wits seemed to be slowed by a jumble of conflicting sensations. Unlike her pulse, which had quickened considerably in the last few moments. She drew in a gulp of air, only to find that her breathing had gone rather ragged as well.

Now was not the time for a flutter of schoolgirl nerves. She had been expecting the earl to seek her out, so there was no reason to feel...whatever it was that was turning her knees to the consistency of jelly. Not if she wished to impress upon him the fact that she was his equal, not just on paper but in worldly aplomb.

"Lady Alexa."

Somehow, she managed not to jump out of her skin at the rumble of his voice.

"Lord Killingworth." She turned with deliberate slowness.

He moved a step closer, the black of his evening clothes a stark contrast to the bouquets of creamy lilies and alabaster urns decorating the alcove. "If you are not too engrossed in the study of botany, might I request the pleasure of your company for the next dance."

There was no mistaking the mockery of his politeness, nor the fact that his words were more of an order than a request.

"I would be delighted." She had recovered enough from her odd little lurch in composure to respond with an equal measure of sardonic formality.

A flash of teeth. Which she doubted was meant to be taken as a smile.

Still, the subtle heat of his body and the light pressure of his gloved hands drawing her close were oddly reassuring. A certain harmony seemed to flow between them, allowing her to follow his lead without thinking, though she usually felt awkward and unsure on the dance floor.

But as the first figures of the waltz drew them far enough from the other couples to ensure some privacy, the earl wasted no time in dispelling such a fantasy. Dropping any pretense of pleasantries, he said curtly, "Enough foolishness, Lady Alexa. You have had your fun with Haddan, but don't think you can make me jump through hoops like some trained lapdog. You have something that belongs to me. I expect it returned—at once."

So much for striking a chord of camaraderie.

Stung by the condescension in his tone, she felt all her well-rehearsed reasonings skitter away. "You must be mistaken, sir. I have nothing in my possession that is not rightfully mine."

His eyes daggered to quicksilver points of anger. "Don't play games with me, Lady Alexa."

"Why not? I seem to be better at them than most gentlemen—including Lord Haddan." The retort slipped out before she could stop it. The conversation was taking an entirely different turn than she had intended.

"I am warning you..." The approach of another couple forced him to bite off his words.

Alexa's gaze dropped to folds of his neckcloth. As usual, she had allowed her bluntness to get the better of her. Instead of appearing polished and poised, she had only managed to goad the earl into a real temper.

She drew in a breath, which proved yet another mistake. Overpowering the subtle scent of bay rum and shaving soap was the essence of aroused pride and raw masculinity. The pulsing of anger was visible at his throat, and beneath her gloved fingers, the rippling of taut muscle hinted at an inner beast that might be unleashed at any moment.

Dangerous. She didn't need his growled warning to tell her of that. Yet his aura of untamed, unpredictable passions was not frightening. Quite the opposite. The Irish Wolfhound was the most intriguing, interesting man she had ever met.

"You may have bested a bunch of brandylogged nodcocks, but if you think you are any match for me, you will find yourself in for a very rude awakening," continued the earl, once he was sure they could no longer be overheard.

Ruder than your manner at this moment? She rather doubted that was possible.

Quickening his steps, he spun her through a series of intricate figures that seemed designed to show off the ease with which he assumed control. "Perhaps I did not make it clear that I am not expecting you to walk away empty-handed. I mean to pay you the fair value for the note, as well as an extra premium for Haddan's carelessness."

"I am not interested in your money, Lord Killingworth."

He looked somewhat surprised. "What, precisely, are you interested in?

You. The truth nearly tripped right then and there from her tongue. *Another lush kiss. The grip of desire upon my naked flesh.* All the things that seemed unlikely to come her way again. Would he think her mad if she dared voice such desires aloud?

Or merely pathetic.

"I cannot quite picture you playing an active role in The Wolf's Lair," he added tightly.

"Why?" she blurted out.

There was a fraction of a pause before the earl answered. "I don't think you possess the attributes necessary for the job."

"How would you know, without giving me a chance to prove my worth?" she demanded hotly. "I have a number of skills that would prove very useful."

She was, of course, thinking purely in terms of the practical skills needed to run a business. But clearly the earl assumed she was referring to something else.

His chiseled lips thinned to a lordly sneer. "You must be joking, Lady Alexa." His gloved fingers tightened around hers. Even had she wished to cause a scandalous scene she could not have escaped their grip. "Need I remind you that I have had an intimate enough acquaintance of you to form a judgment."

Her outspoken independence had drawn enough criticism over the years that Alexa considered herself impervious to insult.

Apparently she was much mistaken.

The room suddenly seemed to be spinning. She was well aware she had none of the physical attractions that might tempt a gentleman like the Irish Wolfhound to look twice. But hearing it said to her face was painful beyond words.

She was of no more interest to him than a mouse in the molding...

No—there was nothing mousy about her. Mice at least

were cute and cuddly. She was more like a stork, with long legs and ungainly feet.

One of which chose that moment to trip over the earl's shoe.

Mortified, Alexa squeezed her eyes shut. Why, oh why couldn't she be more like the other young ladies, with their porcelain prettiness and their tiny, graceful little creampuff slippers that moved so effortlessly across the dancefloor?

The sting of tears burned against her eyelids. *Stork*, she repeated. *A bird-witted stork with feathers for brains.*

"Lady Alexa?"

Though Alexa wished she might sprout wings and fly straight through the open windows, she forced her eyes open. Mouse or stork, she would not be so cowardly as to flee from him.

The Wolfhound's mouth had softened to a quizzical line, and he was regarding her with a strange flicker to the steel of his gaze. The look upset her even more. She would much rather be subject to his anger than his pity.

"Is something wrong?" he asked quietly. "Are you feeling...faint?"

"Of course I'm not feeling faint! I'm merely annoyed at your abominable arrogance and unspeakable rudeness," she snapped, restoking her courage with a show of indignation. After a moment, she added, "I never feel faint. As you have so kindly pointed out, my looks are not those of a polished and proper young lady. And neither are my sensibilities."

To her surprise, the earl did not react.

Drawing in a lungful of air, she went on, "Go ahead and snarl all the insults you want, sir. It does not alter the fact that, whether you like it or not, I now own half of The Wolf's Lair. And unless you plan to renege on a debt of honor, there is precious little you can do about it."

His expression betrayed no sign of emotion, save for a tiny tic of his jaw. "My honor, unlike a good many things about me, has never been called into question." His eyes had gone flat and opaque as pewter plates. "As to my options, they may depend on what you intend to do with your half."

"I haven't decided," she muttered. "When I do, I shall let you know. In the meantime, please return me to my aunt as soon as this dratted dance is over. I don't see that we have any further business to discuss tonight."

Given how badly she stumbled through the last few steps, Alexa imagined that the earl now had several bruised toes to go along with his bruised pride. As a rule, gentlemen did not take well to losing at anything, and given his fearsome reputation, the Wolfhound was unlikely to be an exception. Indeed, she was rather surprised he was not trying to bite her head off instead of maintaining a stoic silence.

The effort must be costing him dearly.

It wasn't until the last notes had melted into the murmurs of the crowd that Connor leaned in for a last word. "Not now, perhaps, Lady Alexa. But I am surprised that a player of your reputed skills would stake a claim to victory when there are still a great many cards that lie unturned. This is merely the first round of play. Be assured that the game is far from over."

Chapter Six

Hell and damnation.

Connor frowned as he swallowed the last of his brandy. What the devil had brought tears to the young lady's eyes? To her credit, she had not attempted to use them to her advantage. She had tried her best to blink away the telltale drops, but several had formed luminous little pearls on the fringe of her lashes. Oddly enough, he had been sorely tempted to reach up and blot them away with a gentle brush of his lips.

He hadn't meant to hurt her. But he had.

Well, it served the chit right, he reminded himself. It was not his fault if she had mistaken his cultivated cynicism for deliberate cruelty. Perhaps it was even for the best. For all her show of spark and spirit, she had little experience in the ways of the world. It was high time she learned that life was, for the most part, a bare-knuckled brawl.

Flicking the butt of his cheroot into the hearth, Connor resumed his restless pacing, moving from the overheated card room out to the upper terrace of the gardens.

Torches set along the carved balustrades cast a flickering light over the stone. Leaning up against the cool granite, he stretched out his legs and flexed his shoulders. The afternoon hours spent hunched over ledgers and sifting through recent rumors had left his muscles knotted and his patience frayed. It had not helped any that the interlude with Lady Alexa had been yet another exercise in frustration.

The swirl of mist and muddled moonlight gave the clipped hedges and topiary trees a vaguely sinister air. The blurred outlines and indistinct shapes kept shifting under his brooding gaze, while spreading shadows threatened to engulf the grounds in a pool of blackness.

All in all, it mirrored his current mood. He was still no closer to puzzling out who was seeking to destroy The Wolf's Lair. Or why.

The business, while beginning to turn a decent profit, was no threat to anyone, save for the few wives who resented the fact that their husbands sought pleasure in places other than the marriage bed. Yet it was nigh on impossible to picture the very proper Lady Burke or the straightlaced Lady Wilford conspiring with a gang of hired thugs. The fine points of card sharping and burglary discussed over tea and cream cakes?

Absurd. But no more so than any of the other possibilities that had come to mind.

"I thought you might care for another brandy." Gryff perched a hip on the smooth stone. "That is, unless you would prefer to be alone with your thoughts."

"They are proving damned depressing company. Even your phiz presents a welcome sight." The earl accepted the drink and quaffed it in one gulp.

The marquess raised a brow. "Turned you down flat, did she?"

A grunt confirmed the surmise.

"I feared as much. Never met a female with such steel in her spine. And elsewhere." There was a touch of wry admiration in his tone. "Unfortunately for us, she has the iron cojones to stand up to a man."

Cojones. Connor's mouth tweaked up at hearing the expression used by their Spanish allies. He supposed she did have iron balls. In a manner of speaking.

Gryff fingered his chin. "Perhaps we should appeal to Sebastian."

The earl found the idea repugnant for a variety of reasons. It seemed a betrayal of the lowest order. And aside from the ethical questions of turning tattlemonger, he did not care to test whether his old army comrade had lost any prowess with a saber. Their friendship was a tenuous one at best, and while Sebastian Hendrie did owe him a favor—a rather large one—expecting the fellow to throw his sister to the wolves, as it were, was rather overdoing it.

"Let us leave Seb out of it."

After brief consideration, the marquess nodded. "I suppose you are right. Two battlehardened veterans of the Peninsular campaign ought to be able to handle a skirmish with a lone lass." His scowl turned a touch more sanguine. "Or make that three, now that Cameron has rejoined our ranks. With his imagination, he can always be counted on to come up with an unexpected strategy."

Connor gave a snort. "That's what I am afraid of. I have had enough bloody surprises, if you don't mind."

Gryff shot him a quizzing glance. "Speaking of surprises, were you aware that he steals jewels?"

"Yes. In fact, he's wanted for theft in at least four different countries. You remember his sojourn in Rome? I heard his precipitate departure had something to do with the fact that his partners in a smuggling venture were threatening to fry his testicles in olive oil and garlic."

A bark of laughter. "I wonder why he takes such outrageous risks?"

"I imagine he has his reasons." Connor finished his brandy in one long swallow "Don't we all."

"Er, Lady Alexa..."

Her head jerked up as Mr. Givens—he of the enameled snuffboxes—added a nervous cough. *Dear God. Not another lecture on Russian cloisonné.* At the moment, she wasn't sure she could stand to hear any more details on pigments and alloys.

However his next words were nothing of the sort. "Please allow me to introduce you to Mr. Daggett."

She wasn't sure she could stand acquaintance with another Hellhound, either, but it did not appear she had any choice.

Givens quickly sidled away, leaving her to face the tall, elegant gentleman who was looming over her chair.

"Forgive me for using the pup to gain an introduction, but none of the tabbies were likely to throw you to the dogs—proverbial or otherwise." He sketched a graceful bow. "However, seeing as I am a old friend of Sebastian, might I have the pleasure of the next dance? That is," he added dryly, "if your card is not full."

Alexa saw his eyes were angled at the bit of pasteboard dangling from her wrist. Its pristine white surface was blinding in its blankness.

"If this is yet another attempt to intimidate me, you

may save your breath, sir—and your toes," she muttered. "I don't intend to dance to Lord Killingworth's tune."

"Clumsy, was he?" Cameron moved so smoothly that before Alexa quite realized what was happening, her hand was tucked in the crook of his arm and they were on the dance floor, ready to step into the first figures of a waltz. "The Wolfhound is usually a bit more agile on his feet."

Seeking a moment to regain her equilibrium, she deflected his question with one of her own. "Do you also have a nickname, Mr. Daggett?"

"Yes. My friends call me the Bloodhound—or, as the ancient Scots called it, the Sleuth hound."

Alexa blinked. With his lean height, chiseled features and mocking eyes, her partner's resemblance to a lugubrious, wrinkle-faced dog was difficult to discern.

Her consternation must have showed for Cameron gave a light laugh. "You see, I have a nose for trouble, if you will, and once I'm on a scent, I usually follow it to the bitter end."

A gentleman who could make fun of himself? She couldn't help but smile back. "And like a bloodhound, do you always catch what you are chasing?"

His eyes turned a darker, more enigmatic shade of green. "Bloodhounds are very stubborn, persistent creatures, Lady Alexa." There was a fraction of a pause. "In that we appear to have something in common."

She fell back on the defensive. "You may insult me all you want, but I am not giving back the vowel. I won it fairly and squarely." Seeing that her retort did not bring the slightest hitch to his step provoked her to add, "Why is it that qualities that are considered laudable in men are looked on as shocking in a female?"

"A good question." His gaze was once again lit with amusement. "My observation was not meant as an insult. Though I suppose any proper young lady would take umbrage at being compared to a Hellhound."

"As you seem aware of my recent activities, you know very well that I am hardly a pattern card for propriety."

"Yes, that's what makes you so intriguing." Moving with an effortless grace, Cameron twirled her through a series of turns. Above the whisper of silk brushing the parquet, he murmured, "What is it you are after, Lady Alexa?"

She was sure her cheeks were turning the same hue as his neckcloth. "I—I don't quite follow you."

"I rather doubt that you are having any difficulty in keeping pace."

The light pressure of his hand had her suddenly reversing direction. Alexa drew in a deep breath, trying to keep her head from spinning.

"Judging from all I have heard, you have a very quick mind." He regarded her thoughtfully. "And, I might add, the imagination to stay a step ahead of the game. Do take care to go slowly, and not let such admirable traits lead you into trouble."

Her chin came up. "I assure you, I am used to looking out for myself."

As the violins finished the last notes of the crescendo, Cameron's gliding step brought them into the shadows of the potted palms. "Then far be it for me to offer advice. As you say, you seem to be finding your way in Town without any help. But bear in mind that it is easy to stray into danger, even for those who are familiar with all its hidden twists and turns." In the shifting patterns of light and dark, she wasn't aware of the small calling card until he tucked it into her glove. "Don't hesitate to send word if I can ever be of service to you."

"I—"

He was already gone, the faint stirring of fronds quickly settling back into a leafy silence.

"What the devil were you doing with Lady Alexa?"

"A waltz," replied Cameron, after quaffing a mouthful of champagne. "Perhaps the two of you ought to go out more often in civilized society if you have forgotten how to dance."

Gryff swallowed a snort. "When I take a lady in my arms, I prefer her to be naked."

"Keep your paws off that particular one. Our old comrade Sebastian would not take it kindly were you to ravish his sister." Cameron savored another sip of his wine. "Though she really is quite ravishing, don't you think? Stands head and shoulders above the crowd. All those milk and water misses look pale in comparison—"

"Damn it, you ought not be sniffing around her skirts, either." Connor spoke more sharply than he intended. "I'll handle this on my own."

"No need to bare your fangs, Wolf. I merely wished to meet the girl and form my own opinion of what you have gotten yourself into."

"And?" prompted Gryff.

Cameron didn't take the bait. His gaze remained on the bubbling of tiny explosion in his glass. "Is there a reason she seems to react so viscerally to the mention of your name, Connor? Other than the fact that you trod on her toes earlier tonight. My guess is you have met before."

"Once," replied the earl through gritted teeth. "Or

twice. We ran into each other during Sebastian's recent troubles."

"You didn't mention that to me." Gryff's voice held a note of reproach.

"For a damn good reason. It has nothing to do with the fact that you are a bloody idiot for playing cards when what few wits you have are soused in brandy." Connor turned abruptly on his heel, causing a clutch of nearby couples to edge back into the woodwork. "You two may do as you please, but I have had enough of polite entertainment for one night."

"Heading back to the Lair?" asked the marquess.

"Yes." His scowl turned a touch fiercer. "Assuming my half is still open for business."

What was she after? With the Bloodhound's probing question thrumming in her head, Alexa twisted the sash of her dressing gown into a string of knots. No amount of reasoning seemed able to unravel the tangle of her emotions. Or the answer to why she was so desperate to win the Wolfhound's regard.

A shiver ran through her, as if his arms were still encircling her. As shadows from the mullioned window danced across the wall of her bedchamber, she could picture the angled leanness of his jaw, the faint whiskering on his cheeks, the refracted glow of the candelabras illuminating the silvery highlights of his hair.

A lordly wolf. She had never in her life encountered such a magnificent beast.

But physical attraction, though undeniably powerful, was only part of the earl's allure. Oddly enough, the more she learned about him, the more she admired him.

Like her, he was...different. He had chosen not to fall
in line with the usual expectations. Whereas most men
would have married for money, the earl had refused to
take the easy way of recouping his fortune. Instead, he
had applied himself to a difficult task with dogged de-
termination and great resourcefulness, despite the risk of
being shunned by his peers.

Oh, he was a rogue, to be sure, but while most people
saw him only in black and white, Alexa was aware of an
infinite range of grays in between. She sensed the earl
was a man of subtle nuances, most of which were over-
shadowed by the glare of his notoriety. A more intimate
acquaintance might...

Alexa gave herself a mental shake. Not that Killingworth would ever willingly seek her out.

When it came to companionship, the man had no dearth
of choices. She had seen for herself the come hither
glances from highborn ladies of the *ton*. And he did not
have to look far if it were other company he sought. Under
his own roof were exactly the sort of women skilled in satisfying the primal urges of any man.

A scudding of clouds dimmed the dappling of moonlight. In light of reality, how had she ever dreamed that
she could measure up? It was absurd to imagine that a
man like the Wolfhound might appreciate any of the qualities she had to offer.

*Of which there were pitifully few she could point to at
this moment.*

Avoiding her own reflection, Alexa took up her brush
from the night table and began to comb through her unruly
curls. If only she were more like other young ladies, who
seemed to fall in and out of love at the drop of a feather.

Oh, but longing for what could never be was too heavy a weight on the spirit.

Heaving a sigh, Alexa blew out the candle. The evening had quickly snuffed out her schoolgirl fantasies about dealing with Connor Linsley as an equal. She had taken a gamble, but played her cards badly. Was it time to cut her losses while she still had a shred of dignity left? Or was she willing to chance another match of wills with the Irish Wolfhound?

Luck versus experience. The odds favored the earl. And yet...

As she slid beneath the sheets, the whisper of linen seemed to echo the earl's earlier words.

The game was far from over.

Chapter Seven

Good day, Lady Alexa." The gentleman's voice, though a trifle rough around the edges, at least sounded sober. "Seeing as our paths have crossed, might I walk with you a bit?"

Rather embarrassed at any reminder of their previous encounter, Alexa was slow to look up from unwrapping the book she had just purchased at Hatchards. "It does appear we are headed in the same direction, Lord Haddan."

Gryff caught a scrap of the brown paper before it could fall to the graveled walkway. "I won't bite," he said softly. "And you needn't fear any harm to your reputation. Even the tabbies will acknowledge that it's perfectly respectable to be seen strolling with me in broad daylight."

"I am not overly worried about my reputation, sir. As you have reason to know."

"Then your reluctance must be due to thinking I mean to hound you about…a certain subject." Falling into step, the marquess cast a meaningful look at the abigail who had accompanied Alexa on the round of shopping.

Alexa murmured a few words to the girl, who fell back a discreet distance. "Are you?" she asked.

"Yes." His austere countenance was softened by a faint smile. "But you may kick me away, as you would a stray cur, if I become too annoying."

"I am never cruel to animals." She ducked her head to hide her own upturned lips. Cupshot, the marquess had not made an overly favorable first impression. But it was hard not to respond in kind to his self-deprecating humor. "Especially strays, who are subject to enough abuse from those more fortunate than they are."

"Ah. A soft spot for animals. And canines in particular. I am particularly pleased to hear it, given the turn our conversation may take."

So, he had a quick wit as well. Keeping her expression shaded by the brim of her bonnet, she replied, "Don't press your luck, sir."

Gryff's half-smile tweaked into a wry grimace.

In the light of day, Alexa could see why half the *ton*—the female half, of course—was ready to fling themselves at his feet. With the haze of smoke and brandy cleared from his chiseled features, he was sinfully attractive. She could see how that lazy, lidded gaze, fringed by indecently thick sable lashes, drove women wild.

No wonder the Hellhounds stirred such a visceral reaction in Society.

"Luck," repeated Gryff. "Clearly I have none to speak of." After a step, he added, "No doubt you are questioning my intelligence as well. Only a jug-witted fool would keep playing when odds were so clearly not in his favor."

"Live and learn." Alexa hoped that she didn't sound too priggish.

The rumble in his throat may have been a laugh or merely a clearing of his throat. There was, however, no mistaking the twinkle in his eye, though it lasted for only an instant. "I'll drink to that. With orgeat, not brandy. However, I draw the line at ratafia punch. I don't know how you young ladies tolerate such vile stuff."

"We aren't given much of a choice, sir."

"Ah. I hadn't thought of it from that angle." The crunch of his boots on the stones was accompanied by a lengthy silence. "From a lady's point of view, quite a lot of things must take on a different perspective."

"The opposite holds equally true—as I can well attest."

A whoop of laughter drew her attention to a young boy up ahead, who had just sent his wooden hoop careening into the shin of an elderly gentleman. Dodging away from the ringing scold of his governess and the flaying cane of the injured party, he flashed her a mischievous grin that seemed to say cutting loose once in a while was worth the consequences.

Alexa smiled back. One's backside might end up bruised on occasion, but it never hurt to experience a dash of freedom. She waited another few steps, until the shouts had died away, before asking, "Is there something you wish to dislodge from your throat, sir, other than the taste of stale punch?"

"As a matter of fact, yes…" He gave another cough "Thing is, it's a rather delicate subject to broach…"

"You may have noticed that I am not easily shocked," she murmured.

"Then I won't mince words, Lady Alexa," replied Gryff. "The Wolfhound would likely chew my carcass into crow bait if he knew I was speaking to you. But the fact is, I have caused him a great deal of grief at a time when he can ill-afford it."

"Indeed?" Alexa had, of course, been dying to know why Haddan had held the earl's note in the first place. Her curiosity piqued, she kept her reply deliberately neutral in hopes of drawing out a more detailed explanation.

"Yes. You see, he has suffered a string of business reversals—through no fault of his own, I might add."

An arch of her brows punctuated what she hoped was a look of worldly skepticism.

"Truly. I assure you, he devotes a goodly amount of energy to his affairs—" The marquess grimaced. "What I mean to say, is, he manages his business establishment with a great deal of enthusiasm...Curse it, this is a deucedly difficult subject to discuss with a young lady."

"If it makes it any easier, I was aware that the earl runs a gaming hell and bawdy house well before our chance encounter, Lord Haddan."

Gryff looked somewhat relieved. "In that case...the fact is, he is careful and cautious when it comes to business, and has worked hard to master the fine points of profits and losses." The marquess hesitated again. "No doubt such praise sounds shocking to your ears, but despite his reputation as an unprincipled cad, and his current means of livelihood, the Wolfhound is not nearly the beast he is made out to be. He is loyal, and generous—and humorous, when he chooses to show that side of his nature. Those few who know him well would attest to the fact that he is an altogether great gun."

Save when an errant rub of flint in the form of a sharp-tongued lady causes the primed powder to explode in a shower of sparks.

"What with the robbery and a run of cheating by a cut-throat Captain Sharpe coming one on top of the other," continued Gryff, "it is not Killingworth's fault that he finds himself on the brink of financial ruin."

Ruin?

"Lord Killingworth the random victim of a thief *and* a cardsharp?" Alexa could not keep the shock from her voice. "That part of Town may be rough, but the odds of two such strikes being unrelated seem quite low."

"You are right," agreed the marquess. "It's no coincidence. I am convinced someone is out to destroy both the Lair and the Wolfhound."

Alexa could easily imagine any number of reasons why some man—or woman—might wish the earl ill. Still, she felt a pain in the pit of her stomach for having contributed to his troubles. "Why?" she asked in a taut whisper.

"I have no idea. And neither does Killingworth."

Somehow the answer made her feel even worse.

"My own recklessness has only compounded his woes. The Wolfhound refused an informal loan of funds, insisting that I hold a formal pledge for the money. He trusted me to keep it safe. Instead I . . . well, I hardly need explain to you what happened."

"I am sorry for the role I played, and for putting you in an awkward position with your friend."

Gryff turned in stark profile. "It is not for you to apologize. The fault is mine."

Alexa drew in a deep breath. Like the other Hellhounds, he was a striking figure, his harshly handsome features chiseled with an untamed arrogance. And yet in a certain light, the edges took on a gentler cut. *Hard, yet soft.* She couldn't define it any better than that. But though no expert in games of seduction, she imagined it was a quality most women found alluring.

"It's of little consolation to Killingworth, but the incident taught me that perhaps it's time...for an old dog to learn some new tricks."

She looked away. "You think that is possible?"

"Hope springs eternal." His cultivated cynicism was back. "If it did not, then life might be too bleak to contemplate."

"I—I see."

"I rather hope you don't." A strange sort of sadness seemed to shadow his features. "It's not a sight I would wish for a lady of your tender years." Before she could muster a reply, he gave a brusque bow. "Good day, Lady Alexa. I'll leave you here, with a last reminder that you have only to name your price for your share of the Lair."

As Alexa watched him walk away, she couldn't help thinking...

Would the cost be too dear?

The glass was but a hair's breath from his lips when Connor yanked it back. Another jerk smacked it down on the desk, drowning his disgruntled oath in a loud thump.

"Hell, I had better send out for a cheap tot of blue ruin and save these last few precious drops," he muttered, staring balefully at the decanter. His quarterly delivery of aged French brandy was now a viscous puddle of ooze in the Iron Nun alleyway. God only knew what was diluting the delicate balance of oak and grape. *Cat hair? Rat droppings? Rotting cabbage?* Not to speak of the substances whose amorphous shapes and hues defied identification.

It made him quite sick to think of it.

"Every last barrel, smashed to smithereens," announced McTavish, his doleful burr for once all too understandable.

"Must have used smithy hammers to reduce oak to splinters of that wee size."

"My, aren't you a fount of interesting information," snapped Connor. He immediately regretted the show of sarcasm on seeing the look of confusion on the hulking Highlander's face. Normally he did not stoop to venting his spleen on subordinates. "If you wish to spout off gruesome details, you might at least try to discover something that might help us in tracking down the scurvy weasels who attacked the wagon."

"Aye, sir." The man rubbed at his flattened nose. "Rufus is on his way to the Badger's burrow. Some of his lads who lift tickers from the gents in Covent Garden come home about that time. One of them might have seen something."

"Perhaps." The earl made a face. "But their memory usually requires a certain amount of jiggling before the picture becomes clear. At the moment I lack a sufficent amount of coins to do the trick.

"Don't you fret about that, sir. The Wolf's Lair ain't been stripped of all its treasures." The other man's grin revealed a number of ominous gaps where the teeth had gone missing. "The girls are offering a free poke to anyone what can supply information leading to the capture of them bastards."

"Bloody hell, that will certainly stimulate a steady stream of hyperbole."

"Er, is that good?"

"I would not bet on it." A conversation with one of his ex-pugilists usually provided a note of comic relief, but at present Connor was in no laughing mood. "Why don't you toddle around to The Great Gabriel and see if any of his Avenging Angels might have the grace to come clean with what they know."

"Aye, sir."

As soon as McTavish had stomped off, Connor forced his attention back to the various sets of notebooks and ledgers arranged on the desk. From the roll of the ivories to the tumblings of the lasses, he was going over every record of the last six months with a fine-tooth comb, looking for any clue as to who might have a grudge.

So far, the search had turned up nothing, save for a few elementary mistakes in addition and subtraction.

He skipped over any equation involving simple division, needing no reminder of fractions. The concept of "half" was not a particularly edifying one at the moment.

"Damn Gryff," he muttered aloud. If the curse were multiplied by the number of times he had said it each hour...

"M'lord, and exalted scion of County Kerry." O'Toole added a knock for good measure.

"Don't bother me," growled Connor. "Not unless the bloody place is on fire."

"Things are likely to get a bit hot around here, but not on account of coals or conflagration."

"Stubble the Hibernian histrionics, if you don't mind, and get to the point."

Folding his hands behind his back, the Irishman heaved a lugubrious sigh. "There is a visitor to see you, milord."

"Send him away."

"I'm afraid that is beyond my power."

"Is that so? Well, be advised that it is not beyond my power to boot your emerald arse from here to Dublin if you don't." The earl swatted at one of the pages. "Given the present precarious state of the Lair's finances, we may all be seeking new employment opportunities, whether it be here or abroad."

"I was not being impertinent, sir." O'Toole gave an aggrieved sniff. "Merely truthful. Seeing as the 'he' is a—"

"She," finished Alexa. Unknotting the strings of her bonnet, she dropped it in the outstretched hands of the Irishman, who for once appeared bereft of speech. A moment later it was joined by a heavy pelisse of charcoal gray napped wool. "Now, if you don't mind, the earl and I have business to discuss in private."

Taking his cue with a good deal more speed than he usually showed, O'Toole backed out of the room and drew the door shut.

Connor watched as she crossed the carpet in several measured strides, kicking up an enticing little swirl of shimmering indigo silk and frothy cream lace. Dragging his gaze away from the sight, he drew in a sharp breath, only to find himself distracted by the wafting of verbena and jasmine through the stale smokiness of countless cheroots.

He cleared his throat just as she gathered her skirts and took a seat. "Forgive me for not offering you a drink, Lady Alexa. But seeing as *our* coffers are just about drained dry, I am afraid I cannot afford even the most basic show of hospitality."

Her eyes, luminous in the intensity of their color, did not flinch in the face of his deliberate sarcasm.

Brave girl, he applauded, even as he tried to goad her into losing her composure. And her temper. Their previous encounters had proved she had one nearly the equal of his own.

"Though I doubt you have any notion what it is like to have creditors snapping at your heels," he continued. "I assure you that we have no choice but to impose the strictest measures of economy to keep the wolves from our door."

"Actually I know the feeling all too well, having spent the last few years trying to keep the slate and granite of Becton Manor from crumbling down around my family's ears." She fell silent, lowering her gaze to the ledgers and loose papers spread across the scarred desk.

There was no resentment or self-pity in her voice, only a note of wry irony. Connor certainly hadn't expected an aristocratic young lady to have experienced the grim realities of encroaching poverty. Somewhat taken aback, he covered his uncertainty by propping his elbows upon the desk and steepling his fingers.

Damn. He couldn't afford to feel sympathy for the chit. Or any emotion, for that matter.

Regrouping, Connor tried another line of attack. "Look, despite the dribble of ink on a rip of foolscap, you have no business being here," He flung a hand out to indicate the roughhewn file cabinets and hard back chairs crammed into the cramped space, the empty bottles scattered across the threadbare carpet and the peeling plaster walls, dulled by the tallowed film of cheap candles. "This is hardly the sort of environment that a gently reared young lady should be exposed to."

His grand gesture ended up emphasizing his point to a greater degree than he had intended.

Set behind his desk, atop one of empty crates of rum shoved up against the wainscoting, sat a statue of a phallus, anatomically correct in every little detail, save for being over three feet tall. In the dingy shadows, the pristine whiteness of its smooth marble stood out like...a sore thumb.

Bloody hell.

Snatching his coat from the back of his chair, Connor quickly draped it over the offending member.

On turning back, he found that Alexa's head had dropped so low that all he could see was a topknot of wheaten curls. The silky strands were bobbing about as her shoulders quivered, and though muffled by the folds of her India shawl, a choked hiccuping was audible.

Bloody hell. Next time he wished to reduce an innocent young lady to hysterics, he would cut right to the chase and haul out an oversized penis.

Not his own, he might add. It would be conspicuously absent from his body, along with his testicles, if Sebastian ever got wind of what had just occurred.

"Accept my apologies, Lady Alexa." With a gruff cough, he fished a handkerchief from his waistcoat pocket and held it out. "I intended to be uncivil, but not offensive."

Her only reaction was a more pronounced rocking to and fro.

Worried that she was about to fall into a dead faint, he half rose from his chair. "Shall I fetch you a glass of sherry? I'm sure there must be a drop left somewhere—"

Alexa finally looked up, her cheeks wet with tears of suppressed mirth. "Oh, no need to waste the last of our precious stock on me," she gasped. After several deep breaths, she steadied herself and angled a glance over his left shoulder. "How very interesting. Though I only caught a fleeting look, there appear to be a number of differences from that of a ram or a stallion. But I imagine the thrust is the same."

Connor dropped like a hunk of stone back into his chair. He opened his mouth, fully intending to let fly with a curse that would send any female fleeing from the room.

What came out instead was a bark of laughter. "Don't tell me you are acquainted with the breeding of sheep and horses?"

Her mouth curved upward, revealing a peek of pink as the tip of her tongue briefly touched her lower lip. "Intimately."

Another rumble sounded deep in his throat. "You are, without question, the most audaciously outrageous young lady I have ever encountered."

"So I have been told. *Ad nauseam.*"

"A scholar of Latin, as well as animal husbandry?"

"And Greek," she replied. "Along with geometry, trigonometry, biology, soil chemistry, and a host of other subjects considered unfit for females. But then again, 'feminine' is not usually an adjective used to describe me."

No? To his eyes, she looked unquestionably feminine. *Alluringly feminine.* So much so that he had to lace his hands behind his head to keep them from stealing across the expanse of wood that separated them.

"How does Sebastian manage to keep you out of trouble?" he asked, hoping the mention of her brother would serve to distract his attention from her physical charms.

"He doesn't. Never has, though not for lack of trying." She picked at the hem of her glove. "And now, of course, he has his hands full with his new bride. Which, in some ways, is rather like shifting one's fingers from the frying pan to the fire."

The earl's lips twitched.

"But Nicola always appears extraordinarily calm, collected, and ladylike when she is defying a direct order, or issuing commands of her own. So Seb doesn't even notice the heat. While I, on the other hand, only manage to singe everyone's nerves when I kick up a dust. Including my own."

She said the words so softly, Connor wondered whether they were meant more for her than for him. Still, he could not help but respond. "You ought not compare yourself to Lady Becton."

"Ha! Believe me, I am more than aware of that, sir."

Her laugh had brittleness to it. For an instant, the layers of clever retorts and feisty attitude slipped and he caught a glimpse of just how fragile she was.

Prickly pride. Uncertain anger. Pinching vulnerability. Oh, she might hide behind a pugnacious attitude and dowdy gown, but right now she was naked to his eye. Perhaps because he recognized the feelings all too well.

"The qualities you describe are not the only ones that appeal to a gentleman, Lady Alexa."

"You certainly have a great deal of empirical knowledge in that subject, sir," said Alexa tartly, her armor back in place. "Though from what I have witnessed, you aren't overly discriminating." She hesitated for just a fraction. "It seems anyone who wears a skirt will do. After all, you kissed *me*."

"You needn't worry. It won't happen again."

She looked away, but not before he caught the overbright sparkle of unshed tears in her eyes. "I am well aware of that, sir."

Damnation. It wasn't often that a stab of guilt—or any other emotion—penetrated his hide, and he found the feel-

ing damned uncomfortable. The sooner the meeting came
to an end, the better it would be for both of them.

With a brusque sweep, he cleared several of the ledgers
from his blotter. "Seeing as I have already offended you,
I might as well continue speaking bluntly. I can ill-afford
to waste time in idle conversation, so unless there is some
specific reason you are here, Lady Alexa, and not just
idle curiosity, I suggest you return as quickly as possible
to more genteel surroundings. And stay there. I meant it
when I said you don't belong here."

Her lowered lashes hid any reaction to the deliberate
roughness of his voice. "In fact, sir, there is—"

Alexa's voice cut off abruptly. She had been regarding
one of the ruled pages rather than his face and was now
leaning in for a closer look.

"There is a mistake here," she announced. Peeling off
a glove, Alexa pointed out the sum entered beneath one of
the accounts receivable columns. Her finger then shifted
slightly. "And here."

"You needn't take your role as half-owner quite so
literally," he growled. "I was just about to make those cor-
rections."

A faint flush rose up from the collar of her gown, but
her only reply to his sarcasm was a dignified silence.

Which only made him feel more of a beast.

Alexa started to close the ledger when the pages fell
open to a section on expenses. A frown crossed her face
as she looked up. "You are paying far too much for bed
linens. Given the quantity listed here, you could order
straight from a mill and get much better price."

"Hmmph." Loath though he was to admit it, the suggestion was an astute one.

"You know, you could also consider joining with some of the other establishments to buy in bulk," she went on. "Which would result in an even more substantial saving." As she spoke, she thumbed quickly through several more of the pages. "If you like, I could make a more thorough study of the monthly purchases and give you a list of other suggestions. I may be ignorant about certain aspects of this business, as you have taken pains to point out, but I do have a great deal of experience in ordering supplies on a limited budget. I have learned a number of ways to cut costs."

Connor's fingers began to drum upon the ink-stained blotter. He had caught the flicker of uncertainty in her eyes. And vulnerability. All it would take was another casual slap of sarcasm to send the young lady on her way. The sting would fade soon enough. She would recover.

He flexed his hand. Then rubbed at his jaw. "I would never have thought to say it, but I admit that a partnership with a lady of your talents would have great potential...to be profitable." Softly, almost gently, he added, "However, what you suggest is impossible."

"Why?"

Unwilling to witness the disappointment he knew was writ on her face, the earl looked at the still-open ledger. "Come now. If I added up all the reasons, I should fill the rest of those pages."

A sigh sounded in response, along with a faint rustle of silk as she folded her hands in her lap. "And then some, I suppose."

Somehow, it now didn't surprise him that she met adversity with show of dry humor rather than a torrent of tears.

"But it is deucedly unfair," she quickly added, the defiant little tilt of her chin accentuating the graceful arch of her neck. "I could do a better job of it than most men, if given half a chance."

"I don't doubt it," he said gruffly.

She blushed and for some unaccountable reason, it brought a warmth to his own blood that he had given her a small spark of pleasure.

Still gripping the ledgers, Alexa shifted in her seat. "However, to rail at the reality of the situation is not the real reason I came here tonight."

"If you are seeking to arouse my curiosity, I confess you have done so. In spades." Alexa had also given rise to a far more visceral reaction. Her movement had pulled her bodice tight to her breasts, allowing a tantalizing hint of the nubbed tips to show through the wool.

Beast. Connor felt an overwhelming urge to thrust his hands inside her bodice and caress her lush curves, just as he had done once before. He could still recall the heat of her flesh, and the fire in her eyes as she had melted at his touch. The memory made him feel even more like a ravening wolf, ready to devour every tender morsel of flesh…

"I owe you an apology, my lord."

Drawing in a measured breath, he wrenched his attention away from such evil thoughts.

"It was wrong to take this from Lord Haddan by means of deceit." Alexa laid the vowel on the table. "That is, by dressing as a man." A martial gleam came to her gaze and she couldn't help but add, "Aside from that, I did win it fair and square."

Connor found himself smiling. "Yes, Haddan says you

are very skilled at cards. A shame we can't have a game—
mano a mano, as our Spanish allies would say."

"Hand to hand," she repeated softly.

"It strips the conflict down to the bare essentials...in a
manner of speaking. I confess, I should like to see you in
action."

"We could deal the cards and engage in a round or two
of hand-to-hand combat...in a manner of speaking."

Connor steeled his expression. "Not tonight, Lady
Alexa. Luck is a fickle mistress, as perhaps you will learn
one day. I've learned from experience when not to tempt
her ire." His nails dug into his palms. "Nor do I care to
rouse Sebastian's fury. Let us leave it at that."

The scrap of paper still lay untouched.

"As for this..." With a flick of his hand, the earl
nudged the promissory note back across the scarred oak.
"The way it works among honorable gentlemen is, I redeem it when I have the money. Which I don't. Not at the
present moment." He pushed back from the desk. "You
keep it. But unlike Haddan, try not to sink all my hopes
in a bout of deep play, if you please. It should only be for
another few days."

"However long, you need not worry. I am not usually
reckless, and after tonight, I shall no doubt revert to my
normal, staid self," she replied. "So your future is safe
with me, Lord Killingworth."

He didn't feel nearly so sanguine. Perhaps his current
run of bad luck had his nerves on edge, but instinct warned
him that things might not play out quite so easily.

Alexa took the scrape of his chair as a note of dismissal.
She rose quickly, gathering her reticule along with the
vowel, and turned for the door—not without a last longing

look at the ledgers. "I shall let you get back to…whatever it is you do within these walls, sir."

"A moment." He reached for his coat.

"You needn't stir from your Lair, sir. I came here on my own, and I am perfectly capable of leaving in the same manner. I paid the hackney to wait at the end of the lane."

"That may be. But as we are partners, at least for the next little while, I have a vested interest in seeing you safely to the vehicle."

She fixed him with an odd look. "So it's business before pleasure?"

"Don't try to goad me into a temper, Lady Alexa." The earl took her arm. "Surely we can make it through another few minutes in each other's company without another outburst of hostilities."

Chapter Eight

$\mathcal{A}$ damp fog had crept in, bringing with it an oppressive closeness and noxious scent of the surrounding stews. Drawing the collar of her cloak up over her nose, Alexa peered up and down the narrow street. The hackney she had come in was nowhere to be seen.

"He must not have heard me ask him to wait."

"No matter." The earl took her elbow. "It's but a short walk up to the right where the jarvies tend to gather and wait for the gentlemen to finish with their revels."

She allowed herself to be led around a trickle of raw sewage and into a sliver of an alleyway. "Lud, would not a more...pleasant location be better for business?"

"The filth and the danger are part of the allure of a place like The Wolf's Lair," replied the earl as he drew her even closer to avoid scraping up against the grimy brick. "You needn't fear, though. No one in the neighborhood will seek to make trouble with me."

Alexa wasn't the least bit afraid. Absurdly enough, despite the muddled squish of garbage and the scratching of feral scavengers, she felt at ease in the crook of his arm. A good deal more so than when she had been dancing amid the glitter and splendor of Mayfair.

Closing her eyes, she could almost imagine the creak of the rusting hinge was the bass note of a cello, and the whistle of the wind through a broken window was the trilling of a flute.

The irony of such imaginings was not lost on her. She sighed into the thick folds of his greatcoat. How like her to find a slog through the muck more romantic than a waltz over polished parquet.

"Pull up your hood."

So much for girlish reveries. This was, she reminded herself, business, not pleasure for the earl.

A faint spill of light from one of the shuttered windows showed they were coming to a gap between buildings. From there, another maze of passageways branched out in a series of bewildering twists.

"That hardly seems necessary, sir," protested Alexa. "It's pitch black and I am wearing a bonnet and a cloak that comes down to my toes."

"As soon as we pass through the next alleyway, we come out into the street where the hackneys wait. There are always a few lanterns lit and those glorious guinea-colored curls of yours are much too recognizable, even when half covered by a bonnet."

Killlingworth considered her hair "glorious"? She had always thought it a rather drab shade of light brown. "Really, sir, I am quite...unremarkable."

He stopped abruptly, his gloved hands brushing over her shoulders. "I would rather be safe than sorry—"

For an instant, Alexa thought the loud crack that cut him off was just another of the menacing sounds of the

Southwark stews. But then he suddenly slumped forward, his spasming fingers shoving her roughly aside.

With the echo of the gunshot still ringing in her ears, she hit up hard against a planked doorway, the jagged wood spearing through her cloak and tearing the tangled wool. The shadows seemed to come alive, the dark, distorted shapes spinning like whirling-dervish demons. Twisting free of the splinters, she saw that Connor had recovered his footing, though he appeared bent at an odd angle.

An eerie silence hung for a heartbeat over the alleyway, and then was shattered by running footsteps crunching over broken glass.

In blur of black, a figure came barreling out of the heavy mist to their rear.

"Run, Lady Alexa! Ahead, and to the right!" The earl turned awkwardly to block the attack.

Alexa cried out a warning as a pistol shot up, its snout silhouetted against a swirl of ghostly vapor.

Sparks flashed, punctuated by the harsh click of a misfire.

"Run, damn it, *run*!"

Ignoring Connor's muffled shout, she started toward him, but her foot slipped and she fell heavily against a rusty iron bar sticking out from the planks. It snapped off in her hand.

A guttural curse followed on the heels of the earl's oath. Coming on at a dead run, his assailant slashed out with the spent weapon, aiming a vicious blow at Connor's head, just as he started to yell again.

"Lady Alexa—" Forced back, he managed to parry it with his forearm, but the force sent him staggering back.

The other man's momentum carried him past the earl, and in the few seconds it took to spin around, Connor had dropped into a defensive crouch. Shifting warily, he seemed to be searching for firmer footing.

But even amid the confusion of yawing shadows and scudding light, Alexa could see something was seriously wrong. Despite the danger, he kept one arm clenched to his side, and his movements were sluggish. His breathing was ragged as well, its rasp rough with pain.

She dared not make a sound, for fear of distracting him.

Like a predator scenting blood, the earl's assailant moved in for the kill. Whipping a blade from his boot, the man began jabbing a flurry of quick thrusts through the air.

"The Irish Wolfhound, eh?" he sneered, angling sharply to his right in a move that forced Connor to edge back closer to the dark wall. "Yer more like a bloody French lapdog, fer all the fight ye be putting up."

Another lunge cut off any further retreat. A quick sidestep and he would have the earl pinned against the pitted bricks.

The squelch of mud covered the sound of Alexa's rush forward. As the blade flashed up, she swung the bar as hard as she could. Iron collided with bone in a shivering thud.

"Never turn your back on a Yorkshire terrier," she muttered as the man collapsed in a heap at her feet. Quickly kicking the knife from his limp fingers, she looked up.

"Don't you ever obey orders?" grunted Connor.

"Very rarely." Alexa drew in a gulp of air to steady her voice. "For which you ought to be profoundly grateful."

There was no word from his lips, thanks or otherwise, for he, too, suddenly toppled forward.

She managed to keep a grip on his coat, though his weight nearly knocked her over. Fear hit her with just as much force.

"S-sir?"

His continued silence was even more frightening. Now that the first rush of unthinking bravado was spent, Alexa suddenly realized how scared she was. Despite being fisted in folds of melton wool, her hands began to tremble.

"Killingworth!"

The slight shake had no effect. His long hair, now slick with sweat, brushed against her chest, but still no answer.

With a low groan, the man at her feet began to move.

"Killingworth, we must be gone from here." *But which way?* She tried desperately to recall his exact words. Had he said "right"?

Think! Think! Her mind was numb, but a hoarse shout from close by roused her to action.

"Bull! Ye got him?"

Wrapping her arms around Connor's chest, Alexa managed to stagger forward. He was a large man, broad-shouldered and well muscled. She didn't know for how long she would be able to handle such a dead weight—

No. She would *not* allow herself to think in those terms.

Praying that her memory was not as faltering as her courage, she squeezed through the gap in the rookeries and staggered headlong into the alley on the far right. She dared not look back.

"Killingworth," she gasped between gulps of air. Surely the bumps and scrapes, if not her urgent pleas, would jar him to his senses. "Dear God, can you hear me?"

As if in mocking answer, she heard another shout.

"Bloody 'ell!" The echo, though distorted by the maze of angled walls, did not deflect the note of rage. "Ye let him get away!"

A second voice rose in reply. "'E's hurt—I know 'e is. Woulda 'ad him dead to rights if he hadn't had a bloody she-bitch helping him. Nobody said nuffink about there being two o' dem, but I swear, they won't get far—"

"Aw, shut yer gob and get up. Which way did they go?"

Spurred on by the sound of pursuit, Alexa summoned an extra surge of strength to maneuver through the twisting passageways. But she knew she couldn't keep up such a pace for any distance. And while the ruffians might be slowed by a wrong turn or two, they would soon pick up the trail.

Fighting off panic, she paused for a moment to shift her hold on Connor's coat. Her cheek, already scraped raw from several near falls, hit up against a broken board. In fear and frustration, she wrenched the earl around and gave him a hard shove. "Damnation, sir! Try to move your feet."

This time, her urgings finally stirred some sign of life, if only a faint groan.

Tears of relief flooded her eyes as she saw his lids flutter open.

"What the devil..."

"Not one, but two of them. Hot on our heels." Another push inched him forward. "We must hurry."

Whether or not he comprehended her disjointed explanation, Connor roused himself. Hooking his arm around her shoulders, he gritted his teeth and managed a scuff of his boots.

Still, their progress seemed painfully slow. At any moment, Alexa expected a bullet or a blade to cut them down.

"One more step, one more step." Over and over, she repeated the words aloud. She had not the energy to think of anything else.

Finally, she spotted a flicker of a light up ahead, and nearly wept for joy.

Another oath richoceted from out of the gloom. Aware of steps drawing ever closer, Alexa pressed on with one last, frantic burst of speed.

She and Connor emerged into a roughly cobbled street. As he had promised, a pair of hackneys were drawn to a halt. One of the nags raised its head and gave a desultory swish of its tail. The drivers, however, remained unmoving, hats pulled low, trying to stay warm on their perches as the wind rattled the bits of worn brass and leather.

It took another cry and a thump on the nearest vehicle to rouse any reaction. "Help me!"

"Help ye?" From beneath the twist of scarf came a harsh cackle. "Ye must be new at this, duckie," replied the driver. "Ye'll learn quick enuff that out here, ye got te fend fer yerself."

"Aye, sweeting," called the driver's cohort. "If the toff's drunk hisself into a stupor, it's time fer ye te be doing the thrusting. Shove him inside and help yerself to his purse."

As Connor gave a querulous mutter, Alexa worked the door latch free. "Step up," she ordered, giving a sharp tug to his trousers.

"That's the spirit, luv." Clearly amused by her struggles, the driver held out his whip. "Want to try a touch o' the lash on his arse? There's some gennelmon wot like a taste o' leather."

"I'd rather you turn it on your horse's rump." A last heave, and Connor landed heavily onto the floor of the cab. Alexa started to climb up after him. "Get us away from here fast, and I'll split the gentleman's purse with you instead of the jackals on our heels."

The driver fumbled for the reins. "A pleasure doin' business with ye."

Her foot had barely cleared the iron step when Alexa felt a grab catch at her skirts. Falling backwards, she yanked with all her might.

A rip rent the air, and the outstretched hand was left holding naught but a scrap of lace petticoat.

"Spring 'em!" she screamed, slamming the door shut.

The hackney lurched forward.

"Lady Alexa! Lady Alexa!" Along with the clatter of the iron-rimmed wheels, her name rang off the uneven pavement. "Don't think we'll ferget the Wolfhound's bitch."

"Where to, duckie?" yelled the driver, after the first few careening turns.

Alexa bit her lip. Her aunt's townhouse was out of the question. *Henry?* She didn't have much faith in her cousin to keep a cool head in a crisis. *The earl's own residence?* Good Lord, she hadn't a clue as to where he lived…

She felt the vehicle starting to slow.

Mouthing a silent prayer that she was making the right decision, Alexa quickly called out a direction.

"Dear me." After wiping the blood from his well-tended hands, Cameron Daggett smoothed at his cravat, though none of the intricate folds were a fraction out of place. "The coat and shirt appear quite ruined. Not that it is any great loss, seeing as they were fashioned by a far more clumsy hand than Weston or Stutz."

"T—to hell with my bloody tailor." Connor's whisper was barely more than a breath of air.

"Yes, I've been telling you that for ages, Wolf. The man ought to have his patterns burned to a crisp and red hot needles stuck under his fingernails."

Alexa's clutch on her glass of brandy relaxed slightly. Connor's halting words were only a ghost of the earl's usual snarl but they were still somewhat reassuring. He hadn't uttered a sound during the long ride, not even when she had been forced to be rather rough in wrestling him up from the floorboards.

The Wolfhound muzzled? She had begun to fear the worst.

After a sip to steady her nerves, she leaned in for a closer look at the jagged hole in his side. And then wished she hadn't. The sight of blood and gore was nothing new. She had witnessed a good many accidents in the course of managing an estate. But somehow, a bullet wound seemed so very much more...personal.

Quickly averting her eyes, Alexa fought to keep her voice from cracking. "D-don't you think we should summon a surgeon, Mr. Daggett?"

"I have done so, Lady A." The earl's friend had peeled open the torn shirt and was probing gently at the wound. "The bullet does not appear to have penetrated the lung—"

Apparently not, she observed, for the earl managed a sharp snarl. "Goddamn it, Cam, no!"

"Still, it should be removed as soon as possible," continued Cameron, calmly ignoring the interruption.

"No surgeon," added Connor through clenched teeth. "Prefer to keep this... quiet."

"That thought had occurred to me," replied his friend lightly. "The fellow in question is, like us, a former military man and understands how certain situations call for the utmost discretion." He paused to take up a pair of scissors and snip away a piece of singed linen. "He can be counted on to keep mum."

"How can you be so sure?"

Cameron smiled. "First of all, because I pay an obscene amount of money for his silence concerning the occasional services he renders to me. And secondly..." Another bit of cloth was expertly removed. "...Because he knows if he fails to keep his end of the bargain I will break all 27 bones in his right hand."

The earl didn't bother inquiring whether the man was right-handed.

"Mr. Daggett, can't you..." Concern squeezed Alexa's appeal to little more than a whisper.

Connor's face had turned alarmingly ashen, the contours of his profile nearly indistinguishable from the white damask of the pillows. In contrast, the tangle of dark hair and the harsh shadows beneath his cheekbone stood out like smudges of cinder. By the clench of his jaw, it was apparent he was in a great deal of pain.

"If you have finished your brandy, Lady A, perhaps you would be so kind as to pour a small draught for His Lordship. And then come around and hold this basin." Cameron had staunched the worst of the bleeding. After coaxing a swallow of the spirits—to which he had surreptitiously added a liberal dose of laudanum—through the earl's compressed lips, he reached for a sponge.

"Lady Alexa." It was only then that Connor so much as acknowledged her presence in the room, and then only obliquely. "Damnation," he swore weakly. "S-she's in danger…"

"Rest easy, Wolf. She is safe now."

"No, she is not. I—I said her name. M-must get her away," insisted the earl. "Away from T-Town…" The words trailed off in a fuzzed groan.

Seeing the earl had lapsed back into unconsciousness, Cameron set to the grim task of cleaning the ugly wound.

Her own hands so unsteady that water was in danger of sloshing onto the counterpane, Alexa was grateful for his show of cool efficiency. He worked in methodical silence, so she, too, refrained from speech, content to watch the skill with which he handled the delicate job.

"Have I sprouted purple spots, Lady A?"

She realized he had finished with the last bit of sponging and was now regarding her with an expression of quizzical amusement.

"Perhaps you do not care for the colors of champagne and salmon in a gentleman's waistcoat? Or is it the diamond stud in my earlobe?"

"Forgive me. I was staring, wasn't I? How abominably rude." Alexa tried to match his note of detached humor. Yet she couldn't keep a slight quiver from her lips. "B-but then, I have trespassed terribly on your good will already, barging in on you at such an ungodly hour, and b-bearing an armful of trouble."

He dismissed her apology with an airy wave. "You are welcome in my humble abode at any hour."

Her eyes could not help but follow the sweep of his hand. Taking in the refined elegance of the carved mahogany armoire, the rich brocades and slubbed silks of the furnishings, and the delicate watercolor sketches of Venice hung over the mantel, she found her expression turning quizzical. The juxtapositions were unexpected. Intriguing. Mysterious.

Rather like the man himself.

"Well, perhaps not precisely humble." He grinned, as if reading her mind. "I may be known as one of the rapacious Hellhounds—a wild, dangerous beast. But in private I do enjoy my creature comforts."

She replied with a tentative smile.

"I trust you won't ruin my reputation," he murmured. "Very few people have ever seen the inside of my home."

"I don't have a wagging tongue, Mr. Daggett. I promise that your secret is safe with me."

"Speaking of secrets…" He fingered the tip of his chin. "We are faced with a devilishly delicate situation."

Alexa suddenly realized that perhaps she had placed the gentleman in an awkward position. "I—I hope you don't mind that I brought Lord Killingworth here. I couldn't think of where else to go with a half-dead gentleman draped around my neck—that is, I pray he is only half dead."

"I assure you, it will take more than a shot in the dark to drop the Irish Wolfhound in his tracks. Over the years, he has dodged a great many efforts to put a period to his existence. No reason to think his luck is going to run out now."

"Have you and the earl been friends for a long time? You seem to know a great deal about him."

"Since we were young pups, assigned to General Broughton's staff in Lisbon. As for being acquainted with his history, I'm afraid to say, our escapades since then could fill a rather good-sized book."

Alexa looked down at one of the Moroccan bound volumes on the bedside table. *Oh, what I wouldn't give to read those pages!*

"Not, you understand, that the earl's personal particulars are of any interest to me," she hastened to add, hoping she sounded suitably indifferent.

"Of course not." Cameron's mouth twitched. "Why would they be?"

Fearing that if her face turned any pinker, it would match the puce in the draperies, she rose abruptly and carried the basin back to the dressing table.

She was saved from any further embarrassment by a knock on the door.

"That will be Thurlowe." He called for the surgeon to enter and made room by the bedside.

The ex-soldier wasted no time in pleasantries. Nodding a cursory greeting to Cameron, he rolled up sleeves and made a quick examination of the unconscious earl. "I've seen worse," he muttered laconically. Opening his bag, he removed several sharp instruments. "Send the lady out," he ordered without looking up. "Unless you intend to pay me for tending to more than one patient."

"I'll have you know I have never fainted in my life," said Alexa, summoning a show of indignation. However, to herself she admitted there was always the possibility of a first time. The scalpel bore a rather gruesome resemblance to an implement from the Spanish Inquisition.

"He has a point, Lady A," said Cameron softly.

Several, in fact. The other items laid out on the table looked equally menacing.

"Why not step out into the hallway? Thurlowe will assure you I have ample experience in serving as his assistant."

The surgeon grunted as he tested the edge of the blade against his thumb.

"Very well," she agreed, marching for the door before another little lurch of her insides necessitated a headlong flight.

Chapter Nine

$\mathcal{I}$t was all over rather quickly. Thurlowe emerged wearing a satisfied smile. He passed by her without a word, intent on tucking a bulging purse—along with what looked to be a ball of misshapen lead—into his waistcoat pocket.

Cameron was a bit more forthcoming. "All is well," he murmured. "The bullet came out cleanly. The Wolfhound won't be waking any time soon, as Thurlowe thought it best to administer another dose of laudanum." Taking her arm, he turned her away from the bedchamber door. "If you don't mind me saying so, you, too, look as though you could do with a medicinal draught. I have an excellent Amontillado sherry downstairs..."

Even if she had wished to do so, Alexa realized protest was futile. Like the ocean tides, Cameron Daggett exerted a subtle yet inexorable pull. It was impossible to resist. *Caught in a silky, swirling current.* And if rumor was true, she was not the only female to feel that way. It was said...

Such musings were drowned by the soft splash of the wine. He handed her a drink, then poured one for himself.

"You know, Lady A, I think we had better have a little

talk—a council of war, if you will." He expelled a small sigh. "Would you care to start by telling me how the Wolfhound came to have a large hole drilled between his ribs?"

Alexa proceeded to do so. The account, however, took rather longer than she anticipated. Even though the earl's friend knew about the wager, she decided she might as well tell the whole story, starting with her night in disguise.

In for a penny, in for a pound. Seeing as she had come this far, there was no point in holding anything back.

To his credit, Cameron listened without so much as batting an eye.

"Hmmm." He moved to the Sheraton sideboard and topped off his sherry. Perching a hip on the inlaid wood, he raised his glass in silent contemplation of the amber spirits. The candlelight winking off the faceted crystal hid his expression. Save for the swish of the liquid there was silence.

Alexa was beginning to fear she had been too candid. Even a man of admittedly less-than-rigid moral scruples could have his tolerance bent to the point of snapping.

But when Cameron finally spoke, there was no hint of censure. "I am beginning to understand why your brother was not overly shocked by some of the exploits you detailed in your letters. Stunned, perhaps, but not shocked. It seems he was used to your unconventional behavior."

"If you mean I am not a typical milk and water miss, I take that as a compliment," replied Alexa.

"It was meant as one." The wry note in his voice then deepened to a more serious tone. "All joking aside, Lady A, the fact that whoever is responsible for the attack now knows your name, and your, er, association with the Wolfhound, is cause for grave concern."

"But there is no possible way they can be privy to our business connection!" she protested. "Both Henry and Lord Haddan promised not to breathe a word of the wager to anyone."

"It doesn't matter whether your assailants know of the vowel," he reasoned. "That you and the earl were together, at such an hour and such a place, bespeaks of a certain intimacy—regardless of whether that is true or not." Cameron smoothed a wrinkle from his sleeve. "I must agree with Connor's opinion that is too dangerous for you to remain in London. Indeed, all things considered, I think you ought not return to your aunt's townhouse."

Alexa set down her glass rather heavily.

"I shall spin a convincing story—with all due modesty, I am rather good at that. And ladies of a certain age tend to trust me." He rose. "In the morning, she shall spread the word that a family emergency required your immediate return home. It's a reasonable explanation, and one that is eminently believable. The *ton* won't think to question it." He rose. "I will have you on the road to Yorkshire, just as soon as I can arrange a carriage—"

"No!" The fierceness of her objection echoed the earl's earlier growl.

His brow arched in mild surprise. "But your brother—"

"Has just set off with his new bride to visit our father in Scotland," said Alexa quickly. "And it promises to be a bit of an ordeal, seeing as he means to settle a number of thorny issues between them." Her chin edged up. "Seb and Nicola deserve some peace and quiet in which to settle into marriage. There is no reason to turn their lives topsy-turvy. I—I would rather handle this on my own."

"Ah." The pause was barely perceptible. "I see."

Was she so transparent? With laughable ease, his gaze seemed to penetrate the arguments she had sought to wrap around her innermost desires.

"Is there, perchance, another reason you are so adamantly opposed to returning home?" he asked softly.

She left off pleating the folds of her skirts, deciding she might as well abandon her clumsy attempts at hiding the truth. "I can't simply up and abandon the earl. We are partners, after all, and I feel partly responsible for his current troubles. If he had not been worried over the vowel…if he had not felt obliged to escort me to the hackney…" Recalling his torn coat and bloodied shirt, she felt her throat constrict. "He can't remain in Town either."

"That's true." A frown pinched at the corners of Cameron's mouth. "Clearly he can't go to ground in the Lair. And this place isn't safe either, given that our friendship is common knowledge." He swore softly. "It's the devil's own timing. Haddan has been called away by his mother's illness, and I…"

Alexa followed his gaze to the doorway, where a black greatcoat and kidskin gloves lay folded atop a small satchel.

"…I was just on my way out of Town. The matter is quite urgent, but if I must—"

"No!" interrupted Alexa. "I don't wish to wreak havoc in your life, as well as the earl's." Still staring at his luggage, she found herself adding, "Given the reputation of the Hellhounds, I imagine you have a *cher ami* set up somewhere whom you are anxious to meet with."

"My dear girl, I do indeed have an assignation with a lady, but it is not what you think." A hint of amusement edged his tone. "She has been dead for several hundred years. However, her ethereal beauty has been immortalized on canvas, and I've a client in Shropshire who is just dying to have her hanging in his bedchamber."

It took a moment for his meaning to sink in. "You mean to say you are planning to…purloin a painting?" Despite her concern for the earl, she couldn't help being intrigued.

"As you see, I have rather expensive tastes, and given my present position in life, I should be hard-pressed to afford them if I did not find a way to augment my meager savings." He gave her a conspiratorial wink. "The Wolfhound is not the only gentleman who works for a living. But again, I trust that you will keep my little secret."

She was beginning to understand why ladies were fascinated by the Hellhounds.

"You and Connor are certainly a most unconventional set of rogues." Her mouth crooked. "I don't dare venture to guess what Lord Haddan does when he is not drinking or gambling."

"Oh, Haddan's activities are actually quite respectable, though also a trifle unorthodox. He…" Cameron slid down from his perch. "But never mind. Gryff's private affairs are not of paramount concern right now—nor are mine."

His boots moved lightly, noiselessly across the Turkey carpet as he took a turn before the hearth. "To keep a step ahead of the jackals on Connor's trail, I see no other way to deal with this, save to put off my rendezvous." He sighed. "A pity, seeing as the lady sails for Rotterdam in the morning."

"You don't strike me as the sort of man who gives up so easily, Mr. Daggett," she appealed. "Surely between the two of us, we can think of an alternative."

"The thing is, given the Wolfhound's ferocious temperament, there aren't many people he can count as friends. Your brother is one of the few who might be willing to help."

"I told you, I would rather not appeal to Sebastian," she said quickly. "There *must* be somewhere else."

Cameron gave the matter some thought. "Well, now that you mention it…" He left off twisting at the fob dangling from his watch chain. "Connor did inherit the ancestral estate—a bit of barren hilltop located along a remote part of the South Dorset coastline."

Alexa held her breath.

"On account of the entail, it was the one family possession his father could not gamble away," he mused. "But it has been pretty much abandoned since the death of the old earl. From what I gather, there's naught but an old housekeeper and her husband in residence. The Wolfhound himself hasn't visited the place in years."

"Which makes it an ideal choice." Alexa needed no more than an instant to make her decision. "No one will guess that is where we have gone."

"*We?*" For the first time in their acquaintance, Alexa saw Cameron react with unmasked emotion. "Lady A, you cannot mean to accompany him?"

"Why not?" she countered. "We both need a place to hide, and as he is in no condition to travel by himself, it kills two birds with one stone."

His usual sardonic humor was by this time back in place. "It will kill a great deal more than that. Starting with your own reputation if a whisper of such impropriety reaches the *ton*."

"I am willing to take the chance."

"Are you? The wave of scandal would make a typhoon look like a tempest in a teapot. And its fury would drag down not only you, but the rest of your family."

Alexa swallowed a tiny gulp and tried to sound a good deal more confident than she felt. "Well, I shall just have to take care it doesn't come to that."

An oath escaped his lips, followed quickly by a harried sigh. "You appear deucedly determined to flirt with fire, despite the danger of being burned to a crisp."

"Ha! Coming from a Hellhound, I would venture to say that's rather like the pot calling the kettle black," she countered.

He had the grace to color. "It's different. Because... er...because..."

"Because I am a female? What utter fustian!" Sensing she had struck a sensitive nerve, she plunged on. "We are just as capable of decisive thought and action—despite the quirk of plumbing."

"At times like these, I wish I might turn off the spigot," he replied. "I have the utmost respect for a lady's intellect but there are the practical considerations I have mentioned. Along with the very real threat of physical harm to your person." He fingered the silky tails of his cravat. "And speaking of killings, Sebastian would likely stick my head on a pikestaff if I were to go along with this."

"That should not be intimidating to a man whose penchant for writing lewd limericks had a certain foreign prince threatening to feed his testicles to the Tower ravens."

"Ah, so you heard that rumor, did you?" He paused. "Actually it was the dancing bears at Pierson's Circus. And your source left out the part about the bits of my person being sautéed with garlic and white wine. If nothing else, Montoni—he was Italian, of course—had a delicious sense of humor."

Alexa bit back a laugh.

"In retrospect, my peccadilloes may appear humorous, but this present situation is no laughing matter, Lady A."

"Please." She cut off any further debate with a simple plea. "Won't you help me? I feel I owe it to Lord Killingworth to see him safely out of Town and away from his enemies. Once he's out of danger, I can continue on to Yorkshire without anyone being the wiser."

Cameron rubbed at his jaw.

"I am sure that a man of your colorful imagination can help my aunt quell any gossip here in Town," she went on. "You seem to have quite a bit of experience in fabricating a..."

"Lie?" he suggested.

"I would rather think of it as a red herring."

"Ah, well, if you put it that way..." He exaggerated a sigh. "Scarlet is one of my favorite hues." His steps were already angling for the Louis XIV escritoire set in the far corner of the room. "Let me think—we shall need an unmarked carriage and a competent coachman...a quick visit to your aunt...a carefully worded message for Sebastian..."

"Thank you, Mr. Daggett," she called softly. "I promise, you won't regret this."

"Oh, it is not *my* hide that I am worried about, Lady A."

Chapter Ten

$\mathcal{W}$here am I?"

"In a carriage, Lord Killingworth," replied an oddly familiar female voice.

"I am aware of that fact," he growled. The wheels hit a rut. "Painfully so."

Hell, his ribs felt as if a thousand red-hot pitchforks were jabbing against sinew and bone.

"More precisely, why am I in a carriage?" He dimly recalled the darkened alley, the flash of sparks and the searing bite of red-hot lead. But from there, it was all just bits and fragments in his head. *Stumbling steps. A jarring ride at breakneck speed. A helping hand from Cameron. The muffled voice of Lady Alexa . . .*

LADY ALEXA?

He struggled to sit up. "And confound it all, why are *you* in it with me?"

"You are in a carriage because you did not appear to be in any condition to walk the distance to Devonshire," she answered. "Which also explains my presence. In your current state, we could hardly have sent you rattling off on your own."

Far from providing a satisfactory answer to either question, her words only raised a sense of dire foreboding.

Connor raised a hand to massage at his temple, only to find that the movement sent another stab of pain knifing through his left side. "Why the devil am I going to Devonshire?" he demanded.

"Do try to stop thrashing about, sir." Alexa paused to tuck a corner of the loosened blanket back into place. "Otherwise you will open the bullet wound."

So, he had been shot? No wonder he felt like an Egyptian mummy, wrapped tight in layers of linen strips.

"Bloody hell."

"Quite," she agreed. "A most unpleasant sight, even at a distance."

"It doesn't improve on closer acquaintance," he said through gritted teeth. "How bad is it?"

"The bullet nicked a rib, but other than that, the surgeon said it was a clean wound. He doesn't expect there to be any lasting damage."

"Hmmph."

"Would you care for another sip of laudanum? It will take the edge off the pain until we reach our destination." She didn't wait for an answer but brought the vial to his lips.

He hadn't the strength to resist.

Lying back, Connor could catch only a glimpse of scudding gray clouds and swaying treetops through the sliver of window. The slender branches, their leaves still furled in tiny buds, had a certain delicate grace as they bent one way, then another, buffeted by the whims of the gusting wind.

Why was he suddenly reminded of his mother's hands?

They, too, were slim and graceful. *And distant.* Always in motion, always grasping at naught but air. He couldn't recall ever being held in her arms.

The flickers of green brought back other haunting images as well. She had worn a large emerald ring on her right hand. As a child he had been fascinated by its angled facets and how the luminous color changed constantly with the shifting light. Later, it had disappeared, along with rest of her valuables, feeding his father's insatiable appetite for gaming.

Connor tried to shake off the memories. *Strange, he hadn't thought of his mother in years.* She had been a beautiful woman, but like the windbent twigs, she had found herself at the mercy of a force she had no control over. She, too, had been resilient at first, then slowly hope had withered away to a dry brittleness.

The fights between his parents had become more tempestuous, until something had snapped. She became even more distant. Detached. Six months later, she died in a carriage accident. With a man other than his father.

Closing his eyes, Connor swore a silent oath. It must be the disorienting drug, or the loss of blood that had him in such an oddly maudlin mood. Or perhaps it was the sharp scent of wet loam and sea salt now wafting through the carriage, bringing with it the unbidden, unsettling recollections of childhood.

Another jolt drew a groan from the creaking wheels. Was it just another figment of his feverish imagination, or was the coach lumbering into a twisting ascent?

Still muzzy from the laudanum, Connor tried to sit up and reach for the curtain.

"Steady, sir." Alexa scooted forward and caught him

by the shoulders to keep him from rolling onto the floor-boards. "We are nearly there."

Though he had a sinking suspicion that he knew the answer to the question, he asked it anyway. "Where?"

"Linsley Close."

No.

"Absolutely not." He meant to muster his most intimidating snarl, but to his chagrin, it came out sounding more like a rather pitiful whimper.

Not paying him the slightest heed, Alexa went back to reading the book in her lap.

"Do you hear me? I refuse to set foot in the cursed place."

"You won't have to," she replied. "The coachman will carry you up to a bedchamber."

"If I have to crawl away on my hands and knees, I am *not* staying here."

She didn't look up. "Why? Is there a reason you are so adamantly opposed to a visit?"

"I don't have to explain myself," growled Connor. "Not to you or to anyone."

The pages snapped shut. "For a grown man you are sounding remarkably childish, sir."

The truth of her words only goaded him to greater ire. "Be damned with what you think of me. I demand that you turn this cursed carriage around!"

"Impossible." Her voice remained maddeningly calm. "Even if I were inclined to accede to such an idiotic request, the road is much too narrow for such a dangerous maneuver." As if to confirm the observation, she craned her neck for a glimpse of the passing landscape. "Frankly, I have had enough excitement for one night. Having escaped flying bullets, slashing knives, and the clutches of a hulking brute, I do not fancy a drop of a hundred feet onto jagged rocks and pounding surf."

Connor clamped his jaw shut. *The devil take it.* It suddenly occurred to him that there was only one way that he could have escaped his attacker.

Alexa Hendrie hadn't panicked. Instead, she had somehow found a way to bring him to Cameron's house.

A sidelong glance showed that her curls had come loose from their pins, and one scraggled twist now hung over a smudged cheek. Its shadow deepened the hollows under her eyes, accentuating a look of utter exhaustion. Her clothing—the mud of Southwark still clinging to her skirts—was rumpled from the hours spent cramped in the carriage.

Yet she had not voiced a peep of protest.

It was, he admitted, churlish in the extreme to make her a target of his anger. What she deserved was a medal. Maybe two. Most chits would have swooned at the first crack of trouble. She, on the other hand, had shown amazing pluck and resourcefulness in getting them both to safety.

But grudging admiration quickly gave way to harried exasperation. That was the trouble—she was too brave and too clever for her own good. She should never have come this far in the first place. And with every turn of the wheel, she was moving farther along a path that might lead to her ruin.

Or worse.

His brow, though hot as Hades, felt a momentary touch of ice. Sebastian would not forgive him if it came to that. Nor, for that matter, would he forgive himself. Whatever tentative bond of camaraderie had formed between them last night, it must be quickly and unequivocally severed.

The task should not be a difficult one. Scaring people off had become second nature to him.

What his voice lacked in volume, it made up for in sarcasm. "In retrospect, you have only yourself to blame, Lady Alexa. You wouldn't be in this mess if you had behaved like a normal young lady and not strayed from the cozy confines of Mayfair."

"Hindsight always appears clearer than ordinary vision."

"I wouldn't know," shot back the earl. "I make it a point of never looking back."

Her response, when it came, took him by surprise. "Do you never have regrets?" she asked softly.

"Never."

The harshness of his tone brought a slight quiver to her lips. Brushing aside a twinge of guilt, Connor drew himself to a sitting position. The uneven crunch of gravel indicated that the coach had turned off the rutted road. All too familiar with the drive, he waited in surly silence until the last of the twisting turn had been negotiated before announcing, "Now, seeing as we are about to enter a courtyard of ample dimensions, there is little danger in executing a reversal of direction. As soon as we come to a halt, I will descend and give the order."

"Sir, that is not a wise move. You are likely to faint if—"

"Men don't faint, Lady Alexa," he replied with a mocking smile. His stockinged feet hit the floor—followed promptly by his knees as his legs gave way.

* * *

"No, men don't faint, they simply pass out cold," muttered Alexa, somehow managing to keep the earl's chin from smacking against the facing seat.

She had not really expected him to fall at her feet in gratitude upon regaining consciousness, but a word or two of thanks might have been nice, rather than the angry, deliberately abrasive attitude he had adopted since opening his eyes.

Lord, he must dislike me something fierce. There was no other explanation for why her presence provoked such ill-tempered snaps and snarls. Clearly he found her as irritating and unwelcome as the hole in his side. A small lump formed in her throat. She had thought some sort of understanding had formed between them during the meeting at The Wolf's Lair. Not precisely a friendship, but at least a wary tolerance based on mutual respect.

Evidently she was much mistaken.

Which, she thought with a tiny sigh, was hardly surprising, since most of her recent decisions had revealed a sorry lack of judgment.

The earl, steadied between her arms and the edge of the seat, was now no longer in imminent danger of collapse, but a ghost of a groan drew her thoughts away from her own inward hurt. Seeing an unhealthy flush had burned away his previous pallor, she felt a frisson of alarm.

"Jenkins!" She called to the coachman.

An answering "Arrumph" sounded from outside.

That was as close to a coherent word as she had heard out of the man hired by Cameron to handle the ribbons. Thick as a barrel, with hunched shoulders, massive arms, and a lumbering gait, he brought to mind the performing bear she had once seen tethered to a Gypsy caravan. His long beard took up where his shaggy hair left off, which only reinforced the unfortunate resemblance.

Yet despite all appearances, he had proved a godsend throughout the arduous journey, enduring the lashing rains and frightful roads without a word of complaint. During the hurried stopovers to change the horses, he had somehow always contrived to have steaming tea and a warming meat pie delivered to her, along with hot bricks.

The door pulled open and he climbed in, shaking a spatter of raindrops from his wide brimmed hat.

"Please wait here with His Lordship," asked Alexa. "While I look for someone to inform of our arrival."

"Arrumph." The earl, though not by any means a small man, looked rather dwarfed by the spread of Jenkins's caped shoulders.

Stumbling down the narrow rungs, Alexa felt her knees buckle as her half boots hit the rough gravel. She had managed a few hours of fitful sleep during the journey, but it wasn't until now that she realized how utterly spent she was.

The immediate surroundings did little to lift her spirits. Dark clouds had rolled in to obscure the waning sun, casting an oppressive half-light over the unclipped hedges and unpruned gardens. Beyond them, the landscape rolled off in an unremitting tumble of craggy rocks and wild grasses, their color leached to a dull palette of grays and ochres. As if things were not bad enough, a drizzle started up again, giving the air a despondent chill.

The manor house itself looked even more forbidding. An air of neglect hung over the weathered stone. Not a wisp of smoke curled up from the chimney pots, and the heavy oak door, black with age, looked as if its massive hinges might well be rusted shut.

Repressing a shiver, Alexa found herself wondering whether Mr. Daggett had been wrong in his information. The place certainly looked desolate, deserted.

What if no one was there? She wasn't sure she had the strength to continue on. Besides, where on earth would they go?

Anxiety added an extra measure of urgency to the rap of the iron knocker.

Its echo clanged in her ears, then died away to a dreary silence.

She knocked again.

Just when she was beginning to look up at the mullioned window and calculate the length of cudgel that Jenkins would need to break the glass, she heard a faint scuffling from within. It was followed by a jangling of keys and the labored rasp of metal on metal.

Slowly the door opened a crack

"If you be lost, you had best turn back for the inn at Wyke." The voice was female—that much Alexa could tell. "It's trouble enough scraping together enough for our own meager hearth and table, let alone harboring any unexpected guests."

Squinting, Alexa could just make out the fringe of a mobcap in the gloom. A peek of silvery hair, pulled back in a tight bun, seemed to indicate its wearer was well advanced in years, but other than that, she could make out no other features.

"I do apologize for the lack of notice—" began Alexa.

Stepping forward, the housekeeper made a shooing gesture with her keyring. She then looked up, and though crinkled with age, her pale eyes appeared sharp and observant. "I don't want your apologies...milady." The pause between words made obvious her skepticism over whether the disheveled stranger on the steps deserved such a distinction. "They are naught but a waste of breath if you are thinking they may garner an invitation to stay for the night."

Acutely aware of the sorry state of her appearance, Alexa couldn't say that she blamed the woman. Still, she stood her ground.

Another rattle of brass and iron emphasized the curt dismissal. "You can't stay, I tell you."

"Unexpected—and unwelcome—as our arrival may be, I am afraid you cannot simply turn away the master of the house."

The housekeeper's face, now limned in a spill of dull light, betrayed a look of dawning horror. The keys fell back against her apron, the gnarled fingers fisting twining together so tightly that the frail bones looked ready to crack.

"M-master Connor? But that's impossible! He hasn't come here since he was a wee b-bairn!"

Alexa managed a fleeting smile. "Nonetheless, he is here now."

Rather than soothe the woman's distress, her words only elicited a more agitated wringing of hands. "Lord, have mercy. The house in holland covers, and the larder all but empty. The earl—the present one, that is, and not his nipcheese pater—sends a bit of blunt each quarter. Not much, ye understand. Just enough fer Joseph and me to keep the slates from sliding into the sea. He made it abundant clear he never meant to come here again."

"I am sorry for the sudden change in plans," replied Alexa. "But His Lordship is in need a place of peace and quiet where he won't be disturbed by any acquaintances from Town."

"Is he ill?" Concern was evident in the tautness of the woman's tone. "Poor mite—bit of a frail child he was, quiet and prone to fits of fever."

Alexa nearly laughed aloud at the idea of anyone referring to the Irish Wolfhound as a "poor mite." However, she controlled the quirk of her lips and nodded gravely. "Yes, I'm afraid he is ill." It might be stretching the truth a bit, but it relieved her of having to make a more detailed explanation.

The announcement brought on a new chorus of clucking. "The chill...the dust...the damp..."

"We'll manage." She might be unfamiliar with the workings of a brothel or how to dodge murderous thugs, but in taking charge of a penny-pinched household, Alexa was right at home. "First things first, Mrs...."

"Callaway, milady," replied the housekeeper with a bob of her head.

"Mrs. Callaway," she repeated. "To start with, please summon Joseph. Our coachman could use some assistance in carrying the earl to his room. I shall go inform him that help is on the way, and then, if you will show me the choice of chambers, I shall decide which one is most suitable..." She turned while speaking, already engaged in making a mental checklist of what needed to be done next.

"Just as you say, Lady Killingworth,"

Alexa nearly tripped over the granite step. *Hell's Bells!* The woman thought she was the Wolfhound's wife? It was, she realized, a logical assumption. And one that might prove awfully awkward to correct.

But for now, she would...let sleeping dogs lie.

The pattern hadn't changed, the colors had merely faded to a ghost of their former hues...

Connor wished he might say the same for his memories of the room. He looked away from the damask draperies framing the narrow, diamond-paned windows and let his eyes skim over the heavy oak armoire and matching chest of drawers. Devoid of any decorative details, they looked to be relics of an earlier century, the sort consigned to the attics by anyone with a modicum of taste, he thought. Or a bonfire.

Ah, but beggars can't be choosy. His mouth thinned to a sardonic sneer. His father had long ago stripped the house of any valuable pieces of furniture, leaving precious little choice from the cast-offs of previous occupants.

Damn the chit for bringing him here.

He turned abruptly, tangling the linen sheets and eiderdown coverlet around his limbs. To his relief, he found the pain in his side had lessened considerably. No doubt the bottles of vile-looking liquid arrayed on the bedside table had something to do with his current condition. Still, the fact that the fever seemed to be gone was encouraging. He was determined to be on his feet as soon as possible. Avoiding, of course, any repeat of the highly embarrassing incident in the carriage.

Tugging at the pillows behind his head, the earl swore under his breath. Had he really fainted...

The oath had barely died away when a tentative knock

sounded on the door. "Are you awake, sir?" Without waiting for confirmation, a female bustled in, bearing a tea tray.

The years had altered her appearance considerably. Her face, coarsened by exposure to the salt air and chill winds, was now a sea of wrinkles and her fingers were as gnarled as driftwood. She was also much stouter. And grayer.

But then again, so was he.

Her voice, however, had not changed a whit from the brusque brogue he recalled so clearly from his childhood. Nor had her manner of not mincing words. "Tis about time you paid a visit to Linsley Close, Master Connor— or I should say, Lord Killingworth."

What, he wondered, did she see? A lad whose thin, bony features had grown even harsher, chiseled by years of dissipation and disappointment? No doubt he, too, was much changed, and not for the better.

His reply was a gruff "Hmmph."

Undeterred by the growl, the housekeeper set down the tray and began to stir a splash of cream into the bowl of steaming porridge. "We thought you should try to take a bit of nourishment."

As his stomach gave a loud rumble, he realized that he was ravenous. "Thank you for the warm welcome, Mrs. Callaway." He eyed the gruel with a grimace of distaste. "But in case you have forgotten, I have never been overly fond of boiled oats. I would prefer a slab of beefsteak."

"There is none."

"Mayhap you might—mmmph!" The earl was forced to swallow the rest of his words, along with a helping of the porridge. "If you don't mind, I am now of an age to be capable of feeding myself," he grumbled, reaching up to remove the spoon from his mouth.

Mrs. Callaway handed over the bowl, but remained standing by his side. "Very well." Crossing her arms, she fixed him with a basilisk stare, as if to ensure he didn't slip the stuff to the large marmalade cat who now lay purring at the foot of the bed. "If you finish every bite, Her Ladyship allows that you *might* be permitted a bit of boiled fowl for supper."

It took the earl a moment to digest the meaning of her words.

"May I be the first to offer my congratulations, milord. It's high time you settled down," she continued. "Isolated as we are here, we rarely hear a word about your doings in Town—save for the occasional bits of scandalous gossip." Ignoring the earl's sputter, she poured him some tea. "She seems a very sensible and capable lady."

"You may quickly revise that opinion when you get to know her better," muttered Connor, once he had recovered his voice.

"Eh? What's that?" She cocked an ear and bent in closer. "I am afraid my hearing isn't as good as it used to be."

"Just as well." Feeling in need of something a good deal stronger than tea, he waved away the cup. "Bring me some brandy, if you please."

Mrs. Callaway pulled a face. "Oh, I don't know, sir. I had better consult with Lady Killingworth—"

"On second thought, I shall ask her myself." He braced his shoulders against the pillows. "Kindly tell my...lady that I wish to see her. Immediately."

"I'm afraid you may have to wait for a while, milord.

She has just gone out for a walk."

So the impertinent chit thought she could run tame at Linsley Close?

He would soon see that notion put to rest.

Along with a number of other gross misconceptions.

Alexa climbed over the stile, careful to avoid the sections of rotted wood. Despite the musty sheets, sagging mattress, and pervasive chill of the drafty bedchamber, she had dropped off into a deep slumber earlier in the day. But on waking, she had suddenly needed to escape from the manor house and...

Think.

Lud, everything had happened so quickly! She had been too shocked by the attack, too worried about the Wolfhound, to think clearly, and had relied on instinct rather than intellect.

In the light of day, however, her position appeared a good deal more precarious than she had first imagined. She didn't need the slip of her boot to remind her she was on very slippery footing.

One little misstep...

Gathering her skirts, she jumped down to firmer ground. As the earl had taken pains to point out, looking back was an exercise in futility. Better to keep moving ahead, though she couldn't help feeling it was not always easy to escape the past.

Regrets, remorse, and old mistakes seemed to have no trouble keeping pace.

At least she had the quick-thinking Mr. Daggett to help keep her one step ahead of disaster. She had no doubt that the rogue—who could likely mesmerize a cobra with his silver-tongued charm—had won over Aunt Adelaide, and that all was going according to plan back in London. The elderly lady had a soft spot for handsome, well-spoken gentlemen.

Sebastian, on the other hand, would be not be easily fobbed off with some farradiddle. With any luck, the message would take some time to make its way north to the family hunting box in Scotland. After that, if all hell broke loose, she would simply have to face it.

Turning sharply, Alexa crested the hill and found herself looking out over the sea. Whitecaps frothed upon the wind-whipped water, foam and spray thrown up by the collision of two such powerful forces of nature. The dull roar of the surf against the cliffs echoed the same message.

As if she needed any reminder of the tumult caused when opposites hit up against each other.

Still, the scene had a stark, elemental beauty to it. A spattering of sunlight sent quicksilver highlights dancing across the rough seas. High above the shimmering water a lone kestrel floated on the swirling air currents, while gulls skimmed along the deserted strand. She stood for a moment longer, listening to their raucous cries, before turning back to the narrow footpath.

It led around a high outcropping of granite, its weathered crags fringed with tufts of wild grasses and whin, then skirted a stone fence and followed the twists and dips of the rugged hillside down to the distant paddocks. The going was steep, and Alexa had to pause more than once to catch her breath. Looking around as she leaned up against a broken gatepost, she noted that the land had the same untended, abandoned look as the manor house.

Land left fallow. Structures allowed to crumble. Lord Killingworth clearly had no interest in preventing his property from falling into a state of ruinous disrepair.

She wondered why.

There was no sign of another soul. Indeed, the only other living creatures she had seen were the soaring sea birds and a small vole scurrying through...

A stirring in the tall grass close by caught her eye. Bleating softly, several shaggy goats rose from behind a sheltering mound of sandy soil and began to graze, accompanied by a pair of tiny kids. She had to look twice. Their appearance—coats of long, finespun strands of pale ochre and gray—was very different from that of any livestock she was accustomed to seeing.

Intrigued, she climbed atop the fence and reached out to touch one of the animals. In spite of the tangled knots and clinging burrs, the wool was soft as silk beneath her fingertips.

Looking up from its munching, the animal gave a grumpy snort and pulled away.

Alexa stared thoughtfully at the twist of hair left in her hand, then tucked it away in the pocket of her pelisse. The sun had dipped behind a covering of clouds and the wind was beginning to cut through the felted wool. Chilled, she hurried her steps toward the house.

Not that she expected an overly warm welcome when she got there.

Chapter Eleven

"I understand that felicitations are in order," said Connor with scathing politeness. "I wasn't aware that you were married."

"I assure you, sir, I am no more happy about this unfortunate misunderstanding than you are." As Alexa's cheeks were already flushed from the wind, it was hard to tell whether she had colored at his sarcasm. "If you have any suggestions on how to correct the erroneous assumption without stirring up trouble, I would be delighted to hear them."

His jaw tightened. *She had a point.*

Apparently taking his silence for agreement, Alexa continued, "It seems that the best way to avoid a scandal is to go along with the charade for the short time we are together here. There are only two elderly servants, and the place is remote enough that word of a Wolfly wife will never reach Town."

"It can't be short enough," growled Connor. It was, he knew, an ungracious remark but during the long wait for her to return from her walk, he had worked himself into a truly foul mood.

Uncomfortably aware of his tangled locks, unshaven face, and sapped strength, he felt helpless. *Humiliated.* He resented her intrusion into his life—all the more so for the unwanted spark of attraction she set off in the deep, dark places he didn't want to think about.

Damn the chit. Even if he wished to like her, he couldn't afford any such tender sentiment. Not for a whole regiment of reasons.

"That dressing on your wound has to be changed," said Alexa, patently ignoring his rudeness. "And as the fact that you have been shot is best kept under wraps, I had best see to it myself."

Though he wished to object, Connor realized that a relapse would only make the present situation more untenable. Gritting his teeth, he leaned back and submitted to her ministrations.

As she leaned closer, her slim fingers working at the fastenings of his nightshirt, Connor couldn't help noticing that the long walk had restored a bit of life to her features. The blue of her eyes was no longer washed out and the salt air had brought a glow back to her creamy skin. She had, he also noted, removed the pins from her hair and tied it back with a simple ribbon. The dampness had given it a sinuous curl. Like a waterfall of burnished gold, it cascaded down her back, stirring a tantalizing scent...

"Lift your shoulders, sir," murmured Alexa.

He shifted so that she could slide the nightshirt down off his arms and his chest.

"Now turn to your right."

Damnation. He was beginning to have a notion of how a horse must feel on the blocks at Tattersall's, poked and prodded for every little imperfection. Laid nearly naked, the rumpled linen bunched around his hips, Connor felt uncomfortably vulnerable. Stripped of his pride.

Snipping away the bandages, Alexa leaned in to examine the wound. "No sign of infection," she announced, making one last swab of the stitched flesh before starting to apply the ointment supplied by Cameron's army surgeon. "The fever seems to have passed as well. How are you feeling, sir?"

Weak as a newborn kitten. Snappish as a cornered wolf. Which made him all the more angry at her for witnessing his pitiful state. In a bedroom, he wasn't used to feeling awkward, unsure.

Unperturbed by his surly silence, Alexa methodically folded a padding of lint and tore off a fresh length of linen. "Lean forward, so that I may ensure that the bandage is wrapped snugly." Her voice betrayed no emotion. She might have been speaking of tying up a parcel of candlesticks or broken forks.

By God, if he were to suffer embarrassment, so would she!

Slipping his arms around her, he gave a little yank.

Taken by surprise, she fell awkwardly against his bare chest, the momentum tumbling both of them back into the pillows.

Her cheek was soft as a sun-ripened peach, the flesh like velvet against his bristly chin as she struggled to right herself.

"Sir!" she squeaked, her lips pursing in outrage just inches above his.

Damn, but her mouth looked lush and tantalizingly sweet...

Connor had intended all along to kiss her, but not quite so hungrily.

Though lacking their usual strength, his hands framed her face in a sure hold, tilting her head back to open her more fully to his advance. His tongue slid inside her, tasting the salt of the sea, the tang of wild heather, and some ethereal spice that was indescribably feminine.

A groan, undeniably male, rumbled deep in his throat.

His fingers twined up through her curls, still damp with drizzle, and worked the ribbon free. Ringlets fell like a shower of silk across his shoulders. Another groan sounded as he traced the delicate shell of her ear. The tip of his thumb lingered in a stroking caress of its sensitive lobe, and though the sea was half a mile away, he was aware of a strange sound in his ears, like the pounding of surf.

The desire to tease her into confusion had now crested into something far more powerful. Swept up in its current, Connor deepened his embrace.

In her twistings and turnings, Alexa had come to be straddling his middle, her skirts rucked up about her waist, her stockings sliding down her shapely legs. Only a ruffle of lace and a thin layering of lawn cotton and linen lay between the heat of her innermost thighs and the fast-steeling ridge of his arousal. The force of his embrace pitched her forward, and as she slid along his length, Connor felt a stab of exquisite fire.

The flames licked hotter as he realized she was no longer fighting off his advances. The shock of the first assault had softened from her mouth. Her lips had parted and needed little coaxing to open fully to him. He nipped at her flesh, then filled her with another long, lapping kiss.

Her tongue touched his in tentative response.

"Hellion," he murmured, slowly releasing her. "You like playing with fire, don't you?"

"I—I..." Her dazed reply trailed off to an inarticulate gasp as he arched his hips into her. Knees clenching around him, she began moving again, back and forth in a slow, rocking movement that threatened to explode every last vestige of self-control. Her palms, pressed flat against his nipples, were also teasing the sensitive nubs of flesh into arousal.

A wave of liquid heat, far more potent than the costliest brandy or champagne, surged through him, rousing another groan from deep within his throat. He was already cupping her breasts, and it was tantalizingly clear through the rain-damp wool, that their tips were turning to hot little points of flame beneath his touch.

"Sweeting." Connor hadn't meant to say it aloud, but was gratified to hear her moan in response. He ran his hands to her waist, then slowly caressed the curves of her hips. She arched into his arms.

Women had always come easily to him. They seemed to take his aloofness as a challenge, though in truth it wasn't. Apparently Alexa Hendrie was no different.

And yet she was. Utterly different. He had never desired anyone in quite the way he wanted her. Perhaps need was a better word...

Need.

Connor could feel her growing damp. By now, her passage would be slick with honeyed heat. He ached to thrust himself inside her, to be enveloped by sweet, sweet warmth. Mayhap she could light a spark in his chest, one strong enough to thaw the chill that gripped his core.

Hell, his devil-benighted bones were getting tired of the unremitting cold.

His hands suddenly froze on her thighs.

Ye God—what was he doing? She was an inexperienced young lady and he was a world-weary rake. Despite his many faults, he had never preyed on innocents.

And yet...

Just how innocent could she be? She had dared to disguise herself as a man, she had dared gamble with rakish gamesters. What other rules had she flaunted? What other risks had she taken? He was still sure she hadn't much experience in being kissed. But that didn't necessarily mean she hadn't much experience with men.

The thrumming of his blood grew louder. He knew enough of Alexa Hendrie to have learned that her passions—be they anger, compassion, or some other elemental emotion—were easily aroused. That there was a powerful physical attraction between them was undeniable. If she had already indulged in the forbidden pleasure of an illicit affair, surely that released him from all strictures of honor?

Fair game. That was how it was played among the members of the *ton* who craved excitement. The young lady had made it clear she thought herself up to the challenge of hazarding her chances with rogues and reprobates. But did she truly understand the rules?

It took him a moment to realize the sound in his ears was not the echoing of his own doubts, his own searching questions.

"S-sir, this must s-stop. At once!" His fleeting hesitation had allowed her to recapture her breath. And with it a measure of reason. Drawing in ragged little gulps of air, she sought to disentangle herself from his arms. "Any overexertion may bring on a relapse of fever." A flutter of her hand grazed his forehead. "Indeed, your brow is burning. I—I had better mix a draught of willow bark."

The earl was quite sure the heat of his flesh had nothing to do with any recurring illness. Still, reluctant as he was to lose the intimacy of her warmth, he had no choice but to let her go.

"I am in no danger of expiring, Lady Alexa." He decided the best course of action was to make a sardonic joke of what had just occurred, rather than admit that these odd flares of fire between them were as confusing to him as they were to her. "But neither herbs nor drams will have the least effect on what ails me. Cold water, perhaps, but only if applied somewhat lower than my brow."

Alexa blinked, clearing the last smolderings of passion from her gaze. "No doubt you are quite unused to going more than a night or two without a female warming your sheets."

"And polishing the knob of my bedpost." Connor shifted under her weight. Would that he were as ruthless as his reputation implied. He had no doubt she had been his for the taking. Gentlemanly scruples could be a deucedly inconvenient—and uncomfortable—encumbrance. Especially when the lady in question showed not a whit of appreciation for his noble sacrifice.

"Then I breakfast on virgins. All depraved rakehells do, you know."

"Oh, you are..." Her words cut off in a gasp as her wriggling pulled the rumpled nightshirt—along with the last shred of decency—down from his groin.

"Wicked?" he suggested with a lascivious grin. Oh,

yes, it was truly, truly wicked to take such sinful amusement in seeing her eyes grow wide as saucers. "I did warn you of the dangers in consorting with a Wolf."

Her gaze remained riveted on his rampant arousal. That she appeared more fascinated than shocked goaded him to even greater wickedness.

"You are welcome to touch it, if you like."

The movement seemed to recall her to the utter impropriety of her position. With a faint gasp, Alexa scrambled off him, her feet finding the floor amid a welter of flapping skirts and flailing limbs. Bodice askew, garters fallen around her ankles, hair tangled in wanton disarray, she looked delightfully *en déshabillé*, as if she had just been tumbled up against a tavern wall.

Honor be damned. At that moment, he was sorely tempted to follow her out of bed and do just that. Instead, he contented himself with a crooked grin.

"You are tantalizingly lovely."

"You are dangerously delirious."

"Then perhaps you ought to come back to bed and minister to my dying needs."

The purse of her lips, still swollen with the force of his kisses, suddenly curled from indignation to an expression of outright horror.

Connor turned to see the source of her dismay. The housekeeper, her arms loaded with a tray of tea and freshly baked scones, had nudged the door open without a warning knock. "I thought Your Lordship and Your Ladyship might be wanting a bit of refreshment—" One look at Alexa sent her crabbing backward with an audible gasp. "I beg your pardon," she stammered. "I hadn't thought...I didn't mean..."

"That's quite all right, Mrs. Callaway. You may put it on the dressing table," said Connor easily. He couldn't resist adding, "I am sure that my...lady would welcome a reviving cup of tea after all her strenuous exercise."

A daggered glare was accompanied by a very unladylike word, said just loud enough for him to hear it.

The housekeeper set the tray down, gave a quick bob of her head and lost no time in hurrying from the room, taking great care to close the door behind her.

Alexa was still for a moment. As she turned to mix up a glass of the medicine, the earl saw that her hands were shaking slightly. He certainly accomplished his goal of embarrassing her, but the fact gave him precious little satisfaction.

"Look, it was you who suggested the charade of newlyweds," he said, seeking to temper his earlier sardonic comments with a note of gentler humor. "I was merely playing my role as the besotted husband."

"Playing it to the hilt," she muttered.

He couldn't help but chuckle as he took the glass she had prepared. The young lady might nearly have lost her virtue to a rakehell rogue, but her spirit—and her sense of humor—were still intact. "Our acquaintance does seem to be marked by flair for dramatic scenes."

"It was you who began the first act by shoving me up against an erotic etching and kissing me."

"It was you who chose to barge onto the stage of a bawdy house," he countered, enjoying the fact that quick wits and clever retorts were among her repertoire of charms. Indeed, dialogue with her was nearly as exhilarating as the sexual play. "Besides, you have to admit you like being kissed."

Her cheeks took on a guilty flush. "Being ravished by a lecherous libertine? I most certainly do not!"

"Your words say one thing, but your body, when I touch you, says quite another. Had I delved within your folds and caressed your most secret spot, I could have easily brought you to ultimate ecstasy."

Her hot denial suddenly died away, and in her face he saw the confusion aroused by her own, undeniable passions. Which only made her appear more sweetly desirable.

All the more reason to send her away from Linsley Close, he reminded himself roughly. And the sooner the better, for both of them.

"W-what do you mean?" whispered Alexa.

"Never mind," he growled.

"That first encounter at The Wolf's Lair was not a role I had rehearsed, sir," she finally stammered. "It just...happened. I thought my brother might be in danger, and so I acted."

"I do not question your motivations, Lady Alexa, merely your sense of timing. Courage and loyalty are admirable qualities. But you have an unfortunate tendency to charge in without thinking of the consequences."

"Perhaps you ought to be glad of that. Otherwise the script might have taken a tragic turn—murder on top of intrigue and foul play."

"If you expect me to play the role of grateful hero, you have greatly misjudged my character."

She had taken up a position by the tea tray, but made no move to pour. Her hands remained clenched by her sides.

"And as for a happy ending to this farce, it will come

when you exit the stage." Connor took care to keep his gaze leveled at the leaded glass window. He would far rather face the bleak view of dark clouds, heavy with the rains of an impending squall, than the look on her face.

"I mean to send off some letters this afternoon. Just as soon as I am assured that it is safe for you to leave, I will arrange for your departure."

Leaving the tea and the pastries untouched, Alexa turned without a word and quitted the room.

Bloody hell. The earl drank the draught of medicine she had prepared, finding it more bitter than usual on his tongue.

Tallow. Alexa added the item to her list, then looked up from her notebook. "Anything else you can think of, Mrs. Callaway?"

"No, milady." The housekeeper cast a doubtful glance at the dusty holland covers, faded draperies, and unwaxed floors. "But begging your pardon, I am not sure how it can be done. There is no staff here, save Joseph and myself." She hesitated. "And even if the blunt was available, I would have a hard time convincing any of the local lasses to work here."

"Why is that?"

Ducking her head, the older woman fell to a nervous twisting of the keyring at her waist.

"Mrs. Callaway?"

"If you must know, milady, the earl—the old earl, that is—was a lecherous old goat who was always trying to slip a hand up their skirts."

"Well, you may assure them that things have changed at Linsley Close."

The other woman scuffed her shoe over the threadbare carpet. "To be frank, that is not going to be easy. Even in an isolated spot such as this, we get wind of the gossip from London."

"Regardless of what you or others have heard, the present Lord Killingworth is not the sort of gentleman who would ever force his attentions on a unwilling female," replied Alexa. The new earl might be just as randy as his father, but he had no need to chase after skirts. They tended to fall right in his lap. With an inward sigh, she recalled the buxom beauty who had so obviously enjoyed her waltz with him. No doubt the lady was just one of his many paramours...

She quickly cleared her throat and went on. "As you have known him since childhood, I imagine you can convince the local folk that it is now safe to pass through these portals."

An odd little look flitted across the housekeeper's face before she bobbed her head, "Yes, milady."

Enough of the Irish Wolfhound. She would not think of his wickedly wanton mouth. Or his rampantly male...maleness. *Cock. Pizzle. Pego. Tallywag*—oh yes, she had overheard all the cant terms her farmworkers used for the male reproductive organ. Such whispers of forbidden things had been mildly titillating. Her barnyard experience had given her some idea of what to expect. And yet, she couldn't help but be curious as to how a man looked in the flesh.

Well, now I know. She should have screamed. Fainted. Melted into a puddle of shame. Instead she had sighed. Stared. *Oh, I admit it—I was tempted to take his challenge and touch him.* The tantalizing textures—the coarse dark curls, the ruddy velvet flesh, so impossibly hard and soft...

She closed her eyes for an instant, trying to squeeze away a stab of longing. It was unlikely that she would ever have the chance again to experience such shocking intimacies with a reprobate rake. *For which I should be profoundly grateful.*

And yet...

Tightening her grip on the pencil, Alexa quickly thumbed to a fresh page of her notebook. She would soon be gone from here. But in the meantime, rather than sit around mooning over foolish girlish fantasies, she might as well occupy her time with doing the sort of things she was good at.

"I believe we can budget a small sum to hire help for some of the larger jobs," she murmured. Cameron had provided her with a generous purse to cover contingencies. "As for the other tasks, I am sure that between the three of us, we shall manage quite nicely."

There was a sharp jangling as the heavy iron ring slipped from the housekeeper's fingers. "Oh, milady, surely *you* can't be meaning to be donning an apron and taking part in the actual work!"

"Why ever not?"

If possible, Mrs. Callaway looked even more shocked than when she had walked into the bedroom and discovered Alexa in a near scandalous state of undress. "Because you are a fine lady, with a lofty title!"

"I am a down-to-earth country miss," she replied with a wry smile. "Not some pampered Town belle. If need be, I am perfectly capable of rolling up my sleeves and wielding a broom or a dust mop."

The assurance did not appear to put the housekeeper's mind at rest. She voiced no further protest, but her fisted hands and furrowed brow spoke clearly of how little enthusiasm she had for the plan.

Stifling a sigh, Alexa consulted the lists she had drawn up, then jotted down several more notes. "I suggest we start in the drawing room. By your accounting, we have an ample supply of beeswax, ash, and lye."

A stiff nod bobbed in answer.

"Excellent." Forcing a brisk cheerfulness, she slapped her book shut. "We shall also need buckets, mops, brooms, and dusting cloths."

"As you wish, milady."

One would have thought she had just ordered up a coffin and gravestone.

"Excellent, excellent. Then let us count on beginning first thing on the morrow."

"I will see to it, milady." Clutching at her skirts, Mrs. Callaway edged back a step, clearly anxious to be dismissed. "Is there anything else, milady?"

"No, that is all."

The housekeeper scuttled away, leaving her standing alone in the shadows of the neglected room.

Hell, she seemed to be out of place wherever she went. Unwelcome, unappreciated, unattractive, un... Alexa bit back the quivering of her lip. No, she would *not* come undone at this latest rebuff. If she wished to take gambles in life, she must be willing to accept the losses as well as the victories, whatever the cost.

But unlike Lord Haddan, she would fold her hand before she had lost everything, including her dignity—or what remained of it.

Lifting her chin, Alexa managed a rueful smile. At least she could give a good polish to the table before making her exit.

Her spirits thus uplifted, she tucked her notebook back in her pocket and turned for a last look around at what needed to be done to make the place habitable. Reaching up for a closer inspection of the soot stains on the mantel, she found that the twist of goat hair she had tucked away earlier had become twined around her fingers.

Alexa was about to toss it into the empty hearth when something about it caused her to hesitate. Light as a puff of air, the gossamer fibers were intriguingly soft against her skin. She stared for a long moment, slowly spinning them between her thumb and forefinger.

The smudges of smoke forgotten, Alexa hurried off in search of the library.

Chapter Twelve

Taking a momentary break from her work, Alexa leaned back to admire the newly burnished glow of the sherry-colored paneling. Now that years of accumulated salt and dust had been cleaned from the bank of leaded windows, sunlight spilled into the room, illuminating the fine grain of the oak and the delicate detailing of the acanthus leaf moldings.

Ah, yet another task could be crossed off her list.

She looked over to where Mrs. Callaway was running a vinegar-soaked rag over the last pane of glass. The draperies, lank folds of emerald velvet that had long ago lost their luster, would have to go. Something much lighter was in order. But nothing too feminine. This was, after all, a bachelor's retreat. A contrasting stripe, perhaps.

She made a mental to note to ask the housekeeper about paying a visit to the attics. There might be some suitable material stored away in a trunk.

"What the devil is going on here?"

The deep baritone rumble sent a tingling through her fingertips. The cursed Wolfhound was right—her mutinous body reacted in the most shameful ways when he was near.

Gripping the polishing cloth more tightly, she gave the wood another rub. "I should think that is rather obvious, sir. We are making the place habitable."

"Don't bother." The earl had managed to shave and make himself presentable in an old silk dressing gown, but his voice was bristly as ever. "I have no intention of spending any length of time here."

Why was it that a gentleman could look raffishly handsome in a hodgepodge of borrowed clothing?

Alexa brushed at a straggle of hair, belatedly realizing she had left a streak of beeswax and dust on the tip of her nose. It was a good thing she had abandoned all illusions of appearing attractive or alluring to his eye. A droopy mobcap, dusty apron and shapeless gown were not likely to elicit any sighs of admiration.

"Nonetheless, I prefer to keep busy," she replied. "Besides, on a purely practical level, it's a prudent business investment to keep a house in good repair."

"I can never sell it," he snapped. "It's entailed. Otherwise I would have gotten rid of the cursed place long ago."

She raised an eyebrow. "It's actually quite a wonderful house, with lovely architectural lines, airy rooms, and a marvelous view. Why do you hate it so?"

Ignoring the question, Connor shuffled past her. Aside from a slight limp and a deeper chiseling to his features, he appeared to be recovering nicely from the gunshot wound. Staring up at his back, the broad expanse of shoulders and narrow waist limned in the sunlight, Alexa felt her breath catch in her throat. It had been some time since she had seen him standing on his own, and she had almost forgotten what a large, imposing man he was.

"I am afraid that my lady may have become carried away with her role as mistress of the house," he said to the housekeeper. "It is, after all, a position that is quite new to her." Another glance around only deepened his scowl. "She seems to have forgotten that we will only be here a short while. There is no need for all this fuss. A simple sweeping of the bedchambers and an adequate fire is all that is required."

"I don't mind, milord. As Her Ladyship says, it is good to be busy. A body should have a useful purpose, rather than engage in frivolous pursuits." Mrs. Callaway wrung out her cleaning cloth and picked up the bucket. "Or just sit around brooding himself into a black study."

The earl glowered.

Ducking her head, Alexa bit back smile. The housekeeper must still see a sickly little mite, and not the notoriously dangerous Irish Wolfhound looming over her.

"Shall I fix you a cup of tea while I mix up a batch of fresh suds?" Mrs. Callaway directed the question at Alexa. Her frosty manner had thawed somewhat over the course of the morning, and her tone, while still reserved, betrayed a grudging note of respect. "You have been working since daybreak without a respite. Wouldn't do for you to fall ill, too."

"Yes, that would be lovely." Straightening with a wince, Alexa realized that her muscles were indeed cramped with fatigue. Besides, if the earl was intent on ringing a peal over her head, she would much prefer not to have an audience witness her humiliation.

Connor waited until the other woman had gathered up

her things and left the room before turning his gaze from the freshly dusted curio table back to her. A brief glint of teeth was followed by a gruff cough. "My apologies for what occurred yesterday."

"None are necessary, my lord. If we could go back and repeat the last week, I am sure both of us would choose to do a great many things differently."

"Still, I have placed you in an awkward position—"

"More than one, actually," murmured Alexa.

Her rueful attempt at humor did not extract a glimmer of amusement. Angling his face away from the light, Connor picked up an enamel snuffbox from the curio table and turned it slowly between his fingers. Shadows darkened the faint lines crinkling out from the corners of his eyes, accentuating their hooded heaviness. He looked immensely weary, in a way that was more than physical.

Some of the reasons she could guess. As to the others, the Earl of Killingworth deserved his reputation as a supremely skilled card player. She had never seen anyone keep his hand—and his feelings—so closely guarded.

"As I said, I am sorry that you have been dragged into danger." Connor put down the box and took up another item, this one a Celtic cross, its intricate patterns finely worked in silver. Just as abruptly, he changed the subject. "How did you come to have an Irish name?"

"I am called after my grandmother," she said softly. "Who hailed from Donegal."

"I should have known from the red highlights in your hair that you had a spark of Hibernian fire in you."

"By all accounts, she was an even greater hellion than I." Alexa sighed. "At age seventy, she still rode to the hounds, danced till dawn, and enjoyed a daily tipple of Bushmills."

"A remarkable lady." He shifted his stance. "It appears to run in the family."

Her head jerked up. *Was that a compliment?* Or simply an oblique way of indicating how little he approved of her conduct.

Alexa had little chance to reflect on the question, as she found herself staring at his outstretched hand.

"Come, you have spent long enough on your hands and knees." She allowed him to help her up. "If you have need of vigorous exertion, perhaps you will consent to join me in a walk to the cliffs after you have taken your refreshment."

"But the hearth has yet to be polished—"

"It has lasted this long without crumbling to ashes. Another hour or two will make no difference," pointed out Connor. "You, on the other hand, look as if you could use a breath of fresh air. As do I. I also would like a private word with you."

"Very well, sir. Let me just inform Mrs. Callaway of our plans and change into more respectable clothes."

"Thank you..." A pause. "Alexa."

Don't be a goose, she chided herself. Still, the intimacy of her name without a title, spoken just as a lover or husband might say it—set her heart to fluttering.

The crunch of gravel punctuated his labored steps. Connor had brought along one of his father's old walking sticks from the entrance hall, but still his progress was painfully slow. Determined to recover his stamina as quickly as possible, he tightened his grasp on the silver knob and forced himself to pick up the pace.

"You know, sir, it is not necessary to hike up into the moors in order to have a private conversation," pointed out Alexa after they had traversed a steep ascent. "You have a perfectly comfortable library."

"I would prefer that Mrs. Callaway does not become privy to our deception." His mouth quirked. "I wouldn't want my reputation ruined in the eyes of an old family retainer."

"She indicated to me that she is hard of hearing."

"When it comes to matters of a confidential nature, I have always found that servants, no matter their age or proclaimed infirmity, have extremely sharp ears," replied Connor.

Beneath the poke of her bonnet, he detected a smile. "A point well taken, sir. What is it you wish to discuss?"

"How the devil I am going to send you back to Seb without kicking up a terrible dust?" he said.

She stopped short. "What makes you think I shall consent to being trundled home, as if I am a naughty child in need of a spanking?"

"Because you have no other option."

Her half boot scuffed at the ground, and a large pebble skittered perilously close to his ankles.

He sympathized with her anger and frustration. For an independent, intelligent young lady, the strictures of Society must feel like a cage, no matter how gilded the bars.

However, he was in no position to offer her an escape.

"I've dispatched Jenkins back to Town," said Connor dispassionately. "With orders to return as soon as possible with the latest news from Cameron, as well as a portmanteau of your clothing and a conveyance suitable for a fast journey north."

A sharp inhale of breath was her only response.

"Cam is extremely capable when it comes to dealing with delicate situations," he went on. "I'm sure that he has been able to squash any unpleasant gossip concerning your abrupt disappearance from Town. Without the cloud of public scandal hanging over your head, your family won't have any problem in accepting your innocence— that is, as long as you exercise a bit of discretion."

"You seem to have given this a great deal of thought," said Alexa slowly.

"Not really," he lied. "I have a good many more important things on my mind than a headstrong hellion. However, as I would rather not be distracted by the demands of an outraged brother, I strongly advise that we play down some of the particulars of this predicament. For both of our sakes."

She stood stony-faced as the surrounding crags as he went on to suggest a highly edited version of the recent events. "If you stick to this script," he finished, "you should suffer no serious consequences."

"Nor will you, if that is what you are worried about." No longer impassive, her features betrayed a twist of indignation. "You odious, arrogant beast. Are you implying that I set out to *deliberately* snare your paw in the parson's mousetrap?"

"I meant no—" he began, only to be cut off.

"Ha! I may be an aging antidote, but I am not *that* desperate for a husband. Even if I was, I should not wish to shackle myself to one who is an unmannered, ungrateful lout!"

"As I do not seek a wife, we are in perfect accord on one thing," he said evenly. "My intention was not to offer insult, Lady Alexa. Merely to make certain things are clear between us."

"Never fear, sir." Brushing by him, she started back in the direction they had come. "Your sentiments are egregiously clear."

The path was narrow and steep, but that did not stop her from lengthening her stride to put some distance between them.

The uneven stones made it impossible for him to go any faster. Swearing, he limped over the loose scree, swatting with his stick at the occasional sprig of gorse that hung in his way.

Marriage? Bloody hell. Even a sham one was proving decidedly difficult.

On making his way around a sharp outcropping of rock, Connor spotted Alexa up ahead. She had stopped at one of the stiles that dotted the stone fences, and as he came closer, he saw that she was feeding a handful of meadow grass to what looked like a walking skein of unraveled wool.

"Where did these animals come from?" The recent quarrel seemed forgotten as she pointed out several other longhaired animals grazing over the hardscrabble terrain.

He paused to catch his breath. "Haven't a clue. The same place, I imagine, where most farmers buy their sheep."

She made a pained face. "First of all, they are *goats*, not sheep. And ones that would not have been easy to acquire."

"Well, then it can't have been my father who brought

them here. His interest in livestock was confined to the two-legged variety." Not that he could claim to be an authority on the hairy beasts either. "Why do you ask?"

The sun suddenly appeared from behind a scattering of clouds, but the glint in her eye was more than a reflection of the slanting rays. "I thought I recognized the characteristics, and so I did a little research in your library last night." She tugged gently at the animal's beard. "These are Kashmir goats, which come from India. They are rare here in England and the wool is quite valuable, you know. With the numbers you appear to have running wild here, you could start a highly profitable business."

"Too much hard work involved." Connor shrugged. "I would rather fleece reprobates of the *ton* than be a cursed farmer."

And yet, why did he feel a strange clenching in his chest at the thought of returning to his ancestral home? Shading his eyes, Connor darted a look back at the facade of the manor house, its mortised limestone warming to a honeyed glow in the changing light.

Ah yes, what a pretty picture that would make, he scoffed. The Irish Wolfhound turning into a domesticated herder of wool on the hoof.

Next he would be imagining a wife for real and a litter of squawling brats.

Perish the thought.

"It would not entail all that much effort," persisted Alexa. "Or initial expense. They are very self-sufficient, and you would not require more than one or two shepherds to handle the shearing. Of course, the marketing of the product would need some careful consideration—"

"Hell and damnation!" he exclaimed. "Fate may have

thrown us together as nominal partners in The Wolf's Lair, but the arrangement is purely temporary, and does not give you the right to try to order the rest of my life."

Spooked by his shout, the goat gave a startled bleat and pulled away from Alexa's grasp.

"This is *not* my home," he finished. "Or yours."

"Damn you, Connor Linsley!" She, too, was shouting. "I need no cruel taunts from you to remind me I have no real place to call home. Just as I need no hostile insults or pawing liberties to tell me how much my presence irks you."

Her chin had taken on a defiant tilt, but he saw that her lashes were wet with tears. Still, she did not allow them to fall.

"I was only trying to help. If I have offended you, I am sorry." Alexa drew in a ragged breath. "Why do you hate me so? Because I see something in you that frightens your own perceptions?"

Connor didn't answer right away. "I don't hate you, Lady Alexa," he finally said. "Far from it."

"Then why—why do you treat me so abominably?" she demanded.

Connor was close enough to see the subtle sparks of red and gold in her loosened tresses. "Because you send fire through my veins. And it chills me to the bone." Reaching out, he traced his fingertips along the line of her jaw. "It's not me I'm afraid of, but you, *álainn*.

"I—I don't understand."

He captured her mouth in a sudden fierce kiss. *It was wrong—oh-so wrong*. His brain was shouting a warning, but for a wild moment, the blood was thrumming too loudly in his head for him to hear it. *Be damned with reason.* Frustration, longing—along with a pelter of emotions he dared not name—welled up inside him.

With a deep, feral groan, Connor sucked in her lower lip, savoring the clean, herb-sweet taste of her essence. His hands came up to frame her face, and the warmth of her skin suffused his callused palms.

"Ohhhh." With a breathy sigh, Alexa swayed and yielded to his embrace, opening up to him with an eagerness that made his chest clench. Her hands fisted in his hair, pulling him closer.

"*Álainn,*" he rasped, the Gaelic endearment lost in a gust of wind as he crushed her body against his. Heat flared as Alexa arched and allowed his rampant arousal to nudge between her skirt-swirled legs.

Oh, this was wicked—truly wicked. She deserved more than a snabbering, lustful beast pawing at her innocence. The dim roar of Reason finally penetrated the primitive pulsing of need. Connor held tight to the feel of her for an instant longer, then roughly released his hold and stepped back.

"I don't understand," repeated Alexa, her voice sounding a little dazed as she lifted her fingertips to touch the swell of her lips.

"God Almighty, neither do I," he muttered as he turned his back and stalked away. "Let us leave it at that."

Hot and cold.

Men were a complete mystery, while stoves...

Alexa jiggled the thin blade a fraction more to the left and managed to tighten the screw. "There, that ought to rectify the problem." Shimmying out from inside the unlit oven, she adjusted the iron griddle. Sure enough, it stayed level.

"Why, thank you, milady. Joseph's fingers have grown too stiff to work such tools, so I had resigned myself to making due with a broken stove." Mrs. Callaway's lined face wreathed in a broad smile as she inspected the handiwork. "We are fortunate, indeed to have such a clever mistress of the house. I daresay there is nothing at Linsley Close that you cannot put to rights."

Nothing save my own off-kilter emotions, thought Alexa with an inward grimace. However, she took a measure of satisfaction in having earned Mrs. Callaway's praise. The housekeeper's initial reserve had softened enough that she actually felt welcome.

"Oh, aye, m'lady." The girl who had been hired to help with the cleaning bobbed her head in vigorous agreement. "I was telling me mam that I never dreamed that a fine lady could know all the things ye know."

"Necessity is a good teacher." Alexa smiled as she wiped her sooty hands on a rag. "I am sure that you know a great deal more useful skills than I do, Becky."

The girl blushed with pleasure. "Yer awfully kind, Lady Killingworth."

Alexa caught herself from looking over her shoulder.

"Me mam sent along the bit of beefsteak ye requested, along with the lamb chops and a slab of bacon." Becky placed the parcels on the table, then added a basket of eggs. "Mrs. Deevers asked me te bring these te ye as well. Everyone is right pleased te hear a new countess is in residence at Linsley Close."

"I am happy to be here as well." Alexa hoped that the powdering of ash hid her guilty flush.

She felt badly about the deception, but consoled herself with the thought that it was doing no harm—and perhaps even a bit of good. Yesterday she had ventured a visit to the small village and had made several purchases. Though modest, they had elicited a shy gratitude, and she planned to return with a list of various other sundries to acquire.

"Will ye and the earl be staying fer long?" asked Becky.

"That is, of course, for His Lordship to decide," she replied slowly. "But I rather doubt it."

"Oh."

The girl looked a bit disappointed, and to her surprise, Alexa found that she, too, was regretting her imminent departure. She much preferred the wild ruggedness of the moors and the honest pleasures of country life to the artificial glitter and carefully choreographed rituals of London. Here, as in Yorkshire, she could breathe freely of fresh air and tramp about outdoors without fear that the tabbies were watching her every step. And the sea— she would miss the elemental rhythm of the surf breaking upon the craggy cliffs.

But as the earl had said, regrets were best left in the dust.

As Becky took her leave through the kitchen door, Alexa caught a glimpse of Connor in the distance, wending his way up to the cliffs overlooking the sea. He seemed to have taken his own words to heart, she mused, for he had spent much of the past few days walking the moors. With his wind-whipped hair and flapping cloak, he had stood out against the weathered rock and gorse, a solitary figure, buffeted by the elements.

A lone wolf. Did he never tire of his self-imposed isolation, both physical and emotional?

Apparently not, for he had taken great pains to avoid her since their harsh words and strange kiss. He had his meals in his own chamber, and spent the evenings locked away in his library until the wee hours. Mrs. Callaway had made mention of several letters being sent out, but as of yet, no replies had come in. Nor had anything been heard from Mr. Daggett.

For now, there was naught to do but wait.

However Alexa had no intention of sitting still. "I find there are several other things I wish to buy in the village," she announced, after setting the rag aside. "Is there anything else we need, aside from candles and a tin of tea?"

"No, milady. But Joseph can make the trek if you wish."

"I have been inside all day and look forward to the walk. I shall just change out of these garments and wash the dirt from my face—"

A rapping at the front door cut her short.

"Perhaps it's Jenkins," said Alexa as Mrs. Callaway straightened her apron and hurried to answer the knock. Anxious to know what word had come from Town, she was quick to follow.

Only to find herself wishing that she could crawl back inside a black hole. Preferably one that burrowed down all the way to China.

It was not the bearish coachman standing on the landing, but rather an elegant lady, stylishly attired in what Alexa ruefully recognized as the latest fashion from Paris.

The charming little chip straw bonnet, trimmed in a luscious shade of cherry red, showed off the caller's glossy mahogany curls to perfection. But even had her hair been hidden under a basket and her stunning figure

clothed in a gunnysack, Alexa would instantly have iden-
tified recognized her. *It was the buxom lady who had
waltzed so intimately with the earl in London.*

And here she was, dancing attendance on him at an
isolated country estate.

Why, the nerve of the dratted man to invite her here!

Much as she wished to deny it, Alexa felt an irrational
wave of jealousy sweep over her. Their marriage may be
a complete hum, but she would not tolerate him inviting
another woman into his bed right under her nose.

"Is the earl in?" The question was accompanied by a
dimpled smile.

"His Lordship is out at present," replied Mrs. Callaway. There was a slight hesitation before she added, "but
Lady Killingworth is at home."

Alexa took a rather spiteful pleasure in seeing that the
announcement caused the perfectly shaped brows to arch
so high that they disappeared completely beneath the poke
of the bonnet.

But to her credit, the lady evinced no other sign of
shock. She merely murmured, "Indeed? He did not mention having taken a wife." Slipping a calling card from
her beaded reticule, she held it out to the housekeeper.
"Would you kindly send someone to ask if Her Ladyship
will see me."

Mrs. Callaway took it and passed it on to Alexa.

Quelling the urge to crumple it up and toss it over her
shoulder, she stared mutely at the engraved script.

The Honorable Mrs. Andrew Blake Chatsworth.

It could have read the Queen of Siam or the Man in the
Moon, and Alexa would still have felt the same frisson of
dislike prickle through her fingertips.

Noting that the figure in the dusty mobcap and much-abused apron seemed in no hurry to seek out the lady of the house, Mrs. Chatsworth's expression turned a touch quizzical. "She does not know me, but you might make mention that I am an old friend of her husband."

Alexa looked up, doing her best to assume an air of un-ruffled dignity. Which, she admitted, was a trifle difficult while looking like something the cat had dragged up from the root cellar. "There is no need to pass on your message. I am Lady Killingworth." Somehow she got the name out with tripping over her own tongue.

"Indeed! How delightful to make your acquaintance!" The dimple reappeared. "Naughty man—I mean to ring a peal over Connor's head when he returns! Not only for keeping his nuptials a secret but for failing to invite us to the ceremony."

Connor. The implied intimacy set her teeth on edge. "It all happened rather suddenly, Mrs. Chatsworth."

"Oh, do call me Suzy. All my friends do." Suzy grinned. "Swept you off your feet, did he?"

"In a manner of speaking," replied Alexa tightly, re-calling how the unconscious earl's slumping weight had nearly knocked her on her backside.

There was a brief silence, then the earl's lady friend gave a tiny cough. "Er, might I come in?"

So much for appearing the gracious hostess.

Blushing to the roots of her bedraggled hair, Alexa hopped back a step. "Yes. Of course." Her fingers fum-bled at the folds of her faded skirts, seeking to scrub away any lingering traces of kitchen grease.

"Shall I bring tea to the drawing room, milady?"

Alexa nodded, grateful that the housekeeper had the

presence of mind to recall common courtesy. Her own brain had gone rather blank.

"Please follow me," she mumbled.

The clomp of her own half boots echoed in mocking contrast to the dainty patter of the visitor's silk-trimmed slippers, an all-too-vivid reminder that she was going to have to tiptoe very carefully to avoid sliding down the slippery slope of disaster.

For an instant she contemplated falling ill or feigning a twisted ankle, but after several steps, she regained her footing. She had bluffed her way through an even more brazen charade, she reminded herself. Surely she could play the role of a countess, despite smelling of bacon fat and looking like a chimney sweep.

The drawing room, at least, was not a source of further embarrassment. Sunlight sparkled through the scrubbed glass, illuminating the polished marble, freshly swept carpets and gleaming woodwork, still redolent of lemon oil and beeswax. Centered on the sideboard was a ginger jar, filled with the bouquet of wildflowers she had picked on yesterday's walk back from the village.

"Oh, what a cheery room," exclaimed Suzy, darting a glance around as she peeled off a pair of pale pink kidskin gloves and untied the strings of her bonnet.

Alexa couldn't help noting that beneath the breezy nonchalance was a certain air of alertness. Suzy's eyes, wide and set at a slight slant, were feline in their intensity. Though shaded with a thick fringe of lashes, they did not appear to miss much.

A kitten. That was the image that flashed to mind. But a kitten with claws, and no compunction about using them if the need arose.

Once again, Alexa felt rather like a mouse, surrounded by predators.

"Of course you will wish to add your own individual touches once you have settled in." Dropping her bonnet on the sofa, the earl's lady friend moved to the window. "Do you plan on taking up residence here?"

"That is up to... Connor."

"Ah, yes. A newly married lady is always quick to defer to her husband. But you'll soon learn the knack of how to bring a man around to your way of thinking."

Alexa's eyes narrowed. Was that a wink of secret amusement she detected in the other lady's hazel gaze?

"By the by, when did the two of you become man and wife?"

Aware she was treading on treacherous ground, Alexa took a moment to remove her mobcap. "Oh, a week ago. Or was it two?" She kept her reply deliberately vague. "Time flies, you know, when... when..."

"When you are having fun?" suggested Suzy. "You must tell me all the delightful details! Beginning with where the two of you met."

How much did the earl's lady friend know? And how much did she suspect? Alexa considered her options. More lies? That was dangerous, and yet so was the alternative.

To hell with the consequences. Drawing a deep breath, she decided to tell the truth.

"We met in a brothel..." A small part of her wanted to shock the insouciant smile off of her guest's face.

Suzy did not so much as bat an eye.

"And actually, I'm not really the Wolfhound's wife, but his partner—his business partner," she added, fully expecting that the bombshell would knock buxom beauty into a dead swoon.

Instead there came a peal of delighted laughter. "How marvelous! Do you mean to say, you have an interest in The Wolf's Lair?"

It was Alexa who found herself reeling. "You know about The Wolf's Lair?"

"Why, yes—I used to work there."

Talk about bombshells. The news certainly gave her a new perspective on the Honorable Mrs. Andrew Blake Chatsworth. Not that a different view of the luscious curves made her any more inclined to like the other lady. It was all too obvious what one of her primary jobs at the Lair had entailed.

Not, admitted Alexa, that warming the earl's sheets would have proved an onerous task.

Suzy did not seem the least bit perturbed at discovering Alexa's relationship to the Wolfhound. Indeed, she seemed genuinely amused by the connection. "How on earth did you ever convince Connor to give up a share of the Lair? I know him well enough to be sure he would never do it for money alone."

"No, he wouldn't. And he didn't. I won it in a game of cards," admitted Alexa. "Not from the earl himself. From his friend, Lord Haddan, who had temporary possession of…that is to say, it was all a rather egregious mistake." A harried sigh escaped her lips. "I'm afraid it's a rather complicated story. Much to Killingworth's annoyance. He wishes me to the devil."

"This is getting better and better!" Suzy settled herself on the sofa with an air of expectation. "Do go on."

"There is not really that much more to tell." Alexa was

quick with the rest of the account, glossing over a good many of the details. In retrospect, she wasn't overly proud of her actions.

Suzy, however, appeared genuinely impressed. "Dressed in breeches…beat the gentlemen at their own game…" she murmured to herself. "And knocked the teeth out of the Irish Wolfhound…"

Her ruminations were cut short by the appearance in the doorway of the Wolfhound in the flesh. Shaking droplets of rain from his coat, Connor stalked into the room.

With a cry of delight, Suzy bounced up and hurried to press a kiss upon his cheek. "Dear Connor, allow me to offer my heartfelt congratulations! It seems you have finally met your match."

Chapter Thirteen

$\mathcal{K}$indly stubble the show of hilarity, Suzy. At the present time, I'm in no mood for it." Wincing, Connor pulled away from his erstwhile employee's embrace. "Dare I hope that your unexpected appearance here indicates Drew has learned something useful?"

"It is a good thing that I know your bark is a good deal worse than your bite. Otherwise I might feel hurt at such a snappish welcome for an old friend," she replied.

"He has been even more ill-tempered than usual lately," offered Alexa. "Though I suppose being shot in the ribs would tend to make anyone feel out of sorts."

"*Shot?*" Fisting a hand on each hip, Suzy fixed him with an accusing glare. "It seems that your letter omitted quite a number of interesting details."

Women! Had the Almighty put them on earth simply to plague his peace of mind?

Connor made a face. "I didn't think it necessary to give any more than the bare-bones facts."

"Even when those bones were in danger of shuffling off their mortal coil?"

"That danger is well past." He had no intention of allowing Suzy to put him on the defensive. "The threat to the Lair is what is of paramount concern. I'm anxious to hear what you have discovered."

"I had better let Drew explain," replied his old friend. "He had to stop off at Goat Cove to pick up something from Spotted Dick. I expect him here shortly."

"We are expecting more guests?" asked Alexa faintly.

"My husband," explained Suzy brightly. "What fun! I hadn't expected that we could make an intimate little a party of the visit."

"Neither had I," said his pretend wife.

Bloody hell, swore Connor to himself.

"Please excuse me while I go upstairs and change into something more presentable." Alexa was twisting a dusty mobcap in her hands—and by the look she shot him as she swept by, it was clear she would like to do the same to his neck.

He rubbed at his temples. The years of working in close proximity to a houseful of lightskirts should have given him an intimate understanding of feminine logic. But apparently he hadn't a clue as to what made it tick.

No sane man could, he thought glumly. It wasn't murderous assault, attack on her virtue, or threat to her reputation that had Alexa Hendrie upset, but the fact that she was wearing an unbecoming outfit when company called.

Still, as he watched the swish of her ill-fitting skirts, draggles of dust clinging to the trailing hems, he couldn't help feeling an odd pinch of protectiveness override irritation. She was embarrassed, and she did not deserve to be.

"An extremely intriguing young lady." Suzy waited until the door fell firmly shut. "But then, I expected no less of your choice of a partner."

His teeth clenched. "The partnership—in every sense of the word—is purely temporary."

"Is it? I wonder."

"Well, don't," he said curtly.

"Who knows what lies in the cards?" she said, slipping a hand inside her reticule. To Connor's annoyance, there came the faint sound of shuffling paper. "You have suffered a number of setbacks of late, but I have a feeling your luck may be about to turn."

He scowled. "You might have had a real knack for playing *vingt-et-un* while at the Lair, but I don't recall you having any experience with predicting the future from bits of colored pasteboard."

"No?" She regarded him with an inscrutable expression. "Despite all warnings to the contrary, I predicted that you would be the sort of gentleman who would help a girl in need."

"That was different," he said gruffly. "Besides, I would hardly mention this particular lady in the same breath as 'luck.' She has proved to be anything but."

"Who is she?"

How to answer? A torment? A temptation? A wish for redemption?

"Lady Alexa Hendrie. And unlike the girls who work at The Wolf's Lair, she doesn't need me to offer any help. She has a family of her own. A highly respectable one. Her father is the Earl of Bushnell, her brother Viscount Becton—an old army comrade."

"Perhaps it is *you* who need *her.*"

A sarcastic retort, the sort that had become second nature, somehow eluded his tongue. Turning away, Connor stalked to the sideboard and poured himself a glass of brandy.

"*Sláinte*," he muttered in Gaelic, and then tossed it back in one swallow.

Suzy arched a brow. "You know, I wouldn't blame your wife if she put another bullet into that ornery hide of yours."

"She is *not* my wife," growled Connor.

To his relief, Suzy was distracted from further retort by the sight of a horse and rider galloping up the drive. "Oh, look, here comes Drew."

"The King of Hearts," he muttered, the burn of the brandy helping him recover his usual cynicism. "Let us hope he is bringing aught than the King of Spades. I am dug into a deep enough hole as it is."

No choice.

That was, unfortunately, the depressing truth about quite a few aspects of her life, thought Alexa.

Repressing a grimace, she fingered the lone garment in the armoire. In the haste to flee London she had come away with only the gown on her back—a shapeless indigo sack, chosen to hide any distinguishing feature during her midnight foray.

At least it was freshly laundered. What did it matter if it was hideously unfashionable? There was an old adage that one couldn't make a silk purse out of a sow's ear.

And seeing as she was naught but a plain country miss with a rather loud oink...

Still, as Alexa lifted it from the peg, she could not help but wish the neckline were a little lower, the bodice a little snugger.

She was just tying off the last tapes when a tiny click from across the room caused her look up. In the dusky light, the cheval glass reflected only a blur of shadows. Then, as a figure moved out from the paneled doorway, the earl's features became recognizable.

Lud, she had all but forgotten that her quarters were designed for the mistress of the house—and that they connected to the master's bedchamber.

"You ought not be here, sir," she said sharply. "It is most improper...to leave your friends alone."

His lips curved upward as he approached, a wickedly sensuous smile that stirred a most improper heat between her thighs.

"Ah, but we don't seem to do anything by the rules." Before she could make a move, he reached up and brushed an errant curl from the nape of her neck. "Do we, Alexa?"

His touch sent shivers of fire racing down her spine. There ought to be very strict rules about how a young lady reacted to a rake's touch.

Oh, but there are, she reminded herself. Lots of them. However, as all rational thought seemed to have gone up in a swirl of smoke, she couldn't seem to recall what they were.

"You will soon be rid of all these unruly distractions, sir," whispered Alexa. "And your life will fall back in proper order."

Not that her own existence would ever be quite the same again, she thought. He would quickly forget her and this unwanted interlude. While his lean, chiseled face and these unreasonable, unquenchable flares of longing that it ignited would remain indelibly imprinted on her memory.

On her body.

"Perhaps very soon," she added. Was that why he was here? To tell her that she would be leaving as soon as she finished donning the one gown she could call her own. "Has Mrs. Chatsworth's husband brought the news you have been waiting for?"

Connor shrugged but didn't answer. His fingertips, which were still resting lightly on her skin, shifted to the open armoire door and began to trace over the garland of roses carved into the dark wood. "This was my mother's room," he murmured after a long moment, almost too softly for her to hear.

Feeling even more of an interloper in his world, she edged back abruptly. "You should have told me sooner, sir. I had not realized I was trespassing on cherished memories."

His laugh had a splintered harshness to it. "The only cherished memory I have of Linsley Close is the day that I left it." Leaving off his inspection, Connor clasped his hands behind his back.

Alexa hated seeing him like this. *Bleak, brooding.* Bristling and baring his teeth at anyone who dared to come too close. She was sure that the Wolfhound's hide was not quite so tough as he wished for everyone to think. Including himself.

But how to reach the reclusive man beneath it? Her clumsy approaches seemed only to draw snaps and snarls.

"I will move into one of the other rooms," she said quickly.

"I didn't come to chase you from your quarters," replied Connor.

It took a moment for his words to sink in. Of course. The earl had no wish for her to rejoin the others. He was finally in the company of friends—dear friends, she thought with a pang of jealousy—and would prefer to enjoy the respite without her abrasive presence rubbing his nerves raw.

"I seem to be constantly in the wrong place at the wrong time. Saying or doing the wrong thing." She assumed a note of cold detachment—at least she hoped she had. "Be assured I have no desire to tread on your toes, or embarrass you any further with this unfortunate charade. I shall stay here, well away from you and your guests."

He frowned slightly. "You misunderstand me, Alexa. That's not why I am here."

Alexa. Again, the intimacy of her name, stripped of any formal title, sent a slow, shivering tickle down her spine. On his tongue, it had a lushness, like a murmur through a mouthful of honey.

How sweet it would sound—if only it were real.

"Then why have you come?" she challenged.

"You appeared uncomfortable around our visitor." His mouth quivered. "Having a modicum of experience with females, I have come to know how absurdly sensitive you all are about matters of dress." He withdrew an oblong leather case from his pocket and snapped it open. "So I thought you might wish to wear these."

Nestled on a layer of black velvet was a necklace. The design was exquisite in its simplicity, the luminous luster of a double strand of pearls highlighted by a teardrop sapphire pendant set in filigreed gold. It was flanked by matching ear bobs.

Dear God. The air leached from her lungs.

"H-how lovely." Recovering her breath, she looked up in consternation. "I don't understand—wherever did you get them? And why are you offering them to me?"

"It's on my account that you were forced to flee with

naught but the clothes on your back. I felt beholden to make some amends for your present predicament." Connor lifted the necklace from the case. "As for these, they belonged to my father's mother, who passed them on to my mother as a wedding gift." Entwined in his fingers, the sinuous spill of pearls lay coiled on his callused palm. "When she realized my father was selling every item of value to support his vices, she gave them to me for safe-keeping."

Alexa wished to say something. *But what?*

He closed his fist. "I was only eight years old at the time, but as she had drunk a great deal of champagne before coming to my room, I suppose the irony of asking *me* for help did not occur to her. In any case, like every child, I had a secret hiding place for all my imagined treasures. I put them away, and forgot about their existence." He expelled his breath. "Until now."

"But, sir!" Alexa tried to protest as he undid the clasp and started to drape it around her neck. "You mustn't...you shouldn't..."

He paid no heed. "A Linsley countess should appear in Linsley family jewels."

The pearls were like slivers of ice on her flesh. And then like tongues of fire.

"Don't waste their sparkle on a pretender, sir." Alexa lowered her lashes, fearing that the looking glass would reflect the fierce flash of longing in her eyes. "They should be saved for the real thing."

"We have been playing at pretenses for so long that another night won't make any difference," replied Connor.

The daylight was dying. And with it, the will to keep up her guard. This was a game far beyond her skill, and Alexa suddenly felt powerless to pretend she was anything other than a very inexperienced young lady. Uncertain, confused, and no match for the quixotic contradictions of his character.

Her face wreathed in shadow, Alexa pressed a hand to her bejeweled throat. "I confess, sir, I hardly know how to go on. I feel...lost."

"It is not always easy to find your way in the world," he said softly. "You are not alone in sometimes feeling unsure of which way to turn."

Was it merely her imagination, or did the last dappling of sun catch a glimmer of regret for paths not taken? "But a wolf..." stammered Alexa. "Surely a wolf always knows where he is going."

"The pitfalls are there for all of us."

"You are being kind," she replied.

"No, simply truthful. Do not confuse the two, Alexa." The edge in his voice was back. "You still must watch your step very carefully, else in this wicked world of prowling predators, you might end up being eaten alive."

Confusion caught in her throat.

It didn't help that Connor had moved close—so close that their bodies were only inches apart. The earthy, virile scent of his maleness was suddenly overpowering.

Intoxicating.

Still, she managed to whisper, "I'm not afraid of you, sir."

"You should be, Alexa."

His lips feathered against the nape of her neck. The touch was barely more than a whisper, and for an instant she wondered whether it was just her own wishful longing that sensed the light play of pressure tickling the sensitive skin.

Summoning her courage, Alexa turned to face him and lifted her eyes to meet his gaze. Oddly enough, the silvery color seemed to ripple, the scudding shadows reflecting her own uncertainty. Without thinking, she reached up and slowly traced the hard line of his jaw. The stubbling of whiskers rasped beneath her fingertip, darkly masculine against lightness of her own flesh.

"You should be afraid of me," he growled.

And yet, she wasn't. Placing her palm on the solid slope of his shoulder, Alexa inched up on her toes to brush a kiss to the corner of his mouth. A trace of brandy lingered there, its spice warm and tingling. The taste was meltingly sweet, and as it trickled down her tongue, she felt an aching need begin to burn at the back of her throat.

Connor.

Her lips sought his, and for a magical moment, he softened and responded with a deep, demanding embrace. A thrust of wet heat—

And then, all too quickly, it was gone, leaving naught but the chill air to caress her upturned face.

Drawing back, Connor took her hand and nestled it in the crook of his arm. The contours of smooth muscle fitted her like a glove.

"But for tonight, Alexa, you face no threat."

Chapter Fourteen

This is delicious, Lady Killingworth," murmured Mr. Chatsworth.

Lady Killingworth. Alexa lifted the glass to her lips, and as the wine pooled a pleasant warmth inside her, she didn't feel quite as much of an imposter.

"Delicious," echoed Suzy, adding a saucy wink.

Alexa felt herself blush. A hurried consultation with Mrs. Callaway and their newly hired maid had resulted in a simple but excellent supper being served. Along with fetching lamb cutlets, spring carrots, and fresh cheese from a neighboring farm, Becky had cut a bouquet of wild roses from vines growing rampant along the garden walls. Centered on the dining room table, surrounded by the crystal goblets, Chinese porcelain, and silver flatware that Alexa had carried down from the attics several days ago, the pale pinks and greens added a perfect touch of welcome to the burnished wood and freshly starched linen.

All in all, it was not too shabby for her first attempt at playing a countess.

The two visitors had certainly made her feel at ease.

Both Mrs. Chatsworth and her husband proved to be charmingly informal and brimming with sly humor. Even the earl was drawn out by their teasing, going so far as to flash an occasional grudging grin at their playful comments. Alexa, too, had enjoyed the lively give-and-take and the refreshing lack of artifice. Much as she wished to dislike the other lady, she found that as the meal went on, her initial animosity was fast melting away. It was impossible not to warm up to such forthright friendliness and unfettered frankness. There was none of the stilted drawing room airs and graces to Suzy.

A kindred soul? Given their vast differences in experience...

Alexa couldn't help but slant a glance at Andrew Chatsworth. It was clear that despite Suzy's being a broken vessel, her highborn husband saw her as flawless in every meaningful respect. His regard was evident in any number of subtle ways—the cant of his lips, the tone of his voice, the glimmer in his eyes as they followed her every move, even when his attention appeared to be elsewhere.

Once again, Alexa was aware of a small pinch of jealousy. Though, to her credit, Suzy appeared equally enamored of Andrew. Her attentions to the earl revealed an undeniable closeness, but it was more that of a good friend than a current lover.

And Connor? His emotions were, as usual, unreadable.

If only she could learn the trick of holding a gentleman's gaze in thrall. She watched him for a moment longer, then looked away.

Oh, don't be a fool. Trying to be something she was not would only doom her to another dismal failure. After all, she had already tried masquerading as a young gentleman, as a practiced gamester, as a worldly lady and had fooled no one. *No one but herself.*

Better to drop all pretenses and just be…Alexa Hendrie. An unpolished country hoyden who was more at home fixing a sooty stove than she was dancing an elegant waltz.

The strange thing was, as she relaxed and looked around the room, Alexa realized how much she liked being useful. Really useful. Rolling up her sleeves and getting dirt under her nails was infinitely more rewarding than sketching indifferent watercolors, playing uninspired music or nattering about idle gossip. She would, of course, never be at home in Polite Society.

And perhaps that wasn't so bad.

Her gaze met with Connor's and much to her amazement, he smiled. It was only a tiny quirk around the corners of his mouth. But his eyes, gleaming like buffed silver, seemed to reflect a hint of warmth.

Alexa shifted slightly in her chair, the pearls moving against her skin like a soft caress. The Wolfhound had been wrong about there being no threat to her this evening. The truth was, she was in imminent danger of losing…

"…Linsley Close has been transformed. Your lady has breathed new life into this crumbling hunk of stone timbers, wouldn't you say?"

She blinked, suddenly aware that Suzy's offhand question had been directed at the earl.

Connor raised his crystal goblet, obscuring his expression in a swirl of garnet and ruby refractions.

Did the other lady know of his aversion to the estate? Alexa's fingers tightened around her own wineglass. All reveries evaporated as she steeled herself for one of the Wolfhound's usual biting comments.

The silence stretched a bit longer. Suzy and her husband exchanged looks but refrained from further comment.

"She has worked miracles," he finally agreed.

A compliment, however oblique, from the Irish Wolfhound? Speaking of miracles! Her stomach had an odd fluttering in it, as if she had just swallowed a flock of butterflies instead of a tiny morsel of creamed carrot.

"In more ways than one," murmured Chatsworth, who over the course of the meal had managed to extract, bit by bit, the story of midnight attack from Connor. "Hauling your carcass out of the stews of Southwark must have been no easy feat."

"Surviving the snap of your jaws in the aftermath deserves even more credit," added Suzy. "I know from long experience that your atrocious temper would test the patience of a saint."

"Which, you may be sure, I am not." Alexa could not resist joining in. "Just ask Killingworth."

"Connor?" pressed Suzy.

"As I have never dared lift my eyes heavenward, my answer would be purely speculative." Despite his poker face, the earl still seemed in a light-hearted mood. "However, the lady has been heard to utter an oath. I doubt that saints are allowed to swear."

"Neither are proper ladies," sighed Alexa. "So I suppose that leaves me somewhere in Purgatory."

"The hell it does," said Suzy. "Take my word for it, all ladies swear when sufficiently provoked." She paused ever so slightly. "And as we are usually surrounded by men, the only wonder is that we don't do it a great deal louder and great deal more often."

"I defer to your greater knowledge in this area," responded Alexa.

"A wise move, Lady Killingworth. I tip my hat to your judgment, and your muscle." Chatsworth gave a waggish tweak to his auburn curls. "Metaphorically speaking, that is. Or would you prefer that I genuflect?"

Laughter sounded all around. Alexa could not help wishing that the evening, and the sense of camaraderie, might last...forever.

It was, of course, as unrealistic as her other fantasies. "By the by," she murmured. "You really ought not call me Lady Killingworth. As we have explained, it's a little white lie to avoid scandal."

Chatsworth lifted his glass with a gallant flourish. "A rose by any other name would smell as sweet."

As the chuckles died away, Connor passed the wine to his friend. Leaving his own glass untouched, he scraped his chair back and resumed a sober expression. "Enough of fun and games, metaphorical or otherwise. It's time we got down to plain speaking." Turning to Chatsworth, he demanded, "What have you found out about the cardsharp DeWinter?"

"All work and no play?" His friend murmured one last quip before turning serious. "Oh, very well. To begin with, you were right. He's from Antwerp, where his mother—who, according to Spotted Dick, was a woman from Dover named Mrs. Snow—ran a wharfside tavern."

"Not a black mark against him, I trust," murmured Suzy.

"No, my dear." Chatsworth favored her with a smile.

"That he earned without help from anyone else." Unfolding a paper from his pocket, he skimmed over his notes. "DeWinter was soon unwelcome in any Belgian port, due to accusations of cheating. Apparently his skills soon improved, for when he resurfaced in the Mediterranean several years ago, he began to make quite a profitable living fleecing everyone from the filthy rich to the poor sod with only a few groats in his purse."

Chatsworth turned the page over. "DeWinter worked Marseilles, Nice, and Genoa during Bonaparte's brief flirtation with past glory. Last year, after Waterloo, he moved back north, cutting a swath through the high stakes gaming dens between Brussels and Paris—with a knife, when push came to shove. His three cronies are a Dutchman and two Prussians, all skilled with a blade. Or a hobnailed boot," he added with a grimace of distaste. "A Flemish wool merchant found stomped to death in an alleyway attests to that. So, by all accounts, they are a pack of nasty bastards."

The earl cracked his knuckles in impatience. "Tell me something I haven't figured out for myself."

Ignoring the quibble, Chatsworth refused to be rushed. "Once in Paris, they went to ground. Now pay attention, Connor—here is where it begins to get interesting. In making the inquiries you requested, Spotted Dick learned that six months ago, word started to circulate around the docks of Dover that a plum of a job was available for someone who met the two requisites—fuzzing cards *and* cutting throats. With no compunction about exercising either."

Connor's expression was unreadable.

"Furthermore," went on Chatsworth. "It was said that

if the fellow played his hand right, the reward would be not only money but an extraordinary opportunity—a far more profitable game in the highest circles of the *ton*."

A snap of his fingers caused both Alexa and Suzy to flinch. "Voilà! Who suddenly appears on English soil but Mr. Snow, who now styles himself as Lord DeWinter. Dead-Eye Pete recognized him straight off from a gambling den on the rue d'Anglaise." Drew grinned. "Even with an eyepatch, the old pirate doesn't miss much."

"I don't see why you are looking so pleased with yourself," growled Connor. "I hardly need a rum-swilling old barnacle to tell me DeWinter was hired to put me out of business. Have you any cursed idea of who did the hiring? Or why?"

A rather smug expression tugged at his friend's mouth. "As a matter of fact, I have. It just so happens that Weasel and Jug know the man, too." He grinned at the ladies. "Apparently, it's a small world for those involved in criminal endeavors. Anyway, as I was saying, when they heard I was asking around about DeWinter, they recalled having spotted him coming out of a townhouse on Merton Street during the course of making some routine deliveries of their own. Dick got word of it this morning, and promises that they will keep a close watch on the place to see if he turns up again."

"Bloody hell, Drew—whose townhouse?" Connor emphasized his demand with a thump of his fist.

"I don't know," admitted Chatsworth. "Not yet. But Jug is working on getting that information."

"At least it's somewhere to start. When I return to London on the morrow—"

"Don't." interrupted Chatsworth. "The last thing in the world you should do is return to London."

Connor opened his mouth to protest, but Chatsworth gave him no chance.

"Right now, your disappearance has likely got your unknown enemy and DeWinter off balance. In order to regroup and figure out what to do next, they must move quickly. That, as any good soldier should know, makes them vulnerable. They are liable to be a bit careless."

The Wolfhound scowled. "What are you suggesting?"

"That you do nothing. We now hold the upper hand, so why not wait and see how things unfold?"

"At the very least, surely Lady Alexa can return to Yorkshire."

Chatsworth slanted a quick glance at his wife.

Suzy shook her head. "It's still too dangerous. They will be on the watch for her as well. I think it unwise for either of you to stir from Linsley Close."

"Damnation," swore Connor. "I am not used to inaction."

A glimmer of unholy amusement lit for an instant in his friend's eyes. "Oh, with a bit of imagination, I daresay you can come up with some activities to occupy your time here."

Suzy rolled her eyes, then stood up. "Come, Lady Alexa, I can see that business is over for now. Let us leave them to their port and cheroots. They wish to blow a vile cloud and tell bawdy jokes. It makes them feel smugly superior, and I, for one, don't object to them enjoying a few, fleeting moments of that illusion." She gave a broad wink, making no effort to hide it from the gentlemen. "They will soon grow bored and rejoin us."

Alexa led the way to the drawing room. The fire was banked, but as she stirred the coals and added a fresh log, the flames sprang to life. "Might I ask you a personal question, Mrs. Chatsworth?" she ventured, her gaze remaining on the dancing flickers of red and orange.

Suzy had already taken a seat on the sofa. "You wish to inquire about the relationship between Connor and me."

Rather relieved that there was no need to beat around bush, Alexa nodded. "Yes, I—I suppose I do."

"I gathered as much. Otherwise I should never have bowed to such silly convention as leaving the gentlemen to have all the fun. I am very fond of port and know more naughty jokes than the two of them put together."

"I am sure Chatsworth will save you a tipple." Though Alexa tried to sound the same note of flippancy, her heart wasn't in it.

After a slight adjustment to her skirts, Suzy folded her hands primly in her lap. "Connor hasn't told you anything about us?"

Alexa jabbed the poker into the burning wood, setting up a shower of sparks. "He does not share his personal life with me."

"Nor with anyone, if that's any consolation."

It wasn't, especially as Alexa suspected the statement was not quite true. "Obviously he does with you."

"Oh, ballocks!" jeered Suzy. "Believe me, every time I try to get close, he just about bites my head off."

Even with her face angled to the shadows, Alexa's skepticism must have been evident, for Suzy chuffed a sigh and patted the pillow beside her. "Come, sit here while I explain."

"I would rather . . . pace, if you don't mind."

"Not at all," replied her guest. "However, if you mean to come in my direction, kindly put down that weapon. It's bad enough when a girl has to face a strange man with a red hot poker, but at least she knows what he aims to do with it."

Alexa sucked her breath. And then let it out in a peal of laughter.

"There, now that we have broken the ice, please come join me," said Suzy. "If you truly feel the need to hit something, you can smack that hideous Staffordshire figurine on the sidetable and do us all a favor. But I promise you, it's not at all what you think."

"I wouldn't wager on that—I have a *very* vivid imagination," murmured Alexa as she put aside the poker and took a tentative seat on the sun-bleached chintz.

Suzy flashed an encouraging smile. "Think how boring life would be without it."

A weak twitch of her lips was all Alexa could muster in reply.

"Not that anyone could accuse Connor Linsley of being a boring man. A great many other things, perhaps, but *never* boring." There was a fraction of a pause. "However, you know that."

And would give a monkey to know a great deal more.

As if divining her thoughts, Suzy tapped a finger to her chin. "Let me see how to put this simply and without too much fuss. You are already aware that Connor owns a brothel, and that I was one of the girls that worked there."

Alexa nodded.

"I assume that I needn't go into the sordid details of what that entailed. Suffice it to say that I was born in the slums of Southwark and when my parents succumbed to an outbreak of influenza, leaving me homeless and penniless, I did what I had to in order to survive."

"I—I understand," she whispered.

"Word on the streets was that The Wolf's Lair was a very good place to work, and jobs there were sought after. Connor was known to provide decent wages, decent food, and decent living conditions. He was fair, when most of the bosses in the business were slimier than pond scum. And for those of us who showed an interest in bettering our position in life, as it were, he was more than fair. He became a protector of sorts."

Alexa hadn't realized that her knuckles had turned white until Suzy reached over and gently pried her fingers apart.

"I'm sorry if this is disturbing to you. Shall I stop?"

"No, please. I need to know." To her relief, Suzy was tactful enough not to ask why. "You may, however skip over the blow-by-blow descriptions of his prowess in bed. I am not so innocent that I don't know what 'protector' means."

"In this case you are very wrong." Suzy still had a grip on her wrist. "I did not have sex with Connor. What I meant was, he listened to us, helped us learn about running a business. I had always had a dream of having a tavern—a respectable tavern—of my own some day, and Connor encouraged me to believe it was possible." Suzy's voice betrayed a tiny tremor. "Hell, he would say if an earl could be a pimp, a slut could certainly be a barkeeper."

Alexa didn't know whether to laugh or to cry.

"In short, he became a friend. He let me hang around the stock room and the back office in my spare time, picking up little tricks of the trade while I saved my earnings. And when he heard through one of his suppliers of rum that a snug little place was for sale in Lyme Regis, he insisted on loaning me the additional blunt I needed to make the purchase."

Whatever she had expected, it wasn't this.

"And I owe him for much more than that," went on Suzy. "It was Connor who suggested that Drew stay at my tavern."

"I—I see."

"I wasn't the only girl he helped over the years. Indeed, his present predicament is due in part to him having given a large amount of blunt to Mary McGovern for the down payment on a tavern along the Great Northern Road."

Thinking how her recent actions had compounded the Wolfhound's financial troubles, Alexa felt ashamed of herself. "I have been horribly unfair in my assumptions regarding Killingworth's character. Not to speak of adding an unwelcome complication to his life." She bit her lip. "He is right in thinking that he would be far better off without me here."

"Don't sell yourself short—" Suzy's mouth quirked. "Sorry, that was merely a turn of phrase. No offense meant."

Alexa managed a bleak smile. "None taken."

"What I meant was, you may be just the person to beat him at his own game."

"Ha," she said hollowly. "I'm afraid you greatly overestimate my skills. It's become quite clear to me that I'm no match for the Wolfhound."

"Ha," echoed Suzy, a spark of amusement lighting her

eyes. "Time will tell. Don't be so quick to fold your hand," she counseled. "Connor Linsley may have experience on his side, but I wager that in this particular game of hearts, the two of you are very much equals."

"Hearts?" sighed Alexa. "He claims he doesn't have one."

"That, my dear, is what they all say."

Chapter Fifteen

The visit of his friends seemed to have left a lingering warmth, for the next few days dawned sunny and mild. As Connor climbed through the steep turn in the path, the pale, pearlescent light had already burned off the morning mists. A gentle breeze rippled through the meadow grasses, and overhead a lone hawk floated in lazy circles, intent on its hunt.

He, too, liked the solitary splendor of the moors. He had risen early...

But apparently not early enough.

Connor watched as Alexa twirled something in her fingers and held it up at arm's length. She was so intent on studying it that she wasn't aware of his approach until his shadow fell across her face.

Like a stormcloud. Dark, foreboding.

Would that he could bring more than the threat of thunder and rain into her life.

At the moment, however, her expression was sunny. "Oh, look, sir! Isn't it lovely?"

He squinted, having not the slightest idea what she was talking about.

"The *goat hair*, Killingworth," She gave a little wave and he saw a twist of long, silky fibers unfurl in the breeze. "Lud, and I thought it was only flighty females who walked around woolgathering."

The comment teased a smile to his lips. Their conversations had taken on a more relaxed note, as if they had both become used to each other's presence. For him, he realized wryly, the experience had been rather like breaking in a new pair of boots—the leather stiff and unyielding, rubbing raw against the flesh, then gradually softening, and molding to a very comfortable fit. Her feisty show of spirit was now more apt to provoke a smile than a flare of temper.

As for arousing any other reaction...Connor forced his eyes away from the swell of her bosom. "Should I be impressed?"

"Look at the subtlety of the colors." She turned, her face alight with enthusiasm. "Dove gray, buttery cream, warm ochre."

"I shall take your word for it." Connor held out his hand, but as she made to press the wool into his palm, he kept hold of her. "Might I tear you away from your four-footed companions to walk with me?"

Her brow clouded. "More news from Town?"

"No." A letter had finally arrived from Cameron yesterday, but the gist of it had merely echoed Chatsworth's admonition to remain in hiding. "Though," he added gruffly, "we must soon do something to end the present situation. You cannot remain here much longer."

Alexa watched the wisp of wool float away. "I shall be sorry to go."

So will I, realized Connor. But that was a path he would not allow his thoughts to tread.

Turning abruptly, he started up the hill. "Have you seen the view from the cliffs? It is quite dramatic when the tide is coming in."

Water and rock. Two immutable forces of nature hitting up against each other seemed an apt expression of his current mood. *Duty and desire*.

"You seem quite recovered from your wound." Alexa had no trouble keeping pace, matching him stride for stride. "Indeed, the fresh air and daily walks look to have done you a world of good."

"How impertinent of you to remark on it." In truth, the looking glass reflected much the same thing. The sun had burned the sallowness of the slums from his complexion, and physical exercise had gone a long way to banishing the telltale signs of too little sleep and too much brandy.

"What else do you expect from a fast and forward miss?" she replied with an unrepentant grin.

"Fast and forward, indeed—might I request that you not try to break the track record at Epsom Downs." Connor allowed her to forge a little ahead, just to enjoy the coltish grace of her long legs. "Do you bring such an unbridled enthusiasm to everything you do, Lady Alexa?" he called, after watching her scramble over an outcropping. "It's unusual in a gently bred young lady."

"And unbecoming?" She halted, giving a toss of her loosened curls and lifting her face to the sun. "Uncle Frederick puts it more bluntly, telling Father he has been remiss in not breaking me to saddle." Her mouth pinched. "Lud, how that makes my blood boil! As if I were some filly to be put up for auction at Tattersall's, trained for docility and to serve as a brood mare."

Connor drew even with her. "You don't wish to have children?"

Her hesitation, though slight, did not go unnoticed. "Yes, I would. But not just to service the needs of a gentleman who feels dutybound to beget an heir. I—I should like a more meaningful relationship." She paused again. "One of mutual regard and understanding, not a mere marriage of convenience, where we share nothing in common but a name."

Any man who took Alexa Hendrie to wife would be a bloody fool not to appreciate her unique spirit, mused Connor—then quickly shoved the thought from his mind. He had more than enough trouble to cope with.

"Not that such a thing is likely," she added with a rueful grimace. "I am too bossy and too opinionated. Uncle Frederick says I scare off gentlemen, as no doubt you would agree. And since I am unlikely to change, I have accepted the fact that I am headed down the path of spinsterhood. At a full gallop. But at least there is no one on my back, trying to control me with whip and spurs."

"You want my opinion?" asked Connor slowly.

Alexa shrugged, but he saw her shoulders stiffen as if to steel herself for a blow.

"Your Uncle Frederick sounds like a complete and utter ass."

Her eyes widened in surprise. She appeared uncertain of how to respond and abruptly turned her gaze to the rocky pasture. "Oh, look—*Hallooo!*"

Connor saw that she was waving to a man who was cutting a methodical zigzag through the tall grasses. In front of him, a wiry black and white dog was darting to and fro, nipping at the heels of several balky goats and herding them toward a gate at the far corner of the stone fence.

The man returned her greeting and continued on his way.

"Speaking of my penchant for taking the bull—or in this case a slightly smaller beast—by the horns, sir," said Alexa. "I have taken the liberty of asking Mr. Stellings to round up all the goats from the hills, so that we may get a proper count. He has some experience in shepherding, and the extra bit of money will be welcome to the family."

Not *the* goats, but *his* goats, Connor was about to point out.

However, Alexa seemed to anticipate the remark. "I know you think me interfering, but Mr. Daggett gave me money—a draft that Sebastian will repay, so in a sense it is mine to spend as I see fit. And as the benefit is to your advantage, I should think you would have no objection."

"Such reasoning would put Machiavelli to blush," he replied, though not unkindly. "You are a devilishly shrewd negotiator. But have a care about ever mentioning to Sebastian that the money had anything to do with me. He would not approve."

They walked on for a bit before she asked, "Why? Seb seems to bristle at the mere mention of your name."

"No gentleman of conscience wants a disreputable rake sniffing around his sister's skirts."

Alexa made a face. "Oh, bosh. Surely he knows that you're no threat to me."

"Considering that I have kissed you most thoroughly

and tumbled you half naked into my bed, I doubt he would agree," said Connor.

A flush of color rose to her cheeks. "My brother does not hold the reins to my actions. Nor does any man."

"Apparently not," he replied dryly. "Else you would not be running wild—"

A skittering of stones cut him off as she suddenly leapt forward.

An instant later he heard the noise too—a faint but unmistakable bleat punctuating the crash and ebb of the sea. Following hard on her heels, Connor caught a glimpse of the tiny kid, stuck on a ledge way below the edge of the cliffs.

As Alexa started to scramble over an outcropping of rocks, he grabbed her arm. "What the devil are you doing?"

"It's too frightened to move on its own."

"Bloody hell, Alexa! You can't save every damn stray you stumble upon!"

Her chin took a jut that matched the surrounding stones. "I can try."

Muttering another oath, Connor shifted his grip and led her over a patch of loose scree. Edging past a tumble of boulders, he could now see that there was a narrow trail, barely wider than the span of his hand, leading down to where the frightened animal lay hunched against the whipping wind.

"Stay here," he ordered, slipping off his coat.

"But I can—"

"For God's sake, do as I say! One gust, and your skirts will turn into a kite, flying you straight out to sea."

She had the sense to step back, clutching the balled garment to her chest. "Please—be careful."

"Don't worry," he muttered, inching his boots along the windblown rock. "Having made it made it this far in life, I have no intention of cocking up my toes for a bit of fluff and hooves."

A sliver of shale broke away from beneath his foot and was quickly swallowed up by the pounding surf. *Was he really risking his hide for a baby goat?* Through the linen of his shirt, Connor was aware of the knife-edged rocks cutting against his back.

As if he needed any reminder of his precarious position.

On finally reaching the ledge, he gave silent thanks that the kid was too petrified to kick up any protest as his fingers curled into its shaggy hair. Hell, just one lashing of the spindly legs would send them both tumbling into the surging surf far below.

So far, so good. Hugging the tiny animal to his chest, he started back to the top, taking care to keep his gaze from drifting downward.

Alexa's eager hands steadied his last few steps.

"Oh, sir! You were absolutely magnificent!"

I was absolutely idiotic. And yet, for some reason, Connor felt ridiculously proud of himself.

"You might as well wrap my coat around the cursed little beast," he grumbled. "I am sure that you are going to insist that I carry it back to its mama."

"You see, I told you that you would make a very good farmer." Her voice was soft as the tangle of wool between them.

"Hmmph. I only did it to keep you from breaking your neck."

She paused in arranging the last few folds of the garment. "I don't believe that, sir. Though you take pains to hide it, you take care of your flock."

Damn Suzy.

"Whatever fanciful story you have been told, take it with a grain of salt," he snapped. "Mrs. Chatsworth is a romantic at heart and wishes to see the rest of the world as all sweetness and light. We both know it isn't."

"On the contrary," countered Alexa. "Your friend struck me as someone who has a very clear view of the world as it is. She must also be an excellent judge of human nature, to have survived the adversities she has faced in life."

"Well, she will be damn lucky to survive the paddling of her shapely little bum when next she comes within an arm's length of me," he retorted.

"Ha! I wouldn't care to wager on the outcome. I imagine that she can hold her own in hand-to-hand combat."

Connor snorted to cover his chuckle.

"It puzzles her why you wish to appear all tooth and nails, when at heart—"

"Now it is you who is treading on dangerous ground," he warned.

"Very well, I will back off. I suppose I have pushed you far enough today. But..." Alexa angled her chin up over a tiny hoof. "Don't think I don't see what's right in front of my nose."

Several dozen of the shaggy goats had been herded into one of the fenced fields. Climbing over the stile, Connor released the kid from the confines of his coat. It unfolded its knobby limbs, gave a small shake, and bounded away, seemingly no worse for wear after its recent brush with disaster.

Connor rubbed at his bruised shoulder. Youth had a blessedly short memory. While age brought with it a lingering…

"Are you hurt, sir?"

"Oh, no—I believe there are still a few shreds of flesh attached to my back."

Alexa bit back a laugh. "Show a little backbone, sir. It wasn't all that steep a descent, or all that narrow a way."

"Ungrateful chit." He turned to help her down the planked steps. "A wet noodle would have been easier to slide down, and would have provided firmer footing."

As she made to retort, her half boot slipped on the mossy wood, pitching her into a headlong fall. Connor stumbled back a step but managed to catch her around the waist.

"Sorry," she gasped, before falling into a fit of giggling. "Lud, you really have had your arms full this afternoon."

Her hands had come to be entwined around his neck, her curls tickling his cheek with silky softness and the scent of verbena.

"You feel and smell a good deal more pleasant than a goat, Lady Alexa."

With her breasts pressed flat against his chest and her skirts rucked in a flapping tangle around his hips, she was in no position to argue. "I am no doubt a good deal heavier as well. More like an ox, I would say, so feel free to put me down whenever you like."

He would have liked to hold her a bit longer, but dutifully loosened his grip, just enough to allow her thighs to slip in a slow, tantalizing drag down the front of his breeches.

Her feet touched the ground, yet she seemed unaware that her fingers were still clasped around his neck and her upturned lips, ripe with wry amusement, only inches from his.

Heedless of the consequences, he slanted a kiss over her mouth.

With a shuddering moan, she arched into him.

And gentlemanly scruples went galloping off with the goats. His response was no longer governed by rational thought. Like a randy beast, he was acting out of pure, primal instinct.

Falling back against the oak post, he lifted her up, sliding his hands beneath her skirts. The breeze tugged at muslin and lace, tangling his touch in the finespun cloth and the silky softness of her skin. The heat of her thrummed through his fingertips, steeling his manhood to instant arousal. As he and his comrades had often noted in the aftermath of battle, there was nothing like a brush with mortal danger to enflame the most basic of human passions.

Not that he needed much urging. His desire for her had been on the verge of boiling over for some time now. He had done his best to bank the coals, but now, as Alexa slid her palm between them and skimmed over his shaft, every last vestige of self-control went up in smoke.

Was she wicked to want this?

Oh, yes . . . oh, no.

As the earl's big, broad hand found the slit in her drawers, Alexa's breath was suddenly sucked from her lungs. And with went all reason, all restraint. All rules.

So many rules had bound her before this wild interlude, and likely would again when it was over. But for this moment . . .

He hesitated and started to withdraw.

"No, please!" she begged. "I—I want to know what you meant about ecstasy."

A quicksilver gleam hung for an instant on his dark lashes. "Knowledge is a dangerous thing, Alexa."

"I'm willing to take the risk." She pressed her plea with a bold caress of his arousal.

Connor's response was a raspy growl. "Are you sure?" he demanded.

"Yes." His hand resumed its roving, delving deeper, deeper, deeper with exquisite intimacy. "*Oh, yes.*" Alexa clutched tighter at his neck to keep herself upright.

Whatever his reply, the whispered words were whirled away in a gust of wind. Its chill danced up her half-bared legs, but it was nothing compared to the lick of flames now burning between her thighs.

His fingers found their way through the delicate fabric and were now teasing her flesh in unimaginable ways. She gasped in wonder, feeling herself growing slick beneath his touch.

"*Tá lá breá ann.*" Connor's ragged breath tickled her ear. "That means 'you are beautiful' in Gaelic."

"I'm not," she protested. "I'm all sharp, skinny angles and I have too tart a mouth."

He nipped at her lower lip. "Actually, it's quite delicious. Forget everything your cursed uncle has said—you must yield to my superior knowledge in these things."

Alexa lifted her chin and let a laugh float up to the sun-dappled clouds. She should be ashamed, she supposed, of her wanton behavior. But as she watched his windblown hair wave in silver-sparked splendor around the slope of his shoulders, she felt only elation. Pure and joyous elation.

Connor kissed her again, flicking his tongue in and out of her mouth to match the quickening tempo of his touch.

Sliding her half boots over the soft grass, Alexa widened her stance, allowing his strokings to dip and dance over her flesh. Her pulse skittered as tremors shot like fire through her limbs. His free hand had moved to her breast, and she was aware of her nipple hardening against his palm.

The sensations were wildly, wickedly exciting. It was no wonder that proper young females weren't allowed anywhere near wolfish rakes.

Oh, yes he was a Wolf, a sleek, powerful predator. And she was an innocent little lamb, desperate to be devoured.

A growl—or was it a groan—rumbled in Connor's throat. "Tell me now, while there is still time to stop, if you don't wish to play out this game." He sounded a little uncertain, a little unsteady.

That she could affect his self-control sent another jolt of heat spiraling out from her core. She was trembling all over, her body reacting in ways that defied coherent words.

Connor slowed, the pressure of his touch turning delicate, yet demanding.

"Ohhh." A tiny choking sound slipped from her lips as his thumb circled a tiny pearl hidden beneath her folds.

He smiled.

"W-what…" began Alexa, wonder welling up in her throat.

"Hush," he murmured. "Don't speak." His caress spun faster and faster. "Just feel."

And then, all at once, the thrumming in her head was louder than the surf crashing against the cliffs and all lucid thought was cast to the wind.

Wave after wave of pleasure washed through her. Alexa arched against his hand, dimly aware of her moans mingling with the shrill cry of the gulls overhead.

His body tensed and she heard a sharp intake of breath as his hand slid from her breast to the fastenings of his trousers...

Chapter Sixteen

Thank God for the dog.

Its bark gave just enough warning. Otherwise the elderly tenant farmer and his wife might have discovered him with his bum bare to the breeze, ravishing his all-too-alluring faux wife up against a fence post.

"Good day te ye, Lord Killingworth." The man gave a respectful tug to his forelock, but as he ducked his head, Connor thought he detected a glimmer of mirth. "And te you, Lady Killingworth. A fine afternoon te be enjoying a stroll outdoors, is it not?"

Hoping he did not look like a child caught in the act of filching sweets, Connor nodded a reply. However, one glance at Alexa told him he could consign such wishful thinking to Hades. With her flushed face, lidded eyes, and kiss-swollen mouth, there wasn't a snowball's chance in hell that other couple wouldn't guess what the two of them had been up to.

He gave a mental wince, feeling thoroughly ashamed of himself. *Damn—he hadn't meant to let things get so out of hand.* But Alexa seemed to provoke a potent reaction, one that he was powerless to resist.

The farmer's wife dropped a curtsy. "Welcome te South Dorset Downs, Lady Killingworth. Tis a rough and isolated bit o' the world to be sure, and nuffink like London, I imagine, but we all hope ye might find it to yer liking."

Lady Killingworth.

To his surprise, Connor found that the ring of it didn't send a shiver of horror down his spine.

"That is most kind of you," replied Alexa with a gracious smile. She had smoothed out her skirts, and though a telltale blush still stained her cheeks, she had, like a true countess, recovered her composure with admirable aplomb.

"I am from Yorkshire, so am well used to rugged country life," she went on. "Indeed, I prefer untrammeled moorland and heath to cobbled city streets."

The answer seemed to please the older woman. She turned and wagged a finger under the earl's nose. "Ye was a right impish rascal as a child, Connor Linsley, and there have been some wild stories floating around here concerning yer doings in Town." Ignoring a discreet poke from her husband, she set her hands on her ample hips. "But it seems ye have had the good sense to make an excellent choice fer yer bride. Becky Netters has been telling the village how she be putting Linsley Close back to rights—"

"Sally," hissed her husband. "Mind yer tongue. His Lordship ain't a lad in leading strings any longer."

"That's quite all right." Alexa was quick to put him at ease. "The earl appreciates plain speaking. As do I." After a glance at the woven muffler tucked at his throat, she asked. "Are you perchance Mr. Hibbert?"

"Why, yes, milady."

"Oh, Mr. Stellings has told me all about you and your weaving," she exclaimed.

He gave a nervous little hitch of his head. "The old earl paid no heed to the goats and didna mind if we clipped a bit o' fluff."

"I'm sure he did not," said Alexa. "What I meant was, I have heard you do remarkably fine work."

"Aye, that he does, milady," piped up his wife. "Go on now, Ben, show 'er yer scarf."

He looked a trifle embarrassed by the attention, but slowly unwound the cloth from around his neck."

"It's exquisite." Alexa caressed the delicate weave between her fingertips. "The colors have such a subtle beauty, and I've never felt wool this gossamer soft."

Connor suddenly felt something akin to a whisper of sun-warmed breath kiss up against his cheek. "See, Killingworth. Isn't that magical? It's light as a feather."

"Yes, magical," he murmured, though in truth he found himself more enchanted by the elfin play of her hands. They seemed to have woven a spell of their own around him.

"Might I stop by your cottage some afternoon and see some other examples of your craft?" asked Alexa as she handed back the scarf.

"Er, I..." stammered Hibbert, his tongue tied in knots by the unexpected request. "That is, I would be right honored, milady."

"Ye have only te choose a skein of wool ye like, and Ben will weave up a shawl quick as a whistle," added his wife.

Speak of the devil. Connor shuffled back a step as a shrill sound warned the snuffling terrier away from his feet.

"We best be on our way, Sally," said the farmer, clearly anxious to be off before the dog did any irreparable damage to the lord of the manor.

"You could have shown a tad more enthusiasm," murmured Alexa as she watched the couple hurry off toward the village.

"For what?" asked Connor. "The fact that he is stealing wool from my goats? Or that his mongrel was about to piddle on my boots?"

"Was it?" She brought a hand up to her face, but not in time to hide her grin. "Perhaps it thought you too high in the instep."

"A well-aimed splash would certainly have put a damper on any pretensions to lordly pride," he groused. "Assuming I had any left after playing fetch and carry with a squirming kid."

She plucked at her sleeve in a rather belated attempt to smooth out the wrinkles. "You—and your wardrobe—have suffered more than your share of abuse. I'm sorry. I seem to be a bad influence on you."

"With a good scrubbing, I imagine that both my person and my shirt will no longer reek of goat," he muttered. Her scent would likely tease at his dreams, a beguiling blend of sweet florals and earthy spices that was hers, and hers alone.

"Once it's properly carded and spun, the wool loses any offensive odor." Alexa tapped at her chin. "You know, that gets me to thinking…" Her voice trailed off as her eyes took on a faraway look.

Wool?

Bloody hell. Here he had brought her to the peak of pleasure, and then nearly ravished her up against a fence post—and she seemed to have all but forgotten the incident, dreaming instead of those dratted goats.

Connor lapsed into silence as well, his mood growing more unsettled with every stride.

They simply could not keep going on in this way. She might, in her innocence, be unaware of how close to the brink of ruin she was, but he had not needed the cliffside foray to remind himself of what a perilous path they were treading.

Yet it was becoming harder and harder to watch his step. The footing was growing more treacherous and his self-control was balanced on naught but a razor-thin edge. He had already slipped once. Next time...

"We had best hurry." Head down, he quickened his pace, leaving her behind. "There look to be thunderheads blowing in from the sea."

Chapter Seventeen

*A*lexa stared out at the pelting rain. Between the splattering drops and the dense fog, there was little to see through the mullioned glass but a pall of gray. Even the ivy leaves just outside the windows were no more than indistinct curls of charcoal.

Gray, shadowed by more gray.

What could be more fitting than a sudden storm scudding in from the sea? The Irish Wolfhound was as mercurial as the English weather, aglow with sun-kissed splendor one moment, only to blow dark and thunderous in the blink of an eye.

Drawing her shawl a bit tighter, Alexa turned and retreated to a seat by the hearth, hoping the flames might help brighten her own clouded spirits. A book on weaving techniques lay on the sidetable, but after reading the first few pages, she found her thoughts shuttling far from the subject of wool.

She bit at her lip, only to wince at finding it still tender from the force of Connor's kisses. Or perhaps the sting was due to her own heated passions. She could not deny the ardor of her response to his touch, no matter that the reasons for his advances remained as mysterious as his moods.

Was it naught but animal lust that drove the Wolfhound into kissing her? Or simply boredom?

As for her own feelings, they were painfully obvious. She had been fascinated by Connor Linsley from the moment she had laid eyes on him. Perhaps at first it had been the elemental attraction of opposites. Everything about her own self was so ordinary, save for her unladylike temperament, while the earl radiated a brooding sensuality, sparked with an aura of danger—and hidden passions she could not begin to define.

Like a moth drawn inexorably to a flame, she had been helpless to resist his allure...and the fire he had lit inside her.

Not that she wanted to. Her mouth quivered ever so slightly. She was hard pressed to explain exactly how or why, but even as he had ravished her with that first overpowering embrace, she had sensed that the Wolfhound was not, at heart, the fearsome predator he wished to appear.

If only she could make him see the better side of himself.

If only, if only.

Her fingers tightened on the book. It pained her beyond measure to see him caged by a blackness she could not read. Whatever bitter memories or old mistakes darkened his thoughts, she wished she might help free him from the past. But since returning to the manor house, he had remained locked in his room, choosing solitude and silence over any further contact with her.

A wild, wary wolf.
Alexa forced herself to turn the page.

A tip of the bottle showed it was empty. Connor grimaced. That made two gone. *Or was it three?* It had been an age since he had allowed himself to become this foxed. Though in truth, he admitted, he was worse than foxed— he was three sheets to the wind. Caught in the current of brandy.

Adrift on an ocean of doubt.

Sinking deeper into the armchair, he pressed his palms over his eyes. Like the worn leather, Alexa Hendrie offered a haven for his weary bones. He had grown comfortable with her closeness. And the realization scared him to the very marrow.

Damn. His dressing gown fell open, baring his skin to the night chill. He had not meant to reveal too much of himself, but she was sharper than the gusts knifing through the rain-lashed casement. In her eyes, he had seen a flash of understanding.

Echoing the distant thunder, the earl swore again. "Don't want the demmed chit t' unnerstand," he slurred. Hell, he had worked to become unflinchingly tough. Uncaringly sardonic.

Ah, yes, existence itself was a brutal jest.

So how was it that an innocent young miss had managed to pierce such a hardened heart?

Connor blinked in the blackness as the storm unleashed another downpour against the mullioned glass. Perhaps because Alexa was like spring rain, a fresh warmth that brought with it the promise of new life.

But some things were best left dead.

Reaching for a fresh bottle, he poured himself another drink.

A glance at the mantel clock showed it close to midnight. Setting aside pencil and paper, Alexa snapped the book shut. She had made a few desultory notes, but neither her head nor her heart had been in it. Like the smudged scribbles, her thoughts had become too tangled to make any sense. Perhaps in the light of day, things would sort themselves out.

Ha—and perhaps pigs would launch themselves into the heavens.

She did not usually surrender to cynicism. However, with her mood as heavy as the rainsoaked night, she had not the energy to fight off the gloom.

Snuffing out all but a single candle, she banked the last of the coals and turned for the stairs.

Damp with the chill of the raging storm, her bedchamber offered little comfort. Alexa quickly undressed and pulled on her nightrail. Shivering in naught but the sheer lawn cotton, she was just about to slip beneath the coverlet when a shattering of glass sounded from the adjoining room.

"Sir?"

Her tentative call was answered by only a howl of wind.

She hesitated, uncertain of whether to call out again. A moment later, a jarring thud punctuated the crackling of the wind-whipped oaks. Fearing that a branch might have crashed through the window and reinjured Connor, Alexa rushed to the connecting door and grabbed for the latch. Off balance, she stumbled forward as it sprung open.

And nearly tripped over Connor's outstretched legs.

His feet were bare. So, too, was much of the rest of him. He was wearing very little but a dressing gown of amber silk. It was, she realized, a rather fortuitous choice, seeing as it helped disguise the spill of spirits dribbling down his chest.

"Oh! I thought... that is I..."

"Go 'way." His snarl was slurred.

The broken bottle made it clear enough why. From where she stood she could smell the brandy on his breath.

"These had better be cleared." Finding an empty bowl, she set to gathering the slivers from the carpet. "Before you end up slicing off your toes."

"Out, d'mn it."

Ignoring his curses, Alexa finished the job. Though the harshness of his tone threatened to cut deeper than any physical hurt, she came closer.

"Don't do this," he said in a ragged whisper.

She reached out and touched his cheek.

"I warn you, Alexa. Leave now, or I fear you will regret it."

For an instant she made no move. Then, ever so slowly, her fingers slid up to twine in his hair. She leaned in to kiss the last drops of brandy from his mouth. "I won't regret it."

"Ah, but *I* will." His stubbled jaw rasped against her cheek. "God help me," he growled roughly. "This charade is about to become all too real. Run while you can, for if you persist posing as my wife for another instant, I will no longer be able keep from playing my part as the dutiful husband." Connor lurched unsteadily to his feet. The sash to his dressing gown caught in the chair, tugging the garment down from his shoulders. In a slither of silk it fell to the floor, leaving him entirely naked.

Alexa drew in a gulp of air as the flickering fire limned the contours of corded muscle and jutting manhood.

"Stagefright?" Connor made no attempt to hide his rampant arousal. "There is still time to make an exit. Don't be a bloody fool, Alexa, and turn your life into a farce."

She slowly undid the ribbon from her hair, letting it spill over her shoulders. "As I have never had the opportunity to rehearse my role, I trust you will be patient with any mistakes I might make." Masking her nervousness with what she hoped was a knowing smile, Alexa brushed back a knot of curls. "No doubt there will be a number of them. By now you know how little polish I have in performing by rote."

"There is no script for what is about to happen, sweeting." It may only have been a quirk of candlelight, but the earl's expression appeared oddly tentative. "I have no more experience than you in playing the tender lover, so we will just have to improvise."

His grip was surprising gentle as he gathered her in his arms and carried her to the bed. The scent of him, an overtly masculine mix of smoke, leather, and sandalwood, was intoxicating. She could not resist tracing her tongue along the ridge of his shoulder. "You taste of salt and a wine-dark sea," she whispered.

"You taste of honey," he said, after drinking in a more intimate embrace. "And an ambrosial sweetness beyond words."

There was no way to describe the flare of heat that his kiss ignited inside her. Rough with need, the rasp of his stubbled jaw was like a thousand points of fire against her cheek, and the press of his mouth, hard yet soft, a tongue of flame. "Then no more words, Connor," she begged. "No more warnings. I want you, beyond reason, beyond regret." *Beyond yearning.* "Please."

"I fear I am beyond the point of turning back, no matter that I should." His hands framed her face. "You deserve better, Alexa. So much better."

"But I want *you*." In the firelight, his hair had a quicksilver gleam. She threaded her fingers through the curling strands. Now and forever. Though that was a desire she dared not say aloud. For the moment, this closeness was enough. "Only you."

Guiding his grip to the fastenings of her night rail, she wriggled her shoulders free of the fabric. With a ragged groan, Connor pulled it open all the way, sending a row of the tiny pearl buttons skittering across the counterpane. A last shrug left her naked beneath his gaze. Alexa knew she ought to feel embarrassed, but the gleam in his eyes sparked a fierce joy deep within her.

"Have you any idea how lovely you are?" Connor's callused palms slid over her hips.

She edged closer, so close that the peppering of dark hair on his chest tickled against her skin. "Not nearly as magnificent as you are." The breadth of his shoulders, the sculpted muscles, tapering to a narrow waist, were smooth and hard as marble. Chiseled perfection. "Like a Greek god."

"Lud, I am all too human, Alexa. All too flawed." His hands came up to cup her breasts. She tingled all over as he teased their tips.

"Not to me." She fell back against the pillows, drawing

him with her. "You are..." All coherent thought dissolved in a gasp of delight as his mouth closed over a nipple, laving, suckling the flesh to hard little points of fire.

"...Perfect." The last word crescendoed into a cry. Arching instinctively, she wrapped her arms around his neck, reveling in the silky tangle of his hair, the slope of his back. The bedcovers fell away as he hitched her higher, their legs entwining in the sheets. His erect shaft brushed her thigh, and the thought of him wanting her was wildly arousing.

Somehow she did feel beautiful. Feminine, sultry, seductive. All the things she never dreamed were within her reach. Her hands tightened. She meant to hold on to the moment, savor the splendor of his shape, his strength, his scent.

Everything about him.

"Please!" she whispered, as his lips slanted to the hollow of her throat. The pounding of her pulse echoed her need. In another instant she feared she might shatter like crystal.

His eyes, swirling like liquid steel, met hers.

Alexa felt another jolt of heat course through her. "Don't wait any longer. Come inside me, Connor."

To hell with the rules. Surely love had a code of its own.

Connor lifted her hips, driven on by the exhortation and his own ruthless desire. Her words had unleashed the Wolfhound—his baser instincts now overwhelmed what few scraps of gentlemanly scruples he still possessed.

Damn him for a beast, but he meant to be her first lover. To mark her irrevocably as his own.

"Open yourself to me, Alexa." He coaxed her thighs apart. "Yes, like this afternoon." All pliant curves and creamy flesh, her long legs responded so sweetly to his touch. He nearly came undone.

A sigh, soft as spun silk, reminded him that she had never before had a man inside her. *Slowly, slowly*, he thought, holding himself in check. More than anything else, he wanted to make this night pleasurable for her, no matter what pain the future might hold.

Her honeyed curls, gleaming gold in the dancing light, were damp to his touch. Sucking in his breath, he found the nub within her feminine folds of flesh and circled a slow caress.

"Oh, Connor!" Her voice—wild, wondrous—urged him to quicken his stroke.

Alexa pressed hard into his hand, intuition overcame inexperience, and he took a wicked satisfaction at having awakened her to her own innermost need. Another cry, as his finger found her passage and slipped inside. So tight. So trusting. And so innocent.

With a low groan, he eased back.

"Please," she begged, grabbing at his wrist. "Don't stop. Not now."

"Not so fast, sweeting," he said through gritted teeth. His self-control was perilously close to going up in smoke. "I mean to make this right for you. I don't want to hurt you."

Her eyes were luminous in the flickering light, as if the sun were shining on a clear blue sky. "You could never hurt me."

It was still not too late. A true gentleman would have come to his senses. But he had never claimed to be a saint.

Fueled by drink and desire, primal passion had taken possession of him, body and soul. Angling higher, Connor braced his weight and entered her, slowly, gently as he could.

But after a momentary flinch, Alexa surged to meet him, sheathing his shaft deep in her warmth. He gasped, fighting to keep from going over the edge.

"A-am I doing this right?" Her smile turned tentative.

"Oh-so right," he rasped. And oh-so wrong. He ruthlessly thrust the thought aside. Cynicism, his usual shield, had unraveled, leaving him tangled in a hopeless snarl of emotions. Hope, guilt, fear, longing. But need overpowered all. Somehow he would sort the others out later.

Connor withdrew slightly, giving her body a moment to adjust to his, then eased forward again.

"So right," he whispered again, tipping her face to take her in a long, lush kiss.

Clinging to his shoulders, she eagerly matched his rhythm. Limbs entwined, he felt her heart pounding, in perfect harmony with his own. So close. Her touch awakening hope, even though he had sworn never to make himself so vulnerable.

"Hold me tight, Connor." The words, so trusting, feathered against his cheek. "I shall be lost without you." He could feel the tension mounting within her, straining to break free.

"I have you, Alexa." His hands guided her hips higher, joining them more deeply. Like liquid honey, her warmth enveloped him. Two as one, cresting in yet another exquisite wave of pleasure, before she shuddered beneath him and gave voice to a cry of ethereal sweetness.

His own limbs trembling, Connor was not sure whether

to laugh or cry. Reveling in her wonder, he was only dimly aware of the darker note thrumming through his head. He must withdraw in the next instant or risk getting her with child. The idea of Alexa, growing full and round with his seed, should have added extra urgency to the warning.

And yet rather than heed the danger, he surged forward, his own hoarse exultation echoing the thunder in the distant moors.

Chapter Eighteen

Connor angled his muzzy gaze to the leaded windows, finding that he had awoken to a glorious new world. The storm had blown over, and the first light of the unclouded dawn was spilling across the bed, highlighting the waves of wheaten curls fanned out upon the pillows. Copper and brass intertwined with an ethereal shade of pure gold. It was a treasure to behold, and for a moment he held his breath, feeling rich beyond measure.

Then closing his eyes, he pressed a hand to his brow, roughly reminding himself that it was naught but an illusion.

Fool's gold.

He was no true alchemist, who had created something precious out of base metal, merely a charlatan. Or worse, a plundering pirate. Sailing in on a surfeit of spirits, he had simply stolen what he could not dream of having by any legitimate means.

The dull throbbing in his head grew more. No doubt he deserved to be flogged and hung from the yardarm...

Alexa stirred, rousing him from such grim reveries. Still asleep, she had tugged free of the coverlet and lay in sun-kissed splendor, naked on the sheet still warm and rumpled from their lovemaking. A small smile played on her lips, and as she stretched her shapely legs and rolled onto her side, it grew wider.

"Mmmm." Purring softly, she gave another feline stretch and snuggled closer, the curve of her derriere brushing up against his groin.

Despite his feelings of guilt, Connor felt a savage rush of pleasure at the touch of her flesh. Reaching out, he drew her close, molding her body to his. He lay very still, holding her tight. The scent of sweet verbena and lavender tickled his senses. Yet there was a new undertone to her perfume as well, an earthier musk, seductive in its hints of smoky passion. It took him an instant to realize that part of the lushness was his own essence suffusing her skin. Marking her in some indelible way as his.

What would it be like to awake each morning with her in his arms?

He stifled a groan, not quite sure whether he wished to laugh, or cry, or howl to the heavens.

Lady Luck was a hard mistress. Given the circumstances, he had no honorable right to contemplate such a partnership. In some primal way, the Wolfhound had claimed her as his own. But as dawn took on a harsher glare, he recognized that the situation they now found themselves in was a good deal more complicated than elemental feelings.

An innocent young lady and a hardbitten rake?

As an experienced gambler, he should have known the odds were stacked against them. It was unfair that he had robbed Alexa of her future. Despite all the vicious gossip, Connor had always thought of himself as an honorable man.

But now ...

Ever so gently, the earl loosened his grip. Alexa made a murmur of protest as he pulled away, her hand groping for his. He eluded her sleepy search with ease. After all, he had a great deal of practice in avoiding entanglements. Both his parents had been selfish, uncaring, and over the years he had often wondered whether it was hereditary, like a title. Perhaps that was one of the reasons he had remained aloof. And alone.

Always alone.

Tucking the sheet up over her hips, he gathered up his clothing and quietly quitted the room.

Connor.

Alexa whispered his name to herself several times over, delighting in the lilt of it on her tongue. The sound seemed to fit him—hard, yet soft. Slightly exotic. *Overwhelmingly male.*

"Connor?"

Her outstretched hand touched naught but a twist of linen. Suddenly wide awake, Alexa sat up to find herself alone. The sheet fell away, but despite the draft from the window, her skin took on a tingling heat as she remembered just how she had come to be sleeping naked in the earl's bed.

Shifting slightly, she was vaguely aware of a pinch of soreness between her legs, but the small discomfort quickly gave way to the memory of Connor exploring the length and breath of her body. Recalling the depth of their intimacy sent another little shivering thrill through her core.

Hot and cold—she wasn't quite sure.

All the rules said what had happened between them was wrong. And yet it had felt so...right. No doubt the worldly Suzy Chatsworth could help explain the mystery of it. But Suzy was not here. And as Alexa fingered the pillows, which still bore the faint mark of the Wolfhound's profile, she decided it was a conundrum that she had to figure out for herself.

Where had he gone?

Rising, Alexa retrieved her nightrail from the carpet and went to the windows, wondering if she might catch a glimpse of him walking the hills. *Alone and aloof.* Was that how he meant to go on? The thought that he might already be regretting the night turned the dancing fire inside her into ashes.

She could follow, of course, and convince him there was no reason for recriminations.

Perhaps.

She could reason, she could plead, she could cajole...But what she could not do was make him love her.

Alexa knew that—she knew in her heart. Pressing her cheek to the cool glass, she allowed the truth to seep through her body, though it chilled her to the very marrow.

Soon—all too soon—she would have to leave. So far they had been lucky in skirting scandal, but the charade could not go on forever. Back she would go to Yorkshire, and yet she knew some integral part of her would always remain here. There would always be a tiny void somewhere deep inside and the ache of it would never quite go away. She would survive, of course. Unlike a horrid novel heroine, she was far too practical and pragmatic to fall into a state of permanent decline over love.

Love.

As if that were any consolation.

She stood for a moment longer, watching the sunlight play hide-and-seek among scudding clouds. Her chin rose. She would not let shadows mar the day. If memories of Connor and Linsley Close were all that she would take with her, she would at least try to make the last ones more than bittersweet.

"Her Ladyship has gone out."

"So I have ascertained." Bone tired from hours in the saddle, Connor could not keep the irritation from his voice. "Any idea where?"

"To the upper pastures, I believe."

"Thank you, Mrs. Callaway." Adding a silent grimace, he turned to go. It appeared Alexa was not going to make the course he had decided on any easier. "I suggest you hold supper. Lady Alexa and I have a pressing matter to attend to in Hillington. I cannot say how long it will take."

"Is something wrong, sir?" The housekeeper's face betrayed a spasm of concern.

"No." His fingers tightened on the sheet of paper in his pocket. The edges felt sharp as a knife. "It is simply a formality, but it cannot be put off any longer. We shall return as quickly as possible."

Starting up the steep path, Connor found it difficult to maintain his footing on the loose stone. *And the way was likely to get rougher.* He knew all too well Alexa's sentiments on submitting to a bit or rein. *Damn.* How was she going to react to the prospect of a legshackle?

Not well, he imagined. Not well at all.

He steeled his jaw. It wasn't that he wished to force

her hand. But she had chosen to play a high-stakes game. Debts of honor must be paid...

"As you can see, your companion seems to have suffered no lasting damage from his brush with disaster." Looking up at his approach, Alexa ventured a tentative smile. The tiny kid nipped at her fingers, eager to squirm free. After a last little hug, she let it go.

Connor did not dare soften the grimness of his visage, fearing his will might bend along with his lips. She looked so carefree, with her hair dancing in the breeze and the sunlight dappling her cheeks. Was he about to cast a shadow over the rest of her life?

Seeing his expression, Alexa stood up, a look of hurt chasing the laughter from her eyes. "Oh, don't be...angry."

He could see she was unsure, yet undaunted, her eyes alight with a fire that warmed him to his very core. Perhaps he was being supremely selfish, but the thought that her future was about to be bound irrevocably to his sent a surge of satisfaction through him.

Would that she would forgive him.

"I am not angry," he replied. "Far from it."

"Then why are you scowling like the very devil?"

"Because..." In searching for words, Connor touched at the paper in his pocket. Deciding that the neatly lettered script spoke far more eloquently than he ever could, he unfolded it and held it out.

She hesitated before leaning in to read the lines.

"No." Disbelief flooded across her face. "I...you...we don't wish to be married."

"Desire has naught to do with duty."

He saw her flinch. "But nothing has changed between

us! N-not really. If anyone took advantage of the situation, it was I. You need not worry that I expect any—"

"A great deal has changed between us, Alexa." Indeed, in looking closely, he found that she herself had altered, in a way that defied explanation. She looked the same, and yet so very different. *Mysterious. Sensuous. Feminine.*

"But—"

"No!" His shout echoed off the rocks and drowned the distant roar of the surf. "Be assured, I will not budge on this."

Clutching at her cloak, Alexa fell back a step.

"I stopped in Hillington on my way back from purchasing the special license and spoke with the vicar. It has cost me a baptismal fount, but he has promised his complete cooperation—and discretion. He will marry us this afternoon, and see to it that no awkward questions arise as to the timing of the ceremony."

"I have no say in this?"

"If this were a proposal, you would have a choice, but it is not." Connor saw her lashes were wet with tears, but he kept his voice deliberately hard. "It is a pronouncement. One we both are bound by."

"And if I refuse?"

A sudden gust set the capes of his coat to flapping, the snap of wool a dull thunder between them. "You demanded that Haddan honor his pledge, no matter that he quickly regretted risking its loss. Do you now refuse to play by the rules of the game?"

Alexa looked away to the gamboling goats. "It is not as if you play by the rules," she whispered. "A whole host of them lie broken beneath your boots. Why is this any different?"

"Because despite all my faults, I have always recognized there are certain ones that cannot be tread on. It is a matter of personal honor."

"But no one knows!"

"*I* know," he replied softly. "As it is, the world sees me as bereft of all decency. Would you have me sunk below reproach in my own eyes?"

Despite the whip of the wind, the color leached from her cheeks. She bowed her head to the force of it. "Might I be permitted to wash the dust from my face before we set out?"

Wincing inwardly at the note of flat surrender, the earl managed a dispassionate nod. "I have sent word asking Givens for the use of his gig. It will take at least another quarter hour for it to be brought around." He cleared his throat. "We must also take a moment to pen a note to Sebastian."

Eyes still averted, Alexa turned for the manor house. "By all means, let us inform him of the joyous news."

What goes around, comes around.

The next day, as the wheels of the hired coach spun inexorably toward Town, Alexa stared down at the simple gold band circling her finger. No doubt there were a number of other equally banal platitudes to describe the folly of allowing passion to overcome prudence.

Passion.

Her hand clenched and a burnished glint of light seemed to wink back at her, silently mocking her current predicament. To think that just a few short weeks ago, she had primly rung a peal over her cousin's head for acting without heed of the consequences.

Repressing a sigh, she slanted a look at the facing seat. Connor, too, seemed to be twisting at his ring. Though his shadowed profile betrayed not a whit of emotion, she had a sinking suspicion that he found the pinch of metal against his skin extremely chafing. It was not that he had expressed any tangible complaint. If anything, he had been scrupulously polite since the ceremony binding them as lawful man and wife.

But distant. Oh-so distant. He had spent the previous evening—their wedding night—in his own chamber. And even now, he had chosen to settle himself in the far corner, as far away from her physically as the cramped confines of the coach permitted.

As for his thoughts, she did not dare speculate on where they might be straying.

Alexa's gaze fell back to where her hands lay fisted in the folds of her traveling cloak. As it was, her own head was still spinning. Things had happened with such dizzying speed. In the last forty-eight hours she had not only lost her virginity and gained a husband, but she had also found herself packing her meager possessions for yet another breakneck journey—this one back to London.

A special license had not been the only piece of paper to effect a sudden change at Linsley Close. She and the earl had arrived back from their brief marriage ceremony to find a letter from Mr. Daggett waiting. Its contents did little to lift the cloud from Connor's brow. Paper in hand, he had retreated to the library, and at supper, his terse announcement confirmed what she had already suspected. A new clue had come to light. And no longer content to sit back and leave the job to others, the Wolfhound had determined to set off to Town at first light.

The coach hit a rut, jarring the notebook from her lap.

As Connor leaned down to retrieve it, his eyes fell upon a sketch. "What is this?"

"I—I was just toying with the idea of a few improvements," mumbled Alexa, trying to pluck it from his fingers. To keep occupied, she had been drawing up some plan for how the estate stables might be expanded.

He leaned back out of reach. "I take it the figures noted here detail the cost of materials and labor?" After studying the page more closely, he added, "They seem to be quite low."

"Mr. Givens knows several excellent stonemasons who would work at a very reasonable wage," she replied. "And there is a local quarry, so the expense of transporting stone could kept to a minimum."

"The addition looks to be rather large. What is it meant for?

"The storage of wool."

Alexa watched his brow knit in surprise.

"Wool," he repeated softly.

Connor slowly thumbed through several more pages of notes, and she found herself watching the lithe movement of his hands and recalling their caresses along her thighs. She pressed her palms together, trying to ignore the tingle of heat between her legs. It was all the more unnerving in that she wasn't sure whether she was angry...or aroused.

He paused at a sketch of a simple plaid rendered in colored chalk. "Isn't this the same pattern as Hibbert's scarf?"

"Actually, I made a few changes." Observing his expression grow more questioning, she explained, "By simplifying the design, and eliminating one of the colors, it can be produced a bit more economically. You see, after discovering the herd of goats, I got to thinking and I...I have an idea on how the estate might be made into a profitable enterprise."

"You seem to have given a great deal of thought to all this."

A rush of heat burned the enthusiasm from her face. Did he think she had spun an elaborate snare to trap him in matrimony? It was impossible to tell whether his tone had a mocking edge, and as she looked up, she found that his expression was unreadable.

"They seem practical suggestions." Closing the covers, Connor returned the sketchbook. "Why not go ahead and draft up a more detailed plan of what you have in mind, and the expenses it will entail."

The coach gave another sharp lurch, throwing her back against the paneling. Suddenly feeling bruised, both in body and in spirit, Alexa clutched the dog-eared volume tightly to her chest. "Oh yes, why not? How very convenient to have acquired a new housekeeper, now that Mrs. Callaway is growing too frail to handle the daily chores." The corners dug into her flesh, a sharp reminder of how uncertain she was of her role in his life. "I am rather surprised you didn't leave me behind in the country, to polish and prune, while you go back to your wild affairs—"

Alexa bit down on her lip, horrified to hear herself sounding like a shrew. Dear God, was she already becoming a nagging wife?

"I am sorry if my words upset you," said Connor quietly. "Indeed, I am sorry for...everything."

No doubt he was, she thought, trying not to let any more maudlin sentiments spill forth.

"Despite what you may think, Alexa, I shall do my best to be a good husband to you."

Because duty demanded it? The thought left her feeling even more wretched.

His handkerchief feathered against her wet cheek. The gesture was gentle, but she found it a cold comfort. What she really craved was the heat of his hand to touch her, rather than a wad of linen, however soft.

"Damn," she swore as tears began to stream down her face. "I *never* dissolve into such a watering pot."

"I daresay you have never experienced quite the provocation as you have over the last several days," he replied rather dryly. Taking the book from her grasp, he placed it on the seat and drew the carriage blanket around her waist. "No doubt you are tired. Try to get a bit of rest."

"Stop treating me as if I were naught but a child!" she cried. "I am your wife, in case you have forgotten."

The sliver of space between was barely wider than the breadth of Connor's shoulders, but as their gazes met across it, the gap looked like a vast chasm, dark and unfathomable.

With all the errant stumbles she had made lately, Alexa found herself fearing she would never find a way to cross it.

"No, I have not forgotten," he replied tightly.

Swiping her sleeve across her face, Alexa pulled herself back from the brink of despair. "And remember that I am still an equal partner in The Wolf's Lair. We ought to discuss what sort of strategy you have in mind for taking care of business, once we reach London."

"Strategy?" His mouth curled in rueful irony. "As I am as new at this game as you are, I haven't much expertise to draw on. But it seems to me that before I can start looking for the enemy, we must first make certain basic moves—like establishing ourselves in respectable lodgings, and squashing any ugly rumors that may have arisen over your abrupt absence from Town."

Alexa swallowed hard, realizing she hadn't given a thought as to where they would live, or how they would face Polite Society. A square peg trying to wedge into a round hole—was she never to find a comfortable place in the world? As for how the earl must be feeling...forced to give up his bachelor quarters and dance attendance on the sort of prigs he loathed.

"I have ruined your life," she whispered.

"Most people would say it is the other way around." He looked out at the bleak moors and shrugged. "But there is little to be gained by railing against the cards we have been dealt. Let us try to play them as best we can."

It was hardly a ringing endorsement of their marriage, but what more did she expect? She may have won his hand, but that did not mean she had any claim to his heart.

"Cameron has shown himself to be a bloody magician these last few weeks. Let us hope he has a few more miracles up his sleeve." Connor essayed a faint smile. "I wrote to him with all the details of our imminent arrival. I trust he will have some practical suggestions."

Alexa winced at the word "practical." But mention of the earl's erstwhile comrade reminded her of the urgent missive he had received. "Speaking of Mr. Daggett, you have yet to share what news has compelled you to rush back to London. Has he discovered the identity of your assailant?"

"Not yet," answered Connor. "Several promising clues

have come to light, and I intend it to be me, and not any of the others, who risks moving in for the final confrontation with the villain." He hesitated for a fraction. "But that is not the only reason we are making this journey. Reputations, once ruined, are hard to repair. To quell any scandal, we must do the pretty and appear as couple in Society."

"I thought you did not care what the *ton* thought of you."

"I'll not have you savaged by vicious gossip, ashamed to hold your head high in the ballrooms of the *beau monde*."

There was a certain fire in his voice that kindled a spark of hope in her breast. Perhaps it was not merely duty speaking, but something else.

Pressing her eyes closed, she leaned back against the squabs, pretending the stubbling of his jaw was kissing her cheek and the heat of his mouth was warming her lips. For an instant, the fantasy was so real she could taste it.

"Try to get some sleep, Alexa," murmured her husband.

This time, she made no objection as he began to tuck the blanket around her.

"God knows, we have a rough road ahead of us."

"Allow me to offer a toast to your felicitous union." After passing around glasses of sparkling wine, Cameron eyed the earl from over the rim of his own coupe. "It is *prosecco*— from Italy." Light from the candelabras spilled over the faceted crystal, setting the pale apricot color aglow. "I find it more playful on the palate than French champagne."

Though in no mood to celebrate, Connor took a small

sip. "Thank you," he said gruffly. The taste was flat on his tongue.

Alexa's hand wavered as she brought the drink to her lips. Standing off to the side, half hidden by an exuberant spill of pink roses, she looked so pale as to appear drained of all life.

"But then again," murmured Cameron, "after such a long and tiring journey, perhaps you are not feeling quite up to cavorting in jolly little cartwheels across the carpet."

"How observant, Cam," he growled. "In fact, I was hoping we might get right down to the practical matters at hand. Alexa and I are both anxious to get settled in Town as quickly as possible." Loath to ask more favors from a friend, Connor felt his jaw tighten. "Have you come up with any ideas?"

"As a matter of fact, I have. One that is an ideal arrangement when you think about it." Cameron's expression sobered as he set his drink aside. "I have made arrangements for you to stay at Sebastian's townhouse."

"But it's been shut up for a number of years," exclaimed Alexa. "Family finances didn't permit the expense of keeping it open while Sebastian was abroad."

"Yes, well it's now been aired and staffed with servants who are both highly efficient and highly unobtrusive. So you needn't concern yourself with any domestic matters." He cleared his throat. "And the connection to your family, which implies their approval of the marriage, makes it a perfectly proper choice."

An awkward silence filled the room.

"I trust that meets with your approval?"

Connor forced himself to nod. The last thing he wished

was to accept charity from the Hendrie family. As it was, Sebastian would already be thinking he had taken advantage of Alexa. But there was no alternative.

"Excellent. I have already ordered your carriage to go on with your baggage to Half Moon Street."

"I fear that was hardly necessary." Alexa essayed a wan smile. "As you know, we did not have much to begin with."

Cameron replied with a courtly bow. "My dear Lady A—or rather, K—I also took the liberty of sending around to your aunt's residence and having all of your things moved to your new quarters." Straightening, he turned to the earl. "And I stopped at The Wolf's Lair and told O'Toole you were in need of some essentials. He has already dropped off a valise, so you should both be comfortable for the time being."

His friend's air of easy assurance set Connor's teeth further on edge. He knew he should feel grateful—which only made it more difficult to growl out a civil reply.

Alexa shot him a look of reproach, but once again, Cameron stepped in to relieve the tension. Offering his arm to her, he turned for the entrance hall. "No doubt you are anxious to be off and settle in your new abode."

Connor set down his glass and fell in step behind them, the echoing clink of crystal sounding more like funeral dirge than a joyous wedding march.

It was hardly an auspicious entry into married life.

Chapter Nineteen

A crush of people paraded across the polished parquet—and every one of them appeared to be staring at him and his wife.

Connor cursed under his breath. He was well used to the glare of speculation, but he felt Alexa begin to wilt.

"Chin up," he murmured, drawing her hand a bit tighter into the crook of his arm. She had moved unflinching through the receiving line, ignoring the looks and the whispers of the other guests. But now, as the intense scrutiny followed them into the ballroom, he could sense the effort was taking its toll.

"Trust me, a show of utter indifference will soon cause them to grow bored with us," he went on. "All we have to do is go through the motions, acting as if there is no question as to our acceptance in Society. In another few days, they will find a new focus for their gossip."

"Do we really have to attend any more of these dreadful affairs?" she asked in a small voice. "I feel as if I am one of the oddities on display at the Tower menagerie."

His mouth quirked in sympathy as the musicians struck up a new set. "I'm afraid there is no getting around it. We must dance attendance on every hostess who tenders an invitation, and put our best foot forward."

"Ha." She moved smoothly through the first steps of the dance. "You know how little skill I have in such social graces. By the end of the week, your toes are likely to be black and blue."

The earl chuckled softly. "Just follow my lead and I am sure we can dodge any disaster."

And yet, as he ventured a quick glance around, he did not feel quite so confident. His own dutiful appearance by her side helped stamp out some of the nasty speculation over her sudden nuptials. But in order for Alexa to garner complete acceptance in Polite Society, she had to be seen dancing with other gentlemen of consequence.

However, he knew the lords and ladies of the *ton* all too well—beneath the polish and plumage they were sharks. At the first sign of weakness, they would circle in the water, keen to feast on the latest victim.

A surge of protectiveness coursed through him and Connor drew Alexa closer. He would be damned if he would allow them to savage his wife.

The trouble was, his own teeth had done a fair share of damage over the years. There were precious few gentlemen present who would feel inclined to do the Irish Wolfhound a favor.

He shifted his gaze, only meet the cold stare of a raven-haired marchioness dancing nearby. *Bloody hell.* It had been nearly a year since he had broken off the casual affair. Still, judging by the ice in the lady's eyes, Alexa would find few allies among the females.

Connor was not quite sure where to turn. The music was fast coming to an end...

"I say, Killingworth, I will be deucedly disappointed if you have not saved me the next dance with your lovely bride." Admiral Wendover, a well-respected naval man, stepped out from the milling crowd and bowed over Alexa's hand. The movement revealed that Gryff—who just happened to be the man's cousin by marriage—was standing at his shoulder, a small smile pulling at his mouth.

"Allow me to offer felicitations on your marriage, Lady Killingworth," continued Wendover, a trifle louder than was necessary. "The Wolfhound is a lucky dog."

"Thank you, Gryff," murmured the earl, as Alexa and her new partner moved off to the first notes of a country gavotte.

The marquess nodded. "I ought to warn you, though— it may be some time before you may reclaim your wife's hand. Anderson and Cantwell are next in line for a dance, with Farnam and Wentworth waiting in the wings.

An heir to a dukedom and a minister from Whitehall, followed by two well-respected peers of the realm. In choreographing their tacit approval, Gryff had gone a long way to smoothing Alexa's reentrance into Society. Even the highest sticklers would be hard pressed to find fault with the new countess.

Connor made a mental note to send his friend a case of the most expensive brandy he could lay his hands on...No—on second thought, he would make it a crate of Indian cheroots. Gryff's newfound sobriety had his hearty approval.

"Let me find you some champagne," offered his friend. "You look like you could use a drink."

Left alone, Connor found his gaze straying to his wife. *Beauty and brains.* The combination was considered volatile in a lady. And yet, though sparks might fly and tempers might flare between them, the pyrotechnics lit up the darkness at his very core. His life without her would be like the dawn deprived of the sun.

Black. Cold. Empty of all meaning.

She laughed at something Wendover said and Connor felt his chest constrict.

Her expression had been so solemn of late, her spirits so subdued. Guilt knotted his insides. Unsure of her feelings, he had kept his distance during the day and had avoided her bedchamber at night. It was better to suffer frustration than outright rejection. The crowd would no doubt find it vastly amusing that the fearsome Wolfhound was reduced to skulking around his borrowed lair with his tail between his legs.

But he was going to have to do something about the situation. And soon. His desire was growing more fierce with every passing hour...

"Your new bride looks to have spirit as well as looks." Lord Turnbridge, a frequent patron of The Wolf's Lair, had sidled up behind him. "Still, I would not have imagined a country chit could be clever enough to collar the Wolfhound."

He gritted his teeth, trying to keep his temper leashed.

"But then again, her brother is a war hero, and his prowess with a saber is well known, hah, hah, ha." Turnbridge flashed a knowing wink. "Given the choice between having my liver carved into fishbait or my cock caught in the parson's mousetrap, I, too, would choose matrimony as the lesser of two evils."

Connor looked around slowly. "You omitted a third alternative." His voice was dangerously soft. "You can meet me at dawn and have your skull blown into a thousand bloody little pieces."

The man's head jerked back. "J-just a friendly j-jest. It was meant in good fun," he stammered. "No need to take offense."

"My wife's honor is not a subject I find remotely amusing."

"Yes... No." Turnbridge edged back a step with each word. "That is to say, of course not." Ducking behind a group of chattering matrons, he quickly disappeared into the crowd.

"Hell, can't you be left alone for a moment in civilized surroundings without straying into trouble?" drawled Gryff as he returned with the wine.

"Damn it, I don't go looking out trouble," snapped Connor. "It seems to come looking for me."

"You do seem to be attracting a rather violent interest in your person," replied his friend. "Cam told me what happened as soon as I got back to Town. But I must say, you look none the worse for the experience." Gryff fixed him with an appraising stare. "Indeed, country life seems to agree with you. You've come back with a spot of color in your face." A pause. "Among other things."

Connor felt his cheeks darken.

Gryff grinned and then left off his needling. "Still no idea who tried to put a period to your existence?"

"A few clues have turned up," he answered. "One of the reasons I am in Town is to chase them down."

"Let me know if I can help."

Connor watched Alexa spin through the figures of a quadrille with her next partner. "You already have." The words came out more curtly than he intended. Generosity from others was not something he had much experience in accepting.

"The tattlemongers are more bloodthirsty than Soult's cavalry." Gryff was also following Alexa's progress across the dance floor. "And the first ones they look to attack is anyone who stands out in a crowd."

His wife did that, thought Connor. *In spades*.

Gryff lowered his voice a notch. "You are a lucky dog, Connor. Your wife is a special lady. I trust you will watch over her—and yourself." The faint curl of his lips became more pronounced. "Only a bloody fool would risk breaking up such a unique—and potentially profitable—partnership."

"You don't mind leaving now?"

"No." Alexa settled her hand on Connor's sleeve, enjoying the feel of hard muscle beneath the soft wool. They had touched so little of late that even a fleeting brush of his arm was better than nothing at all.

"You seemed to be enjoying yourself," he said.

Something in his tone made her look up quickly. "I was. More than I imagined." Was it only wishful thinking, or had she seen a flare of jealousy in his eyes? Ha! And next, she would be seeing a cow jump over the moon! If he wanted her, he had only to open the adjoining door to their bedchambers...

"You dance very well."

"I believe my partners escaped with only two broken toes between them tonight," she said lightly.

He laughed, his lips close enough to stir the tendrils of hair at the nape of her neck. A slight shiver raced down her spine.

"Feeling chilled?"

"Tired," she lied.

"The carriage is waiting to take you home."

What she really wanted was for him to take her to his bed.

But she didn't dare say it. Perhaps he felt trapped in a life he did not want. With a wife who bored him to perdition. After all, he had his pick of worldly women, who knew all the tricks of pleasing a man.

Of which there were a great many.

Alexa knew that because she had recently come across a small book tucked at the back of Sebastian's desk. She had been searching for penknife, but when her fingers had brushed up against the crimson kidskin, she had been curious. Opening the covers, she had discovered it to be a graphic manual on the art of pleasure.

There was an old saying that a picture was worth a thousand words—maybe two thousand in this case, given the wealth of details shown. However, she had been rendered speechless as she perused the pages. And not a little intrigued. Paper and ink, however colorful, was no substitute for actual experience.

But it was naive as to think the Wolfhound might find her as alluring as his past lovers.

Grateful that the darkness helped hide her quivering lip, Alexa stepped out into the night. Connor found their barouche among the crush of carriages and helped her inside. A stab of disappointment once again cut though her as he chose the seat opposite hers, rather than a more intimate position.

Why, oh, why didn't he simply send her back to Linsley Close if he did not want her around? At least in the country she knew how to be useful.

Connor reached out to straighten the folds of her cloak. Suddenly unable to bear his casual touch, she jerked away, mortified to find her eyes stinging with salt.

"Alexa?" He switched seats and drew her into the circle of his arms.

She buried her face in his collar, breathing in a scent that was now achingly familiar. Starched linen, smoky cologne, essence of…wolf. The tears suddenly spilled over, hot and heavy as her fingers clutched at his cravat, holding it tight. She would *not* let go of him. Not without a fight.

Connor feathered his lips against her hair. He tilted her face so they touched her forehead, then slid down her wet cheek.

Reaching up, Alexa traced the chiseled curve of his chin. In the flickering lamplight, he looked so austere, so aloof. She felt her hand tremble.

"I'm sorry," he whispered.

Damn him! She didn't want him to be sorry.

"There won't be many more nights like this to endure," he went on. "Once we have appeared in public together enough to forestall any ugly rumors concerning the match, we may avoid any further obligations."

Nor did she want him to speak so dispassionately about duty. Steadying her nerve, Alexa slid her hand between the fastenings of his shirt, ruffling the coarse curls peppering his chest. She felt him hold his breath for an instant, then release it in a rasp of air. Her palm skimmed over the contours of corded muscle, coming to rest over his heart.

The thud of his pulse shuddered against her flesh.

"Alexa." Connor's voice no longer sounded so distant or so detached. A rumbled groan filled her ear as he shifted against the squabs and swung a booted leg over her skirts. His mouth slanted across hers and Alexa tasted the hot spice of wine. Her tongue licked out, seeking a deeper draught.

He kissed her again, and she grasped the soft linen, pulling him close, wanting more. *More.* Twisting, she hitched a knee over his, tangling wool and silk as she dragged him down. Her heart was beating wildly, its thud echoing the quickening rasp of his breathing. With a soft moan, she arched her hips and pushed against him. *Urgent, insistent.*

He was half on top of her, cupping her breasts when the coach lurched to a sudden stop. Swearing, Connor recovered his balance and fell back against the squabs.

Alexa, too, felt like crying out an oath. Righting herself, she saw him reach beneath the seat for a bundle of clothing. As he shook free the knots, a nondescript overcoat and battered hat materialized from the shadows.

"What—" she began.

His expression already hidden by the upturned collar and angled brim, the earl edged for the door. "I must go out."

To where? She bit back the question, hard enough to taste blood. Was he seeking friends as well as foes in his old haunts?

The latch rattled and a cloaked figure climbed into the coach.

"Cam will see you safely home," said Connor. He lingered only long enough for his friend to pass over a note, then dropped down to the cobblestones.

Cameron settled into the vacant space with a jaunty little salute. "Good evening, countess."

It took Alexa a moment to wrest her eyes from the window, though the earl's form had already been swallowed in a swirl of fog. *How very absurd she must appear.* A married lady mooning after her new husband as if she were naught but a silly schoolgirl. That she couldn't put a name to her longing only added to her confusion.

Cameron cocked his head. "Settling comfortably into your new life?"

Alexa muttered something that caused his mouth to twitch. "I'm fluent in Gaelic, Lady K. And what you just said would put a Barbary pirate to blush." Seeing his gentle teasing only darkened her clouded expression, he pursed his lips. "Is something wrong?"

"Nothing…Everything," she blurted out. "As if that makes any sense at all."

"Of course it does. Life rarely rolls along smoothly, my dear," he replied as the carriage started up again. "Or in a straight line. Rather it is a series of twists and turns, ups and downs. You must expect a few jolts and jostles along the way."

Alexa sighed. "I seem to do nothing but bounce along on my…backside."

"Trust me, we all suffer our share of bumps and bruises."

"I—I suppose you are right. Though men do not seem to have such a rough time of it." She twisted at a corner of her cloak. "I wish I might learn how not always to wear my heart on my sleeve."

"Do you wish to talk about it?"

She shook her head. "Not really." But after an interval of watching the flicker of street lamps dodge in and out of the mists, Alexa cleared her throat. "However, if you wouldn't mind, there is a far more pressing matter that I would like to discuss with you."

"Yes?" he encouraged.

"I have been thinking about the attacks on Connor. I want to help."

"I am not sure the Wolfhound would approve," replied Cameron.

"Precious little about his current situation meets with his approval." She meant to match the note of irony in his voice, but managed only to sound like a shrew.

One of Cameron's well-groomed brows arched, but he remained tactfully silent.

Dropping all pretense, Alexa sank back in her seat. "I imagine you have already guessed that ours was not a match of choice."

Still he said nothing.

Swallowing her embarrassment, she went on. "Connor felt compelled to marry me out of gentlemanly honor. I'm afraid he is already regretting his decision."

"My dear girl," he murmured. "That was *not* a look of regret I just glimpsed on the Wolfhound's face."

Her cheeks flushed. "No, it was remorse. And perhaps a touch of resentment. He was merely apologizing for all that has gone wrong between us."

The other brow gave a distinct waggle.

"The point is, I—I should like very much to prove to him that ours can be a partnership in more than mere name. If I were able to help him catch his enemy, I might be in a position to win his regard."

Cameron took out his snuffbox and inhaled a pinch of tobacco. "What you are suggesting is terribly risky, Lady K."

"So is doing nothing," she countered. "I'm willing to take the gamble."

The lid snapped shut. "What did you have in mind?"

"While the earl is out hunting down clues in Southwark, I should like to take a closer look at the gentlemen of the *ton* who have been regular patrons of The Wolf's Lair. It seems a logical place to start..."

The Wolf's Lair seemed to be doing quite well without him.

Connor shrugged out of his overcoat and handed it to O'Toole. The wainscoting in the hallway had been buffed to the warm glow of Spanish sherry, he noted, and a tiny tear in the wallpaper had been repaired. "Things appear to be in order," he said, glancing down at the freshly swept Turkey runner as he peeled off his gloves.

"Aye, milord. Allow me to welcome you back from the dead. Your presence, though sorely—" The Irishman was rarely at a loss for words, but seeing the flash of gold as the earl opened the door to the back office rendered him momentarily speechless. "By the bones of Saint Patrick," he murmured, quickly recovering his voice. "Perhaps we ought to be holding a wake after all."

"Who died?" asked a female voice.

As Connor turned, it took him an instant to recognize Sara Hawkins. Her gray merino gown and primly coiled hair made her look more like a governess than a lightskirt.

"The Wolfhound," replied O'Toole with an exaggerated sigh. "It appears His Lordship has decided to shed his old skin and become a respectable married gentleman."

"Out," growled the earl. "I still have some teeth left, so if I were you I would bite my tongue."

"Why, congratulations, sir." A tiny twinkle winked in Sara's eyes. "Anyone we know?"

O'Toole covered his laugh with a cough.

"As a matter of fact, she *has* visited here on several occasions." Gratified to see that his announcement had wiped some of the mirth from their faces, he sat down at his desk. "Now if you don't mind, let's get down to business. I only have a short time before I must go out again, and I would like to have a look at the finances."

Sara unlocked one of the cabinets and brought over the ledgers. "I took it upon myself te keep the books, milord. As well as make a few small changes to, er, make up fer yer absence at the card tables." She smoothed at her skirts. "I hope you won't be upset."

Connor skimmed over the neatly aligned columns of numbers. Everything seemed to add correctly. Indeed...

He looked up. "I can well understand how revenue went down at the card tables, but how the devil did you manage to turn a profit at dice? Not to speak of the profit we are showing in the sale of spirits."

"Well, I got te thinking about how we might shake things up a bit," answered Sara. "And I came up with the idea of having a few of the girls toss the ivories instead o' their skirts. It proved very popular with the gents. Why, there was nights we had to turn them away at the door. And seeing as those who played weren't always paying close attention to the odds, we were able to roll up quite a handsome profit."

"Very clever." The earl steepled his fingers. "Did you replace O'Toole behind the bar as well?"

"Now that's an idea." Sara tapped thoughtfully at her chin. "It might be worth a try."

"He might have a few words to say about that."

"Paddy do tend te bend yer ear. But the gents seem te like being served up a stream of fancy talk along with a tot of brandy." She grinned. "What we did was come up with a different sort of strategy fer drinks. One night a week, we offer a special fer anyone who shows up before ten o'clock—two fer the price of one. Everyone ends up happy, if ye get me drift. It's a good deal fer them—and fer us. Over the course of the evening, they tend to imbibe a lot more than usual, and we end up making money hand over fist."

A soft clapping from Connor punctuated the end of her explanation. "I applaud your ingenuity. You show a real aptitude for running a business."

Her face turned pink. "It ain't often a girl like me can be put te blush, sir, but… thank you. I could never have done it without you giving me a leg up—so to speak. I owe ye—"

The earl snapped the covers of the ledger shut. "You have more than repaid me. Now, might I convince you to manage things here for a while longer?"

"Of course, sir. But ye have yet to check over the book of expenses. I studied the outline ye left in yer desk, and tried to follow it to the letter, but you may want to order some changes."

"I am sure it is quite satisfactory."

"Still, you ought to have a look yerself, sir." Sara shifted a bit uncomfortably in her seat. "There is one thing in particular I wish te point out. I have been drawing a salary. Seeing as I've been spending a lot less time upstairs, my earnings have taken a real tumble."

"Double it," said the earl brusquely. "Is there anything else about the business that we need to discuss?"

"No, sir." Sara gathered her skirts and stood up. But she reached the door, she hesitated. "Is she...nice?"

Perplexed, Connor frowned. "What?"

"I know that titled toffs and ladies get legshackled fer different reasons than ordinary folk, so I was just wondering whether yer wife is nice."

"Yes," he replied softly. "She is."

Sara smiled. "I am very glad te hear it, sir."

As the door fell closed, Connor picked up the Andalusian dagger on his desk blotter. A farewell gift from a partisan leader in Spain, it was a lethally lovely memento, wrought of solid silver and forged steel. He spun it slowly in his fingers, then ran a thumb along its blade.

The razored metal was a sharp reminder that he was walking a dangerous edge these days. One that required a delicate balance. Over the years, he had learned to fend for himself. Now, suddenly, he seemed surrounded by people who were willing to circle around and protect his flanks. *Suzy, Drew, Gryff, Cam, Sara.* A part of him resented the burden of friendship. It made him feel awkward, unsure.

And Alexa?

His feelings were even more tumultuous concerning his wife. He was trying to keep his distance—both physically and emotionally—for fear he would only end up hurting her. But it was becoming impossible to deny the damnable truth any longer. Much as he had fought it tooth and nail, he had fallen in love with her stalwart courage, her keen intelligence, her indomitable spirit. And her damnably alluring beauty. He had felt a stab of fierce jealousy at seeing her smiling in another man's arms. Then in the carriage, when she had not shied away from his own touch...

His grip spasmed, the blade cutting a tiny nick in his flesh.

Connor stared down at the drop of crimson. The desire simmering in his veins was threatening to boil over, but he had better find out who was out for his blood before the danger consumed them both.

A knock on the door interrupted his thoughts.

"Spotted Dick has arrived." O'Toole stuck his head into the room. "Shall I show his ugly phiz in?"

With a wave of the dagger, Connor motioned both men to enter. In the hallway, the hulking silhouette of McTavish hovered in the shadows.

"Ready te shove off, Wolf?" asked the smuggler. "Me an' 'Arry got summink ineresting to show ye."

The earl took up his overcoat. "Yes. Let us go take care of business."

The big Scotsman cracked his knuckles. "Auch, need some muscle te go along, sir?"

"No." The earl's mouth sharpened to a grim smile. "I don't expect to be needing muscle tonight."

Chapter Twenty

I believe my name is the next one written on your dance card."

Alexa took a moment to consult the slip of pasteboard dangling from her wrist. *Another evening, and yet another ball.* "So it is, sir."

The gentleman's hand pressed against the small of her back and drew her close to his muscled thighs—a fraction closer than was deemed proper.

"People are watching," she protested.

"Let them." With a lithe grace, Connor spun her into the first steps of the waltz, setting her skirts to frothing around his feet. "A man is allowed to take liberties with his wife."

"Ah, yes..." Her pulse quickened at his touch, though she took pains to hide it with a cool retort. "The rules permit gentlemen a good deal of leeway in whatever they choose to do."

He frowned slightly at her tone, but moved through the turn without missing a beat.

Rather than let her eyes linger on the strands of silky hair kissing up against his collar, Alexa stiffened her spine and stared over his left shoulder.

The view gave her a good opportunity to observe the rest of the ballroom. Cameron had been reluctant to help her at first. But once she had made it clear that she meant to be part of the investigations, with or without his aid, he had handed over a short list of suspects. Alexa was looking for three gentlemen in particular, and had reason to believe that at least one of them was in attendance tonight.

Concentrating on her quarry kept her from thinking about...Connor.

He hadn't come home until after dawn. However, when questioned on whether he had learned anything of note, the earl had been evasive. The brusque answers had stirred a niggling suspicion...

"Are you perchance angry at something?"

She could not help replying with an edge of sarcasm. "What makes you think I am angry?"

"Alexa," he began, only to halt as the music came to a flourishing end. They stood facing each other in awkward silence.

"Lady Killingworth, I believe I have the honor of the next set." A gentleman she did not recognize approached and inclined a polite bow.

Without further word, Connor relinquished her hand and walked away.

Alexa exchanged pleasantries with her new partner as they waited for the first chords of the country dance to begin. But out of the corner of her eye, she couldn't help following the glimmer of Wolf-hued hair to the far end of the ballroom. She was about to look away when another figure caught her attention.

So, Lord Bevan *was* here. And he appeared to be heading for the terrace doors.

"Oh, how terribly awkward!" Tugging at her skirts, Alexa made a show of examining her hem. "There seems to be a tear in the ruffle, sir. I pray you will excuse me while I retire and have it repaired."

The withdrawing room was located at the end of a long hallway. Halfway down it, she checked to make sure she was alone, then reversed directions and slipped into the deserted music room, where a set of glass doors opened directly out to the gardens.

Stepping lightly along the graveled path, Alexa saw her quarry pass between a set of marble fauns, then disappear behind a privet hedge. She moved as quickly as she dared, but the way led into a maze of shadowed twists, lit only by the stars and an occasional wink of the crescent moon. After several harried turns brought her around in a circle, she conceded that it was foolhardy to continue her search. All she was likely to do was stumble into trouble.

"Looking for someone, Lady Killingworth?"

Alexa nearly lost her footing on the loose stones. "I—I found it a bit stuffy inside."

"You appear to be going to great lengths for a breath of fresh air." Connor moved in to take her arm. "It is not the thing for a newly wed lady to go wandering off on her own."

Something exploded inside her.

"And what of *you*!" She lifted her furious gaze to confront him. "*You* feel free to prowl the Town at will. Where did you go last night—to The Wolf's Lair?"

He stood very still, moonlight edging the hard line of his jaw. "Yes," he answered softly.

Alexa wrenched away. The shape of his jaw, the angle of his cheekbone, the curve of his mouth—every chiseled nuance of his face had become intimately familiar to her eye. She couldn't bear the idea that another woman had been close enough to see the silvery intensity of his gaze.

"To look at the ledgers," he added. His grip captured her wrist as she spun for the path. "By God, are you jealous?"

The smile playing at his mouth set her blood to a boil. "Don't you *dare* laugh at me, Connor Linsley!" Curling her free hand into a fist, she smacked his chest. "Your marital rights, legion though they be, do not extend to playing me for a fool."

"My marital rights," he repeated, catching her next blow with maddening ease. With both arms now pinned to her sides, Alexa found herself at the mercy of his superior strength. "You are right to remind me—I have been neglecting them of late, haven't I?"

She gasped in outrage as he wedged his thigh between her legs and forced her back against a low ivied wall. "Oh, you *odious* beast!"

"Odious, am I? I seem to recall you crying out quite a number of different endearments when you were naked beneath me, your body arched in ecstasy." His breath was hot on her cheek. "Tell me you aren't panting for another taste of my lovemaking."

"Your arrogance has swelled your head," snapped Alexa.

He gave a low laugh. "Oh, it is a distinctly different part of my anatomy that is growing enlarged, sweeting." Trapping her between the spread of his booted feet, Connor pressed closer. Through the thin layers of silk and stretched wool, the ridge of his arousal was impossible to ignore.

Anger sparked a struggle to break his hold. "Damn you!" And yet, as she squirmed against him, she could not deny that his body was sending all sorts of strange shivers through her that had nothing to do with anger.

"Say it, Alexa!" he challenged. The curl of his mouth hovered a hair's breath above hers. "You have only to say you don't want me and I shall release you."

She twisted away. "I...I..."

But the words that might free her remained caught in her throat.

"Don't fight me, Alexa," he rasped, the teasing turning taut with need. "It's been damnably hard enough battling myself."

She went very still, and when his tongue slowly slid over the swell of her lower lip, she sighed in surrender.

"Ah yes, that's better, sweeting."

Drawing a nip of flesh between his teeth, Connor groaned against her mouth before filling her with another long, lush kiss. He had released her hands, and they had now crept up to caress his shoulders. She shuddered, and softened as his tongue dipped in and out of her, plunging deeper with each sensual stroke.

It was only when he hiked her skirts up and slipped his hand inside her thighs that she made a murmur of protest. "Connor, surely we cannot...someone might see us."

The earl glanced around at the thick screen of foliage Not even the torches on the terrace were visible. "We are well hidden in this corner of the garden," he assured her. "Spread your legs for me, Alexa."

The soles of her slippers slid out slowly over the grass.

"Wider," he whispered.

Her breath quickened, then she did as he asked.

Parting the delicate frothing of lace and lawn cotton, Connor slowly traced a path through her gossamer curls. A fierce pleasure surged through him on finding she was already slick with a honeyed wetness.

"Lean back, my darling" he urged. "Now look at me." He found he loved watching the play of emotions on her face.

Alexa's eyes grew wide as he slipped a finger inside her passage, their color darkening to a swirl of dusky aquamarine. Moonlight bathed her face in a silvery glow. She shifted, and as her head tilted slightly, it seemed to catch in her eyes, reflecting the sparkle of stars in the sky above.

He withdrew, letting his touch circle slowly over the hooded nub at her entrance.

"Connor...please!"

Hearing his name—and her need—sent a lick of heat spiraling through him.

"Yes?" he coaxed, wanting for her to say it again and again.

"Connor," she repeated. "Oh, Connor. Don't stop."

His fingertips glided back through the petals of flesh, but at the last moment he held back. "Is this what you want?"

"Yes," she moaned.

"Then come to me," he whispered.

After a slight hesitation, Alexa rocked her hips forward, driving him deep inside her. She sucked in her breath, then eased back.

"That's it, set your own rhythm, sweeting."

Her skirts were now up around her waist and spilling

over the smooth stone. A breeze rustled the roses, stirring a floral sweetness. Mixing with the musk of her feminine need, it perfumed the air with an overpowering lushness.

Alexa seemed intuitively to understand what he was asking. Tentatively at first, and then with a mounting eagerness, she arched in and out of his grasp. It was her mouth that sought his, hot and demanding.

With the next press of her warmth, Connor inserted a second finger, feeling the tight flesh clench around him. He groaned against her lips, matching the glide of his tongue to the play of his hands.

Never in his wildest dreams had he imagined that making love to a woman who was his wife could be so exquisitely erotic. He had always assumed the marriage bed would be a dead bore. But a great number of his preconceptions had been stripped away of late, along with his jaded cynicism. It left him feeling rather naked. And rather exhilarated. It was almost as if he were a newborn babe...

Perhaps O'Toole had been right after all and the Wolfhound of old was dead, thought the earl. A primal, animal lust surged through his loins, and yet it was tempered by something deeper, something more rooted in his soul.

The earl could feel the tension in her straining to find release. He, too, was the verge of exploding. Suddenly shifting his palms to the curves of her buttocks, he perched her on the lip of the narrow ledge. "Undo my trousers."

Alexa found the fastenings and worked them free, letting the fabric pool down around his ankles.

"My drawers as well."

She might be new at the game of seduction, but she

proved a quick study in grasping the essentials of play. Trailing lightly over the linen, her thumb traced a slow line along the length of his shaft before loosening the knot. They, too, fell away, allowing his shaft to spring loose.

"Take me, Alexa. And quickly."

"Like this?" Her fingers closed around him, soft as silk.

"Sweet Jesus," he groaned as she guided him through the folds of flesh. "Yes." His self control in shreds, he could wait no longer and thrust himself into her warmth. With Alexa clinging to him, all teasing gave way to a burning urgency. His surges came hard and fast.

She cried out, and an instant later his own voice was echoing her release.

Thoroughly spent, they lay back against the stone, still as statues, save for the rise and fall of their breathing and the ruffling of her skirts in the breeze.

It was Alexa who finally lifted her head. "I—I suppose we ought to be going back in, before our absence attracts attention."

One look at her swollen lips, her and her tresses tangled glorious disarray around her bare shoulders brought a smile to Connor's lips. "At the moment, it is our appearance rather than our absence, that would have heads turning. We had better take our leave through the garden gate. A bit of dalliance is one thing, but I fear we are in a most shocking state of deshabille."

"I—I could fix my hairpins." Alexa brushed a twist of curls from her cheek. "And put my clothing to rights."

"But you could do naught about ravaged swell of your lips and the heated flush suffusing your flesh. You are pink with pleasure, sweeting. And the scent of womanly passion exudes from every pore." His mouth sought the hollow at her throat. "Your emotions, when aroused, are quite a sight to behold. Trust me, no amount of steel or silk can hide that, Alexa."

Though loath to break the connection between them, the earl eased back from her warmth. As he fumbled for his own garments, he was surprised at how chilly the night air felt on his flesh.

She shook loose her skirts from the stone, then ventured a shy look. "I know I have much to learn, Connor, but if given a chance, I shall endeavor to meet with your satisfaction."

"Learn?" Distracted by the tumble of ruffles across her bare calves, Connor had trouble catching the drift of her meaning. "About what?"

"About pleasuring a man." The fringe of her lashes lowered to hide her eyes. "I have been doing some research—"

"Bloody hell." The buttons on his trousers were suddenly in danger of cracking into a fistful of fragments. "Is that why you were out here?" The cold now settled in the pit of his stomach though his voice took on a smoldering intensity. "Do not think for an instant that I will allow you to experiment with another man—"

"I was referring to a *book*."

"You mean to say you have been reading up on the subject?" A twist of wry amusement chased the scowl from his lips. Lud, his new wife was a source of constant wonder. He imagined she would never cease to surprise him. The realization sent a fresh jolt of pleasure through him.

"Actually, there are a great many more pictures than

words. I came across a book in Sebastian's study. It is from India…"

"I think I know the one."

"However, a book, no matter how descriptive, is no substitute for…hands-on experience."

"Ah." He lifted her from the wall. "So if I understand you correctly, you are proposing some on-the-job training, so to speak?"

She muffled a laugh against his shoulder. "My estate foreman says I have an uncommon knack for learning new skills quickly."

"If he dares say such a thing to me, he will be retrieving his teeth from deep in his gullet," growled Connor as he set her down.

"Really, sir…"

"But as usual, you have managed an incisive analysis of the problem and come up with a practical suggestion. I think it can be arranged." He stooped to retrieve a hairpin. "Indeed, I would say we are already a step ahead of the game. Consider this evening your first lesson." Gathering a knot of wheaten curls, he secured it behind her ear. "You passed with flying colors."

Her mouth, still lush from their lovemaking, gave a beguiling twitch. "I ought to be methodical in keeping the information organized. What particular topic did we cover tonight?"

"We touched on several." Though sorely tempted to plunge into a new session, the earl kept a grip on his self-control. "First of all, there is nothing methodical about passion, my dear. You do not employ the same approach as you do with waxing the woodwork or cleaning the stove." Taking her hand, he headed for the far reaches of the garden. "Secondly, the choice of venue affects the mood of an intimate interlude. For example, the risk of being seen adds an extra frisson of excitement to the moment.

"Perhaps I should be taking notes."

"Repetition should ensure you will have no trouble remembering the details."

Her hips grazed against his. "Then I imagine the instruction will have to take place on a regular basis."

"A logical deduction." Up ahead, he spotted the small iron gate leading out to the alleyway. "We will go over future plans later tonight, when we are at more leisure to discuss the matter."

Amid the rustle of ivy and creak of the hinges, neither of them heard the soft scuff of footsteps retreat into the shadows.

"There is someone waiting to see you, sir." The butler hired by Cameron stepped out from the shadows of the entrance hall. "In the side parlor."

Connor frowned. "Who in the devil would come calling at this ungodly hour?"

In reply, the servant held out a silver tray. Square and center sat a dogeared calling card.

Alexa craned her neck to read the smudged type. "Why would a magistrate be paying us a visit?"

"Why, indeed?" muttered the earl. "I will see to the man, myself—"

Slipping past him, she opened the door and entered the room.

The fire in the hearth had been rekindled, the candles lit, and tea served. However, the cup was untouched and the chairs unoccupied. Looking around Alexa spotted someone standing by the curio cabinet.

"Good evening, sir," she said. "I take it this is not a social call."

The magistrate turned from his study of the painting hung over the sideboard. "Queer lot of stuff in here," he observed, eyeing the colorful nude with undisguised suspicion.

"My younger brother is a painter," answered Alexa, summoning her most imperious hauteur. She did not like the man's tone or his slitted gaze. "These are his works."

"Hmmph."

"I doubt Mr. Bolt has come here to discuss art." Hands clasped behind his back, Connor walked slowly to her side.

"No accounting for strange preferences," grunted the magistrate.

"Or narrow minds," retorted Alexa. A warning look from the earl caused her to refrain from further comment.

"No doubt you are as anxious as we are to retire for the night, Mr. Bolt," continued Connor. "Shall we get down to business?"

"Speaking of art…" The magistrate pulled an oilskin packet from his coat and unrolled it to reveal an unusual dagger. "Recognize this piece of workmanship, Lord Killingworth?"

"Of course," replied the earl calmly. "Seeing as it belongs to me. Might I inquire how it came to be in your possession?"

"Dug it out of the chest of a gentleman named DeWinter. Found him just before dawn this morning, in an alleyway close to an establishment in Southwark known as The Wolf's Lair."

Alexa darted a glance at Connor. His eyes had darkened to a flat, opaque cast of steel she had never seen before. Feeling the blood drain from her face, she quickly looked away.

Surely he was not capable of...

A chill washed through her veins. The Irish Wolfhound had fought through the brutal Peninsular campaign and faced off against cutthroat competition of the London stews. Of course he was capable of doing whatever it took to survive.

Her expression must have betrayed some hint of her thoughts, for an edge of grim satisfaction sharpened the magistrate's voice. "Know the fellow, do you?"

The earl walked to the sideboard and poured himself a brandy. "I am acquainted with both the person and the place."

Bolt looked slightly disappointed at the lack of denial. "You don't seem surprised that he's dead."

"I'm not."

The magistrate waited, but when Connor did not elaborate, he took out a notebook and made a show of reading over several of the pages. "I've got a number of witnesses who say you had a nasty quarrel with Lord DeWinter several weeks ago."

"Correct," replied Connor.

As Alexa ventured a sidelong glance, she saw that despite his nonchalant pose, the ripple of sleek muscle and lithe power were very much in evidence beneath the fine evening clothes. *The Irish Wolfhound—a fearsome predator.*

Bolt might be narrow-minded but he was not stupid.

Or blind. The traces of mud clinging to the earl's boots, and the small tear in his trousers were telling ev-

idence that he did not spend all of his evening hours
indoors on the dance floor. And of course, the magistrate
would be quick to assume the worst.

"Word also has it that the gentleman won blunt from
you that same night," pressed Bolt. "Quite a bit of it."

Light flashed off the cut crystal wineglass as Connor
raised it to his lips. "That would depend on what you consider a large amount of money."

The barbed reminder of their difference in rank and
privilege did not miss its mark. The magistrate's eyes narrowed and his jaw gave an ominous tic.

*As if Connor needs yet another enemy snapping at his
flanks*, thought Alexa with dismay.

"I wonder why it is you are called the Irish Wolfhound," said Bolt slowly.

The question drew a quick flash of teeth. "Not on account of my docile temperament."

It was a moment before Bolt had recovered enough
command of his emotions to speak. "Where were you last
night?"

"He—" began Alexa, but Connor cut her off.

"I was out."

Bolt didn't deign to look at her. "This female is your
wife?"

"Yes." Connor put down his drink very slowly. "The
lady is indeed my wife."

The warning was clear enough that the magistrate
backed off in his belligerence. "Were the two of you together...milord?"

"We attended Lady Halliburton's soiree. I am sure you
can track down a number of witnesses who will corrobo-
rate that fact."

"And the rest of the night?"

The earl's lips curled in a mocking smile. "Have you ever worked in Mayfair before, Mr. Bolt?"

"Many a time."

"Then I presume you are familiar with the habits of the *ton*."

"Quite." It was said with contempt. As the magistrate searched through his coat for a pencil, a shade of resentment colored his face. "In my experience, the titled gentry are an arrogant lot," he muttered under his breath. "Indulge in all manner of depraved behavior, thinking they can do anything they please. Well, it's my job to see that no one, not even a peer of the realm, gets away with murder."

Alexa bit her lip. The man looked more and more like he was out for blood.

"Anybody to vouch for your whereabouts after you left your wife?" went on Bolt.

Connor's gaze remained unblinking. "None that I intend to name."

Turning away from the piercing stare, the magistrate cleared his throat. "I suppose that will be all for now." He turned to a fresh page and scribbled a few lines. "However I must request that you remain in Town for the next little while, sir. I'm sure I shall have some other questions to ask as the investigation continues."

"Just what are you accusing my husband of?" demanded Alexa.

"Nothing." Bolt snapped his notebook shut. "Yet."

Chapter Twenty-one

$\mathcal{I}$ vow, the news of your marriage came as a great surprise to all of us, my dear Lady Killingworth. The earl had a great reputation...for avoiding Society." Lady Hawthorne took a sip of her tea. "As he was not wont to attend the usual round of balls and soirees, I was not aware the two of you were acquainted."

Alexa took care to ignore the sly exchange of looks between the other ladies seated on the sofa. She had her own compelling reasons for making the rounds of morning calls with her aunt, and so had steeled herself to expect such probing questions. Thankfully, Cameron had helped her cobble together a clever assortment of half-truths into a story that ought to stand up to close scrutiny.

"Killingworth and my brother Sebastian have known each other for some time," she said smoothly. "They fought together in the Peninsular campaign."

Lady Longwell edged forward on her seat. "So the attachment was a longstanding one?"

"Yes, you might call it that." Alexa nibbled on a pastry. She would satisfy their hunger for fresh gossip, knowing the ladies vied with each other to pass on the latest juicy ondits to their friends. But only because she, too, expected to gather some information.

"How very romantic—no doubt you had your reasons for keeping the courtship quiet," added a hatchet-faced baroness with an equally sharp voice. "We were all *so* disappointed that the ceremony did not take place in London. St. George's in Hanover Square is such a lovely venue for a proper Society wedding."

"Indeed, but concern over my father's uncertain health demanded a sudden journey north," answered Alexa. "Given the circumstances, we decided it was best to forego a long engagement and elaborate nuptials."

Lady Hawthorne nodded. "That is very understandable, my dear. Having brought such a handsome rogue up to scratch, you were quite wise to bring him to the altar without delay." She flashed a sugary smile. "Was it a small ceremony?"

"Very small. Killingworth and I prefer a quiet life."

"They say a reformed rake often makes the best sort of husband," murmured Lady Longwell, not without a touch of envy.

The baroness gave a small sniff. "*If* he is reformed," she said, arching her brows before turning to greet a new arrival.

Alexa bit back a tart retort. To her relief, the awkward pause in the conversation lasted only a moment. Someone mentioned a recent entry in the betting book at White's, and the ladies quickly sunk their teeth into a new topic of scandal.

Amid the waving hands and fluttering napkins, Alexa made a surreptitious survey of the room, trying to still the nervous lurching of her heart. The magistrate's visit had added a new sense of urgency to her original plan. It seemed the attacks on Connor were escalating, both in intent and ingenuity. Fuzzed cards had failed, and so had bullets. Now it appeared that his unknown enemy was intent on drawing a noose around the earl's neck.

Her throat tightened. Connor had assured her that he was innocent of the murder. And yet, the evidence was incriminating, especially as he would not reveal, even to her, a full account of his movements that night. Alexa did not wish to dwell on the possible reasons for his silence.

But how could she not? Things were uncertain enough in her marriage without the fear that at any moment, her husband was going to be knifed in an alleyway or hauled off to Newgate.

Since he insisted on keeping her at arm's length—aside from their physical intimacies—there was no choice but to take matters into her own hands.

Setting aside her cup, Alexa rose and began to circle through the crowded room, hoping her gamble was going to pay off. If anyone could dish up any dirt on the trio of gentlemen Cameron had named, it would be the dowager Countess of Kenilston, an inveterate gossip who was reputed to know every naughty secret in Town.

And word had it that Lady Kenilston never missed the lemon tarts served here every Wednesday... Finally spotting the dowager holding court near the hearth, Alexa went to join in.

A short while later, she was well satisfied that her efforts had been rewarded. A few careful questions had elicited some useful information about the three names on her list. One man in particular now seemed the most likely suspect. But much as she wished to know more about him, she didn't dare press her luck. Too much curiosity about Sir Gervaise might attract attention—and for once, she meant to be discreet.

Wishing a moment of solitude in which to mull over what she had just heard, Alexa moved away from the group to study some engravings of exotic animals hung near the garden doors. If it were true that the baronet had recently cheated a young Scottish nobleman out of a fortune, he might have reason to want such an experienced player as Killingworth out of the picture...

Lost in thought, she wasn't aware of having company in the alcove until a voice sounded close to her ear.

"At times, the present company can make the King of Beasts look to be a toothless tabby," murmured a voice close to her ear.

Startled, Alexa fell back a step from the picture of a roaring lion.

"I hope you don't mind me joining you." The lady flashed an apologetic smile. She was dressed in muted tones of mauve and dove gray, which matched the sound of her murmur. "I could not help but overhear Lady Hawthorne and her cronies seek to sink their claws into you, and wished to tell you how much I admire your self-control."

"Was it that obvious that I wished to bite their heads off?" asked Alexa.

"Only to me." The smile took on a rueful curl. "No doubt because I must exercise an even greater restraint to keep my teeth clenched."

The frank admission was unusual enough to draw Alexa's attention from her earlier worries. She slanted another quick sidelong glance at her companion, trying to recall if they had ever met before. However, the finely chiseled Grecian profile was that of a total stranger. Puzzled, Alexa took a fraction longer to study the face.

The lady looked to be close to her own age, but a similarity between them ended there. In marked contrast to Alexa's height and sun-dappled features, the newcomer possessed a petite daintiness and a creamy complexion so perfectly smooth that it might have been carved from Carrera marble. Her jet-black hair, though arranged in a modest chignon, made for a striking counterpoint.

One raven brow lifted, nudging Alexa into the realization that she was staring.

Before she could voice an apology, the other lady spoke again. "You have every right to looked shocked. I have been terribly forward to approach you without a formal introduction, Lady Killingworth. But I could not pass up the chance to meet someone else who does not appear to relish these gatherings."

"Oh no, I am very glad you did," assured Alexa. "I am not one to stand on ceremony."

"I had hoped that might be the case." The lady inclined her head a fraction. "I am Mrs. Weatherly."

"I am pleased to make your acquaintance. It seems I have no need to tell you my name. You are obviously aware of who I am."

"Well, it would be rather hard not to be, seeing as you and the earl have been the talk of the Town."

"Things must be awfully dull for me to be the subject of speculation," replied Alexa. "The *ton* will no doubt be disappointed to discover I am not very interesting."

"I think you are being far too modest." Mrs. Weatherly took a discreet look around before adding, "Anyone whom

the gossips criticize as being too forthright and too opinionated for a proper young lady is certainly someone who
interests *me*."

*Another female who felt stifled by the strictures of Po-
lite Society?* Alexa felt the tightness in her chest ease just
a touch. It was like a breath of fresh air to be conversing within the stuffy confines of a London drawing room
with someone who possessed a self-deprecating sense of
humor. "Are you and your husband in London for the
Season, Mrs. Weatherly?"

"I am a widow," came the soft reply.

Alexa gave an inward wince at her clumsiness. "Oh, I
am very sorry for your loss."

"Don't be." Mrs. Weatherly shrugged off the condo-
lence. "It was a match of mere convenience. To be honest,
I am better off without him."

"Perhaps you will meet a gentleman more to your liking."

A light laugh sounded in answer. "Good heavens, I
have no desire to reenter the Marriage Mart. Indeed, if I
had my druthers, I should prefer to remain in the country. However, my late husband's family has decided that
I should make a convenient chaperone for a niece who is
to be fired off in the Little Season. So in readiness for the
coming campaign, I have been sent to reconnoiter, and
learn the lay of the land, so to speak."

The note of cynicism in Mrs. Weatherly's voice became more pronounced. "In other words, I am expected
to keep my ears and eyes open in order to discern which
modistes are *au courant*, which hostesses wield the most
influence, and most importantly, which gentlemen are
considered eligible—and which are not."

"I cannot say I envy you the task." Alexa smiled in sympathy, but the shared confidence also sparked a more pragmatic reaction. "I imagine you have learned a great many intimate details about a number of individuals," she said slowly, telling herself that she couldn't overlook any possible source of information. "Take, for example, Sir Gervaise, whose activities Lady Kenilston was just speaking of. One would not expect a prominent peer to be capable of such depravity."

"Oh, it is much more common than you might think." The widow's lips compressed in concern. "By the questions you were asking, it appeared you have more than a casual interest in the gentleman."

"I…"

"It is none of my business, of course." Lady Weatherly dropped her voice to a whisper. "But I would counsel great caution. He is said to be dangerous."

Alexa hesitated, then decided to risk revealing a part of the truth. "It is not out of any prurient attraction that I am making inquiries about Sir Gervaise. I have reason to think he may be threatening a… close friend. By learning more about his private affairs, I hope to find something useful. A bargaining chip, if you will."

"I see." Mrs. Weatherly did not press for further details, and Alexa's estimation of the lady rose another notch. "Regrettably, my late husband and Sir Gervaise were part of the same circle of friends. A group that tended to talk rather loudly and in great detail when drunk. So I can warn you that it is a terribly risky gamble."

"I am not afraid of taking chances," responded Alexa.

The widow looked up. From beneath the fringe of ebony lashes, Alexa caught a gleam of what might have been amusement before it took on a more martial cast. "Somehow, that does not surprise me. In that case…" Mrs. Weatherly paused, as if waiting for some encouragement to go on.

"Yes?" Alexa had the distinct impression that the other lady knew something about taking risks.

Mrs. Weatherly made a wry face as she tugged on the fringe of her shawl. "No one pays much attention to a poor relation who takes care to blend into the background. I tend to hear a great many things that are said in confidence."

Their conversation was cut off by a loud hail from the hallway.

"La, there you are, Lady Killingworth!" Alexa did not recognize the broad-beamed matron who was now sailing toward them with all the force of a four-deck ship of the line. "You sly puss, you must come at once and tell me about your whirlwind romance." The stranger's enthusiasm was not the least dampened by Alexa's blank stare. "I spy a vacant seat by Henrietta."

"I am so very glad we met." Alexa managed a last murmur to the widow before being steered away. "And I look forward to continuing the acquaintance."

"As do I." Mrs. Weatherly had been forced to fall back. Even so, the creak of corset stays did not quite drown out her soft reply. "I found our discussion most interesting. If I learn anything more on the subject, I shall let you know."

Candles flickered in the private parlor of The Wolf's Lair, casting hide-and-seek shadows over three men gathered around the table.

"Bloody hell, of course I didn't kill him." Connor grimaced as he regarded his friends. "He was worth a damn sight more to me alive than dead."

Cameron regarded his well-tended hands. "In that case, it seems that pegos are not the only things that slip in and out with ease at your establishment."

Gryff choked on a mouthful of coffee, earning a muttered curse from the Wolfhound. "Try to swallow your levity. This isn't amusing."

"I know, I know. But you have to admit, Cam brings up an excellent point... so to speak."

"I do try to rise to the occasion," murmured Cameron.

Despite the show of sardonic humor, there was an underlying edge to Cameron tonight, thought Connor. It was evident in the way his eyes probed the surroundings.

Sharper than Spanish daggers.

Seeing that both of his friends were watching him, waiting for a reply, the earl cleared his throat. "There is no denying that someone seems able to come and go at will. And you need not ask your next question—no one saw anything suspicious. O'Toole and McTavish are not always as vigilant as they should be."

"One would almost think that you are running a charity ward rather than a business enterprise," observed Cameron.

"I'm not interested in your opinions," he snarled. "How I manage The Wolf's Lair is none of your concern."

Cameron acknowledged the rebuke with an enigmatic smile. "None whatsoever."

"Which still leaves us with the question of who knows the place well enough to slip in and out unobserved," said Gryff. "I thought Spotted Dick and Harry had a suspect under surveillance."

"We are taking turns watching the townhouse where DeWinter visited around the clock," replied Connor. "A cloaked figure left several days ago, but gave Harry the slip, and has yet to return."

Cameron flexed his fingers before slipping on a pair of snug black gloves. "Why don't I have a little look around inside the place this evening."

Gryff blinked. "You mean... breaking and entering?"

A pained expression crossed Cameron's face. "My dear fellow, I am never, ever so clumsy as to *break* anything. The art of a successful sortie hinges on the ability to leave no trace of your having been there."

"Sounds jolly intriguing," responded Gryff. "Perhaps you could use a hand?"

"Have you any experience in wielding a set of picklocks?" asked Cameron. "Or aligning the tumblers of a wall safe?"

Gryff shook his head.

"How about navigating the pitch of a slate roof in the dead of night. Or stringing an escape rope between buildings?"

"Well, er..."

A slight clucking sound left no more to be said. "Unlike the patrons of The Wolf's Lair, I make it a point to be in and out as quickly as possible."

"Might we get back to the subject of entering a town house?" muttered Connor. "Are you sure you don't mind risking..."

"Pfffph." Cameron tugged at his cuff. "There's no risk at all in something as simple as this. Now if you were to ask me something halfway challenging, like removing Prinny's—"

"I am not sure I care to know the full range of your capabilities." Slapping a scrap of paper on table, Connor scribbled a few lines and passed it over. "That is the location of the place. It is my turn to take the eight-to-midnight watch tonight. Meet me at quarter past the hour at the Crowing Cock on St. Alban's Lane."

"That should afford enough time to get the job done." Cameron tucked the note away. "By the by, what does Lady K think of how the investigation is progressing?"

"I have not told her any of the details. Nor do I intend to," said Connor curtly. "I mean to keep her well distanced from any danger."

"You don't feel that leaving her in the dark is dangerous?"

Connor felt himself bristle. "Damn it, man. I am capable of keeping Alexa from harm."

Cameron arched his brows. "In my experience, females often have a mind of their own when it comes to this sort of thing. They do not always take kindly to being ordered away from the action and come up with their own alternatives. Some of which might very well turn your hair from gray to white."

"Trust me, in my line of business I, too, have learned never to underestimate the wiles of a woman," assured Connor.

"Forgive me for pointing it out, but your judgment has not proved infallible of late."

Connor's chair hit the floor with an emphatic thud. "I shall take care not to make any more mistakes." Turning to Gryff, he snarled, "If we are done talking, perhaps you would be so good as to take a stroll through the ale houses along the Strand. It would be useful if we could catch a glimpse of DeWinter's three companions."

His two friends turned and left the room together, leaving the earl to make his own way out.

"*What?*" Limbs weary, temper frayed from the fruitless search, Connor could not keep his voice from rising. He had come home for a quick supper, hoping to avoid any discussion about the investigation. But Alexa had a mind of her own about the matter.

Her chin rose. "There is no need to shout at me. I am simply trying to be methodical in looking at the problem. After making a preliminary inquiry, I thought to—"

"Bloody hell! For once, will you do as I say and stop meddling in my business? It is not your concern."

"*You* are my concern," she countered. "At this point, I should think that would be obvious."

"I don't need—or want—your help in this."

She recoiled as if struck. "So you wish to be partners only when the urge moves you?"

The barb hit a raw nerve. Connor heard the growing anger in her voice but was too furious to care. "Don't twist the meaning of my words!"

"Why not?" she said hotly. "You don't hesitate to manipulate things to your advantage whenever it suits you."

Something inside him snapped.

He was upon her in two quick strides, his palms coming up to trap her face. "That's right, I am a ruthless reprobate used to handling things exactly as I please. Don't pretend to find that surprising. I made my character abundantly clear to you during our first encounter, when I forced you up against the wall and shoved my tongue in your mouth."

"I slapped you at the time for your overbearing arrogance." Her hands clenched. "And at this moment, I am itching to do it again. I will not tolerate being treated as a toy."

He seized her wrists before she could make good on her threat. The bare flesh felt scorching beneath his fingers. "Then don't keep seeking to play at a man's game, Alexa! You ought to have learned by now how high the stakes can run, and how quickly it can turn dangerous."

She struggled but Connor tightened his hold. He, too, was a prisoner, gripped by a need he felt powerless to combat. "Escape is impossible. You will only hurt yourself in trying."

Alexa suddenly went very still. "Is this another lesson?"

"God knows, it was not planned as such," he growled, aware that heat crackling through his limbs was now taking on a decidedly different fire. "Though there is a fine edge between anger and arousal." One that was now dangerously close to slicing through the last shreds of his self-control.

"I think I am fast discovering that for myself." Her mouth, which only a heartbeat ago had been twisted in righteous fury, now pursed to a rueful grimace. "The question is, how does it resolve itself."

"Striking out is one way." His lips feathered against hers. "But seeing as that is not an option at present, you will have to resort to other extremes."

"Y-you are not playing fair," whispered Alexa.

"Life is rarely fair."

Whispering an oath that ghosted into a sigh, she drew him into a deep kiss. The inside of her mouth was velvety smooth, like the skin of a ripe peach. She tasted of freshness, of sunlight. *Simple pleasures, long forgotten.* The fight drained out of him as he surrendered to her sweetness.

Hearing him groan, she slipped a hand inside his shirt, threading a caress through the coarse curls.

God Almighty, it was his wife who was not playing fair.

Was she aware of the power she now wielded over him? With a wordless sound—half curse, half cry—Connor dragged his lips down the arch of her throat. Her lace fichu gave way to a ragged tug, then his mouth closed hungrily over her breast. The dampened muslin clung to her softly rounded flesh as he teased her nipple to arousal.

Fire speared through his body, and his hands tangled in the tapes of her gown before Connor managed to get hold of himself.

"Alexa," he rasped, forcing himself to a semblance of sanity. "Listen to reason."

"I can't." She crooked a tentative smile. "My heart is speaking too loudly to hear anything else."

He didn't dare pay attention to the thudding in his own chest. "In the heat of the moment, don't misinterpret physical—"

"Lust?" Her hands clenched on his coat. "You think all that connects us is the flare of desire and a bit of enflamed flesh?"

Connor closed his eyes, not knowing what to say. How to admit that his existence had grown so intertwined with hers that he could no longer separate the two? The realization was still inexpressibly confusing.

"Damnation, Connor Linsley—I love you!"

She loved him.

A wave of hope crested in his chest, followed by a vortex of desperate fear. *What if he somehow failed her?* He had been on his own for so very long, and the dangers were now so very different.

"I…" Had he ever said the words? It was so long ago that he couldn't remember. Elusive shadows—they swirled beneath the surface of his memory, caught in cross-currents that kept them just out of reach.

Pulling away from her embrace, Connor brushed a kiss across her knuckles before letting go of her hand.

"I…must go out."

Alexa flinched as if struck. "Look at me, Connor. I open myself to you. I let you inside me, and you—you keep me at bay."

"Perhaps an old dog is not capable of learning new tricks." Avoiding her eyes, he moved for the door.

The breath caught in her throat, but she made no effort to release it until his hand touched the latch. Even then, the sound was so soft he wondered whether he was only imagining the words.

"You may turn tail and run from me now. But some day I shall make you say it too."

Connor wasn't sure whether the prospect made him want to laugh or to cry.

Chapter Twenty-two

$\mathcal{T}$his just arrived for you, madam." The footman placed a small tray upon the desk, a letter centered squarely on its surface.

Alexa eyed the missive as though it were a serpent coiled on the polished silver. That word should come from her brother was inevitable, she reminded herself, but that did not make her any more eager to read his reaction.

With the tip of a pen, she drew the paper closer, quelling the urge to shove it unopened into one of the drawers. At least he had kept his venom to a minimum—there appeared to be just a single sheet, and a small one at that. No doubt he was waiting until he arrived in person to sink his fangs into Connor.

Oh, what a tangle she had made of the Wolfhound's life.

And her own.

Her fingers sought the twist of wool she had brought back from the earl's estate. But rather than offer any comfort, its silky softness was a harsh reminder that of late, goats were the only creatures whom she had not rubbed the wrong way.

Repressing a sniff, Alexa looked back down at her notebook and slowly thumbed through the sketches she had been working on. Somehow, she could render the ideas for bold new architectural and agrarian innovations in a sure hand, the details drawn in with unerring precision. She knew where each element fit in and how it worked.

But when it came to designing her personal life, her imagination seemed to run amuck.

She paused at a blank page, wishing she could draw in an ordered outline. Instead, her pen had a mind of its own, scratching a random pattern across the paper. It took her a moment or two to realize the doodle was taking shape as a wolf's head. With several quick strokes, she altered the jawline, softened the nose, and added a pair of eyes crowned by a sweep of windblown hair. Still, it bore only faint, mocking resemblance to Connor. She had failed to add any real life to the dribbles of ink. The essence of the man remained elusive.

Snapping the cover shut, Alexa forced herself to set aside the reminders of Linsley Close and face up to the present predicament. She took up the letter opener…only to feel a stab of relief. It was not her brother's slashing script that confronted her, but an altogether unfamiliar handwriting. Curious, she quickly broke the seal.

The message was succinct, the directions clear. And yet, she took care to read it over several times before setting the sheet down. On her own, she had been having no luck in trying to shuffle the random clues into any meaningful order. But now, fortune appeared to have dealt her a fresh hand. If she played her cards right, with a bold…

Drawing a deep breath, Alexa refolded the letter. *Duty*

versus desire. Connor's own words echoed in her head. For once she would consider the consequences of acting on impulse. Especially as a glance at the clock showed there was time to be true to both her head and her heart.

"No sign of a bloody soul." Splinters scraped against iron. "Mebbe the poxy cove got wind he was being watched and found hisself another bolt hole," grumbled the smuggler as he edged out from his hiding place among the broken barrels.

Connor kicked away the butt of a cheroot and an empty brandy bottle. "From the look of things, a regiment of Foot Guards could have marched down the stairs and you wouldn't have noticed."

"I swear on me mother's grave, Wolf, I didn't take an eye off the place!"

"Mother?" He slipped into the sliver of space, his temper not improved by the sight of his boots sinking up to the ankles in ooze. "I always assumed you crawled out of a barnacle."

Spotted Dick gave a wheeze of laughter. "Well yer guess is as good as mine. Never knew neither of me parents— though mebbe they be clinging to the bottom of 'Arry's boat."

"Stow the chatter and shove off." Wedging his shoulders against the grimy brick, Connor turned up his collar. "And try to keep Harry sober enough to relieve me at midnight."

"Aye, aye, sir. Ye ain't got nuffink te worry about."

As the smuggler's reply floated off in the fog and mizzle, he tried to settle in. But the memory of Alexa's words was still burning in his brain, and the lingering imprint of her body was still hot on his flesh. Even more uncomfortable was the prospect of the bleak hours ahead, stuck with naught but his own thoughts for company.

Cold cheer, indeed.

A crick was already starting to take hold in the back of his neck. The day had been a nightmare. And the way things were going, the evening did not promise to get any better.

"Mary?" called Alexa.

The only answer was a feral scrabbling in the rotting garbage.

"Mary McPhee?" Fog swirled, blurring the words to an indistinct echo. Though her misgivings were mounting, Alexa took another tentative step into the alleyway. *Had she made a mistake?* The directions had seemed clear enough, but once she had stepped down from the hired hackney to continue on foot, there was a chance she had taken a wrong turn.

Despite the thickness of her cloak, she felt a chill steal up her spine. Circumstances had forced her to move more quickly than she would have liked. The note from Mrs. Weatherly had offered a golden opportunity. The widow had made a few discreet inquiries and learned that one of Sir Gervaise's maids was willing to talk. But the girl was frightened, and fleeing Town. The meeting would have to take place that very night, in a secluded spot in Seven Dials.

Or not at all.

True to her promise, Alexa had sent word to Cameron, informing him of the sudden turn of events. But the messenger had come back with news that her husband's

friend was not at home. Nor had Connor returned from
wherever he had run off to. Her mouth quirked at the
irony of it. She had wished to err on the side of caution,
yet when push came to shove...

Alexa had waited until the last minute before slipping
out the side entrance of townhouse. As a salve to her conscience, she had dispatched another servant to Cameron's
residence, this one carrying the letter from Mrs. Weatherly
and a scribbled note explaining her own actions. At least
she had done her best to adhere to the spirit, if not the letter,
of her pledge.

Somewhere close by, a hinge rasped, its rusty groan
startling her into falling back a step.

A last call, decided Alexa as she stopped to catch her
breath. Then she would backtrack and seek to regain her
bearings.

"Mary!"

This time, a wink of light appeared in answer. For an instant it took shape as a lantern, the weak glow illuminating
a shrouded figure before dissolving back into the darkness.

"This way! Quickly!" A brief flicker reappeared,
pointing out a jagged gap in the row of rookeries.

Without stopping to think, Alexa plunged in between
the splintered boards, following the hurried slap of steps.
The way was narrow, and as it twisted left and then right,
she was forced to turn sideways to squeeze through the
space. Blackness shrouded her movements, and the surrounding stench leached the air from her lungs.

She stumbled to a halt, and must have given voice to her
dismay, for from up ahead came a call of encouragement.

"It's just a little farther, then it's safe to talk. Mind your
head as you round the last turn."

Feeling her way along the wall, Alexa inched forward. Cobwebs caught in her hair. Broken glass cracked under her feet. An overhanging beam forced her to bend low. Finally, the scrape of a flint lit a spark and she exhaled a sigh of relief.

"Where—"

As the cudgel came down on her skull, Alexa heard a trill of laughter before sinking back into oblivion.

The drumming in his left ear was becoming more insistent. Roused from his melancholy musings, Connor turned sharply, his hand instinctively going for the knife concealed in his boot.

"Having sweet dreams?"

"Sod off, Cam." He straightened his leg. "Have I ever told you what an extremely irritating prick you can be?"

"I can think of one or two occasions."

"I'll have you know I wasn't napping," added Connor. "I was…thinking."

"I'm glad to hear it. Then perhaps you will have an idea on what to do about this."

Connor felt a crackle of apprehension as his friend unfolded some papers. "I stopped by my townhouse to pick up a few essentials for the job, and found these waiting for me," recounted Cameron. "What do you know of a Mrs. Weatherly?"

"Nothing. Never heard of the lady," he replied. "Why do you ask?"

"Because just hours ago, she sent an urgent missive to your wife." Cameron quickly read both notes aloud. "As you see, it sets out the time and place for a clandestine meeting between Lady K and a servant who works for Sir Gervaise."

"Gervaise?" Connor frowned. "You must be mistaken. The man is a thoroughly dirty dish, but I can think of no reason why Alexa would be interested in looking into his affairs."

"There is no mistake." A sudden ghosting of moonlight showed that Cameron's expression had turned deadly serious. "I am afraid the blame lies partly with me. I supplied her with names of several patrons of The Wolf's Lair who might wish you ill. But only on the condition that she do no more than ask a few questions. She promised not to take any action without seeking my counsel." He looked down at the topmost note. "She did try to honor her part of the bargain—"

Connor grabbed his friend's dark scarf, choking off the rest of the reply. "Damn you to hell. I ought to slice off your tongue and your testicles."

"You are welcome to hack off any appendage you wish—but do it later. If we hurry, we may still be able to catch up with her. I have a hackney waiting one street over."

It wasn't until they were inside the vehicle, and the wheels struck up a clattering over the cobblestones, that Connor spoke again. "Why the devil does she feel she must take such awful risks?"

"Is that a rhetorical question," asked Cameron. "Or do you wish for an honest answer?"

A brusque nod signaled him to go on.

"Because she loves you. She's willing to risk anything to win your heart." Cameron crossed one booted leg over the other. "And you, you ungrateful cur, ought to have your teeth kicked out through your arse if you don't appreciate what a rare and wondrous gift that is."

Their gazes met, steel against steel. Neither of them blinked.

"You think I don't love her?" demanded Connor.

"It doesn't matter what *I* think."

He shifted against the squabs but there was no escape from the piercing stare. "She *must* know how I feel."

"Have you told her?"

"Well...damn it, not in so many words."

"Women are odd creatures," murmured Cameron. "They seem to require hearing it said in no uncertain terms."

Connor covered his confusion with a hot retort. "I had not realized that you were such an authority on what women want, seeing as I never see you spending much time in their company."

Cameron accepted the implied insult with a nonchalant shrug. "I know a great many things that might surprise you." He checked his watch. "Based on the average speed of a hackney coach, we will be arriving at our destination in a touch under five minutes, so might I suggest you check the priming of your pistol." With a quick sleight of hand, he drew a weapon from his own pocket. "I trust you came armed with more than just teeth and claws."

The jolt of the carriage jarred Alexa awake. Her head ached abominably. So, too, did her wrists, which were lashed tightly together with a length of rope. She tried to sit up, but a hard shove forced her back against the cracked leather.

"Y-you?" Alexa blinked twice, trying to bring her muzzy wits and the tilted face into focus.

Mrs. Weatherly resumed her place on the opposite seat

and calmly smoothed the wrinkles from her cloak. "I confess to being a trifle disappointed. From all that I had heard about you, I expected a more difficult challenge in luring you out. However, your intelligence appears to have been greatly exaggerated."

At that moment, Alexa was inclined to agree.

"Only a fool would walk straight into such an obvious trap."

Alexa allowed the gloating to die away before asking, "Why trap me at all? What sort of threat do I pose for you?"

"None whatsoever."

Cast in the glow of the carriage lamp, the widow's prettiness took on a harsh, unyielding edge. Alexa was once again reminded of a marble statue. She shuddered, wondering how she had missed the cold stare, the bloodless smile.

"It's the Irish Wolfhound I am after. You are merely the means to an end." Mrs. Weatherly gave a small laugh. "Or should I say, the bait. Though I shall be glad to get rid of you as well. Without your pesky interference, Killingworth would have been crushed in the jaws of my ingenuity some time ago. He has grown more wary, but with the right morsel to draw him out, I'll not fail again."

A woman scorned? Alexa did not wish to think of Connor's past dalliances, but his animal magnetism had assuredly attracted any number of willing females. Or perhaps it was the lady's husband who had suffered crushing losses on account of the earl's skill at cards.

"I am sure that Killingworth never intended any injury, to you or your husband—"

Laughter, even more shrill than before, cut her off. "There is no Mr. Weatherly. He and his gentry family from the Lake District exist only in lies and rumors."

Still dizzy from the blow to her head, Alexa could only stare in open-mouthed shock.

"But it is astounding how easily you highborn lords and ladies are deceived. A bit of paint, the proper gown, a heartfelt sigh—oh yes, I learned early in life the importance of appearance and the power of suggestion. Despite its penchant for gossip, the *ton* rarely looks beneath the surface. It sees what it expects to see."

Her captor flung open her cloak. "For example, you observed a gown that was modest in both cut and color, but clearly of good quality and styling. So you assumed that the wearer was cut from the same cloth. The widowed Mrs. Weatherly, a lady of genteel birth and education..." The cultured voice turned quite a bit rougher around the edges "...when in truth what you saw was Helen Snow, a lightskirt born on the docks of Dover."

Alexa tried to concentrate. *A prostitute by the name of Snow.* That should be a telling clue, and yet she could not quite fit the person with a motive.

"That does not explain why you seem to hate Killingworth so," she said slowly. "Such relentless pursuit speaks of a grudge far more personal than a general dislike for people of rank and privilege."

"Ah, so you are not quite as dumb as you seem," replied Helen. "Yes, with the Wolfhound, it is a matter of both personal and professional slights." The sculpted lips thinned to an angry slash, the first real show of uncontrolled emotion. "For which he shall pay dearly."

A wave of nausea churned her insides. Swallowing hard, Alexa forced back the bitter taste of bile. "I should like to know why."

"I suppose there is no harm in telling you all the details." Indeed, Helen looked rather eager to do so. "Have you any idea what your highborn husband does to earn his money?"

"He runs a brothel and gaming hell in the stews." It might have been more prudent to remain silent, but Alexa could not help herself.

A spasm crossed Helen's face, betraying that the reply had caught her off guard. But she quickly masked her surprise. "Then perhaps it won't come as too great a shock to your maidenly scruples when I tell you that I used to work at The Wolf's Lair."

Though Alexa had been expecting something of the sort, her expression must have given away a hint of her dismay. The other woman's lips formed into a smug smile. "Oh, yes, I was one of the most popular—and profitable—girls."

"With your particular talents, I can see why," said Alexa evenly.

"Can you?" Helen crossed her shapely ankles, shifting the reticule by her side. From its depth peeked an ivory-handled pistol, sized for a petite palm, and a plain poniard.

Alexa swallowed hard, sure that her captor would show no hesitation in wielding either weapon.

"No, I don't think you appreciate the full range of my talents quite yet." Helen clearly had no compunction about causing pain. Her next words were certainly chosen to draw blood. "I soon drew the Wolfhound's special notice."

"Like Suzy Simmonds?" said Alexa.

"That stupid cow?" The mocking jeer could not quite hide the edge of anger. "She actually enjoyed *talking* with a gentleman."

Realization began to dawn on Alexa. "You mean to say you were disappointed that Killingworth did not invite you into his bed?"

The facade of cool composure shattered with a resounding crack. "How dare he reject my charms!" Her gloved hand slapped into the squabs a second time. "He singled me out. Only to say he admired my *mind*!" The last word was spit out as if it were something obscene.

"There are some females who would have taken that as a great compliment," said Alexa softly.

Helen went on as if she had not heard. "I offered him a wealth of pleasures and all he wished to do was teach me how to add up a column of monthly expenses. For that alone, I shall never forgive him."

The lamp flickered wildly as the carriage lurched through a sharp turn and picked up speed. "But I am curious about something, Alexa Hendrie from Yorkshire." In the yawing play of light and shadows, Helen's eyes took on a more malevolent glitter. "I have attended many of the recent soirees, taking great care to stay in the shadows. Killingworth never spotted me, but I had ample opportunity to observe him. And you."

"Watching several sedate spins around a ballroom could not have been all that entertaining."

"It afforded some interesting moments. As did a stroll in a moonlit garden, where the figures of the dance became a trifle more heated. You and the Wolfhound couple quite well together."

The first flush of embarrassment quickly turned into a surge of outrage at the violation of her most private intimacies. But after a moment, Alexa willed the two hot spots of color on her cheeks to cool. Anger would only further cloud her already shaky judgment, and the clench of her fists only caused the rope to cut more deeply into her flesh.

Helen laughed, but the sound quickly died away. "I have seen the way he watches you, both on and off the dance floor. Connor Linsley—the aloof and arrogant Irish Wolfhound—is besotted with his country bride. It can't be looks, and neither your fortune nor your family offer the prospect of power." Her eyes narrowed. "Tell me, what hold have you over him?"

Despite her fears, Alexa crooked a wry smile. "I own half of his business."

"You lie! The Wolfhound would never sell his Lair."

"No," agreed Alexa. "I won it in a game of cards."

"Ha!" scoffed Helen. And yet, a shadow of a doubt shaded her voice. "You think I am a Bedlamite, to believe such a farrididdle as that?"

"Nonetheless, it is true. We are partners in more than the conventional union of man and wife."

The assertion gave the other woman pause for thought. "Perhaps I underestimated you after all." Her fingers caressed the pistol. "How very convenient that I shall kill two birds with one stone. It would have been very vexing to have gone to all the trouble of exterminating the Wolfhound, only to discover his Lair remained in business."

Alexa was thrown off balance. She had not expected business to enter into the equation. "Why does it matter to you if The Wolf's Lair stays open?"

"The reason is quite simple," said Helen. "Money."

"But you have long since left his employment—"

"To set up my own houseful of whores."

Things were finally beginning to add up.

"Oh yes, Connor Linsley taught me well, but why would I want to waste my talents running a respectable business?" continued Helen. "The prospect for profits is pitiful and the drudgery a bore."

"Still. I don't see why it is necessary to seek the Lair's demise," said Alexa. "From what I have seen of the *ton*, there are plenty of clients to go around."

"More than enough, but the Wolfhound was going to ruin it for all of us in the business! High wages, comfortable quarters, days off—and worst of all, the prospect of a pension for retirement." Helen grimaced. "Damn his hide, he was much too *nice* to the girls. Word was beginning to spread, giving my sluts airs above their station. Rather than being grateful for a place off the street, they were starting to ask for a raise, and other benefits. Revenues would have dropped dramatically."

"So you decided to kill him?"

"Not at first. I would have been satisfied with stripping him of his pride and his purse, which would have put him out of business."

"You were, of course, familiar with Killingworth's private office, and its contents," said Alexa.

"He is rather careless with his possessions. It was absurdly easy to steal his money and his dagger." Using the point of her own poniard, Helen nudged a lock of hair from Alexa's cheek. "And his wife."

Refusing to be intimidated, Alexa continued with her questions. The odds against escape were awfully high, but there was still a chance, and her knowing all the information might come in useful. "However, it must have taken some effort to find someone skilled enough to cheat Killingworth at his own tables."

Helen laughed. "I didn't have to look too far from home."
Snow. DeWinter.

If her foot hadn't been trapped between the seats, Alexa would have kicked herself.

"Cousin Dickie had a certain cleverness with cards," went on her captor. "He was useful...up to a point."

"A rather cold-blooded way of putting it," murmured Alexa.

Helen's smile was chilling. "We had a profitable working relationship going, but then he got greedy, and tried to blackmail me for more. Subtlety was never his strong suit. Or savvy." She gave a casual toss of her head. "One of his friends found my offer quite satisfactory."

A small shiver coursed up the length of Alexa's spine. The woman had ice in her veins.

"But even in death, dear Dickie was good for one last trick. I thought it one of my more inspired ideas to arrange his demise in a way that set yet another hunter on the Wolfhound's tail."

"You may have put a flea in Bolt's ear, but he will require more evidence than a stray dagger to have Killingworth taken up for the crime."

"And he shall have it!" Helen leaned forward, the flare of malice in her eyes overpowering the pale lamplight. "You are a rather dull creature—have you not yet worked it out? I shall use you as the ultimate bait to lure the Wolfhound to a meeting in rookeries. Where Bolt will catch him red-handed with a corpse and apprehend him for murder of his wife."

The laugh had an eerie, inhuman crackle to it. Despite her resolve to appear unmoved by the woman's hatred, Alexa found herself shrinking back from the sound.

"Combined with the incriminating evidence of De-Winter's death, and his well-known wolfish temper, Connor Linsley will hang from the Newgate gibbet," gloated Helen.

"Very clever, indeed." Bracing her shoulders against the squabs, Alexa regained a measure of composure. "What a pity that for all your brilliance, you overlooked one small detail."

A flicker of uncertainty dimmed her captor's smugness. "Impossible. I have worked everything out perfectly."

"You yourself noted that Killingworth does not guard his possessions very carefully. Perhaps it is because he doesn't care overly if he loses them." Alexa drew in a breath. "You mistake his display of desire for something deeper. I wouldn't count on him coming after me."

Helen shifted back into the shadows. "Oh, the Irish Wolfhound will come. I will bet my life on it."

Chapter Twenty-three

Crouching down, Cameron lit the stub of candle. "Footprints. Quite fresh by the look of them."

Connor peered over his friend's shoulder. "It's Alexa, without a doubt. I recognize the shape of her shoe." Lifting his gaze from the mud, he tried to control his rising panic. "Come, let us see if we can discover where they lead."

A quick search of the alleyway brought them to the narrow opening between the buildings. Drawing back the hammer of his pistol, Cameron prepared to step forward.

"No, I'll go first." Though armed with only a knife, Connor elbowed him aside. "Put out the light."

Swearing silently, he moved as quickly as he dared, but the treacherous footing and twisting confines slowed progress to a snail's pace. Sweat began to trickle down his back, and at the thought of stumbling upon Alexa's lifeless body, he felt the hilt of his weapon grow slippery in his fingers.

Dear God Almighty...With a start, Connor realized that his oaths had given way to prayer.

As if in mockery of his appeal to the heavens, the way

pinched in tighter around his head, forcing him to bend over nearly double. He paused to listen, hearing only the harsh echo of his own ragged breathing.

Was it possible that somewhere in this hellhole he had missed a turn?

He inched forward another step and suddenly, his outstretched blade nicked up against an oaken beam. Muttering a warning to Cameron, he slipped beneath it and scrabbled out into a dirt lane.

"Damn."

The scudding moonlight showed that it was deserted.

Striking a flint to his steel, Cameron relit the candle. "Look here," he murmured, picking a flutter of white from debris littering the ground.

Connor was on him in an instant, and snatched it from his hand. "Damn," he repeated, his fingers all too familiar with the delicate pattern of the lace fichu. It still bore the feminine sweetness of verbena and lavender. "Damn, damn, damn."

As the earl stood, clenching the tenuous connection to Alexa, Cameron turned away and began a methodical search of the area. A circling sweep soon turned up a length of iron pipe. Grim-faced, he held it up to the light. "A bit of blood—but not so much as there could be."

Connor stared mutely at the strands of wheaten hair stuck to the pitted metal.

"Come, Wolf." Cameron reached out and, one by one, slowly loosened the earl's fingers from the bit of lace. "You can't pull her back that way."

Connor thrust the crumpled cloth into his pocket. "No," he agreed. "For that I shall have to wrap my hands around the bastard's throat."

"Nor will an explosion of the fearsome Wolfhound temper be of any help," counseled Cameron. "You need to keep a cool head."

"You may feel compelled to offer advice on the female mind. But war is one thing I understand perfectly." Though his insides were molten with worry, he steeled his voice. "What else did you see?"

"A number of footprints. Two, maybe three, different sets, along with scuffmarks of some weight being dragged over the ground. And evidence of a carriage having passed through here recently." Cameron paused for a fraction before adding, "No sign of struggle."

"Or a body," said Connor, trying to keep his voice even. "If they have bothered to take her away, there is a good chance she is still alive." He started to follow the muddy ruts, but Cameron caught hold of his coat.

"Don't be a fool. We haven't a chance in hell of following the tracks once they leave this lane. We need to return to your townhouse, in case there is a clue there."

Kicking at a shard of glass, he clenched his jaw. "I suppose you are right," he said, allowing his friend to lead him away. *Move—he had to keeping moving.* It was the only way to keep one step ahead of the paralyzing dread snapping at his heels.

Cameron walked beside him in silence until they reached the corner where their hackney was waiting. "I have been thinking—it's even more imperative that I have a look inside the place you were watching."

"Our thoughts are marching in line." Connor was already reaching for the door latch. "I am coming with you."

"Think again." Cameron came to a halt. "The same arguments I raised with Gryff hold true for you. Any errant move might further endanger Alexa. You would only be in the way."

Connor opened his mouth to argue, but he knew his friend was right.

"As I said earlier, you must return home, and see if she left any other clues as to the mysterious Mrs. Weatherly. And while it may be too early as of yet, there is a chance that a note is waiting. If Alexa has been abducted, her captors will no doubt seek to use it to their advantage. I'll meet you there as soon as I can."

The earl's hand hovered over the handle. "I am trusting that one of those many skills you mentioned earlier includes being a bloody good cracksman."

"You won't find a better one between Brighton and Bombay." Moving with catlike quickness, Cameron already slipped off into the shadows. "I shall not let you down, Wolf."

That Cameron's strategy was the only logical one did not help quell Connor's feelings of utter helplessness. A careful examination of Alexa's bedchamber yielded nothing save for haunting little reminders of her—an azure hair ribbon, a bottle of lavender water, a strand of pearls. Slamming the dresser drawer shut, he crossed the hallway and entered the study.

The only papers on the desk were a scribbled chronology of the attacks and a list of questions she had drawn up for Mr. Bolt. Setting them aside, Connor picked up the small leather notebook. The pages fell open to an architectural sketch for expanding the stables of Linsley Close. The notations, written in a careful hand, indicated that

Alexa planned shearing pens, a goat barn, and several out buildings for the storage of wool and weavings.

As Connor studied her handiwork, he found his throat growing tight. She had taken blank paper, an empty book, and envisioned... a future. Leafing through the rest of the sketches revealed a number of other details. A Kashmir goat, complete with historical notes on the breed. New brass fittings for pantry cupboards. A design for a new set of drawing room draperies, the pattern and color spelled out in the margin.

And a portrait, unmistakable despite the whimsical curl of the pen strokes.

An odd rumbling sounded deep in his chest. The book slipped from his grasp as Connor sank into the chair and buried his head in his hands.

If only God would grant him a chance to tell her how much he yearned to share in her dreams.

It was, he admitted, supremely ironic. For most of his life, he had viewed the world—and women—with a sense of cynical detachment. There had been many torrid dalliances. But despite the twining of limbs, the heat of flesh against the flesh, he had never been touched by any of them.

Until Alexa had come storming into his Lair.

Passionate. Provocative. She had, from their very first meeting, both exasperated and enthralled him. Her spirit seemed to defy the boundaries of mere words, and ignore the barriers he had so carefully constructed around his innermost self. Alexa Hendrie had gotten not only under his skin but also into his heart, a place he had always thought impregnable. It frightened him to his very core.

Was that love?

Perhaps the plaguey poets were right. Connor had always thought it ridiculously melodramatic to veer from very depths of despair to the heights of ecstasy, all within the space of a sonnet. Now he wasn't so sure. Love inspired doubt and hope, not to speak of confusion. It had wrought a profound change on him, beguiling his jaded senses, awakening elemental longings, making his heart sing.

Which was ridiculous—he was the snarling Wolfhound. *Wasn't he?*

But no matter that his own words were more likely to come out as a rough bark than a polished pentameter, the next chance he had, he would tell her of his feelings.

Alexa strained at her bonds. Her captors had loosened the rope around her wrists after carrying her up to the tiny room, but any hope of escape had been ruthlessly cut off by the snap of the iron manacle around her ankle, chaining her to the bedstead. Still, the thought of gaining a bit of freedom, however illusory, prompted her not to give up in her struggles. She would not feel quite so helpless if she could gain the use of her hands.

Biting back a cry, she gave another hard twist to the knots. The physical discomfort helped keep her mind off a far deeper pain. She ached with regret at how much had been left unsaid between her and Connor. There had been so little time together. She hadn't had a chance to tell him how much she loved the little things about him—the shape of his jaw, the way she fitted into the crook of his arm, his gruff laugh, and the quicksilver flashes of humor in his eyes, though he took pains to hide the lighter side of his nature.

It was wrenching to think she might never see his austere visage again, or hear his growl...

A last desperate tug and she slipped free of the rope. Pushing up to a sitting position, Alexa found her prospects were not greatly improved. The shackle around her leg prevented her from leaving the mattress, and the sight of matching chains attached to the other three bedposts sent a shudder through her limbs. Her wits were still a trifle dulled but it did not require much imagination to think of what they might be used for.

She fell back against the crimson counterpane, averting her gaze to the ceiling. Which proved a mistake. A large oval mirror, held in place by four leering satyrs, covered most of the painted plaster, its dim reflection catching not only her bruised face and torn garments but the assortment of leather whips and spiked rods hanging upon the wall.

Squeezing her eyes shut did not block out the wicked curl of the lashes and menacing bite of the sharpened metal. But after a moment, she steeled her nerve, refusing to give in to despair. She would *not* lie down like a lamb, and submit meekly to being staked out as bait for the Wolf! Twisting back into a sitting position, Alexa tugged at a knot of her hair.

She had once laughed herself silly on reading a popular horrid novel, thinking it an absurd contrivance of plot that the heroine had managed to open a dungeon door with a hairpin. Now, however, she prayed that truth would prove stranger than fiction.

Bending open the bit of metal, she set to work.

"The house appears uninhabited," reported Cameron. "There is no sign of servants and all the rooms are under holland covers, save for a small library on the second floor, which looks to be a meeting place of sorts. The desk is being used, but it's obvious someone is being careful to leave no telltale trace of identity lying around." After peeling off a knitted cap and a pair of skintight black gloves, he removed three items from his coat pocket and, with a theatrical flourish, lined them up on the desk. "But not quite careful enough."

A deck of playing cards, a gold watch fob, a wine merchant's bill.

Without comment, Connor picked up each in turn, making a careful scrutiny before placing them back on the leather blotter. "Bloody hell."

"So you see a connection?"

"It's hard to miss, if you know what to look for." He flipped one of the cards face down, revealing an intricate pattern on the back of the pasteboard. "Two stylized birds, one white, one gray. A rather unique design, made only for The Soiled Dove, an expensive brothel near Regent's Park." His forefinger then grazed over the pair of tiny gold wings. "The fob is given out to special clients, who have dropped a hefty amount of blunt, along with their breeches, in the private parlors on the third floor. And this…"

The paper crackled as Connor smoothed out the accounting from Flood and Taylor. "…This bill is made out to an establishment at the corner of Crescent Street and Gilpin Lane."

"The exact location of The Soiled Dove," finished Cameron. "A curious coincidence, is it not?"

"I shall know more about that once I have plucked some bird bare, feather by filthy feather." The earl's chair scraped back, but Cameron laid a restraining hand on his shoulder.

"Let's not go flying off the handle quite yet, Connor. We need to decide on a strategy before we go hunting." Perching a hip on the edge of the desk, Cameron asked, "Who owns the establishment?"

Connor pulled a face. "I am not the only proprietor who prefers to keep his identity a secret. I have heard rumors, but never paid the matter much heed. It didn't seem overly important." Taking up the gold fob, he turned it slowly between his fingers. "A grave mistake, I see. One of the basic tenets of business is to know the competition."

"If it is of any consolation, I know a great many others who have made the same mistake," murmured his friend. "Such knowledge does not come without a price."

"No," he said softly. "But in this case, I pray that the cost will not prove too dear."

Shuffling through the cards, Cameron turned one of the Queens face up. "Let us not lose heart. We shall have to play our hand very carefully, but I have a feeling Lady Luck will not turn her back on such a stalwart female as your wife."

The earl stared at the painted pasteboard lips, uncertain whether the smile was playing him false.

With a flick of his wrist, Cameron placed the Jack of Diamonds alongside her. "First of all, I suggest that we call in Gryff right away. We might not know who has taken Alexa prisoner, or why, but we have a good idea of where she is being held. Neither you nor I ought to show our faces at The Soiled Dove." The King of Hearts fluttered down to the desk, followed by the Ace of Spades. "But Gryff's carousing is well known throughout Town. He could pay a visit to the place this evening without raising undo suspicions, and have a closer look around."

Until that moment, Connor had not been aware that

night had given way to the first rays of dawn. He looked away from the window, finding the pale reminder of the passing hours inexpressibly bleak. "The Devil take it, there must be a way to do something before then."

Cameron shook his head. "We can't risk tipping our hand. Our opponent doesn't know what cards we hold. When the time comes, we shall have to use that element of surprise to trump his every move. So we must be patient. A man of your experience in high-stakes gambling knows emotion cannot come into play."

Like dice tumbling across a table, Connor's insides began to bounce and roll against his ribs. Keeping a cool head in his old life was easy. Victory or defeat—he had viewed them both with equal detachment.

It was, however, no longer just a game. *And he was no longer the same cynical wolf.*

His expression must have betrayed some hint of his thoughts, for Cameron sought to lighten the moment with a drawl of his usual sardonic humor. "I hear that settling into a marriage is never easy."

The earl expelled a sigh. "You seem to have an answer for everything. I take it you also have an expert strategy for coping with the opposite sex?"

"Of course. I avoid them altogether." Cameron's voice maintained its mocking note, but his movements lost a touch of swagger as he drew a fresh sheet of paper from the desk drawer. "It makes life so much simpler."

Too simple. Connor had watched the body language of too many gamesters to miss the subtle change. Until now, he had not given much thought as to what lay behind Cameron's devil-may-care attitude. *Hell, he had been careless about a good many things . . .*

But Cameron was quick to deflect attention from himself. Uncapping the inkwell, he nudged it to the center of the blotter. "Here, do the note to Gryff, asking him to come around this evening." Paper rustled. "Then write down all the names you've heard mentioned as possible owners of The Soiled Dove and let's take a look at them."

The scratch of the nib dominated the crackle of the banked coals. After sealing the first paper and sending it off with a servant, Connor passed over the list.

"Hmmm." Cameron took his time in studying it. "Not Hingham," he murmured, crossing off the name. "He's running a pack of lightfingers in Pall Mall, not lightskirts. And as for Whitbeck, I can't see him as having the backbone to be in charge of anything like this. He skulks around the stews because he likes to be beaten, rather than the other way around."

"Actually, I would delete Brighton as well," said the earl. "Too stupid. He blackmailed Lord Upton over an affair with another man's wife and nearly ended up eating grass for breakfast."

One by one, they eliminated the rest of the suspects.

"Bloody hell." Connor stared glumly at the row of black slashes on the page. "Are you sure there weren't any other clues as to the villain's identity lying about?"

"Quite sure." A tiny pause. "And yet…" Cameron tapped the pen to his chin.

After several moments, the earl's fingers began to drum a matching rhythm upon the blotter.

"Have you considered the possibility that your enemy is a female?" asked his friend slowly.

"That is absurd," scoffed the earl.

"Is it?" countered Cameron. "Come now, we both

know members of the opposite sex who possess the requisite cleverness and imagination to mastermind such a complex plan."

Connor's gaze stole to Alexa's notebook. *As if he needed to be reminded of that.* "But not the muscle. Don't forget that DeWinter was stabbed in the chest, and he was not a small man."

"Muscle can be easily hired."

"I suppose that is true," he conceded. "Still... what made you think of a woman?"

"Just a feeling," replied Cameron. "Or, rather, a certain scent. There was the trace of perfume lingering in the air. Attar of roses is not something a man would wear."

"Certainly none of my acquaintance," said Connor. "I am familiar with the damn fragrance. It tends to cling to clothing as well."

"Yes, it is one that is more at home in a bordello than in any sort of refined household."

The earl ran a hand over his stubbled jaw. "It seems an awfully insubstantial clue to pursue."

"Perhaps. But it is the only one we have to go on at the moment." There was a slight pause. "Unless you can think of any former employee who might hold a grudge."

"I never mixed business with pleasure," growled Connor.

"Well, it was just a thought." Cameron rose. "Look, I have a few friends in certain circles who owe me favors. Now that we are honing in on what sort of individual we are looking for, I think it wouldn't hurt for me to pay a few morning calls and see what further information I can scare up." His gloves slid back in place with a supple ease. "It may take me a good part of the day, for these particular fellows do not tend to stay in one place for more than a few days at a time."

As Connor watched, he was struck again by how quickly his friend assumed another role. Like the art of disguising his true self had become second nature. The observation made him shift in his seat, for it cut a little too close for comfort.

"In the meantime, do get some sleep," added Cameron. "You are looking a bit pinched around the gills."

The earl made a face. "To sleep, perchance to dream."

Cameron pulled the black cap low on his brow. "Rest easy. We'll get her back."

"Would that I were as sanguine as you are," replied Connor, threading a hand through his hair. And yet, he didn't dare consider the alternative. Life without his wife was...unthinkable.

"My dear Wolf, if you wish to quote Shakespeare, allow me to suggest another line." Cameron paused in the doorway. "All's well that ends well."

Chapter Twenty-four

$\mathcal{T}$he day passed with agonizing slowness, but finally twilight began to tinge the sky, deepening the shadows outside the townhouse windows. Cameron had still not returned from his mysterious errands, but Gryff arrived at the appointed hour, and without preamble asked, "What can I do to help?"

"Pay a visit to The Soiled Dove," replied Connor. "And play the role of a jug-bitten rake on the prowl for more sinful pleasures than can be found in usual haunts of the *ton*."

"That won't be difficult. As you know, I have a great deal of experience in acting like an arse." Gryff cocked a self-mocking smile. "In this case, however, I shall contrive to keep my wits about me." He stared for a moment at the gold fob and playing cards on the desk before going on. "Once I have made myself at home, what is it I should be looking for?"

"I will sketch out a basic layout of the private upstairs chambers, and what sort of activity each one offers," replied Connor. "In cozening up to the girls, try to learn if there is anywhere in the place that is off-limits."

Gryff nodded in grim understanding. "Don't worry, I will find a way to get a look around." He began to toy with the penknife by the inkwell. "But if I find out something important, I shall need an excuse to go outside and then return—"

"No, you won't," said Connor. "Just take your leave. Your job will be done."

"The hell it will." The blade jabbed into the blotter. "Of all the bloody awful things you have snarled at me over the years—many of them deserved—that is perhaps the most insulting."

The Wolfhound stopped dead in his tracks.

"After battling by your side through the brutal heat and savage guerillas of the Peninsular campaign, I'm not about to abandon the field of battle before you have Alexa safe. Besides, you may have need of a diversion inside."

Limned in the glow of the fire, his friend's features suddenly appeared harder, more clearly defined than in the past. Perhaps, realized Connor, that was because he was seeing everyone around him in a whole new light.

"My apologies, Gryff," he murmured. "You may say you have a item you wish to retrieve from your carriage. A…sex toy."

For an instant, the marquess's brows winged up in surprise, then waggled in humor. "You never mentioned *that* sort of thing around the Lair. You know, I remember a certain establishment in Lisbon—"

"Not now," muttered the earl. "This is no time for games."

The smile was gone in a flash. "No. I'm well aware it is deadly serious. And you can trust that I will not gamble with your future a second time." Prying the knife loose,

Gryff carefully inspected the blade. "I take it you and Cam have come up with a strategy for Alexa's rescue. What do you have in mind?"

A good question. Connor looked away. A message had come earlier, setting up a rendezvous at midnight near The Soiled Dove. But Cameron's continued absence was yet another cause for concern. Within the slums of London, even the best-laid plans could easily go awry.

"We have not worked out the exact details."

An odd expression played on his friend's lips. "It's strange to hear you say 'we.' I have never known you to put much faith in other people, not even your fellow Hellhounds."

"Well, I suppose we both have changed of late," replied Connor. "For better or for worse."

The jingle of the lock gave Alexa just enough time to curl up on her side and feign sleep. The folds of her skirts covered the bits of broken metal on the counterpane and the hairpin still clutched in her hand. It was the third one she had tried, but aside from a few maddening snicks, she had achieved nothing save for a bloodied thumb and a broken fingernail.

The hallway sconces cast a flicker of elongated shadows on the far wall. Two figures... and the snout of a long-barreled pistol.

"She's asleep." Alexa heard the soft rustle of silk as Helen turned to her companion. "Leave her alone for the moment."

"I thought ye promised I could have her." The accent sounded Dutch. And none too pleased about being denied his fun.

"You can, but later, when the time comes to finish her off. Right now, I don't want any distractions." Helen tested the bolts of the door. Metal scraped against metal, a harsh echo of the man's grumblings. He added another comment, too low for Alexa to hear.

Whatever was said, it drew a flurry of words from Helen in some foreign language before she reverted to English. "I am in no mood for argument." She sound vexed. "I don't like what I just saw downstairs. Lord Haddan has paid us a visit."

"What of it?" came the sullen reply. "A great many English lords come here to dip their wicks, or indulge in a taste of the rod or whip."

"Not this one," replied Helen. "He has never sought his pleasures here before. That in itself does not mean much—many gentlemen get the urge to try something new. However, as I know Haddan to be one of the Wolfhound's few friends, I cannot help but wonder..."

"I thought ye said this plan was foolproof."

"It is." For all the steel in her voice, a certain shrillness had crept into its ring. "I don't anticipate any trouble, but one of the reasons for my success is that I leave nothing to chance."

"How much longer do we have te wait?" demanded her companion.

"Just an hour longer. Then I shall send the note to the Wolfhound, setting up the exchange. You have Van Dreisen ready to alert the magistrate?"

"Aye, he knows what to say."

"Good. Keep a close watch on the stairwell. I am going to fetch my cloak and have a look around outside."

"And if the gentry mort tries to make his way up here?"

"Tell him the floor is closed for a private party. I am sure you can be convincing."

"A private party—heh, heh, heh, ye are a right clever one, Mistress Helen." The man's laughter had a nasty, razored edge. "Don't be gone too long. It's growing harder and harder to wait fer the fun te begin."

Alexa felt an involuntary shiver cut down her spine.

"You will soon have your fun," promised Helen. The door fell shut and the bolts rammed home, cutting off the scant spill of light.

Alexa fought against the enveloping blackness. Reason might cry out that her tiny twist of metal was no match for the steel of her enemy. And yet her heart whispered that no matter how dark things looked, hope must keep a flame kindled. *Warmth. Light.* The thought of Connor was like a beacon, beckoning in a storm. She had but to reach out and embrace it.

Flexing her stiffened fingers, Alexa renewed her attack on the legshackle. The hairpin jammed into the keyhole, nearly snapping in two as it probed left and right. A faint snick stirred a momentary spark of excitement...and then the point slipped.

Sweat-dampened hair was now sticking to the nape of her neck. Her hands were going numb.

Swearing softly, Alexa tried again.

Lord Haddan was here. Her mind was working as feverishly as her fingers. By now, Cameron would have received her notes. Had he and Connor stumbled over some clue in the alleyway that had led them to add up two and two? Elation was tempered by a sharp squeeze of alarm. The marquess would not have come on his own. Connor would be somewhere close by. And about to walk into a trap.

Imagining her hairpin as a dagger, and the heartless hunk of iron as Helen Snow, Alexa summoned up the strength to give a ruthless thrust.

Click. The tip quivered, but this time kept hold in the catch of the lock. *Click.* With a last little rasp, the metal jaws fell open and slipped free of her ankle.

The buildings were shuttered to all light and a veiling of clouds covered the sky. Connor angled his gaze from the sagging shingles and rotting timbers to the intersection of Plover Alley and Green Street. It was a miserable little place, two trails of dirt that hardly merited the recognition of a name.

Still no sign of Cameron...

To his left, something moved in the shadows.

The earl flattened against wall, alert to the rustle of footfalls approaching the corner. Gripping the butt of his pistol, he drew it noiselessly from his pocket.

A figure, too dark to identify, stepped out from between the remains of an archway. There was, however, something familiar about the tilt of the cloaked head, the angle of the shoulders.

"Cameron," he whispered.

The shape spun around. "Killingworth?"

It was not Cameron's smooth tenor, but a distinctly feminine voice. One that was threatening to dissolve into a sob. "Oh, thank God it is you!"

"Helen Snow?" He stepped out from the alcove, scarcely believing his ears. "What the devil are you doing—"

Flinging her arms around his neck, Helen buried her face in his collar. "L-looking for a hackney. I had to find you...w-warn you..."

"Calm yourself." He brushed a hand over a cluster of raven curls, hoping to still the trembling of her tone. "I won't let any harm come to you."

"You were always...too kind, sir. I should have...but the past cannot be changed."

"It is not important," murmured Connor. His own voice remained steady but his insides were twisting into a knot. Gently untangling himself from her hold, he tipped up her chin. "You wished to warn me of what?"

"Your wife. S-she is a prisoner in The Soiled Dove. They mean to..." Helen pressed a fist to her mouth. "Oh, it's too horrible for words."

Connor gave her a small shake. "I know you to be a clever girl, Helen. Take a deep breath and think. I need you to tell me all that you know."

"Yes. Of course." Blinking back tears, she managed a game smile. "I shall do my best."

Releasing the cock of the hammer, the earl slid the pistol back into his coat and drew her into the shelter of the recessed brick.

"I am not proud to admit it, but I am now employed at the Dove," stammered Helen. "It is not the same as working for you, but..." Her voice trailed off.

"Don't think to apologize to me for your professional choices. We all have our reasons to do as we do to survive."

"Very well, sir. I won't apologize." Drawing a gulp of air, she began a halting account of what she had discovered. "I was taking a respite between clients in one of the back stairwells when I overheard the master of the house going over the plan with several of his henchmen."

"Who?" he interrupted.

She shook her head. "I don't know his name or his face. Only that he speaks with a trace of a foreign tongue."

"Damn," muttered Connor. After a fraction of a pause, he could not help asking, "Are you quite certain the master is indeed a male?"

"You think the owner of The Soiled Dove might be a *female*?" She eyed him as if she were not quite certain of his sanity. "Whatever brought such a thought to your head?"

Said aloud, it did seem absurd. "A wild flight of fancy." He pulled a grimace. "Go on."

Her gaze softened, then slid away from his. "They mean to lure you into a meeting in the stews by offering your wife in exchange for The Wolf's Lair. But in truth, they intend to murder her and make it look as if you committed the foul deed. A magistrate will be tipped off as to the time and place. He will arrive to witness you standing over her body. She—she will have a bloody handkerchief with your monogram clutched in her death grasp."

It took a moment for him to comprehend the full depths of such depravity. Connor had run up against professional killers in the Peninsular campaign, and vicious predators in the London stews. But he had never encountered a...fiend.

"Can you show me a way to enter the building unnoticed?" he demanded.

Helen nodded. "I can do even better than that. There are a number of hidden stairways and passages that connect the upper floors. I can lead you straight to where your wife is being held without any danger of being seen."

Connor hesitated, forced to choose between gentlemanly honor and the law of the wilds. But need quickly overpowered any twinge of guilt. "I don't like asking you to take the risk, but I fear that I must."

"I don't mind taking a risk." Helen's smile turned a touch more pronounced. "After all, I feel I owe you for all you have done for me."

"Consider the debt paid. With interest."

"We shall tally up the accounting when all of this is over." She tugged at his sleeve. "Follow me. It is best that I lead the way. There is a shortcut that will bring us around to the rear of The Soiled Dove."

Helen doubled back and cut through an abandoned warehouse whose doors had long since been smashed for firewood. She seemed confident of her bearings, thought Connor, and moved through the maze of byways with a stealthy quickness he would never have been able to manage on his own. Feeling extraordinarily fortunate at the chance encounter, he took care to keep up.

Perhaps Luck was indeed a lady.

It wasn't until they had traversed the next cross street that he realized he had left Cameron in the dark. His step slowed for an instant, but then he decided not to mention the appointed rendezvous. It was too late to backtrack, and besides, the actual identity of the villain was no longer important. Only that he—or she—be stopped before any harm came to Alexa.

Ducking under a broken shutter, the earl focused his attention straight ahead. He wasn't going to worry about Cameron. His friend had an uncanny knack for improvising. As for Gryff...

Connor checked that his pistol was close at hand. He had no intention of having to fall back on his friends.

A sudden signal from Helen waved him to a halt. She crept back and indicated a thin blade of space cutting between two of the brick buildings. Barely visible in the rising mists was a set of shallow stone steps leading down to a recessed doorway.

"The entrance to the storage rooms," she whispered. "I left it unlocked, but I had better check."

Connor waited, the thud of his quickening pulse a grim reminder of each passing second. It seemed like an age before she beckoned him on.

A damp chill, sharp with the scent of soap and vinegar, hung heavy over the cramped space. His mouth crooked upward. The distinctive mix was intimately familiar. A brothel had specialized housekeeping needs, with laundered linens and necessities for the girls topping the list.

Helen had thought to leave a lantern lit. Turning up its wick, she angled the light to show the way through the crates and cabinets. "The first stairwell leads up to a small anteroom to the rear of the main parlor. It's used to keep extra brandy and champagne close at hand. The porters are rarely called on to pay it a visit, especially at this time of night, but we must go very quietly.

A rat scrabbled away from the beam.

"From there, we must cross the back foyer to gain entrance to one of the hidden stairways." As she started forward, she touched his shoulder. "Have no fear, sir. I promise this will go exactly as planned."

Connor found his throat too tight for words. His fingers covered hers, and squeezed a quick embrace.

At the top of the landing, Helen turned and pressed close to mouth a whisper. "Wait here, while I go upstairs and make sure that it is safe to proceed."

The zephyr of breath stirred a sudden sense of foreboding. He caught at her cloak. "I think I ought to go on alone."

"No—that would be a grave mistake. If I am spotted by one of their guards, I can talk my way out of trouble, while your appearance might force their hand with your wife."

The earl let her shrug off his hold, though he still could not quite let go of the feeling that something was wrong. His instincts did not usually betray him, but of late they seemed to have gone astray.

Helen appeared to hesitate. "Your weapon—perhaps I should take it. Just as a precaution."

He handed it over without question.

"I shall be back as soon as I can. Be prepared to move quickly when you see my signal."

Alexa finished her inspection of the door. It was as she had suspected—the inside key would no doubt release the lock, but a tiny gap in the molding revealed two bolts on the outside, which held the paneled oak firmly in place. No amount of nudging with a hairpin was going to budge them, so she was still a prisoner.

A circling of her cell showed there was no other route of escape. The large leaded window was unlocked, but a quick glance showed her location to be on the top floor of the building. Knotting the bedsheets into a rope—another scene from the horrid novel—would still leave her with a drop of over thirty feet down to a cobbled courtyard.

Alexa closed the casement and turned to the opposite wall. Undistorted by the ceiling mirror, the array of racked implements appeared even more menacing. With a choke of revulsion, she quickly looked away. Bare plaster met her gaze, a stark reminder of how few options were within her grasp.

Swallowing her scruples, she approached the rack and hefted one of the rods, a wicked-looking length of ash crowned with a studded steel ball. It swung through the air with much the same feel as a scythe or pitchfork.

After several more swooshes, she set it aside on the bed and took up the whip. On occasion, she had been forced to take a crack at a recalcitrant bull, so it, too, felt more at home in her hand than the delicate fans or jeweled quizzing glasses favored by ladies of the *ton*. As the braided lash snapped through the air, the end curling around the top of the bedpost, Alexa smiled.

For all her boasting bravado Helen Snow had been wrong to claim she had thought of everything—she had not reckoned with the earl's wife being a rough and tumble country lass.

Alexa recoiled the length of leather and placed it on the edge of the bed. According to her brother, a decorated war hero, the element of surprise could be nearly as powerful a weapon as bullets or blades in a fight.

When the time came, she meant to use it to her full advantage.

Forty-one, forty-two . . . The seconds seemed to be passing with excruciating slowness.

Connor made up his mind. If Helen did not return by the count of sixty, he would make his move.

A moment later, the faint rasp of hinges cut off his mental calculations. "Come along, sir," whispered Helen.

As he rose from a crouch, the thud of steps rose up from below.

"Connor, stop!" called Cameron. "It's *her*!"

No. His friend must be mistaken.

"Hurry!" urged Helen, beckoning to him from the darkened stairwell. "They are coming for Lady Killingworth."

He broke into a run, hand outstretched for the half-open door. As Helen shoved it wider, a breeze stirred her hair.

Attar of roses.

He dove to one side, just as a searing flash exploded from the pistol in her hand.

Chapter Twenty-five

From behind him came a crashing thud, followed by a grunt of pain from Cameron. But as Connor hit the floor and scrambled to regain his footing, he dared not look away from the contorted mask of fury framed in the doorway.

Her second weapon misfired.

Looking like Medusa with her ebony hair snaking in wild waves around her face, Helen spat out a venomous oath. "After him, you ox," she hissed, shoving at the hulking brute by her side. "Show your cursed skill with a blade, and quickly, while Dirk and I see to the Wolfhound's bitch."

Ducking to avoid the now-useless pistol she hurled at his head, Connor caught the gleam of lethal steel, bright against the flutter of dark skirts that were fast disappearing up the stairs. He forced himself to slow his pursuit. The man coming at him was brandishing a butcher's knife, while he was armed with naught but a fierce desperation.

A sneering grin bared yellowed teeth, narrow and jagged as those of a wharf rat. "It will be a pleasure te gut a stinking English lord." The razored edge cut several quick slashes in the air. "Like a pig."

There was no time to fall back and formulate a strategy. Yanking off his cravat, Connor wound the linen around his left hand and darted forward.

The move took his adversary by surprise. The man hesitated, just long enough for Connor to slip in under the outstretched knife and lash a hard kick to the knee. It staggered him, but he managed to stay upright. His smile, however, sunk into a murderous grimace as he countered with a jabbing counterattack.

Sliding sideways, Connor dodged the flashing steel. "Beware—a wolf always seeks to hamstring his prey."

"Ain't me being hunted," snarled the man. "Yer the one wot's defenseless, and about te be slaughtered."

And yet, another of his thrusts hit naught but air.

"You are making a pitiful show of slicing me into gammon," said the earl. "Afraid of an unarmed man?"

Just as he had hoped, the taunt goaded the other man into lunging out with a flurry of wild stabs. Parrying them with his wrapped fist, Connor ignored the bite of the blade, waiting for just the right moment to smash his other hand down on the man's wrist.

The crunch of bone was drowned out by a harsh howl and the clatter of metal as the weapon slipped from his adversary's grip. The man doubled over, groping to regain his advantage, but Connor grabbed his coat collar and rammed him headfirst into the wall.

Blood spurted from the broken nose. The next driving blow sent several broken teeth skittering across the floor. A weak whimper was the only sound now coming from the split lips.

"Enough, Wolf, enough. Leave him alive for the authorities." Lowering his pistol, Gryff pried the earl away, allowing the man to collapse in a heap. "Damn it, I didn't dare risk pulling the trigger." He looked down at Connor's bleeding fingers. "Hell, you should have waited for reinforcements rather than charge into battle barehanded."

"No time for that." Blinking away the momentary haze of bloodlust, Connor flung the shredded remains of his cravat aside. "Lend me your weapon—then hurry and take care of—"

"Don't worry, I'll take care of Cam." Gryff quickly passed over his pistol. "Godspeed—you go save Alexa!"

Spinning around for the stairs, Connor took them two at a time.

The shot warned Alexa that all hell had broken loose. A frisson of fear spiraled through her, but she shook it off, determined not to surrender without a fight. Grabbing up the rod and whip, she took up a position by the door. Its inward swing would cover her for a second or two. Just long enough to seize the advantage.

But she would have to strike quickly.

Footsteps raced down the hallway. The first bolt slammed back with a jarring jolt.

Tucking the heavy coil of leather into her sash, Alexa gripped the rod with both hands and raised it over her head.

Another shudder of iron and the door gave way to a shouldered shove.

"I've got her." Though his back was to her, Alexa recognized Dirk's voice. He came on in a rush, but skidded to an uncertain halt at the sight of the empty bed.

Alexa betrayed no such hesitation. Taking dead aim at the Dutchman's skull, she swung with all the might she could muster.

The studded ball connected with a sickening thud, knocking the rod from her hold. Dirk lurched around, swiping a grab in her direction. She screamed, but after a wavering step, he dropped like a sack of stones.

"You sodding whoreson, this is no time to be wielding your rod!" Helen ducked into the room and delivered a swift kick to her cohort's splayed legs. "Get off of her! Now!"

"Dirk isn't taking any pleasure from his current position," said Alexa.

Framed in an aureole of black, Helen's face appeared white with shock. Then a rush of molten fury turned her flesh to fire. "You are a dogged little bitch, aren't you?"

Alexa watched her draw her poniard. *How odd that the slim little fingers and needled steel could look so dainty. And so deadly.*

"But you have outlived your usefulness. Killingworth is dead. I no longer need you as bait."

Helen started forward.

"Not so fast." Alexa lashed out a flick of leather, forcing a quick retreat.

A laugh, low and nasty. "It takes a good deal of experience to master the art of the whip." Feinting another approach, Helen suddenly whirled and darted toward the bed.

Connor dead? Distracted, Alexa did not react quickly enough to prevent her from reaching the dropped rod. Clenching the whip, she backed away. *Was it a bluff? Or the brutal truth?* There was no way of knowing, so she determined to play her hand to the final card.

"Go ahead, try putting some real snap to it." The new weapon added an extra edge to Helen's malice. She circled around to the window, making Alexa turn with her. "Ha, you will end up with its length wrapped around your throat."

Deciding things had gone far enough, Alexa let fly with a mighty crack.

The glass panes shattered, sending up a shower of slivers. Clutching her weapons, Helen fell back to one side of the casement, a thin beading of red welling up on her cheek.

"On the contrary. It is *your* neck that will be in danger on the next throw," warned Alexa. She quickly recoiled the lash. "Give it up. The game is over, Helen Snow."

Behind her, the Dutchman was showing signs of life. Alexa ventured no more than a sidelong glance but the slight movement gave Helen just enough of an opening to pounce.

But just as the rod came swinging at her head, a yank on her skirts tripped Alexa off balance. She fell, the studded steel missing her by scant inches.

Dirk struggled to his feet. "Let me bash her brains out."

"Get out of my way!" cried Helen as his broad bulk suddenly blocked a blow that would have caught Alexa lying helpless on the floor.

With a roar of rage, the Dutchman wrenched the rod from her grasp. Muscles bulging, he turned to deliver the coup de grâce.

Alexa opened her mouth to scream.

So, too, did Dirk as sparks exploded and a spurt of crimson shot up from his chest.

The impact of the bullet knocked him back into Helen. Buckled by the dead weight of his body, she lost her footing on the slippery shards and toppled toward the open window. Amid the cacophony of cracking metal and flailing curses, Helen hit the low sill. Her fingers clutched at a remnant of the leaded frame but it snapped like a matchstick.

A moment later, the momentum carried both bodies out into the yawing darkness.

When at last Alexa managed a sound, it was more of a whisper than a cry. "Oh, Connor. Against all odds, you came for me."

Lifting her ever so gently, her husband traced the curve of her cheek with his palm, leaving a smudge of red. "I have taken a great many gambles in my life, but I would never risk losing you," he murmured, before enfolding her in his arms.

Shards of glass crunched beneath his boots as Bolt picked his way across the room and peered out through the broken casement. The magistrate had listened to the lengthy story in silence, save for the faint scratch of his pencil. Tapping the tip to his chin, he jotted down a few more lines before finally closing his notebook and tucking it carefully in his pocket.

"There is an old adage about cats having nine lives." His basilisk stare turned on the earl. "Does it apply to canines as well, my lord? For it seems to me you have used up a good number of them here tonight. Both for yourself and your friends."

Connor found himself recalling DeWinter's first slurring taunt. "I believe the saying goes that every dog has his day."

"Hmmph. I had not heard that one before. I shall have to keep it in mind." Bolt actually cracked a smile. "Perhaps in this case, it ought to replace the one that says you can't teach an old dog new tricks."

Connor drew Alexa closer into the crook of his arm. "Yes, let us hope that particular adage has been proven false and may be tossed out the window."

"I should say it has, milord. On more than one account." Bolt leaned down to pick up the snaking length of leather. "It was lucky that your lady proved such a dab hand at cracking the whip."

"I told you I was a country girl," replied Alexa. "There are some benefits to being more at home in a barnyard than a ballroom."

"A great many," said the earl softly. His hand feathered along the shell of her ear as he tucked back a wisp of hair. "But we shall leave that to discuss in greater detail when we are in private." The intimacy was fleeting, yet fire flared in his fingertips. He cleared his throat. "If you don't have any pressing questions, Bolt, I should like to see to my friend's injury and then take my wife away from this place."

"I am sure a few will come to mind, milord, but they can wait until the morrow. For now, I shall tie up loose ends here." The last bit of lash looped in the magistrate's hand. "Though there is one niggling little matter I can't help but wonder about...the wounded gentleman downstairs looks awfully familiar. I could swear I have seen him before."

"I cannot imagine where." Connor kept a straight face. "What with the dim light and play of shadows, it is more than likely that you are mistaken."

"Perhaps that explains it." The magistrate's mouth quirked ever so slightly. "I have, on occasion, been wrong." He stepped aside, allowing Connor and Alexa to pass.

Hurrying down to the foot of the stairs, they found Gryff, stripped of his coat and cravat, doing what he could to make Cameron comfortable. Looking up from looping the linen around the wounded leg, he pursed his lips. "It could be worse."

"Easy for you to say," sniffed Cameron as he raised his head slightly from the pillow of wool.

Gryff helped him to a swallow of brandy. "The bullet doesn't appear to have broken the bone and the bleeding is staunched. At Cam's request I've dispatched a hackney to fetch a surgeon who is experienced in treating this sort of thing."

"Good work, Gryff." Connor crouched down to make his own examination of the wound. "You'll live," he murmured to Cameron.

"You would think the slut could have had the grace to aim a little more to the left." Cameron grimaced. "I fear the damn scar is going to mar the symmetry of my manly thighs."

Alexa, too, had dropped to her knees and began blotting the beads of sweat from his forehead. "My dear Mr. Daggett, no amount of nicks or scrapes could damage your unique charms. You are, to my eye, quite perfect."

Cameron managed a ghost of his usual sardonic smile. "No doubt because your gaze is so firmly focused on another man." His attempt at humor paled as Connor added another turn to the makeshift bandage. "Tell that sawbones Thurlowe that I shall slice off his fingers at the knuckles if he doesn't set a neat, regular stitch," he muttered before lapsing into a faint.

"I'll see Cam safely to his door," assured Gryff.

"We shall have to arrange for proper care—" began Connor.

"Actually we don't," said Gryff. "He's already assured me that he will be convalescing in a warmer clime. More than that, he wouldn't say, but you know Cam." He touched his friend's injured leg. "Never fear, I'll make sure Thurlowe agrees he is fit to travel. Otherwise, I shall see that he goes nowhere, even if I have to chain him to his bed."

"Excellent." Connor blew out a breath. "Though I had been hoping he could keep an eye on the Lair for the next little while."

"Leave that to me. I promise you that this time around it will be in safe hands."

He hesitated. "Leave it to you?"

"Yes, me. Go ahead and take Lady Killingworh home," urged Gryff. "Trust me, I've sworn off any future forays into trouble."

Connor made a wry face. "You and Trouble have been bedfellows for so long, it's had to imagine one without the other. However..."

Home. The word had a compelling ring to it.

"...I'll take your word that you're ready to turn over a new leaf." He slipped his arm around Alexa's waist. "Ready to go?"

Their residence was only a short carriage ride away. A simple trip. But only a waystop on the real journey home. In the past, he had not cared where he had strayed. The path had always appeared too dark and twisted to retrace his steps. *And now?* He had grown weary of his wanderings, a lone wolf at odds with his surroundings. Ahead was a ray of light, and the prospect of coming full circle.

Still, he was not quite there.

Though it was nearly dawn, Alexa scrubbed herself clean of The Soiled Dove and changed into a fresh gown. Connor had insisted on arranging for tea and some sustenance before retiring. Despite a fatigue that weighed heavy on body and spirit, she had been grateful for the suggestion. In truth she was loath to shut her eyes and see darkness rather than the austere angle of his face.

As she waited for him to return from rousing the servants, she fingered the shawl he had settled over her shoulders. A strange pang—something quite apart from the bruises and scrapes she had suffered—squeezed in her chest on looking around the unfamiliar room. Despite comforts of the place, she found it hard to feel truly at home.

Home. Wherever might that be? Her fingers tangled in the knotted fringe. She couldn't help thinking of the sun-bleached chintzes and faded draperies at Linsley Close, waiting for a special touch to give them new life.

"You may set it on the sideboard." Connor came through the doorway, followed by a maid with the tea tray. "We will not be needing anything else."

Steam spiraled up from the pot, filling the room with its earthy fragrance.

"Drink this." Connor added a generous splash of whisky to the tea before passing it over.

Though he had finally consented to having his hand bandaged, some of the cuts were still visible. She shuddered to think how close he had come to falling victim to his former employee's diabolical scheming.

His eyes did not miss the tremor of her hands. A flare of quicksilver emotion added a smoldering intensity to his gaze. "What is it?"

"I...I think I have seen enough of brothels to last me a lifetime," she murmured, trying to make light of all her inner fears.

During the carriage ride, he had held her in his arms, and his closeness had been comforting. She did not doubt that he cared for her in his own way. And the physical passion that sizzled between them was undeniable, and yet...She had gambled she could win his love.

But perhaps it simply was not in the cards.

"Come morning," she added softly. "I shall consign that dratted vowel to the flames, if you don't mind."

"Perhaps that would be best," murmured Connor.

Oh, how quickly he had agreed to turn their partnership into a pile of ashes. Her heart gave a lurch. Was her dream of sharing a real life with him as elusive as a wisp of smoke? She tried to take a sip of the fortified tea but its taste was bitter beyond measure.

"Alexa." Pushing the bottle aside, Connor reached out to cup her chin. "What is wrong? Are you hiding some hurt from me?"

His touch was gentle and still warm from the heat of the tea. She gave a tiny shake of her head. "Truly, I have suffered naught but a few bruises, and they will heal soon enough. Remember—I am country miss, not some delicate Town belle. I have experienced worse in taking a tumble from my horse."

He did not let go of her. "I am not speaking of any physical scrapes."

The ache in her chest made it difficult to draw a breath.

"I fear that at heart, you wish you could also add our marriage lines to the fire," she blurted out. "That it, too, is a partnership forced upon you by duty, not personal choice."

As his hand slipped away, Alexa blinked back a tear.

Rising abruptly, he reached for a small package on the desk and placed it in her lap.

"W-what..." she stammered.

"A belated wedding present." He replied. "I am sorry that with all the confusion in our lives, it has taken me so long to arrange for you to have it."

Alexa slowly untied the pale ribbon and let the paper fall away. Lying in the pasteboard box was a cashmere scarf, soft as a sea breeze, the colors and design right out of her sketchbook.

When she finally looked up, her eyes were brimming over with hope.

Connor leaned down to kiss the salt from her cheek. "I, too, am thinking of giving up my share of The Wolf's Lair. Sara Hawkins has shown a real aptitude for the business, so perhaps now is the right time to retire."

He shook out the wool and twined it around her neck. "But I am used to working for a living and would be bored to flinders living the life of an indolent lord. What say you to forming a new partnership?"

Alexa breathed in the faint country scent of earth and hay. "We could call it The Goat's Retreat."

Connor crooked a smile. "I suppose if we are going to sell weavings to the ladies of the ton, we are going to need a more pastoral name than The Wolf's Lair."

"But before we come to any final decisions, we had better discuss the terms." She hesitated. "Are we speaking of an equal partnership?"

"Not exactly."

Her heart stilled. "What are you saying?"

"That I have much to learn about being a country gen-tleman...a respectable merchant...a worthy husband. It will no doubt require more work on your part in the be-ginning. But I am hoping you are still willing to tackle the job you started of making Linsley Close our home."

"A house needs more than polishing and dusting to make it a home," she whispered.

"Yes, I know. It needs love." His arms came around her in a fierce hug. "Snarls have always come more easily to me than fine words, Alexa. I should have some eloquent speech to tell you what I feel for you. But I can only say I love you." He touched his lips to the corner of her mouth, drawing her into a deep kiss. "And have since the moment you marched into my lair."

"It is enough, Connor. More than enough."

"Then let us seal the deal with another kiss, my love."

The Marquess of Haddan has traded his rakish ways for more serious pursuits. But when his new interest brings him to a magnificent country house, the temptation awaiting inside may be more than he can bear...

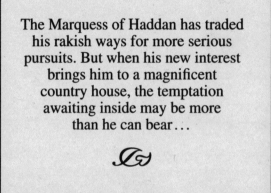

Please turn this page for a preview of

Too Tempting to Resist

Prologue

Oh, I'm *so* glad ye stopped by for a visit, sir. The Wolfhound says ye have a discerning eye fer art, so I'm anxious to get yer opinion on this." Sara Hawkins stripped the last of the wrappings from around a gilt-framed watercolor painting and let out an admiring whistle. "Don't ye think it will look lovely hanging in the Eros Bedchamber?"

Gryffin Owain Dwight, the Marquess of Haddan, shrugged out of his overcoat and came over to take a look. "You intend to hang *that* in *there*?" A dark brow shot up. "I wouldn't advise it."

"Why not?" Sara sounded a little crestfallen. "Roses are my favorite flower and this one is awfully pretty."

"Indeed it is. But in the secret language of flowers, red roses symbolize love—a sentiment that would likely make a number of your patrons rather nervous," said Gryff dryly. Patrons was putting it politely, seeing as Sara's establishment was one of the most notorious gambling hells and brothels in London. "If you must pick a rose for a decorative touch, make it an orange one."

"And what does that mean?"

"Fascination." He curled a wicked smile. "Better yet, find a print of a yellow iris, which means 'passion.' Or sweetpea, which means 'blissful pleasure.'"

She let out a snort of laughter.

"Or a peach blossom, which means 'I am your captive.'"

"Fancy that." Setting aside the painting, Sara perched a shapely hip on the sideboard and gave the marquess her full attention. "Now who would have ever guessed that flowers could talk."

Gryff nodded gravely. "And then there is the grapevine…"

"Which means?" Sara leaned forward, her eyes widening in anticipation.

"Which means, 'I am very thirsty so do you have any more of that expensive Scottish malt stashed away in your private cupboard?'"

A crumpled kidskin glove hit him square in the chest. "Oh, ye horrid man! Here I thought I was learning some fancy bit of knowledge. But ye was just pulling my corset strings." She gave an aggrieved sniff. "Now that I own this establishment, I can make my own rules. So I don't know why I let ye through the doors."

"Because of my *beaux yeux*, of course," quipped Gryff.

"Yer bows-yours?"

"That's French for 'lovely eyes,'" he explained, batting his raven-dark lashes. With all due modesty, the marquess knew that he was a great favorite with females, aristocratic or otherwise. And not only for his *beaux yeux*—though the unusual shade of green-flecked hazel did seem to have a mesmerizing effect on the opposite sex.

However, that fact was proving far less satisfying of late...

"Hmmph." Sara tossed her head, interrupting his private musings. "So Frogs have a language of their own too, eh?"

Gryff gave a bark of laughter. "Touché." Seating himself on the edge of her desk, he loosened his starched cravat, and expelled a long breath. "Now about that malt, Sara."

The door of the Chinoise curio cabinet opened and shut. Glasses clinked as she passed him a silver tray. "Ye may pour me a taste as well."

"I take it that business has been good."

"Aye, very profitable," she replied. "Especially as I'm putting this bottle on your monthly bill."

Gryff splashed a measure of the dark amber spirits into two glasses. "I'd gladly pay double for the pleasure of conversing with you," he murmured, passing one to her.

She exaggerated a leer. "Pay triple and I'll pleasure ye with far more than words, sweetheart."

"Tempting." He eyed her over the rim of his drink. "But I thought you were too busy running the Lair to have private patrons anymore."

Until recently, The Wolf's Lair had been owned by Gryff's good friend Connor Linsley, the Earl of Killingworth. However, Connor had turned over a new leaf in life and had embarked on a new career as a goat farmer after gifting the Lair to his former employee.

Gryff swirled his whisky. His friend had also embarked on a new life as a happily married man, a fact which no doubt had much to do with his own current unsettled mood.

"Lud, I *am* busy," responded Sara. "You have *no* idea how much work it is to run a business." Despite the bantering tone, Sara was watching him carefully, a shade of concern clouding her gaze. "But fer you, I might make an exception."

A smile played on his lips. "Tempting," he repeated. "However, I value the relationship we have now far more than a fleeting tumble in bed." He turned away, his expression blurred by the soft shadows of the private parlor as he stared at the pale painted wall above the bookcase. "Next time I stop by, I shall bring you a picture of ivy to hang here."

"Oh? Does ivy have a special meaning, too?" she asked somewhat warily.

"It signifies 'friendship.' 'Affection.'"

Sara slid over and planted a light kiss on his cheek. "That's sweet, no matter that you're teasing me with all this talk about roses and such having a language of their own."

"Actually, I'm not. The bit about the grapevine was a jest, but the rest is all true," he assured her. "Indeed, the concept has been around for centuries. Lady Mary Wortley Montague, wife of the British ambassador to Constantinople during the early 1700s, brought a Turkish book back to England entitled *The Secret Language of Flowers*. It's quite fascinating. If you like, I'll bring you a copy."

"Thank you." Sara twined a lock of his long black hair around her forefinger. "How is it that a rakehell rogue like you knows so much about flowers?"

Gryff felt himself stiffen. Pulling away, he stalked to the hearth and picked up the poker. Coals crackled as he stirred up a flame. "You know better than to ask your patrons about their private lives. And like them, I don't come here to answer personal questions," he snapped.

"Ye don't come here to dip yer wick or to drink yerself senseless anymore either," retorted Sara, eyeing the very modest amount of whisky he had poured for himself. "Is something wrong? Ye look a little niffy-tiffy. Is something eating at yer insides?"

He stared at the embers, the bits of glowing orange a stark contrast to the surrounding bed of gray-black ashes. *Dark and Light.* "Oh, I don't know. Perhaps I'm sick of…"

Sick of what? Seductions and sousing himself in brandy? Of late, neither swiving nor guzzling a barrel of brandy had held much allure. In fact, he had given up drinking heavily several months ago after his fuzz-witted carelessness had almost cost Connor his livelihood. As for women, strangely enough, these days, he was finding far more satisfaction in dedicating his energy to…other pursuits.

"Perhaps I'm sick of youthful folly," said Gryff slowly, thinking of the books on landscape design stacked up by his bedside, and the unfinished essay on his library desk. "With age comes wisdom…or so one hopes." He made a wry face. "My birthday was last week, and when a man turns thirty, he is forced to take stock of his life."

Folding her arms across her chest. Sara subjected him to a piercing stare.

"Ah, yes…"

Her eyes slowly ran the length of the marquess's lanky form, moving from the crown of his silky, shoulder-length hair, down over the broad slope of muscled shoulders and lean, tapered waist. She let her gaze linger for a moment on the distinctly masculine contours of his thighs before running it down the long stretch of legs.

"Yes," she repeated, raising a mocking brow. "I can see that teetering on the brink of senility can make a man repent of his past sins."

"Of which there are too many to name," he murmured.

"Ain't *that* the truth," drawled Sara. "You and your fellow Hellhounds have a terrible reputation for wildness." Society viewed Gryff and his two friends Connor Linsley and Cameron Daggett as dangerous because of their utter disregard for all the rules and regulations governing Polite Behavior.

"But you, of all people, know our deep, dark secret— we are harmless little lapdogs," replied Gryff. "Our bark is far worse than our bite."

"Ha!" Sara gave a snort. "The Wolfhound may have been domesticated..." Connor's nickname was the Irish Wolfhound, as his mother had hailed from the Emerald Isle. "But you and Mr. Daggett are still devilishly dangerous. And speaking of that devil, how is his leg mending from the bullet—"

A sudden urgent thumping on the door interrupted the question. It was punctuated by a gruff shout. "Oh, no—ye can't go in there, madam!"

"Oh, yes—" The latch sprang open. "I can."

Gryff saw a willowy figure evade the porter's meaty hand and slip inside the private parlor. *Prim bonnet, dowdy gown, sturdy half boots, stern scowl.* An expert in assessing females, he needed only an instant to recognize the type. She was not a lightskirt but a respectable lady.

Definitely a harbinger of trouble.

But thankfully not *his* trouble. Taking a sidelong step

out of the ring of firelight, Gryff slouched a shoulder to the storage cabinet, curious as to what sort of sparks were about to fly.

"Am I to understand that *you* are the proprietor here?" The intruder pointed an indigo-gloved finger at Sara.

"Yes." Sara extended a ladylike hand in greeting. "I'm Sara Hawkins. And you are?"

The intruder eyed it uncertainly, but after a moment, innate good manners prevailed. "Lady Brentford," she said reluctantly.

In contrast to her straitlaced appearance, her voice was low and lush, the sound sending an inexplicable shiver prickling down Gryff's spine. It was soft as silk, yet had a slight nub to its texture.

The effect was unexpected. Erotic.

Gryff gave an inward wince. *Erotic?* Good God, what momentary madness had stirred such a thought? The lady did not look as if the word "erotic" had ever entered her vocabulary.

And yet…

And yet, despite the severe chignon and the subdued, sober hues of her clothes, there was something sensual about Lady Brentford.

"Might I offer you some refreshment, Lady Brentford?" asked Sara politely. "If brandy is not to your taste, I can ring for some tea."

"Thank you." Her tone turned cooler—indeed, it could have chilled all the oolong in India. "But this is *not* a social call."

Gryff tried to shake off the odd current of attraction that kept his gaze held in thrall.

"Ah. Then I assume you are looking for Lord Brentford," said Sara.

"Good God, no." The lady grimaced. "Lord Brentford has been two years in the grave, and I devoutly pray that he remains there."

A small furrow formed between Sara's brows. "Then forgive me, but..."

"It is my brother I seek—Lord Leete."

A delicate cough sounded. "We have a full house tonight, and I do not know every patron by name. Perhaps you could describe him to me?"

Leete. The name stirred a vague flicker somewhere on the edges of Gryff's memory. He closed his eyes for a moment, trying to bring the fellow into sharper focus. *Yes, yes, it had been just last week—an obnoxious puppy, yapping some impertinent question about what type of tassel looked best on a Hessian boot.*

"Average height and reedy," he answered for her. "Blonde hair brushed in an elaborate array of over-oiled curls." A tiny pause. "And sidewhiskers that make him look like a poodle."

"That's the one." Lady Brentford turned slowly to face him. "A friend of yours?"

"Not in the least," replied Gryff. "Actually, he was making a nuisance of himself. I was forced to be rather rude."

"He has a habit of doing that," she said. Her voice remained calm, but her eyes betrayed the depth of her emotion. Beneath the surface hue of azure blue rippled a darker current of stormy slate. "Is he here?"

Sara shot Gryff a questioning look.

"The gaming rooms," murmured he. "Try the *vingt-*

et-un tables in the West Parlor. Word around my club is that Lord Leete plays for high stakes." A pause. "Though only the Devil knows why, as he seems incapable of counting to ten when he's in his cups."

Looking a trifle uncomfortable, Sara cleared her throat. "Lady Brentford, there are, how shall I say it, some unwritten rules regarding establishments such as these. Gentlemen expect discretion from the management, especially concerning interruptions."

"I've come all the way from Oxfordshire to see him." Her tone had turned taut. "It's a matter of pressing importance."

Anger. Though she was trying hard to hide it, Lady Brentford was extremely angry, decided Gryff. *But was there also a touch of fear?* Repressing a frown, he angled a step to the side, trying to get a better read on her face.

"Yes, I can see that it is," said Sara quietly. "So in this case, I shall make an exception."

"Thank you," came the whispered reply.

"If you will excuse me for a few moments, I will go have a look."

Lady Brentford appeared reluctant to be left alone with an unknown gentleman. Slanting a sidelong look at him, she hesitated, and then seemed to decide that he was the lesser of two evils.

"Thank you," she repeated signaling her consent with a curt nod.

As the door clicked shut, she expelled a pent-up breath and turned her back to him. *Swoosh, swoosh.* Her heavy skirts skirled around her ankles as she moved away to study the etching hanging above the bookcase.

Trouble, Gryff reminded himself. He had survived the brutal Peninsular War by listening to the warning voice in his head. And right now it was drumming a martial tattoo against his skull.

Trouble, trouble, trouble.

The wise strategy would be to finish his drink and quietly take his leave. Whatever her reason for being here, it did not involve him.

Instead, he set his glass down and walked across the carpet.

THE DISH

Where authors give you the inside scoop!

♥ ♥

From the desk of Jill Shalvis

Dear Reader,

It's been a fun, exciting year for my Lucky Harbor series. Thanks to you, the readers, I hit the *New York Times* bestseller list with *The Sweetest Thing*. Wow. Talk about making my day! You are all awesome, and I'm still grinning from ear to ear and making everyone call me "N-Y-T." But I digress...

In light of how much you, the readers, have enjoyed this series, my publisher is putting *Simply Irresistible* and *The Sweetest Thing* together as a 2-in-1 volume at a special low price. CHRISTMAS IN LUCKY HARBOR will be in stores in November—just in time to bring new readers up to speed for book three, *Head Over Heels,* in December.

When I first started this series, I wanted it to be about three sisters who run a beach resort together. I figured I'd use my three daughters as inspiration. Only problem, my little darlings are teenagers, and they bicker like fiends. Some inspiration. But then it occurred to me: Their relationships are real, and that's what I like to write. Real people. So I changed things up, and the series became about three ESTRANGED sisters, stuck together running a dilapidated inn falling down on its axis. Now *that* I could pull off for sure. Add in three sexy alpha heroes to go with, and voilà...I was on my way.

So make sure to look for CHRISTMAS IN LUCKY HARBOR, the reprint of books one and two, available both in print and as an ebook wherever books are sold. And right on its heels, book three, *Head Over Heels*. (Heels? Get it?)

Happy reading and holiday hugs!

Jill Shalvis

www.jillshalvis.com

♥ ♥ ♥ ♥ ♥ ♥ ♥ ♥ ♥ ♥ ♥ ♥ ♥ ♥ ♥ ♥ ♥ ♥ ♥ ♥

From the desk of Margaret Mallory

Dear Reader,

Bad boys! What woman doesn't love a rogue—at least in fiction?

I suspect that's the reason I've had readers asking me about Alex MacDonald since he made his appearance as a secondary character in *The Guardian*, Book 1 of the Return of the Highlanders series.

Alex is such an unruly charmer that I was forced to ban him from several chapters of *The Guardian* for misbehavior. Naturally, the scoundrel attempted to steal every scene I put him in. I will admit that I asked Alex to flirt with the heroine to make his cousin jealous, but did he have to enjoy himself quite so thoroughly? Of course, if there had been any real chance of stealing his cousin's true love, Alex would not have done it. A good heart is hidden beneath that brawny chest. All the same, I told the scene-stealer he must wait his turn. When he laughed and refused to cooperate, I threw him out.

Now, at last, this too-handsome, green-eyed warrior has his own book, THE SINNER. I hope readers will agree that a man who has had far too many women fall at his feet must suffer on the road to love.

The first thing I decided to do was give Alex a heroine who was as loath to marry as he was. In fact, Alex would have to travel the length and breadth of Scotland to find a lass as opposed to marriage in general, or to him in particular, as Glynis MacNeil. Glynis's experience with one handsome, philandering Highland warrior was enough to last her a lifetime, and she's prepared to go to any lengths to thwart her chieftain father's attempts to wed her to another.

Alex has sworn—repeatedly and to anyone who would listen—that he will *never* take a wife. So the second thing I decided to do was surprise Alex partway through the book with an utterly compelling reason to wed. (No, I'm not telling here.) I hope readers appreciate the irony of this bad boy's long, uphill battle to persuade Glynis to marry him.

Helping these two untrusting souls find love proved an even bigger challenge than getting them wed. Fortunately, the attraction between Alex and Glynis was so hot my fingers burned on the keys. The last thing I needed to do, then, was force them to trust each other through a series of dangerous adventures that threatened all they held dear. That part was easy, dear readers—such dangers *abound* in the Highlands in the year 1515.

I hope you enjoy the love story of Alex and Glynis in THE SINNER.

Margaret Mallory

www.margaretmallory.com

♥ ♥ ♥ ♥ ♥ ♥ ♥ ♥ ♥ ♥ ♥ ♥ ♥ ♥ ♥ ♥ ♥ ♥ ♥ ♥

From the desk of Cara Elliott

Dear Reader,

Starting a new series is a little like going out on a first date. I mean, doesn't every girl get a little nervous about meeting a guy who is a complete stranger? Well, I have a confession to make: Authors get the heebies-jeebies too. Hey, it's not easy to waltz up to a hunky hero and simply bat your eyelashes and introduce yourself!

Okay, okay, I know what you're thinking. *How hard can it be?* After all, unlike in real life, all I have to do is snap my fingers (or tap them along my keyboard) and presto, as if by magic, he'll turn into a knight in shining armor, or a dashingly debonair prince, or…whatever my fantasies desire!

Strange as it may sound, it doesn't always flow quite so smoothly. Some men have minds of their own. You know…the strong, silent, self-reliant type who would rather eat nails than admit to any vulnerability. Take Connor Linsley, the sinfully sexy rogue who plays the leading role in TOO WICKED TO WED, the first book in my new Lords of Midnight trilogy. Talk about an infuriating man! He snaps, he snarls, he broods. If he didn't have such an intriguing spark in his quicksilver eyes, I might have been tempted to give up on him.

But no, patient person that I am, I persevered, knowing that beneath his show of steel was a softer, more sensitive core. I just had to draw it out. We had to have a number of heart-to-heart talks, but finally he let down his silky dark hair—er, in a manner of speaking—and allowed me to share some of his secrets. (And trust me, Connor has some *very* intriguing secrets!)

I'll have you know that I am also generous, as well as patient, for instead of keeping my new best friend all to myself, I've decided to share this Paragon of Perfection. I hope you enjoy getting to know him! (Pssst, he has two very devil-may-care friends. But that's another story. Or maybe two!)

Please visit my website at www.caraelliott.com to read sample chapters and learn more about this Lord of Midnight.

Cara Elliott

♥ ♥

From the desk of Jami Alden

Dear Reader,

I first met Krista Slater in my first romantic suspense for Grand Central, *Beg for Mercy*. All I knew about her then was that she was tough, no nonsense, dedicated to her work and committed to right, even if it meant admitting she'd made an enormous mistake in sending Sean Flynn to death row. But it was only after I'd spent about a month (and a hundred pages) with her in my latest book, HIDE FROM EVIL, that I learned she's also an automobile expert who can hotwire a car in less than sixty seconds.

And I knew Sean Flynn was loyal and honorable, with a protective streak a mile wide. I also knew that when he was forced into close quarters with Krista, he'd fall and fall hard, despite the fact she'd nearly ruined his life when she prosecuted him for murder. However, I didn't know he listened to Alice in Chains until he popped in his earbuds and clicked on his iPod.

After I finish every book, I'm amazed at the fact that I've written three hundred plus pages about people who exist only in my head. For about six months, I spend nearly every waking hour with them. Even when I'm not actually writing, they're always around, circling the edges of my consciousness while I think up a sexy, scary story for them to inhabit.

When I first started writing, I read books that said I shouldn't start writing until I knew absolutely everything about my hero and heroine. And I mean EVERYTHING—stuff like the name of their best friends from kindergarten and their least favorite food. So I would try to fill out these elaborate questionnaires, wracking my brain to come up a list of my heroine's quirks.

I finally came to accept the fact that it takes me a while to get to know my characters. We need to spend some time together before I get a sense of what makes them tick. It's like getting to know a new friend: You start with the small talk. Then you hang out, have conversations that go beyond the surface. You start to notice the little details that make them unique, and they reveal things from their pasts that have molded them into the people you're coming to know.

That's when things get interesting.

It was definitely interesting getting to know Sean and Krista in HIDE FROM EVIL. Especially finding out why, despite their rocky past, they were absolutely meant for each other. I hope you have as much fun with them as I did.

Enjoy!

Jami Alden

www.jamialden.com

VISIT US ONLINE AT

WWW.HACHETTEBOOKGROUP.COM

FEATURES:

**OPENBOOK BROWSE AND
SEARCH EXCERPTS**

•

AUDIOBOOK EXCERPTS AND PODCASTS

•

AUTHOR ARTICLES AND INTERVIEWS

•

**BESTSELLER AND PUBLISHING
GROUP NEWS**

•

SIGN UP FOR E-NEWSLETTERS

•

**AUTHOR APPEARANCES AND TOUR
INFORMATION**

•

SOCIAL MEDIA FEEDS AND WIDGETS

•

DOWNLOAD FREE APPS

BOOKMARK HACHETTE BOOK GROUP
@ WWW.HACHETTEBOOKGROUP.COM